XOLO

A Novel of Canine Horror

by Peter Hurd

DORRANCE PUBLISHING CO
EST. 1920
PITTSBURGH, PENNSYLVANIA 15238

The contents of this work, including, but not limited to, the accuracy of events, people, and places depicted; opinions expressed; permission to use previously published materials included; and any advice given or actions advocated are solely the responsibility of the author, who assumes all liability for said work and indemnifies the publisher against any claims stemming from publication of the work.

All Rights Reserved
Copyright © 2023 by Peter Hurd

No part of this book may be reproduced or transmitted, downloaded, distributed, reverse engineered, or stored in or introduced into any information storage and retrieval system, in any form or by any means, including photocopying and recording, whether electronic or mechanical, now known or hereinafter invented without permission in writing from the publisher.

Dorrance Publishing Co
585 Alpha Drive
Suite 103
Pittsburgh, PA 15238
Visit our website at *www.dorrancebookstore.com*

ISBN: 979-8-8868-3280-8
eISBN: 979-8-8868-3675-2

XOLO

A NOVEL OF CANINE HORROR

Acknowledgements

First, thanks to my parents and family, who have supported and encouraged me long after the period that familial obligation (or common sense) would have required.

To Sam and Eli, thanks for your constant friendship, your helpful feedback on the early drafts of this novel, and the use of your names in the party scenes.

To my sister Lynn, thank you for introducing me to the Xoloitzcuintli and for first suggesting that I write a horror story inspired by the legends surrounding them.

And to the dogs who inspired this tale, I dedicate this book to you: Moxie, Stella, Rosebud, Henry, and D.O.G.

Finally, to you, dear reader, thank you for your support and for joining me on this journey.

Peter Hurd
May 31, 2022
Forest Lake, MN

Author's Note

The following is a work of imagination. While the myths and legends surrounding the Xoloitzcuintle are very real, I have fictionalized many other aspects of the breed, including their temperament. The Xolo, as well as the other dog breeds featured in this book, are generally loving and kind and rarely present a danger to humans.

Nothing in this book is intended to convey disrespect for any breed presented or for the cultures from which they arise.

PETER HURD

"Throughout the New World, there is the belief in multiple creations, of which the present world is but one. In order to safely reach the next world, human souls needed a canine guide... Xolos were the traditional choice for this service. Xoloitzcuintli can be translated as 'dog that guides human souls to the land of the dead'... Known as 'Mictlan' (The Place of the Dead), the soul had to travel through eight hells to reach Mictlan; a perilous journey, often requiring the assistance of different colored Xolos. Funeral Xolos were bred specifically for these colors and killed during these ceremonies. A common burial custom involved killing a dog by spearing it through the mouth with an arrow and burying it with the deceased. Clay statues of Xolos were interred with the deceased for the same reason."

-Hairless Dogs: The Naked Truth,
by Amy Fernandez and Kelly Rhae

"Our madness engulfs everything and infects innocent victims such as children or animals."

-Unknown,
attributed to Francis Thrive

Prologue

THE HEAT WAS UNBEARABLE.

Mopping sweat from his brow, Derek scanned the crowded square. Even through his sunglasses, the sun blazing off the adobe forced him to squint, his eyes quickly filling with sweat. Between the heat and being the only foreigner in sight, Derek almost felt like one of the *conquistadors* who had once ravaged this land, even if his trip had been filled with endless rounds of golf and five-course dinners instead of raids and battles with the natives.

From across the square, the only other American in the market, not to mention the force behind all those fine dinners and rounds of golf, rudely shoved his way to Derek, earning more than a few sullen looks from the locals. "You see, Derek?" Hector asked, trying to wipe sweat from his face with a handkerchief that was too soaked to accept any more, "these people have plenty of places to go. What makes you think they need more houses?"

"What makes you think they need more golf courses? Besides, what about this scene makes you think there's enough housing?" Derek moved aside as the crowd jostled towards the stands that lined the walls of the ancient market. Derek stepped aside, then regained his position. Hector stood firm while the crowd surged around him, checking the front pocket of his blazer to ensure his wallet and cigars were still there. Finding both, he produced one of the thick, oily cigars and lit it with an antique silver lighter, not seeming to mind the heat or the crowd that thronged around him on all sides.

"I just think you can build the golf course anywhere," Derek continued, knowing Hector would not respond to his question. "And I still think that land belongs to the natives."

Hector puffed his cigar regally, exhaling smoke into the face of a passing woman. "But not anywhere with such great views of the gulf. And I still think that land belongs to you. At least I did when I agreed to take you on this trip."

Derek nodded, looking down at the crumbling brick beneath his feet, as much to avoid Hector's gaze as the miasma of oily smoke that he blew Derek's way. The acrid smell brought to mind the cigars Hector had puffed over every shrimp cocktail, every regular cocktail, and every overly-rich meal Hector had forced Derek to be treated to over the last three days. As the smoke again invaded his head, Derek felt the flavors of them all return to his mouth in one nauseating rush. He tried to double over, but the close-packed crowd made it impossible. People filled every inch of space, bustling to buy meat and vegetables from the creaky wooden stands, where merchants hustled to fill their orders. Their arms full, the crowd surged out in all directions, weaving like the hazy lines the heat made in the air.

Derek felt dizzy watching them, and slowly stumbled towards the nearest wall, hoping he could find a place to discreetly vomit. As he pushed through the crowd, they pushed him back just as hard, keeping him in place like a piece of trash bobbing in the ocean. His feeling of endless floating was anchored by a hand on his shoulder. His relief went up in smoke when he saw the hand still contained the burning cigar, which wafted directly into Derek's nostrils. Derek turned away as much from Hector as from the cigar. "You are sick, my friend?" Hector asked him. "Perhaps something you ate. I will get you some water."

Hector disappeared into the crowd, waving slow-moving shoppers aside with both hands, his cigar held in his lips straight out like a divining rod. Derek laughed internally at the sight of the squat Mexican-American man in the tight white linen suit with sweat stains growing around the armpits, waving aside his fellow Mexicans as imperiously as if he were one of those *conquistadors* of old.

The image took his mind for a moment off the nausea running through him, as well as the doubts of the last few days. Derek had bought the one hundred acres here in Sonora from a friend who was desperately trying to offload his assets before his divorce was settled, but a series of obligations back home and Derek's own lingering doubts about the project had left the land a bare stretch of desert and pristine beach along the coast of the Gulf of California without a single sign of human intervention, which was perfectly fine with Derek. Even his attempts to build a village for the Yoreme people on their native land had run into a lack of interest from investors and a curious dearth of support from the local government, whom Derek suspected of a heartless indifference towards their poorest citizens in favor of wealthy outsiders like Hector Ramirez.

Hector was Mexican by ancestry, but had lived since birth in Colorado, where Derek had met him a few months earlier. Derek had been moving his family to a small development he was building at the foot of the Rocky Mountains a few miles south of Denver, an area where Hector had interests in real estate, restaurants, car dealerships, and other things that Derek knew nothing about but vaguely suspected were illegal. Derek often had the impression that for Hector, the thrill of making an enormous deal was more important than any financial return it could possibly give him, though he certainly received enormous returns, and was not shy about displaying the spoils of them.

Hector had heard through some mutual contacts in the real estate world about Derek's one hundred acres in Mexico even before Derek had moved in and had welcomed him to the area with plying gifts and constant visits, offering to buy the land to build a village of summer homes for himself and a few other wealthy businessmen in the area, (Derek himself included, Hector had always added cursorily) complete with a golf course, yacht club, restaurant, and swimming pool, along with a gated wall and twenty-four-hour security. Derek wasn't keen on the idea of blocking the view of the gulf with brick and barbed wire or of destroying the pristine environment and the locals' native land to build a playground for wealthy foreigners who would leave it abandoned for nine months out of the year. However, his own ideas for the property had stalled out and the cash for his other projects was running low, so he had entertained, half-seriously at first, Hector's offers for the property, entertaining them more seriously as the offers had grown. When Hector had offered to fly Derek in his private jet just, as he said, to "take a look at the property," Derek had flattered himself that he could persuade Hector to both buy the property and to use it for more charitable purposes, but the appeal had fallen on deaf ears, as he should have known it would.

Derek managed to push his way out of the crowd and into a quiet corner of the courtyard, where the crowns of the Spanish-style buildings managed to give a little shade. Being out of the sun and the crowd made Derek feel a little better and he swallowed some of his nausea with a mouthful of cool air. Leaning back, Derek found himself sinking into a post of creaking wood, which bent beneath his weight. He quickly stood and whirled around to see he had been leaning on the edge of a merchant's stand he hadn't noticed before. Derek apologized profusely to the old man sitting behind the stand, who looked up from his tattered paperback for just a moment and smiled.

Wanting to be polite, Derek cast a glance over the hand-woven rugs and textiles that filled the top of the stand, but his eye was drawn to a folding chair next to the old man, where an enormous dog stood a panting watch over the stand and the crowd of customers beyond. It was hairless, except for a thin streak of white fur along the center of its head. Its mottled skin was gray on the exposed underbelly, but tanned nearly black on the backside. Its face was intelligent and curious, with dark, soulful eyes that Derek couldn't help but stare at, although the dog seemed to stare straight through him at the crowd beyond. The dog's limbs and torso were strangely muscular, with an almost human-like six pack protruding from its belly. Its form was noble, its posture graceful and from the way it sat was quite obviously a male, and an unneutered one at that.

Derek was struck by its kingly posture and air of noble grace. "Excuse me, what kind of dog is that?" he asked. The old man again only looked at him and smiled. Derek sighed in frustration. High school Spanish was further away than he wanted it to be and even back then hadn't been his strongest subject. But he remembered the word for "dog" and a word he thought meant "breed," (although he hoped he meant it in the right sense). He pointed a finger at the dog, repeating the two words as slowly and clearly as he could. The old man nodded and said something that sounded like *show-low-its-queentley* in a slow, ominous drawl. The question answered, the man returned to his book, indicating the conversation was over. Derek looked again at the dog, which still seemed to look straight through him.

A bump on his back made Derek turn around. Hector stood behind him, holding pineapples with straws sticking out of the tops. "Closest thing they have to bottled water around here," he said sarcastically. Derek took one and thanked him, but his nausea was already forgotten. He stared at the dog as he took his first sip, not even tasting the sweet, refreshing juice.

Hector followed his gaze and laughed. "You like the dog, eh?" Before Derek could reply, Hector had shoved his way to the stand. "How much for the dog, *amigo*?"

The old man only looked at him, befuddled. "That's alright, Hector, just ask him where we can get one."

Hector snorted. "You can get one right here, mate." He leaned in close to the old man and balanced his pineapple on a stack of rugs, reaching for his wallet with his other hand. "Come on, man, how much for the dog?"

"Is not for sale," the old man said in crisp, perfectly understandable English. Seeing the haughty impatience on his face, Derek recognized his previous silence for what it was, a strategy to dismiss time-wasting tourists. The old man held up a sample of his textiles instead, inviting them to make a real offer.

"We don't want a rug, man," Hector huffed, taking out a wad of bills. "How much for the dog?"

Derek laid a hand on his shoulder. "That's alright, Hector. I thought you spoke Spanish?"

Hector laughed. "They don't speak much Spanish in Denver. You ought to know." He doubled the wad of bills and set them on the stand. "Come on, mate, how much will it take for my friend to walk out of here with the mutt?"

"Is not for sale," the old man said finally, holding up another sample of his textiles with one hand. With the other, he opened a small steel lockbox, as if inviting them to make a contribution. "You want rug, you want carpet…"

Hector looked thoughtfully at the meager clump of torn bills that lined the bottom of the lockbox. Pulling more bills from his wallet, he stuffed the entire pile into the lockbox. "I want dog."

The old man looked down at the lockbox, now overflowing with cash. "Come on, man, I bet you could buy a hundred of 'em with that," Hector drawled, leaning his massive bulk on the wooden stand, which groaned in protest beneath his weight. The old man slammed the lockbox shut hard enough to break a thief's fingers, as if afraid that Hector would change his mind. He stuffed the lockbox, bills still hanging out of the edges, under the table and in the same motion produced a cracked leather leash, which he attached to the dog's worn collar.

Leading the dog around the stand, he handed the leash to Derek. "You must be careful," he said, steadily holding Derek's gaze.

"Why, is he dangerous?" Derek asked, looking back at Hector.

"No, his people believe these dogs are the guardians of the underworld."

"They *are* the guardians of the underworld," the old man corrected, looking sharply at Hector. "They have the power to do great good or great evil. They are the guides through the land of death. Be careful he does not guide you wrong."

Derek kneeled down next to the dog, who sat obediently next to him. "Oh, come on, how could this little guy cause…" His words drifted off as he locked eyes with the dog. His consciousness seemed to sink into the inky blackness of the dog's eyes, where strange visions flittered in each reflected speck of light.

That light caught the jewels of an Aztec priest, dangling across his outthrust chest as he raised a dagger over a young woman who lay struggling on a stone altar. Other priests ringed the large stone chamber, where smoky flames from incensed pots flitted weird shadows across the eldritch carvings on the walls and the graven faces of the priests, which seemed equally made of stone. The dog sat overlooking all of this, sitting regally on an altar of his own, bedecked in a robe lined with jewels.

The dog watched impassively as the dagger came down and the victim ceased her pointless thrashings. The high priest made a slice across her chest and reached into the hollow. A moment later, his blood-soaked hands produced the still-beating heart. Blood ran from the dangling tubes as it gave its final, convulsive shudder.

Crossing the chamber, the high priest kneeled before the dog and offered the heart in sacrifice. For one hideous moment, Derek thought the dog would take a bite of the barely-dead organ, but instead it only leaned in and took a long, slow sniff. Steam rose from every surface of the heart, collecting in the severed tubes and ventricles before jetting out in a thick, grey cloud which disappeared into the dog's nostrils. The high priest prostrated himself and slunk away as the dog sat back, satisfied, its eyes glowing a hideous yellow.

Derek opened his eyes, then pinched them shut as sunlight flooded his brain. When he felt his eyes had adjusted enough to handle the sunlight, he slowly opened them to reveal the sight of Hector standing over him, upending a pineapple so its juice poured on Derek's face, a sight that would have been comical if Derek had any idea how he had ended up on the ground. "You worried me, my friend," Hector said, holding out a hand. "You passed out and I was trying to wake you up. You must really be sick."

"Thanks, I feel much better now." Derek accepted the offered hand and climbed to his feet, seeing the empty wooden stand beside them. At first, he thought the merchant had disappeared like the mad prophet in a bad horror film, then he saw the old man loading his textiles into a wheelbarrow, beneath which was presumably stowed the box of cash that allowed him to take the rest of the day off.

The old man gave Derek a knowing glance as he pushed off with his wheelbarrow. "Remember to be careful with him. I think you know now what I mean, my friend." He pushed into the crowd without waiting for a reply.

The dog still sat by Derek's side, not trying to comfort him or chasing after his old master, but only obediently waiting for his next command. "He watched over you the whole time you were out," Hector said, although the words were more chilling to Derek than comforting. "You see? He is a good pet already."

The dog nuzzled Derek's arm as if to agree, erasing some of the chill Derek felt towards him. "I guess he is," Derek agreed, petting the dog's furrowed brow.

He took a slow sip from the pineapple Hector handed him, feeling the waves of nausea and dread flow out of him. "Thanks, Hector, you didn't have to do that. And you didn't have to throw your money away on the dog."

"It's not thrown away if you like him. Your daughter will love him and with that new house, he will make a good guard dog."

"I'm sure he will," Derek said, patting the dog's head.

"Come on, we have a plane to catch." Derek followed Hector the way they had come in, the dog following obediently on his leash. As they sank into the mass of people crowding the square, Derek looked back for a final glance at the old merchant, but he had already disappeared into the shifting, endless crowd.

ONE

MOUNTAINS SLID BACKWARDS AND DISAPPEARED.

Derek's eyes snapped open the rest of the way at the sight, his mind reeling for an explanation. It didn't take long to find one. He quickly remembered that he was alone in the massive passenger area of a limo either owned or rented by Hector, who had dropped him off in this conveyance after saying his goodbyes and his wishes that they would be working together very soon. Hector himself had stayed at the small private airport outside Denver, having to fly on in his private jet to a business trip in California that would take him away for several weeks, after which he hoped to meet with Derek.

At least that gave Derek a few weeks to make a decision. As the fog of sleep lifted, half-remembered dreams or nightmares disappeared. He lifted his legs off the padded bench and sat upright, gazing at the mountain landscape flying by through the long windows that ringed the vehicle, their peaks sliding backwards through the skylight above him.

Although much of Colorado's Front Range looked the same, Derek had driven this particular narrow country road enough times to recognize even the weedy boulders that lined the shoulders. They were on the crumbling county highway that led into the first rise of the Rocky Mountains, about twenty-five miles Northwest of Castle Rock. Ahead, the crumbling road would be replaced by a stretch of new pavement that would lead to the planned community of Sylvan Springs, the focus of Derek's professional (and often his personal) life for most of the last three years.

"Almost there, Mr. Rains," a flat voice confirmed from the front of the car. Derek had almost forgotten about Hector's valet, Reeve, who had been waiting silently on the stairs to Hector's private plane when they had crossed the dirt runway of the little airstrip in Sonora. He had sat silently in the plane during the entire flight home, giving occasional glances at Derek and his new dog. He was a well-built man who seemed to be in his early thirties and had a few curls of bleached blonde hair sticking out from under the valet's cap that he seemed to be wearing ironically. Whether Reeve was a first name, a last name, or a mononym Derek was unsure, just as he was unsure about everything else concerning his would-be business partner's silent but ever-present companion.

Every time Hector had unexpectedly dropped by Derek's home to "discuss" the land in Mexico, Reeve had been waiting at the edge of Derek's porch or sitting attentively behind the wheel of the still-running car, silently awaiting orders. This flat confirmation of their approaching destination was the first thing Derek had heard him say. The shock was enough to sweep away the last of the sleep clouding Derek's brain.

Intrigued, Derek moved to the front of the cab and sat on a long bench just behind the frosted glass that segregated the driver's compartment. Seeing Derek in the rearview, Reeve rolled down the pane of glass. "I'm sorry I wasn't a very interesting companion," Derek said. "I must have slept the whole ride home."

In the rearview, Derek saw Reeve perform a mechanical baring of teeth that could charitably be called a smile. "Just about, Mr. Rains. Sounded like you were blacked out. You were talking in your sleep the whole time. Good thing you had your new friend back there to look over you."

For a moment, Derek couldn't remember what Reeve was talking about. He followed the driver's gaze from the rearview to the back corner of the cab. Between his troubled dreams and the lingering traces of the sickness that had overcome him in the market, Derek had forgotten all about the dog. It sat, both obedient and regal, on one of the leather benches, as still and statue-like as when Derek had first seen him.

As happy as Derek was to see him, it now took his mind off what he would say to Hector in a few weeks and on to the more immediate problem of what he would say to his wife in a few minutes. Alison had never wanted animals around their young children, let alone an exotic one that could be unpredictable and dangerous, and she had always hated having any kind of decision made about their family life without consulting her first. Derek could only hope that she would be as struck by the dog as he had been, but a large part of him didn't find that likely.

The limo turned off the weed-eaten highway and passed the ornate wooden sign for Sylvan Springs which towered over the newly-paved side road on a mound of artfully arranged rocks. Usually, the sight made Derek feel at home. Today it filled him with dread. "Beautiful neighborhood you've built here, Mr. Rains," Reeve said.

Derek smiled and shrugged. "It's the landscape that makes it beautiful."

Reeve adjusted the rearview slightly. "Mr. Ramirez thinks the landscape on that property in Mexico will make for a beautiful neighborhood, too."

Derek smiled into the mirror, then turned to look out the window. So that was it, was it? Hector had left Derek with his crony in order to have a final shot at buttering him up. It was clever in the heavy-handed way all of Hector's plans were clever, but Derek wasn't going to let it influence him. "Hector thinks it will make a nice playground for him and his rich pals. He doesn't care about the landscape."

Reeve slowly adjusted the rearview until he was staring into Derek's eyes. "You ought to be nicer to Mr. Ramirez. He's a man who can do you great harm, or many favors." He adjusted the mirror again, until the dog was framed in the glass. "And he already has done you a few of those."

Derek said nothing, put off by something in Reeve's tone and the similarity of his admonition to something the old merchant had said. But Derek didn't have time to place it now. The limo was pulling into his driveway.

Emily ran down the darkened corridor, clutching the remains of her dress against her chest with one hand and holding the sputtering lantern with the other. The light was just barely strong enough to see the slimy bricks of the walls and the thin stream of water which ran down the center of the floor, but as she made her way further down the passage, the icy draft from whatever isolated cavern this tunnel ended at grew stronger.

The cold wind tore at her clothes, trying to invade her flesh. As her lantern's flame flickered and went out, the walls of the tunnel seemed to grow closer before they disappeared.

Even if she had pockets to carry them, Emily hadn't had time to grab any matches in her desperate flight from the castle. At least she could take comfort in the icy wind that continued to pry at her, knowing that it meant escape: there was some exit from this subterranean prison ahead and she would find it despite the darkness.

She plunged on, keeping the still-warm lantern against her side and running one hand along the slimy wall of the tunnel. The cold wind picked up, feeling more like fingers picking at her in the dark. Her foot collided with something warm and soft, which scuttled away with a squeak. Emily held in a shout, telling herself it was only a rat. There were far worse things behind her, searching for her in the darkness, things she couldn't allow to hear her.

As if responding to her thoughts, she suddenly heard one of those things. A long, mournful howl echoed through the tunnel, rattling the wall she held onto. She clutched the brick even tighter as her breath escaped in a single sharp burst. She held still and told herself to be quiet, hoping the darkness would increase her other senses enough to hear her pursuer. The echoing had made it impossible to tell how near or far the source of that strangely human howl had been, but she sat and listened for a nearer confirmation.

There was silence for a long moment, then suddenly she heard it: footsteps approaching in the darkness, far behind her but drawing nearer. They sounded as if they were near the beginning of this accursed tunnel, at the point where she had fled from the horrible castle after hearing, but not seeing, the beginning of Michael's transformation, when he had locked himself in the closet of his chambers to protect her. She could still hear the tearing of his clothes and the anguished cries that transformed into horrible wailing howls.

But she had more immediate sounds to worry about. The footsteps were drawing closer and now she thought she knew why she hadn't heard them earlier. The sound was not the distinct leather clicking and metal buckle rattling of Michael's shoes, but the soft scuffling padding of an animal's paws. As she listened, she thought she heard four paws scuffling instead of two. Emily shuddered as she thought of the inhuman howls Michael's voice had devolved into.

She moved deeper into the tunnel, trying to hurry without making any noise that might attract her pursuer. She stopped at a sound that made her blood run colder than the wind that still tore at her. From farther ahead, too distinct to be an echo, came *another* set of shuffling footsteps, two and sometimes four clicking pads approaching. Emily stopped, hearing the footsteps approach her from both sides. She pressed herself against the wall, desperately wondering what to do.

Alison Rains sat back at her keyboard, wondering the same thing. She had written herself into a corner, or near to it. She had trapped her protagonist without a hope for escape, which she hoped would be exciting for a reader someday, but right now was maddeningly frustrating.

A few possibilities ran through her mind and were immediately dismissed. The wall Emily was leaning against could slide backwards, revealing itself to be a trapdoor. No, that was too cliché and obvious; besides, she had already used that trick during the chapter in the library. Emily could find a convenient weapon lying on the ground in the dark. Even worse, it was both predictable and inexplicable. Not to mention this was supposed to be a gothic romance, not a clumsy action-thriller, a fact her fingers seemed to forget every time she started typing.

She decided what she needed was a break. Alison pushed her MacBook away, stood up from the curving oak desk and paced the length of the study. The late-afternoon sunlight poured in through the picture window at the front of the house, dappling the dark wood walls in the same warm glow as the front yard, which curved down from the window to the lonely street at the base of the hill.

The angle of the sunlight reminded her that the kids would soon be home from school. She gazed wistfully at the computer screen, where her cursor blinked as if inviting her back. With a groan, she sat back at her desk, not wanting to write but knowing she had to squeeze in every moment she could. Once the kids got home, she would find herself busy until long after dark, when she would be far too groggy to write.

Since moving to Colorado, she had been working for the first time since Gracie was born, partially as a way to keep her sanity but mostly as a safeguard in case Derek's plans for the development didn't turn out as rosy as he planned, which more and more often seemed would be the case. Several lots still sat unsold in the main development, and investors had cooled on the idea of an expansion. She knew the interest would quickly build on the property Derek had already purchased and she wanted to build up some cash for herself and the kids before they were inevitably left with a mountain of debt, so she had reluctantly taken a job as a secretary at the law firm of Myers, Harim, and Donaldson (the most experienced divorce lawyers in the greater Denver area, as Myers nasally rasped on their late-night ads) for as many hours as taking care of the kids allowed.

Of course, her contributions to the family finances, however minor, were not generally met by a consummate contribution on Derek's part to the rearing of their children, which was often left entirely in her hands while he was away at meetings, surveying new work on the development, or in the latest case, flying off to Mexico for a long weekend with his drinking buddy, ostensibly to look over a few acres of shoreline Derek had lifted from one of his friends trying to unload his property before a divorce.

All of that left precious little time for Alison's true passion, which she had indulged in since she was writing poetry as an English major at the University of Chicago, where she had met Derek, who was a business major but was forced, like all freshmen, to take College Writing, where they had bonded over their boredom at Professor Higginbotham's fastidious lectures on sentence structure and rhetorical flow. Later, while Alison helped Derek with his papers in the student lounge, they had discovered a mutual love for urban design that flowed with nature, which they had indulged in with long walks outside of the city. That had led to her present situation, where the novels she dreamt of writing then were as much dreams nearly a decade and a half later.

She sat down at her desk and attacked the keyboard, determined to put as many words on the screen as she could before the kids got home. She wrote almost at random, improvising a few clumsy sentences where Emily felt around in the dark until she found a small grate where water flowed out of the tunnel. As the footsteps closed in on each side of her, she tugged on this grate and…

The humming of a car engine interrupted her. Curious, Alison stood up and went to the window, where a slight craning of her neck let her see an enormous limo parked in the driveway. A tall man about her age jumped out, ran the length of the car and opened one of the several passenger doors. She snorted as Derek stepped out regally, waiting awkwardly while the valet ran to fetch his bags from the trunk. He always complained about how grueling his business trips were, but here he was being treated like a movie star. It made her wonder how he had been received in Mexico.

As the valet returned with Derek's suitcase, something that resembled a shaved coyote leaped out of the open passenger door and sat next to Derek. She didn't quite recognize the animal as a dog because of its strange gray-black skin, which was entirely visible due to its lack of hair, except a narrow white mohawk along the head, which added to its overall strangeness. The animal sat obediently, looking up at Derek with a strangely intelligent expression.

Any hope she had that the beast was some strange pet of the driver's was dashed when Derek pet the animal on the head and picked up the worn leather leash. He took the suitcase in his other hand and exchanged a few words with the valet before heading for the door, happily leading the dog inside. With a sigh, Alison saved her meager progress, shut the laptop and headed for the front door.

Derek opened the door cautiously, poking his head inside as if searching for danger. A long, gray snout poked out beneath him, sniffing the air, like Scooby looking out for Shaggy. With neither of them apparently sensing any danger, Derek opened the door and led the dog inside.

Alison waited, leaning against the kitchen counter, which was at a right angle to the entryway Derek was scanning. She was thus invisible to him until he stepped fully into the front hall and glanced into the kitchen. Derek froze at the sight of her. "Oh hi, honey. Where are the kids?"

"At school. Remember? That started while you were away on vacation." She could see him struggling not to object so she continued. "But they'll be home any minute."

"Oh, good." He sat down on the bench in the entryway to remove his shoes, slipping the dog's collar off at the same time.

"Why do you ask? Do you have a new friend for them?"

He followed her gaze to the dog, then looked back at her with a lopsided grin. "Well, yeah. Hector got him for us in Mexico. I thought he would make a good guard dog."

Alison looked dubiously at the strange animal, which now roamed freely in the kitchen, sticking its long, bald snout into the crevices around the cupboard doors, its paws leaving faint tracks of dust. "Are you even sure that is a dog? What happened to his hair?"

"That's how they're supposed to look! C'mon, I thought you were a nature lover."

"Yeah, when it's outside, not when it's in my house."

Derek smiled, stuffed his shoes into a cubby, and crossed the kitchen to her. "Come on, you've been saying how you wanted better security around here," he said softly, slipping his arms around her. She didn't know whether she resented more that he thought this would work, or that it almost did.

She pushed his arms away. "I meant some alarms, a camera, not an oversized sewer rat!" The dog looked up at her, as if it had understood the insult. "Is that thing even trained?"

"Yeah, of course. I mean, he was good on the way home."

Alison was unconvinced by his sheepish grin. "Very reassuring. Anyway, I'm glad you had fun on your little vacation."

"Honey, it wasn't a vacation!"

"So that means you got the deal done?"

"Well, I'm not sure if it's the right-"

"Aw, I knew it. Derek, you know we need to downsize the-"

She cut herself off at the sound of the garage door opening. A moment later, the door off the kitchen opened and two balls of pure energy were streaking across the room. Gracie was already throwing off her backpack and running towards Derek (in a way she never ran to Alison) while Max lingered behind, making a show of taking off his shoes. "Dad, how was your trip? Tell me all about it!" Gracie inquired, leaping into her father's arms with all the energy inherent in her eight-year-old frame.

Max, true to his role as older brother, languidly crossed the kitchen with cool indifference, suddenly stopping to point at the thing in the corner. "What the hell is that?" he cried.

Gracie followed his gaze to the corner. Her eyes lit up and her breath escaped in a short gasp. "He's perfect!" she squealed, squirming out of Derek's grip to see the dog, oblivious to how far above the kitchen floor she was. Derek set her down before she could fall.

Alison winced and drew a breath as Gracie bolted towards the dog and threw her arms around it, but the dog accepted the hug calmly, and even leaned its head against hers. "Oh, I love him!" she exclaimed. "Isn't he just perfect, Max?"

Max blew away the hair covering one eye. "He's weird."

"No, he's not, he's handsome! Did you buy him for us in Mexico?" Gracie turned to Derek without letting go of the dog. "They're like the national dog there."

Derek shot Alison a glance over Gracie's head. "I didn't know you knew so much about dogs."

Gracie sat next to the animal, holding his paws as if studying them. "Oh yeah," she said casually, "I read all the books about them, since Mom would never let us have one."

Derek gave Alison a longer look that she struggled to avoid. "Well, I guess you're ready to take care of one then."

"Only if he's well-behaved," Alison cut in.

"Oh, he will be," Gracie cooed, "his breed is known for their great temperament."

"And their leathery hide." Max crinkled his nose as he drew near the dog. "What happened to his hair?"

"It's so he can withstand the desert heat," Gracie explained. "People just think it's weird because they're not used to it. Hey, maybe I can bring him for show and tell tomorrow." She looked up at her mother for approval, who sighed and crossed her arms. "Please, I don't have anything! And he doesn't have fur, so he can't cause any allergies."

Alison thought for a moment as Gracie stared her down. "Well, I guess it would be a good test to see if he can behave himself. I'll call your teacher tonight to make sure it's alright."

Gracie jumped to her feet and hugged the dog again. "Hear that, buddy? You're coming to school with me tomorrow, Mr..." She looked up at Derek. "Hey, what's his name?"

"I never asked. I guess it's whatever you want it to be."

Gracie looked thoughtfully into the dog's eyes. "Hmm, we'll think of something tonight."

"That dog is not sleeping in your room!" Alison warned.

As usual, Gracie looked instantly to Derek to undermine Alison.

As a surprise, Derek stood up for her. "Your mom's right, honey, let's have him sleep down here tonight, make sure you don't give him fleas."

"Gross, dad!" She giggled as she pushed away his hand on her hair.

"Yeah, barf," Max said, pointing a finger towards his open mouth as he headed for his room.

"Will you be able to give her a ride tomorrow?" Alison asked. "Or them, I guess. She won't be able to take the dog on the bus."

"No can do," Derek said with a grin, "I have a meeting early tomorrow with investors for the new expansion."

Alison blew air between pursed lips. "Well, Gracie, looks like mommy will have to drive you to school before she goes to work because of the dog daddy bought for you without saying anything." She shifted her look to Derek, who glanced away to avoid it. "Doesn't that sound like fun?"

TWO

Alison adjusted the rearview, trying to frame the dog out of her view. It sat panting in the back seat, buckled in next to Gracie, who was stroking its smooth chest with one hand and reading from the two single-spaced pages of facts she had gathered for show and tell. She had spent all evening in the study, researching every possible fact about the dog while it sat by her side, accepting unending pets along its single plume of hair. The sight had not so much warmed Alison up to the dog as made her worried about a possible obsession.

The dog was buckled into the backseat, a precaution Gracie had insisted on, though Alison would rather have transported the dog in a carrier, not that Derek had thought of buying one, or anything else for the dog, before bringing it home. They had even fed the dog leftover chicken for dinner last night, with Derek promising to buy some proper dog food on the way home after his meeting.

Alison cringed at the sight of the dog's bare skin, spread flanks, and dirty paws splayed against the clean canvas of her back seat, just as she cringed at the sight of the dog in general. Something about its bare, mottled skin was abhorrent to her. She pushed the rearview up further, exposing more of the weed-eaten country road receding behind them until the dog was completely out of view.

Gracie sat up into view, still laughing and petting the dog. Alison pretended the laughs were meant for her and smiled. Gracie had Alison's flowing blonde hair, but her wide grin and carefree laughter were descended from Derek. Maybe that was why Alison found it easier to love Gracie, seeing in her the form of someone that she already loved. Or that she had loved, she thought and pushed away.

"When are you guys gonna make out already?" Max groaned from the passenger seat. He glanced back at Gracie and the dog in the backseat, rolling his eyes at the faces Gracie was making at the dog. The dark hair that tumbled over his eyes was an unrulier version of Derek's, but his soft features were a smaller version of Alison's, not that she would ever draw that fact to his attention. This similarity was probably the reason for their unspoken alliance within the family, though that alliance seemed to be growing strained as Max entered his pre-teens.

He was ten, two years older than his sister, but the space between their birthdays meant that they were only one grade apart, a grievance for Max only worsened by the fact that their new elementary school had decided to combine the fourth and fifth grades for part of the school day, an exercise meant to provide a feeling of mentorship on the part of the older students, but which only seemed to create more resentment in Max.

Lately he had been growing more distant from the family, but Alison figured that was natural for his age, probably exasperated by their move from Illinois, which had been hard on the whole family, and his entering a new school where he knew no one but his younger sister, and would have to depart again in a year for the unfamiliar world of middle school.

In response to her brother's snark, Gracie wrapped her arms tighter around the dog, giving him a kiss on the head that smacked wetly against his bare skin. "Yuck," Max groaned, "how did I get stuck with this lovefest?"

"Because," Alison reminded him, "you overslept and missed your bus, so your mother was wonderful enough to give you a ride, giving you the privilege of spending more time with your beautiful sister."

"I already spend enough time with her at school. Every time we partner up with the younger kids, I'm always stuck with her. She's two years younger than me, for Chrissake!"

"Max, we've talked about the language. And it's not our fault that the school puts the fourth and fifth grades together for part of the day."

"But it is your fault that you had me just a week too early to put me into the next class."

Alison laughed at that. Max had a strange sense of logic that she always found funny. She turned to him and held up two fingers, just an inch apart.

The kids grew mercifully quiet as they drew near to the school, Max slumped over the armrest on the door, dreading the day ahead, Gracie busy giving admonitions to the dog to be a good boy and show mommy how well behaved he could be. Alison smiled at this, enjoying the rare moment of peace before she had to report to the offices of Myers, Harim, and Donaldson.

As the minivan exited the mountains, the road ahead flattened to a wide plain of breathtakingly green grass. The newly renovated campus of Sunnydale Elementary School was the sole occupant of that plain, surrounded by a thick stretch of forest that backed into the base of the mountains.

Only a few years before, Sunnydale had been a dying farm town whose few acres of downtown still lay moldering some miles distant, a small huddle of single-story buildings grouped around the rusted remnants of the train track that had once stopped there to pick up crops. The town itself had been in danger being swallowed up by those crops until Derek and a few other developers had discovered the many acres of beautiful land tucked away between the ridges of the mountains and spread among the valleys at their base.

Previously considered uninhabitable because of its remote distance from any metropolitan center, the land, and the homes quickly built on it, had proven attractive to upper-middle class families whose parents had learned to work from home during the pandemic. Now that the virus was gone, these software engineers and marketing professionals were desperate to escape metropolises like Denver and raise their families among nature, and were willing to put up with the hour-long commute to Denver on the rare occasions they had to appear in the office.

To educate the sudden influx of young children from these families, the town had let its old elementary school (little more than a schoolhouse) go to seed, while a new high school had been built across town. The new Sunnydale Elementary had been built in the old colonial-style high school building that had once serviced the entire county, with all the latest upgrades that the tax dollars of the new families could afford.

The building was a pleasant one-story strip of faux-colonial brick running along the long and otherwise uninhabited stretch of the state road that connected Sunnydale to a string of dying farm towns before ending at Interstate

25. The building stretched the length of one or two city blocks before ending with a few small wings that girdled a playground and several sports fields, which ended at a thick, dark expanse of woods with only the sheer face of the mountains beyond.

Alison pulled into the narrow curve of road before the school's wide front lawn and stopped the car. "You aren't going to walk us inside, are you?" Max groaned, watching with horror as she pulled the keys out.

"I just want to say hello to your teacher."

"She's not my teacher," Max grumbled, slamming the car door on the way out.

Ms. Lightheart was standing, as she did every day before school, just in front of the school's wide, high-arched main entrance, on the pool of concrete where the rivers of sidewalks snaking through the massive stretch of grass in front of the school ran together. She was young, in her early twenties, and pretty in a non-descript way. She was enthusiastically greeting each student by name, having memorized them all despite school only being in session for a week.

Like Max and Gracie, she was new to the school, having earned her teaching certificate at the University of Colorado, Boulder only the previous spring. She taught the fourth grade, but during the time the two classes were combined, she took over for the fifth-grade teacher, Mr. Franklin, who used that time for an uninterrupted nap in the otherwise deserted teacher's lounge, at least if Max and Gracie could be believed.

As Gracie approached with the dog on a leash, Ms. Lightheart bent down to squeeze the animal's face. "Well, aren't you a nice addition to my class? I hope you stick around." She looked up at Alison, somewhat embarrassed. "Oh, hello, Mrs. Rains."

"Oh, just call me Alison. Thanks for letting Gracie bring the dog in. It means the world to her."

"Oh, my pleasure. I'm an animal lover myself, and I think it's good for the kids to learn how to behave around them."

"And vice versa. Alright, I have to get to work, be good you two." She pointed only at Max and the dog, neither of whom seemed amused. Max rolled his eyes and pretended not to know her, wandering off towards a group of boys his age who waved to him from around a corner of sharp brick.

"I see Max is in a positive mood like always," Ms. Lightheart said with a smirk.

"I'm just glad he's finding friends so quickly."

Ms. Lightheart said nothing, looking at the corner the boys had disappeared around.

Craning his neck around the corner, Eddie Parker scanned the long hallway that led along the outer wall of the school, connecting the square of classrooms to the second gym used by the older students and finally to the storage rooms and loading docks in the back. Apparently seeing nothing, he held up a hand and waved the others towards the single glass door that led outside. "All clear," he announced.

Trevor Soto stopped pretending he was getting something out of his cubby and walked towards the door, casting a final look down the hall as he passed. Max followed nervously, casting long looks behind them that would have been suspicious if there had been anyone around to see them. He and his new friends had quickly noticed that, while the front of the school was a whir of commotion during this brief period between the unloading of the buses and the start of class, the back of school was a ghost town until first period, with the principal and his staff busy sipping coffee in their office, and the teachers commiserating in their lounge or, like Ms. Lightheart, stupidly cooing at their students as they trudged in to start the day.

During this brief respite, Max and his friends had taken to sneaking out through this little-used back entrance into a corner of the school grounds blocked from the view of the classrooms and offices by the humming mass of the school's emergency generator, and hidden from the view of the athletic fields and the streets beyond by the towering bulk of the secondary gym. Here they could safely pass around a loose cigarette given to them by Trevor's older brother or a travel size bottle of alcohol lifted from Eddie's parents.

Today, it was Trevor who had promised the "find of the day," as they called it. Casting a final look around to make sure no one was watching, Trevor rummaged in his backpack and carefully removed a metal cylinder about the length of his hand, which the others stared at vacantly as sunlight glinted off its silver surface.

"Dude, is that… a Züül?" Eddie finally asked, deciphering the cryptic slashes of red metal that formed the logo.

"Yup," Trevor beamed, pressing the single button almost hidden in the metal until a small blue light above it began to blink. "My brother got a new one so he didn't need this one."

"I hear those things really mess you up," Max instantly wished he hadn't said.

Trevor raised an eyebrow at him over the Zuul, which he balanced on his lower lip while holding the single button, the blue light growing brighter, then blinking when it was time to release. Trevor exhaled a massive cloud of blue vapor, which Max tried to wave away.

"Yeah, right," Trevor said, and instantly burst into a coughing fit.

Eddie took the Züül Trevor held out. "So what, man? Don't be a vagina. They say the same thing about Family Guy and Diet Coke. You can't believe everything people tell you." Eddie took a slower, more measured drag on the metal cylinder, exhaling long after the light began to blink. "See? No cough." He instantly broke into a fevered bout of hacking, scattering the blue cloud that had gathered in front of his face with a spray of yellow droplets.

Max looked back at the door, nervously wondering if their hacking would attract any unwanted attention. "You guys gotta keep it down," he warned, trying to keep his voice far cooler than he felt.

Trevor glared at him and struggled to swallow a cough. "Fuck, man, are you gonna be cool or what?" he croaked. "Eddie and I thought you would be when we let you into the Gentlemen's Club."

"The Gentlemen's Club" was Trevor's term for this illicit gathering. Max didn't understand the name, and had a feeling that Trevor didn't either. Trevor had founded the club after discovering this spot the previous year, having transferred to the new Sunnydale Elementary when it had opened two years ago.

Trevor's family had lived since he was born in a development just at the base of the mountain where Sylvan Springs had been built. Max had met Trevor on the bus last week when school had begun. Recognizing a rare new face in the neighborhood, Trevor had struck up a conversation, where they discovered they were to be in the same class. Since then, they had been eating lunch at the same table every day with a few of Trevor's friends, including Eddie, who had lived in the same neighborhood as Trevor since they were born. Trevor and Eddie had been having some form of the Gentlemen's Club since their days at the decaying old elementary school across town, where they had snuck away during recess to a shady tree-lined grove at the back of the playground to pass around Playboys stolen from Trevor's older brother.

When Trevor had invited Max to be the third member of this secret club, Max felt as if he had lucked into the highest rung of his new school's society, washing away the painful memories of being an outcast at his old school in Illinois. The Gentlemen's Club was Max's only truly social time during his day and the only thing he looked forward to at school. He didn't want to lose it over whatever abstract fear he was feeling now.

He took the Züül that Eddie was offering and flipped it around to find the mouthpiece. "What's even in this thing?" he asked.

"Pure fucking happiness," Trevor gasped, stifling another cough in his sleeve. Max wanted to ask whether the amber-like goo visible in the glass pod was weed or tobacco, but he sensed that even having to ask that would be a major strike against him. He wrapped his lips around the mouthpiece and pressed the silver button.

He had meant to take only a brief puff, but with Eddie and Trevor's eyes on him, he felt compelled to hold the button until the light began to blink. A strangely cool vapor filled his mouth and from there seemed to find its way into his nose. He breathed in steadily, filling his lungs, not feeling any pain or irritation. He didn't know what the other guys were so bothered about; he didn't have to cough or hack, he felt fine.

Max released the silver button and let the pen drop to his side. He slowly released the cloud of vapor, confidently blowing it into Trevor's face. As he exhaled the last of the vapor, his lungs suddenly began to burn. A fit of coughing tore through his torso. Trevor laughed as he took back the pen, jokingly slapping Max on the back, making his coughs even worse. "It's alright dude, don't be a pussy."

The coughs racked Max's body until he was sure he would never be able to make them stop. The harder he tried, the stronger the urge became. With each cough, a tingling sensation spread from his head to the rest of his body. Whether this was a high or the result of a lack of oxygen, Max couldn't tell, but the feeling quickly spread through his body, relaxing him. Even his lungs grew slack and gave up the urge to cough. Max straightened cautiously, his abs and back sore.

"Feeling better?" Trevor asked over another hit. Max nodded silently, not wanting to risk another cough. He watched the door as Trevor and Eddie took another hit, but waved the pen away when Trevor offered it again. A peaceful feeling was coursing through his body, and he didn't want to ruin it with another fit of coughing. Trevor shrugged and put the pen away. "About time to get to class anyways. This meeting of the Gentlemen's Club is adjourned."

The peaceful feeling quickly wore away as the morning ground on. As Mr. Franklin resumed yesterday's lecture about long division, Max stared hopelessly at the clock, occasionally comparing it to the schedule written on the far-left side of the whiteboard, which split the day into segments of forty-five minutes. Once the clock reached 8:45, the math lecture mercifully ended and they were on to History, which Max would have enjoyed if it weren't for the reminder written on the schedule that the next section was "mentorship hour," which meant that Mr. Franklin would be marching them over to the fourth-grade classroom.

Max sighed. The peaceful feeling was now completely gone, replaced by a vague irritation he couldn't place. He tried to focus on the history lesson, but found his mind unable to concentrate. Even the tales of heroism from the Revolutionary War couldn't grab his attention. Instead, he doodled aimlessly in his notebook, occasionally stifling a cough in his sweatshirt. At each cough, Trevor would look over and flash him a quick grin.

Finally, the history lesson ended and Mr. Franklin announced it was time for mentorship hour. He made them line up in two rows in front of the door, like they were soldiers preparing to jump out of a boat at Normandy. Trevor jockeyed to be in line next to Max. "How ya feeling, bud?" he asked with a grin. Max shrugged, not wanting to say too much around the other kids.

Mr. Franklin opened the door and led them into the common area between the fourth and fifth grade classrooms. This long octagonal space was sometimes used for presentations to all of the classes, and was capped on one narrow end by a hallway to the library that served as the school's centerpiece, and on the other end by a doorway to the playground.

At each end of this common area was a walled area with openings on each end, flat on the innermost wall and on the outermost mirroring exactly the three walls of the end of the common space. Inside this walled area was a collection of coat hooks and cubbies. The entire common area was underlit and underwhelming despite the dirt-crusted skylights in the center of the ceiling, and today struck Max with more than the usual sensation of being a sort of prison area.

Mr. Franklin led them around this walled area to the fourth-grade classroom. The students took advantage of this moment of freedom to talk excitedly, unleashing a babble of noise that filled the common area. The sound pinged off the walls and doors, piercing Max's skull and filling his brain with static. As they reached the fourth-grade classroom, Mr. Franklin silenced them with a raised hand and opened the door.

In contrast to Mr. Franklin's spartan classroom, with only a few generic motivational posters to liven up the bare brick, Ms. Lightheart's classroom was warm and inviting, with multi-colored artwork covering every inch of the walls. The narrow entryway of the triangular room had been turned into a sort of lounge, with rugs covering the floor and an overstuffed purple chair along the front wall. The barrage of colors hurt Max's eyes, overwhelming his brain no matter where he looked.

Mr. Franklin held the door open and ushered them inside. Ms. Lightheart was finishing a lesson on the planets, but looked up from the whiteboard to welcome them inside. "Think you can handle these animals for a while?" Mr. Franklin growled from beneath his mustache. Max was facing the other way, but thought he could feel Mr. Franklin's eyes on his back.

Ms. Lightheart only smiled and said it wouldn't be a problem. "Good," Mr. Franklin growled, "I have to go work on my lesson plans." He headed for the door, his eyes already glazing over in anticipation of the nap he would soon be taking.

Ms. Lightheart put away her markers as the door slammed shut, sealing the two classes in together. "All right, today we're going to be doing something special. I hope you all brought something fun for show and tell."

Max rolled his eyes. He supposed this was better than helping the fourth graders edit their papers or learn their multiplication tables, but it would still be painfully boring. Ms. Lightheart directed the fifth-graders to sit on the floor in a series of semi-circles around the overstuffed purple chair. The fourth-graders quickly joined them, Gracie walking the dog by its leash.

As the fourth and fifth graders (mostly fourth graders) took turns displaying some treasured toy or boring family heirloom, Max felt his mood and energy levels sinking even further, and he found himself counting down the minutes until lunch. Maybe he and Trevor could find a way to sneak outside while everyone else was eating. Max saw Trevor making faces at him across the semi-circle, but resisted the urge to respond. He had already had a few brushes with Mr. Franklin and didn't want to get himself in trouble in only his first week at a new school.

As a fourth-grade girl finished showing the class a collection of historical family photographs and telling them in painstaking detail who each person in each photo was, Ms. Lightheart led the class in a round of forced applause. "All right, next up is Gracie with her new dog, which I know a lot of you have noticed already!"

An excited murmur spread among the students as Gracie strode to the front of the group, confidently leading the dog behind her. Trevor rolled his eyes at Max, who held back a laugh.

"Gracie, can you tell us what kind of dog that is?" Ms. Lightheart asked.

Gracie cleared her throat and held up her two pages of notes, as if she needed them. "He is a *Xoloitzcuintli*, or Xolo for short. Xolos are the national dog of Mexico, where they were revered by the ancient Aztecs as guardians of the underworld. Their hairless skin derives from-"

Max zoned out as his sister droned on. Looking around the classroom, he saw a ring of fawning faces staring at the dog. Even Ms. Lightheart was staring at the thing in rapt attention. Damn it, what was wrong with all of them? It was just some stupid animal; it wasn't so special.

As Max looked around, his vision settled on Trevor, who was trying to goad Max into something by repeatedly cutting his eyes towards the floor. Max followed his gaze to the dog's leathery, whip-like tail, which was slapping back and forth on the rug just in front of Max, wagging as the stupid animal basked in the mindless attention of the class.

Trevor continued to nod at the tail, which wagged back and forth, back and forth, rhythmically slapping a tuft of carpet just inches from Max's hands. Trevor subtly raised a hand, mimicking yanking the tail, the same way Max and Gracie signaled to truckers to sound their horn to relieve their boredom on one of the interminable road trips their dad dragged them on.

Max looked at the kids mindlessly fawning over the dog and shrugged. He reached a hand across the floor, palm-up, and waited for the leather whip to collide with his palm. When it did, he snapped his fingers shut instantly. As he felt the tail struggling to escape, he pulled. Hard.

The dog's head whirled around, its face contorted into a look of rage that Max wouldn't have believed was possible from an animal. The mouth slid open, revealing fangs far longer than he had expected, all of them yellowed and dripping with slime.

Max dropped the tail, but it was far too late to appease the thing. The dog pounced and knocked him to the ground, pinning him down with its paws on his chest. He saw kids run away screaming on each side of him, tripping over each other in their desperation to get away from the dog. Drool dripped onto Max's face. It filled his mouth as he opened it for a scream. A blast of hot air filled Max's nostrils with a stench like rotting meat.

Beyond the dog, Max saw Ms. Lightheart trying to push her way through the crowd, but he knew it was too late for her to save him. The dog's mouth opened wider to swallow Max's face, until his vision was filled by nothing but fangs and the rolling pink ridges of the thing's mouth. Max tried to scream, but only swallowed a spray of the dog's drool. The weak, gagging sound that followed seemed to echo in the cavernous space of the dog's mouth. Before Max could try to scream again, that massive cavern seemed to close down all around him, blacking out the world around him and leaving him in a realm of darkness.

THREE

FOR THE THIRD TIME THAT DAY, LEROY MYERS QUIETLY POKED HIS HEAD out of his office and found Alison writing in her notebook. He knew she harbored some secret desire to be a poetess or some such, but he thought she could pursue those dreams when not on company time, regardless of whether there were any clients in the practice at the moment. He snuck as close as he could before announcing his presence. "Ms. Rains," he asked evenly, "do you have the files for the Stevenson case?"

He was satisfied to see Alison jump a little. She hid the notebook beneath a stack of papers on her desk and produced the files in the same motion. It amused LeRoy to see that she thought she could keep her writing habit a secret, when the narrow window of his office looked out directly on the desk she manned in the main lobby. He often looked out on her when he wasn't busy, making sure that she kept the office running as he and the other partners had hired her to.

"Here you are, Mr. Myers," Alison said, holding out the file and trying to distract him with a smile. She was still pretty despite being in her mid-thirties, with gentle features and soft blue eyes, her long blonde hair always kept in a fastidious bun, her blazers and skirts kept neatly pressed. He forced his gaze to the little black notebook that was still poking out beneath the stack of work-related papers. He took the files and thanked her brusquely.

"You know, Ms. Rains-"

"It's Missus, actually."

LeRoy gave her a shallow grin and exhaled through his nose to show that she was not to interrupt. "Alison, I do appreciate the work you've done around here the last few weeks. And if my partners were in today, I know they would say the same."

"Thank you, sir," she said, obviously confused where this was going, as he had intended. "I just wish that you would keep your, um, journaling, to your private time." She followed his gaze to the notebook and started to object. He raised a hand to silence her. "Now, I know you have to have your creative output; I just hope that, while you are here, you can find that output in the organization and management of this office."

She swallowed and nodded. "Yes, sir. That shouldn't be a problem." He was satisfied to see her slide the notebook into her purse.

He nodded to show the conversation was over and turned to the front door, where John Stevenson was dragging his massive bulk in from the parking lot. John was one of the longest-serving city council members in Sunnydale, and had recently fallen on hard times with his wife Barbara, which had started with an argument over the best way to spend the town's recent influx of tax dollars (Barb was the city council's treasurer) and had ended with Barb moving in with the city manager, who had conveniently taken her side in the argument.

LeRoy stepped forward and offered John his warmest handshake. "My condolences, John, for how all of this has turned out." Behind him, the phone rang and LeRoy was pleased to hear Alison answer with a warm recital of the firm's name.

John half-heartedly accepted the handshake. "Yeah, well, as long as it turns out to be an amicable split." Then, after a moment's reflection, "I don't want to lose any more money over this than I already have."

"That shouldn't be a problem, John. Alison, could you get Mr. Stevenson some coffee?"

When she didn't answer, he turned to the desk where he saw her glued to the phone, a look of concern spreading across her face. "Yes, this is Mrs. Rains," she said in a hushed tone. "What's Max done this time?"

LeRoy shrugged at John, apologizing for his secretary. "Alison, I'm wondering if you can–"

"I'll be right there!" she yelled, but not at him. She slammed the phone down and shot out of her chair, collecting her purse along the way. "I'm sorry,

Mr. Myers, I have to go. There's been an emergency at my son's school." She rushed to the door, almost knocking Mr. Stevenson over on her way out, leaving both of the men looking after her, perplexed.

Alison's Toyota flew across the narrow lane in front of the school, barely stopping in time to avoid hitting the curb. The Sienna came to a rest across several parking spaces, but Alison took no notice. In her frantic rush she didn't even bother to lock the doors behind her as she left. Her attention was entirely consumed by the ambulance that must have navigated the narrow sidewalks to cross the wide plain of grass in front of the school. It was parked on the pool of cement just in front of the school, where only a few hours before she had said goodbye to her children. As she ran towards the ambulance, she was almost blinded by its lights reflecting off the windows that lined the front of the building, almost obscuring the faces of the children who peeked out from inside in weird shades of red and blue.

As she made her way around the vehicle, she ducked around the doors which hung open at the back. The pristine steel interior sat empty, but that didn't make her feel any better. Her anxiety growing, she turned to the glass doors to the school and found them locked. After rattling the doors desperately for a few moments, a grim-faced old man in something resembling a police uniform appeared in the breezeway. He stepped forward and pushed one door open.

"Mrs. Rains?" he asked without expression.

"Yes. Where's my son?!"

He held the door open for her. "Right this way."

He led her into the school, Alison's anxiety growing in the silence. She didn't even take in the wide, sun-bathed entryway or the deserted cafeteria, filled only by the distant smell of grease and the sound of an invisible fryer sizzling. The hallways beyond were deserted, giving Alison the impression that the kids she had seen from outside were now in hiding.

Alison weaved around the empty library, which stood like a diorama in the center of the school. A few classrooms lined the hall on the other side, their doors shut and their narrow windows covered in construction paper. Disembodied voices whispered from within. Alison knew they were whispering about what had happened to Max, keeping their voices down so she couldn't hear the truth.

Past the library, the security guard or police officer or whatever he was turned left through a pair of doors hanging open on magnets hidden in the wall. Beyond yawned the shadowy throat of a narrow hallway. Alison stepped in cautiously, made subtly nervous by the cold and dark in the windowless stone passage. Coat hooks lined the walls on both sides.

The light jackets the children wore to deal with the unseasonably early onset of fall hung limply, their empty limbs waving slightly in the mild breeze from the air conditioning. The image made her imagine the ghosts of children were animating their former clothing, waving to her in greeting, or farewell. She pushed the thought away and noticed Max and Gracie's coats hung at opposite ends of the hallway. She wondered vaguely if Max would ever wear his again.

Ahead, the hallway forked around a brick wall. The school resource officer (she had suddenly remembered his title from the parents' tour over the summer) led her right, past the classroom she also recognized as Mr. Franklin's from the tour. Around the corner, a tumult of voices was quickly growing louder, echoing off the stone walls around the common area.

The space was incredibly dark. The classroom doors were all shut, allowing no sunlight, and the few fluorescent lights barely illuminated the dark red carpet and brown brick walls. Students milled nervously around the common area, their teachers struggling to keep them contained. The commotion was focused on the center of the area, where several teachers formed a protective ring. Alison pushed through them and saw Max spread out on the floor, bleeding profusely from a massive tear on his hand. A paramedic was bandaging the hand while the school nurse tried to comfort him.

"Max, honey, are you okay?" Alison shrieked, pushing teachers aside in order to be close to him. Max only groaned.

The paramedic, an intelligent-looking, clean-cut man of college age, answered for him. "He'll be fine. He's in a little bit of shock right now, but the bleeding's going to stop. We're taking him to the clinic just for an evaluation. Do you know if the dog's had his rabies shot?"

Alison realized with horror that she didn't. She didn't know anything about the dog, but had let her daughter take it to school just because Gracie and Derek had pressured her. She felt so stupid, so irresponsible. She shook her head to keep back tears.

"That's alright," the paramedic responded. "We should give him the shots just in case."

"Can't you just test the dog?"

"We would have to kill him to do that." The paramedic shrugged, as if to say it was up to her.

"No, don't kill him!" Gracie yelled from somewhere in the crowd. Alison turned to see her emerging from a pack of other kids, wiping tears from her face. "It wasn't his fault. He only bit Max because he pulled his tail."

"Fuck you, Gracie," Max sputtered weakly.

"Max, language," Alison said as sternly as she could muster. "Gracie, everything will be fine. Where is the dog now?"

Gracie turned to Principal Brown, a hefty man in a suit that matched his name. When Alison had met him during the summer tour, he had seemed cool and collected, but since she had walked in, he had been in the corner, furiously berating Ms. Lightheart, admonishing her for allowing an animal in her classroom. When she had responded that he had signed off on the dog as well, he had scolded her for changing the subject and berated her even louder.

Now he cut himself off and turned to Alison. After taking a moment to catch his breath, he pointed to the closed door of Ms. Lightheart's classroom. "We managed to lock the beast in there before he attacked anyone else. Animal Control is on their way. Hopefully once they're done, you *will* be able to test him for rabies."

Alison held up a hand to calm him. "Okay, no need for that. My husband has a bond with the dog, he'll be able to get him out of there. I'll call him right now." With a sigh, she fished her phone out of her purse and began to dial.

FOUR

William Metcalf was already unimpressed. He had been unimpressed on his drive through the barren, rocky landscape between his Denver office and Sylvan Springs, then even more unimpressed when his valet had turned onto a lonely, weed-eaten country road that cut through a narrow pass in the most barren part and unimpressive part of the Front Range. The pathetic wooden sign which was the only indication that the neighborhood had begun was particularly unimpressive, a coating of dirt already collecting in the grooves of the letters, despite being less than two years old.

The narrow lane leading to the development was even more unimpressive than the crumbling county road it branched from. As the road wound deeper into a shadowy, high-walled ravine, William began to fear that the sign had been only a ruse, that bandits would soon line up along the tops of those high walls, emerging from the cracks in the walls to block their car and prevent their escape. Just when he was about to order his valet to turn around, the ravine opened ahead of them, revealing an unimpressive huddle of homes and empty lots that it took William a long moment realize was supposed to be the neighborhood.

Not that it wasn't beautiful, with its rolling streets wound perfectly through the mountain ridges, or that the houses built on its wide green lots weren't grand and impressive. He had been unimpressed simply by how few of them there were, and how many of the weed-choked empty lots had "for sale" signs on them.

When Derek Rains had invited William to Sylvan Springs in order to discuss an investment for an expansion, William had assumed that his intent had been to show off the bustling neighborhood and demonstrate why there was a pressing need for that expansion. Instead, driving through the carless streets and around the empty parks, there was only one word for how he felt: unimpressed.

He was even more unimpressed now, in a conference room in the back of the Sylvan Springs community center (he had noted, unimpressed, that the pool and gym were unoccupied) watching Derek give a presentation on the need for an expansion to his impressively unexpanded community. To be fair, Derek Rains did cut an impressive figure. Still youthful in his mid-thirties, Derek had a handsome, even boyish look, with a clean-shaven face and short brown hair swept neatly to one side. His sport coat was neatly pressed, though William wasn't particularly impressed by his decision to pair it with jeans.

Derek was trying to impress him with a presentation of his plans for the expansion, showing slide after slide of long streets snaking through the forest. Not only were these plans wildly optimistic, with street after street of filled lots, but Derek sounded nervous, almost desperate. Even worse, he had pulled his phone out of his pocket to silence a call a few minutes into his presentation. It had rung again during his presentation, and he had silenced it again after staring at the screen for a long moment. All in all, William was quickly growing more unimpressed.

"Well, I like the plan," he forced out as Derek held on a rendering of bucolic homes among rolling hills, "but is it necessary to keep this much open land?"

"I think it's essential to preserve the character of the land as much as possible." Derek's phone rang again and he silenced it with a long look at the screen.

William sighed. "It just seems like you're leaving a lot of potential lots on the table." He resisted the urge to say that Derek had already left plenty of lots on the table by not selling them.

"Perhaps, but in order to build those lots we would have to completely destroy the value of the land, not to mention their ecological value..." His phone rang again, a few short beeps this time as a series of texts flashed on his screen. Derek glanced at the phone and began to read them. A worried look crossed his face.

"I'm sorry, Derek, am I keeping you from something?"

Derek looked at William as if just noticing he was there. He slapped the phone nervously between his palms. "I'm sorry to do this to you, William, but it's my wife. Apparently, there's been some kind of family emergency, I have to go." Without further explanation, Derek ran for the door, leaving William alone with the rolling hills animated on the screen. William sank back with a sigh, thoroughly unimpressed.

FIVE

By the time Derek arrived at Sunnydale Elementary, the ambulance had already left, bringing his son to the clinic at the base of the mountains, Alison riding along, fretting and fussing over him the whole way. In its place, a bulky van with the logo of Puebla County Animal Control filled up most of two parking spaces behind the Sheriff's patrol car. Alison's minivan filled most of the remaining spots. Derek parked neatly in the last open space and jogged the long sidewalk to the door. The school resource officer let him in and they walked the eerie, silent path to the classroom, the officer filling him in on what had happened so far along the way.

When they arrived at the common area, Derek found the students and teachers somewhat calmer than the resource officer told him Alison had, with the distracting influence of an injured student gone, replaced by the calming but still exciting distraction of two gawky young animal control officers armed with silver-barreled dart guns, and an overweight but imposing county sheriff brazenly brandishing a massive six-shooter on his hip.

This lawman approached Derek as he entered and held out a hand. "Sheriff Garth Chambers. That your animal in there?"

Derek accepted the meaty hand, which almost crushed his own. "I haven't had a chance to look yet, but I'm going to assume so."

Garth cut off his vigorous handshake with a laugh. "Well, we're going to need you to remove it so these kids can get back to their studies."

"Fat chance of that happening," the overweight principal sneered from his perch in a corner near a crying teacher. Derek had met both of them over the summer but couldn't remember their names just now.

He followed the sheriff to the door he had indicated. The narrow windows beside it and the tiny porthole-like opening in the middle of the door were covered on the inside by black construction paper, but one sheet was peeled back just enough for Derek to peer into the darkness. "Why are the lights off?" he asked.

"They're on a motion sensor," the principal answered. "He must not have moved in a while."

"Then he's probably calmed down. I'll go in there and grab him."

"Let me come with you, Dad." Gracie had appeared at his side, pulling at the sleeve of his blazer to stop him. "He's nice to me."

Derek crouched next to his daughter, putting a hand on each of her shoulders. "I know, Gracie, but he could still be angry. Besides, now that he's bit your brother, he might have developed a taste for the family blood." He squeezed her shoulders with a laugh she did not return.

"Then you shouldn't go either."

Derek's laugh died out. "Well, I have to."

"Alright, Mr. Rains," the sheriff drawled, "but if he bites again, animal control will have to take care of him."

He nodded to a young animal control officer, who was nervously loading a dart from a steel lockbox into his enormous silver-barreled gun. Derek's eyes widened at the size of the dart. "Jesus, would that kill him?"

The officer nervously glanced at him, not wanting to look away from his work. "It shouldn't," he said, without confidence.

Gracie pulled on his sleeve again. "Dad, please don't let him die. He didn't do anything wrong. He only attacked because Max was being mean to him."

"Yeah, I believe it." He pulled Gracie's hand away and returned it to her side. "I'm not going to let anything happen to him. Believe me."

Gracie nodded and reluctantly allowed him to lead her away from the door. The sheriff and the principal stepped back as Derek opened the door. Derek exchanged a final look with the sheriff before slipping inside.

Closing the door behind himself, Derek found himself trapped in a world of near-total darkness. The only light came from a small window on the far end of the room, which opened only onto a narrow space before the brick wall of another wing of the school. The day outside had suddenly grown cloudy, and little sunlight pierced the soap-filmed window.

In the darkness, Derek could hear the dog softly snoring, but was unable to see it. He waved a hand through the air, trying to activate the motion sensor, but without success. He thought of what his waving limb might look like to a hungry dog and withdrew his hand. Turning back to the door, he slipped a finger under the construction paper covering the small window in the door, which was already peeled back an inch. Trying not to make enough noise to wake up the dog, he carefully peeled off the construction paper and placed it in a blue bin near the door.

The fluorescent light had seemed dim while Derek was in the hallway, but now that it was concentrated in a narrow beam, the light seemed impossibly bright, glinting off the steel legs of desks and revealing the back paws of the sleeping dog. Derek looked out the small window and gave a thumbs up to Garth. Using the narrow beam of light as his only guide, he moved carefully towards the dog, holding out his arms in search of unseen obstacles. As he drew closer to the dog, it grew invisible as the beam of light suddenly wavered and disappeared. Derek turned back to see the faces of Garth and one of the young animal control officers blocking the window. Garth pressed a meaty hand against the window and gave Derek a silhouetted thumbs up, blocking out the last sliver of light.

Derek rolled his eyes and turned back to the dog, using his memory to crouch near where he had last seen it. A pair of eyes appeared from the darkness, glowing as if the dog's eyes had their own internal light. Derek jumped back as the eyes narrowed at him viciously. As he moved, the room was suddenly flooded with brightness, so intense that Derek jumped, thinking he was seeing the flash of shock as the dog attacked him, long before the pain of the bite entered his nerves. As his eyes adjusted to the light, he saw the dog lying still as before. His eyes moved to the motion sensor on the wall.

"Right," he muttered to himself, then, to the dog: "You wanna go home, buddy?" As he crouched to collect its leash, the dog wearily raised its head, lifting its snout from a pool of reddish drool. As the dog sleepily turned its head towards him, Derek saw dried blood crusted on its lips and nose. He shivered, forcing himself not to think about where that blood had come from. He pushed away the thought of the thing sucking his son's blood like a vampire, feeding off his life energy. Forcing himself to keep calm, Derek spoke in soft tones as he reached past the dog and grabbed its leash.

He froze when he saw the dog eyeing the inside of his arm. For a long moment, Derek stood still, preparing to react in case the dog really had gotten a taste for Rains family flesh. But the dog only glanced at him for a moment, then wearily turned away. Derek let out a breath he didn't know he had been holding and stood up, tugging on the leash to bring the dog with him. "Come on, boy, let's get out of here." The dog followed without a fight.

The sheriff and the animal control officer backed away from the door as Derek stepped into the hallway. Derek held the door open as the dog followed, stopping when it saw the crowd assembled outside. Derek tugged on its leash, leading it away from distraction and a possible attack. He held out his free hand, inviting Gracie to join him. She took it and they walked out together, the dog casually trotting beside them, the crowd behind them still and silent.

Derek expected the sheriff to call him back, to imprison him for having an uncontrolled animal or to confiscate the dog, but he heard nothing as he led Gracie and the dog past the fifth-grade classroom. He led her towards the coat hooks so she could collect her own and her brother's coats. As they and the dog passed out of sight, he heard the students break out as one into an excited chatter, the principal unsuccessfully trying to maintain order, leading a futile charge to continue the day as normal.

SIX

"All I'm saying, Mr. Rains, is if it had been any other child than your own, you and I would be having a very different conversation."

There hadn't been much conversation at all, but Derek didn't think it was wise to make Sheriff Chambers too aware of that fact as he sat in Derek's kitchen, doling out his diatribe. "For your own sake, I suggest you get rid of the dog," he concluded.

"I understand, Sheriff. Sorry for the trouble." Derek was just glad the scolding was over. He watched Garth collect his hat from the kitchen counter and walked the sheriff out the front door, hoping that the neighbors wouldn't see him leaving.

In the living room, Derek found Alison and Max on the couch watching TV. Max had returned from the clinic with stiches on his hand and a bandage across his stomach where they had injected the shots for rabies; nothing serious, but he was shaken up and exhausted. Alison had been doting on him unnecessarily since the moment they had returned from the clinic.

"Where's Gracie?" Derek asked when neither of them acknowledged his entrance.

"Up in her room, crying her eyes out," Alison answered. "Where else would you expect her to be?"

"What's she crying about?" Max groaned. "She didn't have to get stitches. Or those damn shots." He laid back, rubbing his belly with his non-bandaged hand.

"Well, if you hadn't pulled on that dog's tail, you wouldn't have had to either," Derek reminded him sternly.

Max snorted. "Or if you hadn't brought a wild animal into our house."

"This is my house, Max, and I won't-"

"-Derek, can I have a word with you?" Alison cut in, already moving him towards the kitchen. He let her move him, already dreading another scolding. From the living room, he heard the blare of the TV growing softer.

"Can we do this somewhere the kids won't overhear?" he asked.

"Well, Gracie's upstairs. What about the backyard?"

"The dog's out there." He didn't want to have a fight in front of its subject.

Alison rolled her eyes and led him out of the kitchen. She crossed the main hall, between the front entryway and the wide staircase to the second floor, and led him into the study. She closed the door behind them.

Derek dropped himself into the single desk chair while Alison paced in front of the picture window. "You realize we have to get rid of the dog, right?" she said finally.

Derek shrugged. "Gracie seems to have a bond with it. Max probably would too if he could behave himself."

"You're changing the subject. Have you thought about how Max will feel seeing the animal that bit him every day?"

Derek hadn't, and he suspected that the look on his face betrayed that.

Hearing nothing, Alison answered her own question. "He'll be scared to death, and honestly, so will I. I can't stop worrying it will bite one of the kids."

"That's why we have it locked up in the backyard."

"And is it going to stay there all night? All winter? That dog was made for Mexico, he doesn't have any hair, how do you think he's going to like our winters? Did you ever think about that?"

Derek sighed. "I guess I haven't."

Alison's tone and face softened. "So, you'll get rid of it?"

Derek nodded, more to indicate thought than acceptance. "Well, I don't have the paperwork for it, we can't sell it. And we can't rightly give it away if we know it's going to misbehave."

"What about a pound?" Alison suggested.

"No, don't bring him to a pound!" Gracie shrieked, bursting through the door she had been holding open an inch.

"Gracie, we talked about the sneaking around," Alison said, bemused.

Gracie continued as if her mother hadn't spoken. "Mom, don't send him to a pound, please! They'll just kill him; he doesn't deserve that."

Alison didn't know what to say.

Derek took Gracie by the arms and gently turned her around. "Don't worry, Grace, the shelter around here is really good. They always find a home for animals, and if they can't, they take care of them themselves." Derek caught an appreciative glance from Alison over Gracie's head.

"You promise?" Gracie asked. Derek nodded. "Are you taking him there tonight?"

"I have to."

"Can I come with you?"

"Sorry, kiddo. The shelter is way on the other side of the mountains. It's a two-hour drive each way, so I won't be back until late, and you have school in the morning."

"But, Dad, I want to–"

Derek cut off her tantrum before it could start. "No buts. Just stay here. If you're good, we can get you a new dog, one that's better behaved."

Neither Gracie nor Alison looked happy about that. "But only if you're good," he attempted to recover, then slipped out before he could do any more damage.

As Derek stepped out to the backyard, the sun was just beginning to set behind the mountains. The dog was on a chain tied to a stake in the center of the backyard. His back was turned to the house, and he sat slumped and dejected, as if he knew he was being shamed. Derek zipped his jacket against the suddenly chilly night. Maybe Alison was right about the dog not being able to survive the winter, he thought as he watched its huddled posture.

As Derek walked across the yard towards him, the dog stared intently at the thick woods behind the house, as if ignoring him. "You're curious about the world out there, aren't you?" Derek said, approaching cautiously. The dog did not react. "Well, let's go for a ride and you can see it."

He carefully slipped the leash off the stake and gave it a tug. He froze as the dog turned back to him. In the glow of the setting sun, the dog's eyes seemed to glow again. He paused for a moment, instinctively feeling the bearer of those hideous eyes would attack him, but nothing happened. He shuddered and led the dog through a gate to the front yard.

He was almost to his car when he heard the front door burst open. "I have to say goodbye," Gracie cried, her arms held wide as she dashed across the front yard. Derek held his breath as she threw her arms around the dog, but the animal did not react as Gracie enveloped it in a hug. Kissing the dog on its forehead, she gave it a final squeeze. "I'll miss you, Mr. Ed."

"Wait, you gave him a name?" He knew that Gracie religiously watched reruns of the old show about the talking horse whenever it was on the channel aimed at elderly shut-ins, but had no idea she had enough of a bond with the dog to name it after the fictional animal. He had to look away as Gracie nodded and gave the dog a final hug.

Wiping away tears, Gracie walked back towards the house, casting a final look back at the dog. Waving goodbye to Gracie, Derek adjusted the rearview until he was looking the dog in the eye. "Well, thanks for not biting her at least."

The dog said nothing as Derek backed out of the driveway and started down the road.

SEVEN

Because the only pound in Puebla County was the dingy and rather frightening county animal shelter, Derek decided to make good on his promise to Gracie and take the dog to the nearest private shelter, where the beast might have at least a chance of being adopted. The only one a search on his phone returned was on the far side of the mountains, so Derek reluctantly set out on the 110-mile drive down the twisting, lonely county highway which was the only route west into the smaller villages scattered among the peaks and valleys of the Rockies.

The sun was just setting behind the mountains as the road descended into a deep valley of forest, the shadows of the trees reaching out like skeletal hands across the highway. As the road dipped into a layer of darkness that looked like a solid sea his car was sinking into, Derek glanced in the rearview at the dog, who sat placidly in the backseat, seeming to fear or expect nothing. Derek looked forward into the eternal night, wishing he could do the same.

After a long stretch in which he was sure he had missed the turn in the impenetrable blackness that had settled around his car, Derek finally found the building long after dark, an animal hospital and shelter that served the small towns along the banks of the South Platte River and scattered among the Rocky Mountains, performing surgeries on horses and cattle brought from the farms that filled the narrow valleys while housing the strays that wandered off from the towns hidden between the peaks.

The shelter was the only structure on the top of a ridge overlooking the river on one side and a series of dramatic peaks on the other, though none of that was visible in the darkness. Even the building itself was little more than a small, boxy outline of shadow against the deeper darkness of the infinite sky. The only light in the area came from a floodlight posted on the building's roof, which unevenly lit the packed dirt of the parking lot. The only vehicle there besides Derek's was an oversized, amazingly dirty van with the logo of the shelter barely visible below a crust of mud. As Derek dragged the reluctant dog across the empty parking lot, the only sound was the rushing of the river far below. Even the woods seemed to be empty of birds and insects.

The lobby was equally deserted. A few broken plastic chairs and a dying potted plant were all that lined the wood-paneled walls. The fluorescent lights put off more noise than light. Derek's shoes stuck to the gummy linoleum. The dog curiously sniffed the air, and after a moment Derek did likewise, taking in a heavy scent of antiseptic that seemed designed to drown out the curious dingy smell that seemed soaked into every surface. The dog took another whiff and turned to whine at Derek. "I know, buddy," he said, uneasily patting the dog's head.

As he walked the dog to the empty counter at the far end of the lobby, Derek heard a soft electronic chime from deeper in the building. Immediately, a series of small sounds he hadn't been aware of stopped, replaced by a shuffling set of footsteps. A moment later, a small, wiry woman of about sixty appeared at one of the two doors in the back corner.

Her features were sharp and weathered, as if all the concern they had expressed in life had been written permanently on her face, but her eyes were still striking and bright, seeming to stare into Derek with an almost aggressive intelligence. She wore a knee-length white lab coat streaked with shockingly red blood. She stood in the doorway for a moment, staring at Derek over thick-framed bifocals which were also coated with blood along the temples. "Can I help you?" she asked in a sharp, impatient voice, seeming to direct the question equally between Derek and the dog.

For a moment, Derek was unable to answer, too distracted by the massive volume of blood coating her. She followed his gaze and emitted a humorless laugh. "That's nothing. Just working on a horse with a nosebleed. You here to drop off the dog?"

Xolo

Derek looked down at the Xolo and wondered if he could really leave him in a dismal mountaintop pound with this brusque, blood-soaked vet. He thought of the animal as he had first seen it, standing proud and noble in the Mexican sun. This was no place for him to end his story.

"Um, actually I'm here to find a friend for this guy," he improvised. The vet cast an even sharper glance at him over her bifocals, letting them slide so far down her face that Derek thought they would tumble to the floor. "I want to find one that gets along with him," Derek continued with a forced laugh.

The vet let out a long sigh. "This is a little later than most people shop for strays," she explained wearily. "I usually use this time for my surgeries, but you're welcome to take a look." She pushed open the door opposite the one she had entered from and held it open for Derek. He entered a narrow room of concrete and brick with rows of steel cages lining both walls and stacked to the ceiling. A voice at his shoulder almost made him jump, having already forgotten about the vet as she sat silently at the door.

"I have to get back to my horse, but you take a look around and see how they get along. I'll be back in a bit." He heard the door slam shut as she left. Derek led the hesitant Xolo inside, walking him into the narrow aisle between the two walls of cages. A dog filled every cage, more than three dozen in total. By their shape and size, there seemed to be a representative of almost every breed imaginable, but determining the exact breed of any one was impossible through their matted, dirty fur and the shadows they hid themselves in at the backs of their cages. They shrunk back even further as the Xolo neared their cages, like frightened servants hiding from a cruel master.

A red nose pit bull locked eyes with the Xolo and immediately began to bark, clawing furiously at the bars of its cage. The barking soon spread to the other dogs, who threw themselves against the bars like prisoners demanding liberation. Their barks and howls joined together in a ululating chorus which seemed to grow threefold as it bounced off the brick walls and the hard concrete floor. Through it all, the Xolo sat calmly, observing each dog in turn, never responding or even reacting to their barks.

Derek tugged on the Xolo's leash, trying to drag him from the room, unable to stand the barking any longer. The vet burst through the door she had disappeared behind, the lines on her face deepening in fury. "Sorry, I don't think any of these dogs will be a good friend for him!" Derek yelled over the howls. The vet did not seem amused.

When the Xolo still refused to move, Derek took a chance and scooped him up. To his surprise, the dog did not struggle or react, but only positioned himself to look over Derek's shoulder, casting a final glance back at the other dogs as Derek fled the room, trying to avoid the reproachful gaze of the vet. The howls followed him outside and echoed across the parking lot. Even as Derek approached his car and fumbled in his pocket for the keys, the muffled braying filled the air, occasionally mingled with the vet's unsuccessful orders for them to stop.

Derek hastily threw the dog in the passenger seat and started the car, speeding back onto the county highway without bothering to look for traffic. He sped through the dark without thinking where he was going, only trying to escape the noise and shame of the animal shelter. "What the hell was that, buddy?!" he asked the silent dog. "I can't even drop you off at the pound without you causing a scene!"

The dog only stared at him impassively. "I know, I know, that wasn't technically your fault, but you must have done something to set them off. It's a good thing I didn't leave you there after all." The dog only looked ahead into the night.

The road was lost in darkness, just as Derek's mind was lost in thought. He wondered what he could possibly do with the dog. He would have to bring him home tonight, but what could he possibly say to Alison? What would Max think when he woke up and saw the dog that had bit him in the house? And what would he ultimately do with the dog?

Derek's thoughts were interrupted by a sudden flash of white across his headlights, followed almost instantaneously by a sickening thump and a jolt that rattled his entire car. Derek slammed on his brakes, not bothering to pull off into the narrow dirt shoulder. He slipped the car into park, focusing on slowing the beating of his heart. He had clearly hit something; he could only hope it wasn't a stranded motorist or one of the homeless children that allegedly lived in this stretch of the mountains.

Throwing open the door, he saw nothing. No stranded car on the side of the road, no sign of an injured child, no body at all. The only hint that there had been an accident was his cracked headlight, smeared with thick streaks of blood which smoked as it dripped through the narrow cracks in the glass and sizzled against the bulb. Derek began to think that whatever animal had jumped in front of him had managed to run away just as fast.

Then he saw the body. The broken form of a female deer lay across the opposite lane, about twenty feet behind his car. The body was barely visible in the glow from his tail lights. Derek ran towards it, unsure whether to hope it was alive or dead. As he drew near the doe, it gently raised its head, as if looking for its attacker. Derek was struck with guilt and desperation. He looked out at the endless night around him, as if expecting the forest and the mountains to render aid.

Sensing movement near his side, Derek feared that his guilt was to be increased by the appearance of the doe's mate, or even worse, its children. Instead, he was surprised by the appearance of the dog at his side. Turning back to his car, Derek realized he had left the door open in his haste. The dog trotted towards the body, his leash bouncing on the pavement behind him.

At first Derek thought the animal would start eating the deer or try to lap up the blood pooling on the pavement, but as he rushed to stop the dog, he realized the Xolo was only staring the doe in its eyes, holding its gaze as the deer died. As Derek watched, transfixed, steam rose from the deer's mouth and nostrils, and from the jagged lines where the impact of the car had torn its flesh. This steam, heavy, yellow, and viscous, curled heavily through the air, the various jets converging before the dog's eyes, where they vanished as he took a deep breath. As the dog continued to inhale, the flow of steam gradually slowed and the deer settled heavily, the last light fading from its eyes. At the same time, the dog's eyes seemed to grow brighter. Finally, the deer's empty eyes shut slowly and its body relaxed.

The night seemed to grow chillier. Standing on the empty road, surrounded by nothing but darkness, the dog, and the body of a dead deer, Derek suddenly felt afraid of the Xolo. He remembered the vision he had after first looking into the dog's eyes, of Aztec priests committing a human sacrifice for the dog, the dog sitting regally on its throne while breathing in the steam that rose from the still-beating heart. At the time, Derek had been content to call it a hallucination, the fevered result of heat exposure and food poisoning, but now he couldn't help but acknowledge it as a vision, a glimpse of the past provided by some unknown force coming forth from the Xolo, or using it as a conduit.

That thought reminded him of something the old man who sold him the dog had said. "Guardian of the underworld, right?" he asked the dog. "You… helped him die, sucked his soul out, right? How'd you do that?"

As if to answer, the dog sat calmly on the pavement and turned to look at Derek. Its eyes glowed a horrible yellow, standing out in the darkness like a pair of headlights. Derek felt himself slipping into that light, the glow becoming the glint of fire reflecting off the jewels of an Aztec priest's necklace, but he pulled himself away, forcing himself to turn away from the dog. As he stared into the darkness beyond the road, he felt his mind begin to clear.

He couldn't bring the dog home, not now that he knew what it was. At the same time, the dog had already shown him it couldn't live among others of its own kind. As Derek's eyes adjusted to the darkness, the endless forest beyond the road came into view. Looking at the tangled, wild mass that stretched as far into the darkness as he could see, Derek realized that this was the perfect place for the dog.

In the rush of leaving the animal shelter, Derek had driven much farther than he had realized. He was now at the low point of a long valley, surrounded by nothing but unbroken forest for miles in every direction, cut off from all human communities by the high mountain ridges. If the dog tried to use the road to escape this valley, he would most likely end up like the deer. If not, he would live in the woods until he was starved or killed by some larger predator. If he somehow managed to survive until winter, the cold would surely kill him.

Some part of Derek still loved and pitied the dog, no matter how much he feared it now. That part of him rationalized his abandonment of the dog with the thought that the dog would be happier here in nature, free to hunt and follow its natural instincts. Hadn't Gracie said something about him being a primitive breed? Even if he died, at least he would die in nature, going down fighting as a noble animal like him deserved. Besides, with his temperament, the dog didn't stand a chance of being adopted. He would be on death row at the county animal shelter in less than a day. Out here, he had a chance to last much longer.

Now that he had convinced himself to ditch the dog, Derek had only to execute his plan. He looked both ways down the long, straight highway and saw nothing but the empty lanes disappearing into the night. He looked back towards his car, an island of light in the darkness, his door hanging open as if an invisible valet was welcoming him. He moved casually towards the light, hoping not to attract the dog's attention with sudden movements. When he heard the dog moving beside him, Derek broke into a run.

Before he could reach the car, the dog jumped into the front seat, turning back as if waiting for him to take it on a ride. Before he could convince himself it was a bad idea, Derek grabbed the dog by the collar and yanked it from the car. The dog immediately lashed out, sinking its teeth into the back of Derek's right hand. He screamed and tossed the dog to the street. He felt its teeth rip through his flesh as it fell, opening a massive strip of pain from his knuckles to his wrist, a flow of warm blood running down his fingers.

Derek had no time to worry about that. As the dog hit the pavement with a heavy thump, Derek dashed for the door, pulling it shut as he climbed in. As he instinctively locked the doors, the dog suddenly filled his window, its outstretched jaws spread against the pane, its drool smearing across the window as its breath fogged the glass.

Derek threw the car in gear and hit the gas. The dog fell from the window as the car took off. In the rearview, Derek saw a brief glimpse of the animal rolling across the pavement, then forced his eyes to the road ahead, knowing his car wouldn't survive another impact. He clutched the steering wheel until his knuckles turned white, knowing the pressure was forcing blood to jet from his hand, but not caring. He kept his foot on the gas, speeding through the endless darkness until he knew the dog was far behind. Even then, he kept speeding, secretly fearing that the dog was tracking him by the smell of his blood.

It was only when a semi, the first vehicle he had seen since leaving the animal shelter, sped past him that he consciously remembered the bite on his hand. A blinding flash of blue-white halogen flooded his car, illuminating the ragged strip of flesh that hung from the back of his hand and the blood that dripped from it. With the sight came pain, and soon he was so overwhelmed by the intense, burning agony in his hand that he could think of nothing else.

He pulled off where the dirt shoulder widened just before a narrow bridge. Ahead of him was a steep cliff looking over a wide expanse of forest, both forest and cliff cut off by the South Platte River far below. The dark forest and the wide expanse of stars above disappeared as he turned on the dome light, replaced by the blood-soaked interior of his car. Blood was splattered across his console, his radio, his steering wheel, his jeans, and the upholstery of his seat. He grabbed a handful of left-over fast-food napkins, the closest thing he had to a proper bandage, and pressed them against the back of his hand, squeezing his eyes shut against the pain. The crumpled napkins immediately bloomed a flowery red, then darkened and wilted as they grew heavy and collapsed on themselves. Blood continued to ooze around the crumpled remnants and drip across Derek's lap.

He knew he had to get to a hospital. Reaching across his lap with his uninjured left hand, Derek struggled for a moment to pull his phone from his right pocket, but the awkward angle made it impossible. He considered climbing out of the car so he could stand and easily reach down into his tangled pocket, but lingered with his hand over the door handle, imagining the dog lurking just outside. He tried to tell himself that was crazy, that he had left the dog behind miles ago, but it didn't help.

Knowing he had no other choice, Derek took a deep breath and reached into his pocket with his injured right hand. The tight seam scraped away the layer of dried tissues, then tore at the skin beneath as he held in a scream. The denim on his hip began to bloom red as he pressed his hand deeper into his pocket. After a few agonizing fumbles, Derek felt his fingers wrap around the phone, his hand bulging against the denim as he secured his grasp. As he dragged the phone out, his torn flesh scraped against the denim. He held in a scream, emptying his lungs through his nostrils as the loose skin bent back and tore further, the exposed nerves firing until the phone suddenly came free. Derek slumped back in his seat, taking in a new breath through his mouth as he let the pain subside.

When he finally worked up the strength to raise the phone, he found that the blood smeared across the screen made it impossible for the camera to recognize his face. Even when he tried to enter his passcode, his fingers could only swipe uselessly across the blood-slickened surface of the screen. Retrieving the last of his napkins from the storage area on the inside of his door, he wiped away enough of the blood to be able to enter his passcode. Opening Apple Maps, he searched for the nearest hospital. After a long moment of searching, the map dropped only a single red pin into the dark and otherwise unmarked territory around him, a twenty-four-hour emergency clinic just a few miles further up the county highway.

The place was strangely parallel to the animal shelter on the opposite side of the valley. It faced in the opposite direction over another steep cliff, looking over a majestic view of mountains and the swirling river far below. But this time the parking lot was made of asphalt and the small building was brightly lit. The lobby was again empty, but far more inviting, with a smiling nurse waiting at the desk on the far end. Derek had to reach into his back pocket this time, wincing at the pain and soaking another patch of denim with blood, to retrieve his wallet. He placed his insurance card on the desk, being careful not to get blood on the desk or the card. The nurse smiled at him, unfazed by his condition, and entered his information.

The doctor appeared without any obvious communication having taken place. He was a tall Indian man with a large black beard and a shockingly red turban that looked regal above his doctor's coat. He reached out a hand to shake Derek's, but withdrew it upon seeing the blood running down Derek's hand. "Come back, my friend," he said heartily, his voice a mixture of the rich tones of India and the clipped, precise diction of England.

As he rinsed Derek's wound and began to wrap it with bandages, he asked Derek how he had received such a nasty bite. Derek told him about the dog, about it biting Max, then told the doctor he had brought the dog to the pound, where the dog had bit him while Derek was dropping him off. Dr. Acharya nodded at this, only raising his head from the bandages at the point when the truth became a lie. "The vet couldn't do an emergency bandage? She let you drive all this way with that wound?"

Derek's mind reeled, desperate not to reveal any information that could reveal a hole in his story. "She was alone at the shelter; she was in the middle of a surgery. I told her it would be fine; I wasn't bleeding that badly when I left."

Dr. Acharya nodded, cut off the roll of gauze with a small pair of scissors, and taped the end of the strand to Derek's hand. The nurse appeared with a tray containing some syringes. "These will help to prevent rabies and tetanus, if the dog had it."

Derek winced at the sight of the syringes. He had always hated needles, and knowing that he had to get several shots in a row made the anticipation that much worse. To take his mind off the pain, Derek asked him if there were any other possible effects of a dog bite.

"Not really. In my village, it was believed that a dog bite was a prophecy of trouble to come in your marriage and family. But I'm afraid I don't have a shot for that." Derek laughed, but not too much.

As he left the clinic, Derek walked to the small fence surrounding the parking lot and looked out over the darkened mountains, breathing the clean air and trying to clear his head. He decided that when Alison asked him about the bandages, he would tell her the same story he had told the doctor. There was no need to upset her or Gracie with the fact that he had abandoned the dog in the woods. For Gracie's sake, he might even tell them it was another dog that had attacked him.

Turning away from the mountains, Derek realized he would have to clean one thing up in order for his story to work. The Xolo's drool still hung in heavy strands across his window, seeming to glow in the moonlight. Derek hurried towards his car, vaguely wondering if the dog would be able to track its own scent.

After some fruitless searching down the dark back roads, his phone having long since died, Derek found the only gas station in the area, an oasis of excessive brightness surrounded by a desert of dark mountains and a lonely county road that curved away into untouched forest in both directions. The little convenience store was locked and unmanned at this hour, but the pumps still beckoned for his credit card. As one pump silently filled his car, Derek grabbed a handful of paper towels from the dispenser on a nearby pillar and wiped away most of the drool, following it with a splash of the clear blue liquid in the squeegee dispenser. A swipe of the rubber blade revealed the bloodied interior of the car. After a few dabs of the upholstery with paper towels, Derek decided that he would need something stronger and that it would have to wait until morning.

Waiting for the gas to finish pumping, Derek walked across the parking lot towards the edge of the cliff the gas station was built on. Out of the blinding glare of the lights, his eyes could take in the endless forest below. Looking at its expanse and wildness, he decided again that it was the perfect place for the dog. He would have endless room to explore, endless animals to hunt. His instincts and his body would be put to good use, and he could live out the rest of his days in tranquility. Still, Derek couldn't help but feel a twinge of guilt for abandoning the dog.

As if in response to his thoughts, a long, mournful howl sounded from somewhere in the forest below, echoing off the endless cliffs. At the sound, the wound on Derek's hand began to burn, as if responding to its maker. Derek told himself that was silly and grabbed the wound with his other hand, squeezing the bandages to ease the pain, which only created more. But at least the pain took his mind off the sound, which reached a ululating crescendo, then cut off, leaving a haunting echo among the mountains.

Derek told himself he had only heard a coyote, but found it hard to make himself believe. He had heard the sadness in that cry and could not forget it. Behind him, he heard the gas pump click as it turned off. Before leaving, he stood at the cliff a moment longer, waiting for another cry, but heard nothing.

EIGHT

Derek struggled to keep his eyes open against the flickering light.

As the darkened chamber came into focus, he saw the Xolo over him. He tried to jump away in fright, but found he couldn't move. He turned his head as much as he could and realized he was lying on a large slab. The stone was cold and rough against his bare skin. His wrists and ankles were bound with what felt like rope, but his shoulders were free, allowing him to move his upper body.

As he struggled to sit up, he felt strong hands pushing him back down, pressing him against the slab. He tilted his head back to see one of the stone-faced priests holding him, his expression as emotionless and grave as when Derek had seen him before. Another priest appeared above him with a large dagger, which Derek realized the priest intended to use on him.

Raising the blade over Derek's head, the priest let it hang agonizingly in the air for a moment, then gently lowered it, setting the jewel-bedecked dagger on the slab next to Derek. He craned his head towards the Xolo, who stood like a statue on his own altar, adorned with a robe covered in gems. The priest carefully removed the robe, like a trainer revealing a boxer before a prize fight, and stood back. The Xolo bared its fangs; its hungry eyes began to glow. Derek realized that the priest had no need to remove his heart; the dog was going to do that itself.

Derek screamed and tried to struggle, but the priest held him firmly against the slab. As if attracted by his screams, the Xolo leapt down from his altar, his snout fixed on Derek like a heat-seeking missile. As he landed on Derek's chest, his claws began to swipe away large swaths of flesh. Derek screamed as the snout burrowed between his ribs. He felt the jaws lock around his still-beating heart and with a powerful bite, begin to squeeze the life out of him.

Derek woke up with a start. He still lay on his back and a shadowy figure still stood over him, holding his shoulders, pinning him down. He struggled to get away as the figure shook him. "Derek, wake up!" Alison yelled.

Once Derek heard his wife's voice, her face came into focus. A moment later, the high, wood-paneled ceiling of the living room also came into view. He had only looked at it before from a design point of view, never from the point of view of one drowsily waking up on the couch. Alison shook him again and let go of his shoulders. "What is it? What's wrong?" he asked lethargically, finally registering the angry tone of her voice and the sullen look on her rapidly focusing face.

"What's wrong?!" she asked sarcastically, her face growing even more upset. "Why don't you tell me?! Your car looks like you ran someone over, and there's blood all over the inside."

For a moment, Derek couldn't remember. Then the memories came flooding back to him, a series of disconnected fragments mixed with shadowy, mystical images. He raised his arms to rub sleep out of his eyes, trying to separate reality from nightmares. He remembered the bandages on his hand only when they rubbed against his eyes. "And what happened to your hand?!" Alison yelled, noticing the bandages at the same time he did.

He struggled to sit up, motioning to her to be quiet. His head was pounding, and sleep still conspired to drag his eyelids down. "The dog bit me while I was dropping him off at the pound," he said sleepily, proud of himself for remembering his lie in his condition.

Alison gasped, seeming to accept his story. "Oh my God! You have to go see a doctor!"

"I did," he reassured her, holding up the bandaged hand as proof. "He said I'll be fine. But I bled all over my car on the way."

"Oh, my goodness. But what happened to your car?"

"I hit a deer on the way to the clinic," he said, secretly pleased at his ability to mesh the truth and a lie so seamlessly, "I was in a rush and got distracted, but the car's okay, it will just need a little body work."

"I'm not worried about the car. I thought at first that you had decided to just run the dog over instead of dropping him off."

"Come on, I couldn't be that heartless." Derek wondered if that was really true.

"Glad to hear it. Just get the car cleaned up before the kids see it; they'll be traumatized. And make sure they get on the bus, okay? I have to get to work."

Derek mumbled sleepily that he would, then lay back on the couch as soon as he heard the front door closing. Within seconds, he had fallen back into a troubled sleep, interrupted by eldritch images that could have been dreams or memories. He awoke with no conception of how long he had been asleep, though the changed angle of the sunlight through the picture windows told him it had been at least an hour. He remembered with a start his promise to Alison and leapt off the couch, his head spinning as he realized he had stood up too fast. As he stood still, trying to get the room to stop spinning, he realized that the house was too quiet. The kids must have caught the bus while he was asleep.

Walking to the kitchen, Derek tried to remember how he had come to fall asleep on the couch. After the clinic, the night became a blur as the need for sleep had overtaken his mind. He must have stumbled inside and fallen asleep on the first convenient surface that presented itself, even the stairs to the second floor proving too much of an obstacle.

Derek downed several glasses of water, realizing more after each one how thirsty he had been. The pounding in his head began to subside and the sleep lifted from his brain. He wondered how much of his dehydration was due to the dog bite, then remembered distantly that extreme thirst was a symptom of rabies. Good thing the doctor had given him that shot, though he worried vaguely if the medication might have expired in that remote mountain clinic.

Over the chugging of his fifth glass of water, he heard a noise across the kitchen. Through the bottom of the glass, Derek saw the blurred outline of Max's back. Derek wondered how long he had been there. "How'd you sleep?" he asked, setting down his glass.

Max shrugged without turning around. "Did you have any weird dreams?" Derek continued.

Now Max turned around, but only to sneer at him. "Why is that your next question?"

"I just wanted to check if the dog bite had any effect on you." Derek realized that he and his son had matching bandages on their hands, and from a matching cause, but Max didn't look at him long enough to notice the bandages on his father's hand.

"It's fine," Max said, turning his attention back to the toaster in front of him. Derek reached for his glass and noticed the clock on the oven next to it. "Hey, it's getting late, aren't you gonna miss your bus?"

"Already did," Max said. "It's fine, I'm getting a ride."

This was news to Derek. "Oh? I hope you're not planning on getting that ride from me. And your mother already left for work."

"I know," Max said. He reached for the toaster just as a pair of Pop-Tarts sprang up with a clang. He caught them mid-air, not seeming to mind the heat.

"Well, last I checked, you are in fifth grade and shouldn't have any friends that can drive." Derek followed Max as he walked out of the kitchen and towards the entryway, holding a Pop-Tart in each hand.

"It's fine," he said once again, this time muffled by his first huge exploring bite. "My buddy's older brother goes to the high school down the street and offered to give us both a ride." He held the Pop-Tarts in his mouth as he pulled on his coat and backpack, gingerly pulling a sleeve over his bandaged hand.

"And who is this friend of yours?"

"My buddy Trevor Soto from class. You met him."

Derek didn't remember that. "Have I met his brother?" he asked.

Max swallowed another enormous bite of strawberry filling and shrugged. "I guess not." The sound of a rattling engine outside was followed by the squeak of a horn. "That's them. See ya later."

Derek stopped him by holding the door shut with one hand. "Hang on, I want to meet this friend of yours." Seeing that his dad would take no refusal, Max sighed. Derek let him leave and followed a moment later.

A rusted Buick LeSabre filled the driveway, the putting of its strained engine echoing off the mountains. As Derek approached, a tall, lanky teenager who appeared to be about sixteen climbed out from the driver's seat. Like his car, he looked a little rough around the edges, but not unreliable. He approached Derek with a confident greeting and offered an enthusiastic handshake, introducing himself as Jeremy Soto. He seemed charming enough, despite his air of a wannabe-gangster, helped by his dated look of baggy jeans, skate company t-shirt, snapback hat, and a thin goatee.

"Just wanted to say thanks for giving Max a ride." Max was climbing into the backseat with a scrawny boy his own age. Max handed the boy his second Pop-Tart and ate the rest of the first in a single giant bite.

"No problem, Mr. Rains, it's right on the way for us." He pointed to a burned-out-looking boy his own age in the passenger seat, who waved distractedly when Jeremy motioned to him. "That's my friend Steve and my little brother Trevor. He and Max get along really well from what I hear."

"Well, it's the first I heard of it," Derek said, leaving the boy somewhat puzzled. "Drive safe, Jeremy." Jeremy thanked him and climbed back into the car. Derek waved goodbye to Max, who pretended not to notice. The Buick struggled out of the driveway, its brakes squealing as Jeremy carefully sailed the massive bulk into the street.

Derek went back inside, making a note to himself that he should call the school later to make sure Max got there, just in case Jeremy's charming exterior was not as trustworthy as might seem. This thought, however, was forgotten as soon as Derek stepped inside the silent and now empty house. Flopping down into his previous spot on the couch, Derek fell into a deep and dreamless sleep.

Max heard the others suppressing a laugh as his dad waved goodbye to him from the driveway. He held in a laugh himself until Jeremy had turned the corner and they were out of sight of the house. "What a dork," Trevor said, spewing Pop-Tart crumbs across the backseat.

"Total dork," Max agreed. "He wants to watch over me constantly."

"Well, it's a good thing he can't do that now," Jeremy said, guiding the Buick out of Sylvan Springs and onto the uninhabited county road that led down the mountain. After a quick glance to ensure no one else was on the road, Jeremy nodded to Steve. After a long moment, Steve caught his glance and shook himself into action, sleepily reaching for the glovebox, from which he pulled out a crumpled cigarette carton. He opened it and turned it over, letting a foil-wrapped object fall into his palm.

He unwrapped the foil carefully and revealed a long, fat joint, its wrapping paper nearly bursting in the middle. The weed inside shone through as green as an emerald as Steve held it up to the windshield. "You guys smoke that before school?" Max said nervously, looking out between them to make sure no one passing on the road could see their rather obvious display.

Steve laughed, still turning the joint over in the sunlight. "Hell yeah, man," he sneered. "Before, during, and after..." He trailed off with a cackle, holding up the joint to admire the light refracting through the crystals of THC.

"But we're not going to school today," Jeremy cut in, giving Max an excited look in the rearview.

"We're not?" Max hoped the others didn't hear the nervous tremor in his voice. Jeremy shook his head as he took the joint and clenched between his teeth the long bit of rolled paper that made up the filter. He lit the joint with a brief spark from a tie-dye Bic lighter and took a series of long, deep drags, blocking out the windshield with a cloud of smoke before handing the joint back to Steve.

"Naw, I thought you could use a day off after your little injury yesterday, so I called the school and pretended to be your dad."

Max sank back into his seat. "At least someone thought so. Where are we going?"

"Everywhere and nowhere," Steve said through a series of coughs, "Everywhere and nowhere."

They drove down the county highway to the base of the mountain, Jeremy and Steve exchanging hits on the joint, filling the front of the car with smoke, while Max looked out the window, wondering where they were going. They drove, rather brazenly he thought, past the elementary school. Max felt like he should duck below the seat while they drove past, and wished that Jeremy and Steve would put the joint out for just a minute.

Past the school, the road led deeper into the countryside, little more than a flat strip of pavement over a flatter plain of grass, no buildings or trees on either side, even the mountains little more than a picturesque backdrop amongst the clouds. After a sign telling them they were leaving Puebla County, the only trees in the area loomed ahead in a thick wall, pierced only by a narrow gap where the road became a small steel bridge over the North Fork River.

Jeremy slowed as he crossed the bridge, then turned off the road and onto a narrow strip of dirt cut into the forest. "This is where the cops wait to catch speeders coming in to the county from Denver, sort of a welcoming committee."

Max stopped with his hand on the door. "Then are you sure that's where we want to be?"

"Yeah, they don't bother coming here until rush hour. No one's here during the day, that's why I love coming here."

"To the woods?"

"Better. Just come on, I'll show ya." Max followed the others out of the car. The dirt inlet ended just past Jeremy's bumper, the wall of woods pressing in on each side.

The brush was littered with empty plastic bottles, cigarette butts, coffee cups, and empty packages of Hostess' and Little Debbie's. Jeremy led them to the edge of the woods, where a narrow trail was cut through the brush. The others followed him single file, digging their feet into the soft dirt as the trail angled steeply downhill.

The woods were thick enough to block the sunlight. Steve took advantage of the situation to sneak another hit on the joint. "You sure nobody's gonna see your car up there?" Max called ahead, growing nervous now that the vehicle was out of sight.

"Will you relax? This is the very edge of the county, on the road between here and nowheresville. Nobody ever comes out here during the day." Jeremy brushed some branches aside and let a little sunlight in. Ahead, the massive steel bulk of the bridge towered over them. Max followed the others onto the soft mud of the river bank. Just ahead was the sloping concrete that formed the base of the bridge. Jeremy and Steve climbed up, helping the younger kids up the slope.

The concrete extended around the beams that held up the bridge, forming a sort of narrow ledge just above the river. Max followed the others carefully, looking upwards for traffic before plunging into the shadows beneath the bridge. The air instantly changed, as if they were stepping onto a different planet. The crispness of impending fall was replaced by a soggy, polluted dampness.

The narrow ledge of concrete extended only a foot or two from the pillars. A few feet down from the ledge was a bank of uneven rocks, which extended into the river, growing slimier and more uneven as they grew closer to the ruddy water. Jeremy and Steve dropped down to the rocks, clambering across them as if they knew each step already. Trevor followed them, uneasily at first, but quickly finding his footing. Max lowered himself carefully off the ledge, keeping one hand on the concrete above him.

The rocks shifted and settled beneath his feet, and he took a few stumbling steps to reorient himself. The others cast sharp looks at him until he found his footing. The boys spread out along the rocky bank. Jeremy relit the joint and took a heavy drag before holding it out to Max. "Just be careful not to exhale when you hear a car coming. If a cruiser does drive by here, we don't need them to see smoke coming up."

Max eyed the joint suspiciously, remembering the strange, nervous-excited feeling the Züül had instilled in him. If what was in the vape pen had been distilled from what was in that joint, he didn't think he needed to feel the effects of the original. "Uh, I think I'm good," he said, trying to avoid the reproachful looks of the others by pretending to study the graffiti that covered the concrete beneath the bridge.

"What's the matter, noob?" Steve asked. "Don't you smoke?"

"Uh, only a few hits off Trevor's Züül, but I think that's harmless."

The two teens looked at each other and laughed.

"Yeah, so's this," Jeremy said, holding the joint out more forcefully, almost stabbing it into Max's eyes.

Trevor snatched the joint from his outstretched hand and took a deep drag. His eyes seemed to glow as the tip burned red. Trevor lowered the joint and blew an enormous cloud into Max's face. "C'mon, man, I told them you were cool," he said weakly, the last of the smoke still escaping his lips. He held the joint so close to Max that Max had to take it in order to avoid getting burned.

Max turned the joint end over end, as if unsure what end to smoke out of. "You better hit that thing before it goes out," Steve warned.

Max held the joint unsteadily to his lips and took a drag, not feeling any smoke in his mouth until he had inhaled a massive amount of it, all of which rushed down his throat as he tried to hold it in. He pulled the joint away from his lips, looking at the others as they waited for his reaction. When he felt his eyes watering, he turned away from them, letting his eyes wander over the graffiti covering the concrete. The shakily painted letters seemed to vibrate and pulse, sliding across the concrete like brightly colored slugs.

A painted penis that spanned the length of the bridge began to pulse and thrust, the uneven blobs of paint ejaculating from its tip seeming to drip down the wall and be forever replaced by new ones. Max squeezed his eyes shut, hoping to block out the nervous, spinning feeling he felt overtaking him. The feeling only grew stronger in the darkness, accompanied by an unbearable pressure in his chest which had to be relieved.

The others laughed as Max began to cough, weakly holding out the joint until someone took it. He turned from them, the coughs racking his body, stumbling towards daylight and not knowing why, hoping somehow that the fresh air would revive him. As he escaped from the soggy damp beneath the bridge, the crisp air of early fall invaded his lungs. His cough grew even stronger, but felt as if it were finally pushing the smoke out, and with it the strange, nervous feeling overtaking his body. He stepped as close as he could to the river bank and gave a final, enormous heave, finally pushing all the smoke from his lungs.

He stood there for a moment, his hands on his knees, still doubled over on the edge of the river, waiting for his lungs to refill and his heart to slow. He idly spit into the river, hoping to purge the last of the nervous feeling from his body. As he watched his globs of spit float along the surface, he noticed something else in the water: the vague shape of a reflection which the unconscious part of his mind recognized long before the conscious part, and filled him with an instinctive terror before his rational mind could figure out why.

The Xolo was reflected in the water, standing on top of the hill just above and behind him. He froze, not wanting to turn around and confirm his fear, hoping to write the reflection off as just another hallucination, but the shape stayed firm in the water. Max knew he had to turn around in case the thing attacked him. He turned slowly, careful not to make any sudden movements. His eyes scanned slowly up the hill, as if still refusing to cooperate. When they reached the top, the xolo stood like a general surveying a battle, looking straight at Max with eyes so yellow they seemed to glow even in the daylight. Max's cough had been entirely forgotten.

He began to take slow backwards steps towards the bridge, afraid to turn his back on the thing. The dog watched him carefully, following him only with its eyes as Max slowly, unevenly found one foothold after another among the scattered rocks.

Max screamed as something grabbed him from behind. He whirled around to find Jeremy, laughing and holding his hands up to show he meant no harm. "You alright?" he asked with a smile.

Instead of answering, Max looked back at the embankment above, which now stood empty. His eye traced the path through the woods that led down to where they were standing, but he saw no movement among the branches. He turned back to Jeremy with a sigh of relief. "I thought- I thought I saw something. I guess I was just tripping."

"Let's hope not that fast. At least your cough is gone."

With a pat on his back, Jeremy led Max back under the bridge, where Trevor and Steve were waiting. They passed the joint around again, this time without Max participating. The four boys stood around beneath the bridge for some time, Trevor and the two teens idly talking about the current generation of video games versus the classics the older boys had grown up with.

Max stood apart from them, quietly throwing rocks into the river, trying to decide if what he had seen had been real or a hallucination.

The strange nervous feeling began to lift from him as he decided that the sight of the Xolo had been nothing but an effect of the joint. How could the dog be out here in the woods anyway, when his dad had dropped it off at the pound last night? He shook off the shock of seeing the dog and tried to rejoin the conversation, but the lingering effects of the joint made it hard to keep up with the conversation.

Eventually, the four boys grew bored. Trevor suggested they go exploring in the woods, but Max, still fearful of what he had seen, or thought he had seen, objected. They finally decided they would drive to the McDonald's in Castle Rock for lunch, where they could be sure no one would recognize them, then spend the afternoon on some trails nearby, where Steve knew they would be able to smoke without being bothered.

As Jeremy led them back up the hill, Max was careful to stay in the middle of the group, peering into the deep forest that pressed in on both sides of the trail, but saw nothing. When they reached the car, Max saw a trail of paw prints leading towards an open edge of the embankment which overlooked the river. He told himself they could have been from any dog, but he also knew he hadn't seen them on the way down. As he climbed into the car and cast a final nervous glance into the woods, he found himself unconsciously scratching the bandages that wrapped the wound on his hand, which burned and itched again, as if the dog had just now bitten his flesh.

NINE

For weeks, the dog had been forced to survive in the wilderness. Ever since the Master had abandoned him, he had been scourging a living in the wild, fighting off predators, hunting for his food, and sleeping when and where he could. On the night the Master had abandoned him, he had stood in the middle of the road, watching the lights disappear in the darkness, wondering when the Master would realize he had forgotten his dog.

The dog had only attacked him because the Master had attacked him first, grabbing him by the neck and slamming him against the ground. The dog had assumed that by winning the fight, he would be able to prove his worthiness to remain a member of the pack, but apparently the Master had misunderstood. He had waited in the road for what felt like days, eventually realizing the Master was not coming back. Returning to the deer's body, he ate a little, but wasn't satisfied, having earlier consumed the best part of the animal.

His meal was interrupted by bright lights that fell across the road from the direction the Master had disappeared. He turned eagerly from the carcass, awaiting his Master's return. The lights were at the top of the hill his Master had disappeared over, and rapidly growing larger. With them grew an enormous rushing sound, completely unlike the sound made by the thing his Master had left in. The lights grew larger and brighter, then were suddenly joined by a violent, piercing sound.

The dog scrambled out of the way, hiding in the ditch next to the road as the long, metallic object slid past him. After several moments, the noise subsided and the lights disappeared in the opposite direction of the Master's. The dog warily climbed back to the road and looked around. Seeing no more lights coming, he returned to the deer, which had been flattened and destroyed by the long shiny object, parts of the body scattered across the road and pressed into the pavement. He ate as much as he could, peeling scraps of flesh and skin from the road, but was soon doing no more than licking the asphalt, hoping to get a few more drops of the sweet red liquid.

It occurred to him that if he hadn't gotten out of the way of the long, shiny object, he would have been destroyed just like this deer and some other predator would probably be licking up his scraps right now. It dawned on him that his Master had left him here to die. The only other human he had encountered since had simply sped on, indifferent to his life or death. He realized he couldn't count on humans for his survival anymore, as he had for so long.

The night air was quickly growing colder. The wind tore into his exposed skin, stinging the spot where his former master had slammed him into the pavement. He walked away from the road, looking for a place to sleep in the woods. His leash dragged on the roots and branches. He tried to disconnect the leather strip where the Master had attached it to his collar, but his teeth were unable to force the clasp. In desperation, he bit into the leash, finding the weakest spot in the cracked leather and chewing until his mouth ran dry.

After his gums had started to bleed and his teeth felt like they would fall out, he finally bit through the last scrap of leather. The amputated leash disappeared among the weeds. The final wet stump of leather still hung from the collar, irritating him as it brushed against his chest, but at least he could move freely.

He dashed deeper into the woods, desperately looking for shelter. He found only a den burrowed beneath a deadfall. When he poked his head inside, a cluster of furry heads poked out. They could have been others of his own kind, but smaller and leaner, with thin, cruel lips, and long, sharp teeth. They snapped and bit at him, one of those long, thin teeth carving a jagged line across his snout. He felt blood drip into his mouth as he turned and ran, hoping the animals weren't chasing him. When he stopped and turned around, he saw nothing behind him. In fact, there was nothing around him but trees in every direction.

He realized this was as good a place as he would find to rest for the night. He had thought the world of nature, the world he belonged to, would accept him, but it had rejected him even more violently than the world of man. He smeared his snout along the ground, feeling some relief as the dirt filled his wound. He burrowed beneath a bed of fallen leaves, creating as much cover as he could against the increasingly cold wind.

After a night of restless and fearful sleep, he woke up still tired and hungry. The first had gone away as much as it would after he had walked around the forest for a while, but the second had only been cured after several hours of chasing after the small furry animals that crowded the forest floor. The smaller brown ones had been able to scramble up the trees where he could not follow, and the slightly larger white ones were able to burrow beneath the leaves and among the roots to their secret hiding places. Finally, he found one of the smaller white animals limping across the forest floor, dragging its broken leg behind it.

The dog pounced on the animal as its helpless companions scattered. A single bite to the neck stopped its useless struggle and brought a spray of delicious warmth into the dog's mouth. Even better was the rush of energy he absorbed as he looked into the dying thing's eyes, which quickly relaxed, then dimmed, then grew dark. The dog felt the creature's hopes, fears, and memories as they were absorbed into him. The dog felt rejuvenated, invincible.

He bit through the outer layer of fur, which was bitter and made the inside of his mouth dry out. He burrowed through the skin and pulled the pelt back, revealing the warm flesh beneath. The dog ate greedily, feeling more of the creature's hopes and fears enter him through the quickly-cooling flesh. The rush of energy from the animal's spirit was quickly dissipating, and before he knew it he had eaten the animal down to a flat-spread pelt lined with broken bones. His stomach roared as he licked the bones clean.

He needed more, but knew his opportunities would be limited here. Everything in this forest was able to run from him or fight him off. Perhaps he could still return to his human masters, persuade them to take him in again. Perhaps this had all been a misunderstanding, an accident. Perhaps his master had just grown frightened over seeing his first display of the dog's ability to absorb the lifeforce of his prey. He would grow used to it, even grow to love it once he realized how it could be used against the predators outside their home.

The dog had heard them scratching through the woods at night while he slept comfortably in his cage. It had taken every ounce of his willpower not to try to chase after them, to bark and strike furiously at the bars of his cage until one of the humans let him out to hunt. But he wanted to be what the humans called a GOOD BOY, knew how vital it was to his survival. He had never realized just how vital.

In the early morning sunlight, he set off towards the road where he had last seen the Master. Once he reached it, he began to walk in the direction the lights had disappeared in, staying within sight of the road, just far enough into the woods to remain invisible among the branches to the loud, shiny objects that occasionally whizzed by.

Once he had followed the road until the shadows of the trees had reversed direction, he picked up a familiar smell, not the smell of the Master or his family, which were too distant and too mingled with the smells of millions of other humans to be identifiable even to the dog's sensitive nose. Instead, he picked up a nearer and even more familiar scent: the dried but unmistakable smell left by his own saliva, the hormonal trace of his own bite. He was sure the Master had washed the saliva out of the bite on his hand by now, but the pheromones remained, dried in his wound and circulating through his blood, oozing out through his skin and forming a beacon the dog could follow home.

He ran through the woods as quickly as he could, eventually leaving the road behind in order to crash blindly through the heavy branches, guided only by his nose. The scent continually changed location and occasionally grew weaker, but its general direction stayed the same. Eventually, he left the main stretch of forest and followed the scent through a thin band of trees along a narrow river. On both sides, past the trees, stretched vast plains of grass. Although no human presence betrayed itself in those wide-open spaces, the dog still feared to show itself there, feeling that even allowing himself to be seen would bring danger.

Up ahead, the plains were briefly interrupted by a thin stretch of road. None of the long, shiny objects were whizzing by, but one of them rested among the trees ahead. The familiar pheromonal scent came strongly from this object. Cautiously looking out for humans, the dog crossed the road and smelled the object. The scent of the pheromones came strongly from one of the outcroppings in the back that the humans used to open the object, but there were no people inside.

The scent continued on a narrow trail leading downwards. The dog, fearful of trapping himself in a confined situation, looked for another way down. Just beyond the shiny object, the trees cleared out, leaving room to look down at the river. The dog approached carefully, hearing human voices just below.

Slinking to the edge of the cliff, he saw movement below. A familiar human figure emerged from beneath the bridge, bearing the unmistakable scent of the dog's bite. It was the Boy, the one who had cruelly pulled his tail. The dog realized he had been mistaken, that he had forgotten about this second trace of his bite and accidentally followed the wrong trail.

Still, perhaps the Boy could lead him back to the rest of his family. Maybe he would even take the dog in as atonement for attacking him. The Boy was bent over the edge of the water, trying to puke or cough. The dog waited at the edge of the cliff, not wanting to risk alarming the Boy. Nevertheless, the Boy seemed to suddenly grow aware of the dog, as if by instinct, and turned around, staring straight into his eyes. Perhaps his sense of smell was just as good as the dog's.

The Boy froze, then stiffened as terror stole over his face. The dog remained motionless, not wanting to alarm him, but the Boy slowly backed up, raising his hands in defense as if the dog would dive from the cliff and attack him. Another human, an older and taller boy, appeared from the darkened cave behind the Boy and grabbed him around the shoulders. The Boy screamed and then laughed at this newcomer, who the dog did not recognize. The dog heard more voices from within the cave, reacting to the screams outside. The dog backed away from the cliff, knowing he would be in danger if several humans decided to come after him at once. From below, he heard the Boy's excited shouts, probably calling the others to action.

The dog retreated into the woods, cowering among the bushes as he listened to the voices below. They grew louder before the Boy emerged from the woods, part of a group of four now, all of whom climbed into the long shiny object together. The dog jumped back at the roar the object made, and the cloud of black smoke that emerged from it, filling his nose and for a moment eclipsing his otherwise perfect sense of smell with an acrid, oily stench. The object began to lumber away, making fearful pops and rattles that frightened the dog even more. As it lumbered onto the road, the dog thought about chasing after the metal object, but knew from experience that he would never be able to keep up with it, even if he were willing to risk exposing himself in the wide grassy plains on each side of the road.

Digging himself as deep into those woods as he could, the dog watched the metallic object disappear over the horizon. Scanning the landscape, the dog realized that although the land on either side of the road was a long stretch of open grass, eventually that grass was interrupted by a line of scraggly trees on the horizon. By remaining among them, he might be able to follow the road the Boy had taken, eventually picking up on his scent in order to find his way back to the family home, where the Master had taken him in and the Girl had loved him, the only home where he had truly felt safe, if only for a night.

Taking the risk of being seen in the open grass, the dog ran to the thin line of trees, following them as far as he could, keeping the road just barely in sight most of the time. When the road swung away from the trees towards a small collection of human habitations, the dog took a more indirect path, dodging between a few clumps of open forest, hoping to pick up on the Boy's scent. The Boy's smell was long gone, but the acrid stench of the metal object still lingered in the air, much heavier on the nearest of the four roads that sprouted from the collection of human dens. Cutting across a stretch of forest to that street, the dog followed the smell through a winding mountain road that led through miles of forest and open rocky terrain.

With only one path to follow, the dog followed as best he could, taking several days and nights to make his way through the wilderness, occasionally stopping to eat one of the small furry animals that scampered in the woods along the road, enjoying the taste of their flesh and even more the rush of energy he absorbed from their dying eyes. Occasionally, he found already dead animals along the side of the road, bigger ones like the animal his Master had killed or smaller ones like the ones he hunted. Exhausted from his travels and too tired to hunt, or finding no game in the more remote parts of the wilderness, he ate the flesh of these creatures, sustaining his own in the process, but enjoying none of the spiritual, energetic refreshment he received when killing creatures on his own.

For water, he diverted into the woods to drink from clear mountain streams or lapped up brown pools from the side of the road. When the humans' shiny objects came rushing by, he hid in the woods, afraid to be seen, yet always peering out to see if the object was one he recognized, sniffing the air for a familiar scent.

Eventually, he reached a fork in the road, a split in the center of a deep valley. The oily smell of the metallic object was long gone and the scent of the boy was undetectable. The dog had no choice but to guess which way to go, hoping that he picked the right direction and would eventually pick up the scent.

Scanning the landscape, he saw a thick forest on a sloping hill across a long valley, which looked somewhat like the wild land behind the Master's house. Having no better ideas and fearing the open land around the roads in every other direction, the dog set off into the woods, hoping they would at least afford him shelter and easy prey.

Instead, they brought him hardship and competition. While there were plenty of the brown fluffy animals bounding across the forest floor and scampering up the trees, there were far more of the orange furry animals that he had seen poking their heads out of their nest, snapping and nipping at him, on his first night in the woods.

They seemed to be of a species similar to his own, but they acted as if he were an intruder from another world. They howled and bit at him, chasing him away from the small dens that could have provided his only shelter, eating the small, brown furry animals before he could hunt them, sometimes killing them only to spite him. Every once in a while, he managed to kill one of the small furry animals, and once even managed to kill one of the orange predators, a juvenile he caught away from its pack, but its dying howls had brought several of the adults running before he could even harvest the energy from its dying eyes.

His mind grew dull and his body grew weak. He trudged through the forest as best as his tired, broken paws would carry him. Sources of water grew fewer and further between, his body barely able to make the journey from stream to stream. The orange predators increasingly seemed to be hunting him, banding together to force the intruder from their land.

Through the weeks he wandered in this endless forest, the nights grew increasingly cold. The leaves began to fall from the trees, exposing him to the blinding sunlight during the day and the brutal winds at night. He slept in what shelter he could, but the strange orange predators seemed to be hiding in every available hole and cove, forcing him to take what shelter he could in the roots of trees or behind large rocks.

He began to think this had been a mistake, that he should have stuck to human roads until he found the familiar scent again, or simply looked for another human family to make his own. But his experience among the strangers who had run from him in panic after he defended himself against the Boy had taught him that he wasn't safe among most humans. Only the Master and the little girl had taken him in, shown him affection.

Then, one night when the air was getting just cold enough for him to see his breath at night, he had heard a sound that proved all his hopes well-founded. Waking from a light and restless sleep, he cocked his head and perked up his ears to make sure he had heard correctly. After a moment, he caught the distant but distinct sound of barking, not the sound of the orange predators but one of his own kind, or at least similar enough to live with humans. A human voice trying to silence the dog a moment later confirmed it: he was near a human settlement and could perhaps find his way to the Master, or at least escape from the endless woods.

Rising from the scant shelter of a deadfall, the dog made his way towards the sound, not even waiting for first light to traverse the woods. When that light did arrive, he found himself on the edge of a human settlement, the trees thinning out before the barriers that surrounded the flat areas around their homes. Taking a deep whiff of the air, the dog picked up the scent of hundreds of humans, almost as many dogs, and the million other conflicting smells of humanity, some of them sweet and lovely, most of them acrid and terrible. Searching through these smells again, he picked out just the faintest trace of himself, the slight pheromonal scent drying inside the wounds of the Boy or the Master.

The scent wasn't powerful enough to pinpoint, but by sticking to the edge of the human settlement, he thought he could eventually find the Master. For days, he walked through the woods on the edge of the human settlement and along the sides of roads, the scent growing stronger all the time. Finally, he followed the scent through a narrow mountain pass, hiding among the scant underbrush when the metal objects sped by.

Eventually he reached the settlement where the Master lived. He recognized it from the lone entrance he had made to the community in one of the long metal objects, and knew the Master's den was not far ahead. With his long-sought goal so near and the pheromonal scent overwhelming his mind, the dog wanted nothing more than to run down the street to his Master's home, to throw himself at the humans' mercy and hope they took him in. But he knew that could be dangerous; the metal objects could run him over or one of the other humans might attack him.

Forcing himself to play it safe, the dog slunk into the woods surrounding the settlement. Finding his way more by smell than memory, he climbed up a hill and eventually came to the stretch of woods just behind the Master's den. He heard the other dogs in the neighborhood barking when they sensed his presence, but he ignored them. His excitement grew as the shape of the house grew visible through the chain-link fence and the smell of the pheromones grew overwhelming.

Another scent was mixed with them, one so exciting and overwhelming that he didn't dare let himself hope it was real until his eyes confirmed it. The Girl, the only person who had truly cared for him, was alone in the backyard. She was sitting in the grass near where he had been tied up, playing with a few small objects that looked like miniature dogs.

The dog pressed himself to the edge of the of the chain-link fence, trying to decide how to make his presence known, when he heard a familiar voice from inside the house: the Master. The dog grew nervous. He had been searching for the Master for so long, confident he would be taken in, but now that the dog was near, he was suddenly sure the Master would only reject him again, take him even further into the wilderness to die, or perhaps even kill the dog himself.

The Master called again in an enticing, welcoming tone. The girl still ignored him, only went on playing with her miniature, inanimate dogs. The clear, sliding door opened and the Master appeared. The dog couldn't help but grow excited. His tail wagged, then fell at the sight of the dog next to the Master. He was tall and broad, with a friendly face and a bright golden coat that gleamed in the sunlight.

After another call from the Master, the Girl turned around, at first seeming not to notice the new arrival. She turned back to her miniature dogs for a moment, then whirled back towards the real one, apparently seeing it for the first time. Excitedly yelling to her father, the Girl ran to the new dog and threw her arms around it, the same way she had run to him that first day. The xolo stepped back from the chain-link fence, not wanting to be seen now, but continued to watch from among the branches.

The Master and the Girl were excitedly yelling to each other when the Master's mate appeared, the woman who had seemed to hate the dog but had never harmed him. When she saw the new dog, she grew agitated and began to yell at the Master, but both he and the Girl stepped in to the dog's defense. Over the woman's excited yelling, they voiced their approval, even gathered around the dog as if physically protecting him.

So, they had replaced him. The dog had journeyed for weeks through the wilderness and risked his life fighting predators, all just to make his way back to them, only to find they had replaced him without a second thought. Instead of watching their new happiness a moment longer, he snuck off into the woods before they could see him, hearing the excited cries of the Girl and the happy barking of the new dog echoing behind him as he ran.

He realized now he had no home among the humans. His old master in the old land had given him up without a word of goodbye after many years of loyalty; his new family had attacked him, then dumped him in the woods for defending himself; now they had completely forgotten him. Even when the Master had taken him to that awful building, where the abandoned dogs had been locked up in cages, the woman in charge had obviously disliked him. Even the dogs in that place had seemed to hate him, barking at him wildly as if he were a dangerous outsider.

There was no place for him but the wild. That hostile, unforgiving wilderness, that was his true home. The struggle, the deprivation, the fights with predators, those were his true birthright and lot in life. All of this he felt instinctively as he ran through the woods, not looking where he was going or even caring, only trudging deeper into the wilderness.

Eventually he came to a clearing in the woods, a little-used dirt road that led through the deepest stretches of this forest. He ran into this road, not aware enough of his surroundings to look for danger, not happy enough to care if there were any. The screeching sound of one of the long metal objects snapped him out of his trance.

The dog hadn't noticed the black van as it sped around the corner. The driver, not used to encountering anything on the road in this desolate stretch of woods, hadn't slammed on the brakes until it was almost too late. The van slowed, raising a massive cloud of dust, the rusted body spinning out on the dirt road, almost in danger of flipping over on the narrow roadway. The Xolo sat still in the middle of the road, as if he had already accepted his fate.

The rusted hulk screeched to a halt just inches from his snout. He sniffed the acrid fumes emerging from the hood, which continued to emit a rattling, thumping beat. There was a whining groan as the driver put the van in park, then the rusted creak of the driver's door opening. A pair of worn leather boots hit the ground with a thump of dirt and a splash of sand.

The driver stepped around his door and slammed it shut, never taking his eyes off the dog. He was as pale and thin as the cigarette dangling from his lips, and his ripped jeans and faded flannel matched his worn cowboy boots, although the baseball cap and aviator sunglasses threw off the look. The dog did not react as the man crossed the road and crouched next to it, even when he blew a heavy cloud of smoke in its face. "Oh, boy, ain't you a weird one?" he drawled.

The passenger door opened and a second man, with dark brown hair, a wide face, and the body of an ex-football player stepped out. "What the hell is that, Darren?" Mark asked, "A coyote with mange?"

Darren took another drag of his cigarette and smiled. "Oh no, it's a dog. Just lookit his face." He reached out and stroked the side of the dog's face, running his fingers along the torn flesh. The dog winced and drew back, baring his teeth in a vicious snarl. Darren's cigarette lit up along with his grin. "Oh, you're perfect," he rasped through a cloud of smoke.

The groan of the van's back door sliding open made both Darren and the dog turn their heads. Darren's other passenger, Billy, was impatiently striding from the van, his long black hair and the straps of his cracked leather jacket blowing in the wind. "C'mon, Darren, the boss just told us to find a dog, any dog. And I guess this overgrown sewer rat is close enough, so let's go."

"Alright, hang on, Billy." Darren fingered the amputated stump of leash hanging from the collar and tried to work it loose. "He doesn't have a leash; do we have an extra?"

"You kidding me? Of course we fucking do." Billy reached back into the van and pulled out a selection of leather leashes, some with collars hanging from them. He tossed Darren a length of red leather and Darren confidently replaced the torn stump of leash with the new one. The dog never objected as Darren snapped on the leash and led him towards the van.

"Come on, buddy," Darren said as he loaded the dog into the van. "You wanna come with us? You can be a fighter."

Mark laughed as he climbed into the passenger seat. "Yeah, you can be a gladiator!"

As Billy climbed into the driver's seat and threw the vehicle back in gear, the Xolo happily followed Darren into the van.

Because they had already picked up a dog, Billy was able to take the winding dirt road all the way up the mountain, skipping the newly-built neighborhood nearby. That was just as well with him; it made him nervous to be plucking pets off neighborhood streets where anyone could see them, even if the boss was in desperate need of another dog to even out the card tonight. Besides, in a prissy suburban development like that, full of fancy McMansions and wannabe country folk, they were likely to find only yippy little chihuahuas and poodles, and they already had plenty of bait dogs.

They had been damn lucky to find a healthy fighting dog all alone, and even luckier that he hadn't given Darren any trouble. His collar showed that he had recently had an owner, though why they would abandon him Billy couldn't say. It couldn't have been too long ago, since he still seemed to be civilized, though Billy hoped that some of that civility would melt away once they reached the fights.

They took this backwoods service street to another rarely-used dirt road, little more than a trail which would have been long ago absorbed by the forest if not for the occasional traffic to the building at the end, which was carefully hidden by a thick stand of evergreens. This structure was built in the style of a log cabin, although it was far too big to have ever been a simple summer residence. Perhaps it had once been a restaurant or supper club, but whatever it was, no evidence of any past life remained.

The roof of its once-inviting front porch was sagging and filled with dead leaves, and the wide front picture windows were covered on the inside with black paper. No signage indicated its current purpose, and nothing on the road pointed it out, but that hadn't stopped the field of dirt that served as its parking lot from filling up with a mix of rusting work trucks that looked barely able to function and high-end luxury cars that would have looked out of place even in the suburban neighborhoods they had just passed.

Billy found an open spot at the end of the lot and they all climbed out, Darren guiding the dog on a leash. The dog tried to remain near the van, as if he sensed what was going on inside, but Darren pulled harder on the leash, coaxing the dog, telling him that everything would be alright. Billy almost had to laugh; the gentle, loving tone was so discordant with the fate that Darren was literally dragging the animal to. "It almost seems like you love the thing, Darren," Billy said with a laugh.

Running ahead of the others, Billy jumped up onto the patio, the sagging floorboards groaning beneath his sudden weight, and knocked on the door in the idiotic pattern The Boss forced them to use. A metal panel in the door slid aside and a pair of eyes studied them, still covered by mirrored sunglasses despite the darkness inside. "New contender, Billy?" a gruff voice said, followed by a sucking puff on a cigarette. The sunglasses flared orange for a moment, then a puff of smoke billowed out through the panel.

"That's right, man, you mind letting us in before he runs away?" Billy waved to Darren, who was struggling to pull the dog onto the porch while Mark stood helplessly by. The eyes bobbed up and down and the panel slid shut. A moment later, the door opened wide, revealing a vortex of darkness that sunlight seemed unable to penetrate. Stale smoke drifted out in a cloud, mixed with the scents of liquor, sweat, and desperation.

The bald-headed bouncer waved them inside, holding the door open as the trio entered, Darren practically dragging the dog across the threshold. The bouncer finally took off his sunglasses and crouched next to the dog. "You think you got yourselves a real fighter?" he asked Billy.

Billy shrugged. "We hope so, man." He couldn't remember this bouncer's name, couldn't tell him apart from the half-dozen or so others who drifted through the clubhouse. They all shaved their heads and wore the same dark suits and mirrored sunglasses, like they all got the idea of what a bouncer should look like from the same dumb movie. Billy couldn't stand any of them and tried to avoid conversation with them the same way he tried to avoid the customers of this place.

The bouncer, old what's-his-name, reached out a hand and put it beneath the dog's nose. When that earned him only a curious sniff, he slapped the dog's face hard, dragging the flesh around the torn wounds. The dog leaped forward, stopped only by Darren tugging the leash backwards at the same time, and snapped the air where the bouncer's hand had been just a moment before. The bouncer's grin was deep and wicked. "That's better." He stood and waved to the three men. "Come on, guys, I'll bring you to The Boss."

The trio followed him deeper into the clubhouse. The main room was a large, high-ceilinged bar with wood walls and a ceiling of exposed beams. Halogen work lights were strung around the beams on dirty cords, providing a dim, uneven light, aided only by the few beams of sunlight that snuck in through the rips in the tarpaper covering the windows. A brass-railed bar lined one wall, backed by racks of top-shelf liquor and a mirror so dusty Billy could never see his own reflection, even if there were enough light, which there never was. That never bothered the regulars, who were, as usual, lined up along the bar or huddled in groups around the wobbly card tables that filled the main room.

The men drank cocktails, played cards, and smoked cigars and blunts. Half of them were dressed in thousand-dollar suits with hundred-dollar haircuts; the other half were unshaven, with rotted or missing teeth, and wrapped in greasy overalls that looked like they would peel the paint off the cheap wooden chairs. Strangely enough, these two groups were not segregated to their own tables, but made an almost even mix at each table.

The men looked at the trio of newcomers suspiciously as they walked by, and then even more suspiciously at their dog. One poker player even took off his sunglasses (God only knew why he needed them in here, or how he could see his cards) in order to get a better look at the dog. As they passed, Billy heard the murmuring start behind them, like an audible dropping the dog had left behind. The suits were speculating what kind of odds the dog would get, and the slacks wondered loudly and crudely how vicious his kills would be. Darren felt a perverse pride swelling inside his chest, despite having nothing to do with this dog's potential victories besides being the one to drag him to his fate. Perhaps it was the perpetual outsider in himself that had to root for this strange, scrappy dog they had found in the woods.

Billy, however, was strictly business as usual. "When do we get our money?" he asked.

The bouncer stopped in front of a small door in the back of the room and smiled. "Once The Boss inspects him. You know he doesn't let us handle the money."

"Yeah, I wouldn't let you handle jack shit," Mark muttered under his breath.

The bouncer pretended not to hear that and threw the door open, guiding them into an even darker space, a narrow passageway between the main building and the outbuilding just beyond. This cavernous wooden space had once been a barn or cow palace, but the only animals inside it now (besides the customers) were dogs.

As the bouncer led the men out of the damp darkness, the dogs began to bark. The tiny cages they were crammed into filled much of the short wall to the right. Most of the dogs were pit bulls or rottweilers, experienced fighting dogs straining at the bars of their cages, directing their barks at the newcomer, pushing their scarred faces through the bars in an attempt to bite him. The xolo strolled casually in front of their cages, only sniffing them curiously. He jumped back as one of the rottweilers snapped at his nose. His tensed claws scraped against the worn concrete.

A deep laugh resounded from across the room. "You call that a fighting dog?" the voice mocked. The trio turned to see its source, a squat Mexican-American man in a tight white linen suit, emerging from a cloud of his own cigar smoke. "More like a bait dog," Hector sneered.

Darren scoffed, trying to hide his wounded pride. "Hey, he's scrappy. We found him living by himself in the woods, and it looked like he had been there for a while. You try doing that this time of year without any hair. And just lookit the scars on his face, he's seen some shit."

Hector nodded and took another puff of his cigar. "Is that so?" He stepped closer to the dog, suddenly looking as if he recognized the animal. He crouched down and grabbed its face as if trying to study its features. "Perhaps he will be alright. Where did you find him?"

"Out in the woods, by that new development up the road."

"Sylvan Springs?"

Darren hesitated for a moment, unsure what to say. He had heard vaguely that Hector was involved in real estate, but was unsure whether Sylvan Springs was one of his projects. Perhaps the dog had been stolen from one of Hector's neighbors, maybe even from the man himself. Darren pursed his lips, but Hector saw the answer on his face anyways and grinned. "Yeah, just by there," Darren confirmed. "Looked like he had been out in the woods for weeks."

Hector shrugged, trying to make this information look like no big deal, but Darren spied him stealthily checking the collar for an address tag. "Well, he should do fine anyway."

"Damn, right," Billy said. "So, can we get our money now?"

Hector chuckled and struggled to lift his bulk onto his feet. He nodded to his bouncer, who took the dog's leash and led the animal towards an empty cage. Hector reached into his breast pocket and pulled out a wad of cash that Billy eyed hungrily. Being careful not to burn the cash with his cigar, Hector split the wad into three small even piles, handing one to each man.

Billy looked resentfully at the few bills Hector handed him. "You promised us three hundred."

Hector grinned smarmily over his cigar. "Three hundred per dog, not three hundred per man."

As Billy crumpled the bills in his fist, Hector clapped him on the shoulder. "You wanna make some real money, why don't you stick around for the fight? You really believe in that mutt, you can bet your earnings on him."

Darren watched as the bouncer stuffed the hairless dog into a small cage. The dogs on either side started nipping at him through the bars on the side of his cage. After securing the Xolo's cage, the bouncer walked to the end of the line and opened a small kennel stacked on top of the larger cages. Pulling out a small, malnourished toy poodle, he dangled the dog like a treat, pacing in front of the cages, holding the poodle just beyond the bars. The starved dogs went crazy, slamming themselves against the doors of their cages until the bars began to bend outwards and the latches looked ready to break.

Alone among the dogs, the Xolo remained still and calm, only furrowing his brow in puzzlement as he watched the other dogs. Darren watched the bouncer rile up the other dogs with a mixture of excitement and disgust, but couldn't help but be impressed by the Xolo's stoicism.

Other men had begun to file into the arena without Darren noticing, the regulars from the bar and others who had just arrived. They spread across a raised wooden platform that filled most of the building, surrounding a pit with a bloodstained wooden floor. They leaned against the railing surrounding this pit and filled the space around it, yelling encouragement to the dogs and lighting up fresh cigarettes or joints, filling the space between the roof beams with smoke, which glimmered in the hazy glow of the halogen work-lights that dangled from the ceiling beams or stood on precarious metal stands.

Mark bought cans of beer from a man with a cooler and handed two to Billy and Darren. "Might as well enjoy the show," he said with a shrug. The trio took a spot along the railing.

Two sullen, hard-edged men wearing leather gloves and faded t-shirts opened two of the dog cages, carefully leading out a pair of the meanest-looking dogs by long leashes. Another handler opened a wooden gate that led into the arena from the lower floor, through a tunnel beneath the viewing platform.

The audience cheered as the handlers led the dogs into the arena. An old man in an expensive Italian suit accepted the wads of bills the cheering men held out, writing down their bets in a small notebook. The man outside closed the gate while the handlers led the dogs to opposite corners of the arena. Bouncers pushed the spectators back from the railings as the handlers climbed out of the arena and over the railings, still holding the long leashes, keeping the dogs away from each other, the leashes pulling on their necks and revving them up to fight.

The spectators pushed back as one of the bouncers held the poodle over the railing, dangling it over the center of the arena between the two dogs. Both dogs pulled at their leashes, biting the air as if they could possibly reach the poodle. Their handlers pulled back, riling them up even more. The poodle squirmed helplessly, trying to escape the bouncer's grip without realizing how dangerous that would be. The cheers of the crowd drowned out the cries of the dogs.

Darren saw Hector across the arena, calmly smoking a cigar in the back of the crowd, waiting for his audience to reach the peak of their excitement. When he saw the last of the bets being placed, he waved his cigar as a signal to the bouncer, who instantly dropped the poodle. At the same moment, the handlers let go of the long leashes. The dogs charged forward, descending on the helpless poodle in an instant. Its whimpering cries were quickly replaced by the sound of tearing flesh and the crunch of bone. As the dogs ripped the poodle's body apart, their jaws bit into each other's, and soon they were fighting over the few remaining scraps of flesh. The cheers from the crowd grew louder as the dogs began to tear into each other.

Darren grimaced at the blood that flowed from their necks and sides. He had seen a few fights before, but the violence had never bothered him. He looked over to the Xolo, who sat in his cage with a worried look on his face, his brow furrowed as he watched the dogs fighting. Darren could almost hear the whimpers he was sure the dog was emitting. As the dogs continued to tear into each other, Darren had to avert his eyes. He saw only floorboards, heard only the yelps and cries of pained dogs and the wild cheering of the crowd.

Half the cheers turned to boos as one of the dogs hit the floor with a thud. Darren looked up to see the larger of the fighting dogs eating the loser, ripping open his neck as the crowd cheered. The winning dog's handler grabbed his leash and pulled him away from the loser, who was still feebly twitching on the floor.

Darren looked back at the Xolo, who was barking at the men and scratching at the bars of his cage. Mark tapped one of the bouncers on the shoulder and pointed to the Xolo. "Looks like that sewer rat is ready to fight next!"

The bouncer followed his gaze and called across the arena. "Bring in that hairless thing!"

One handler dropped the leash connected to the dying loser and climbed off the platform. The Xolo nipped and bit at him as the handler violently tugged the dog from his cage and pulled his leash toward the arena. The Xolo pulled back, trying to remain near the cage, but the dog was no match for the enormous bulk of the man.

Darren felt a surge of pity for the dog. All of the dogs showed a willingness to fight for their lives, but the Xolo was the only one who had shown a willingness to fight in order not to fight, to avoid the conflict between its own kind entirely. The handler, however, was doing all he could to create that conflict, using the leash to pull the dog's nose higher in the air as he tugged him towards the arena in a series of short, violent bursts. "You smell that?!" the handler screamed. "You smell that blood in the air, you freak?! You wanna eat that, don't you?!"

A bouncer swung the gate open while the other handler held the previous round's winner back, raising his bloodlust even further. The winning dog barked and struggled as blood, both his own and the other dog's, dripped from his jaws. The Xolo shrunk back from this out-of-control animal, but his handler pulled him into the arena, bringing him close to the dying dog. "You wanna eat him, don't you?"

The Xolo only looked the dying dog in the eyes. Darren leaned over the railing to see what he would do. The Xolo kept his gaze steady and even as the dying dog's thrashing slowed and then stopped. A thin stream of what looked like yellow steam rose up from the dying dog's mouth and the wounds in his neck. The Xolo breathed in the steam as the other dog grew stiff and died. When the Xolo opened his eyes, they seemed to be glowing yellow.

Darren glanced around the crowd, trying to see if anyone else had seen what he had just seen. The handler holding the Xolo's leash was behind the dog and had apparently only seen the animal's back, while the other handler was busy with his own dog. The people in the crowd were busy placing bets, buying beers, or just lighting up a fresh smoke. None of them were looking in the arena. Darren turned back to Mark and Billy, who were both placing bets.

"Did you guys see that?"

"See what?!" Mark handed the old man a wad of bills. "Put it all on the winner of the last round. I ain't betting on that hairless mutt!"

"You might want to," Darren cautioned, "he just sucked the life out of that other dog."

Mark looked at him blankly, as if not quite comprehending what his friend had just said. Finally, the realization came to him and he could only laugh. "Man, you are way too connected to that dog," he said, shaking his head. Darren turned to Billy, trying to protest, but saw it would do no good. No one could possibly believe what he had seen; even he had trouble accepting it. He gave up and leaned against the railing, realizing there was nothing he could do but watch.

The handler pulled the Xolo away from the corpse and into one corner of the cage. Across the arena, the Xolo saw the other dog being pulled back, rearing on its leash, struggling to pull free. The Xolo realized with horror that they intended for him to fight this dog.

The Xolo was sickened. He was unable to even imagine fighting another of his own kind. Even those strange orange predators in the woods had been too similar for him to fight if it hadn't been necessary to stay alive. The humans could have at least allowed the victor to eat the losing dog's body, then at least some good could have come from this violence.

Looking up at the humans gathered around the arena, hearing their loud, excited yells, the Xolo realized that it was impossible for dogs to live in the society of humans. None of them had good intentions for dogs, only selfish uses that they tricked dogs in order to obtain. These men only wanted dogs to kill each other for their own sick pleasure; the Master had only wanted him to protect his family, and hadn't even bothered to protect the dog from his family in return. Even the little Girl had moved on as soon as he was gone, proving she only wanted companionship and didn't care who she got it from.

The Xolo realized he could never have a family among these creatures, could never have a place in their society. But since the wilderness had also proven unforgiving, the only answer was to build a society of his own, a family of creatures of his own kind. But right now, the humans were trying to actively destroy that society before it could be made, forcing the dogs to kill others of their own kind. The madness had to stop now; the new society had to be built.

Thankfully, he had been able to absorb the energy of the dying dog. After not killing for days, his powers had felt depleted, but now they were back to full strength. He would have to use the powers that he remembered only vaguely, and had never actually put into practice, the powers passed down from his ancestors to rally others of their own kind, something they had had to use when the humans had tried to destroy their kind once, long ago.

The handler let out a bit of the other dog's leash, letting him get closer to the dead dog in the center, but not quite close enough to reach it. As the Xolo stepped forward, the other dog growled at him, warning him to back away from his prize. The Xolo calmly locked eyes with him, staring deep into his eyes. The other dog looked confused, but calm.

At a cry from above, the handlers let go of both dog's leashes, crying out for a fight. The Xolo stood his ground. The other dog remained calm, confused and overwhelmed by the Xolo's powers. The Xolo focused those powers further, trying to transform their effect from a passive ceasing of violence into positive action. He urged the other dog to help him break free, to free all the dogs in the arena so they could have a new and better life. After a moment's struggle, the dog seemed to understand.

"Come on, let's have a fight!" yelled one of the men from above. The other dog's handler grumbled and climbed over the railing, reaching down to grab the other dog's leash. He gave the leash several violent pulls, hoping to rile up the dog's fighting instinct, but the dog remained still and calm. With a groan, the handler hung from the railings and reached into the arena with one arm, pushing on the dog's back.

At the man's touch, the dog whirled around and bit his hand, swallowing all four fingers to the knuckle. The man screamed as the teeth sunk into his flesh, raising a squirting ring of blood. The man pounded on the dog's head with his free hand, trying in vain to free himself. The Xolo rushed forward and sunk his teeth into the man's other arm. Together, the dogs pulled the man off the railing and into the pit.

The men in the crowd screamed as the dogs began to bite the man's face and neck. Panic ran through the crowd as several men climbed over the railings, rushing to help. The handler outside the arena threw open the gate, leaving it open as he rushed towards the dogs. The Xolo saw its chance and bolted for the gate, biting at the few men who tried to stop it and then running past them. Still watching from above, Darren was amazed by its speed; none of the men in the arena had a chance of catching it. Even if they could, most of them were still busy with the other dog, which was tearing into the handler's face as he desperately tried to push it off.

The Xolo ran to the cages, where the other dogs were excitedly howling. Grasping a metal pin in his jaws, he unlocked the first cage as he had seen the humans do. The cage swung open just as the few men chasing the Xolo caught up to him. A vicious rottweiler burst from the cage and lunged at the humans, knocking one man to the ground while his companions tried to pull it off. With the humans distracted, the Xolo moved to the next cage, and then the next.

The doors to the cages swung open almost in unison. The men trying to free their friend from the rottweiler saw the animals and tried to run, but it was too late. The dogs ran them down and knocked them to the floor, sinking their teeth into the men's necks as they screamed helplessly.

The screams echoed in the cavernous wooden space, bringing terror to the men still gathered on the platform. Darren watched as panic ran through the crowd. Below, the men in the pit had managed to pull the fighting dog off his handler, but the man was already dead. As they tried to pull the animal away, it attacked the next man, biting his hands and then his face. The other men finally panicked and ran, some moving for the gate while others tried to climb the railings to escape.

Their movements seemed to inspire the men in the crowd, who began to surge backwards and move as one towards the sole exit. The surging crowd jostled an improvised light stand, sending it tumbling over, landing in the midst of the crowd. The old man in the expensive Italian suit was knocked unconscious as the halogen bulb shattered over his head. The exposed filament roared flame, igniting the pomade in the man's hair, quickly spreading to the fine linen of his suit. The flames quickly engulfed the unconscious man.

Darren wanted to stop, do something to help, but the man's clothes and hair were already blazing. As the surging crowd pushed Darren on, the old man regained consciousness and began to scream, helplessly struggling as he realized the flames were overtaking him. After a long moment, he mercifully grew still. The flames quickly consumed what was left of him and spread to the wooden floorboards around him, quickly snaking their way up a wooden pillar nearby.

The crowd surged forward even faster at the sight of the smoke and fire, pushing each other out of the way to reach the exit. Darren saw Mark trip over one of the twisted cables that lined the floor. The crowd didn't even stop, trampling him as they made for the exit. Darren tried to stop but was unable; the rushing crowd pushed him forward like an ocean wave. Between the jostling bodies, he caught only occasional glimpses of Mark's face, each more bloodied and bruised than the last, like the pictures in some demented flipbook. In the final image, Mark was unconscious, most of his teeth missing and his face a bloodied pulp, before the crowd pushed Darren forward and swept Mark out of his sight forever.

As the crowd reached the only door, several dogs rushed in from the direction of the cages, cutting off their escape. The crowd stopped as more dogs emerged from the darkness, blocking the exit. "Go back!" a man in greasy overalls shouted just before a dog leaped on him. The men in the crowd scattered, each of them looking for another way out. Darren saw one man stop to force open an ancient wooden door only to reveal a supply closet. A dog leaped on his back while he was still gaping at the empty space, knocking him to the floor. As the door slammed shut behind them, Darren heard the man's screams as the dog tore him apart.

As if making their decisions in some sort of hive mind, the crowd ran for the back of the building, perhaps hoping that a door would magically appear once they got closer. A few tried to push open the heavy windows that lined the walls, but couldn't get them to budge. Darren saw Billy climb to the top of a stack of milk crates to reach a higher window. As he tried to turn the rusted crank, the smoke filling the space swept over him. He coughed a few times, holding his head, trying to maintain his balance, then fell, the milk crates tumbling out beneath him. As he hit the ground, two dogs appeared and began to tear his unconscious body apart.

The fire was quickly spreading across the beams on the ceiling, filling the entire building with smoke. The other halogens shorted out as their electrical cables burned, leaving the room lit only by the crazy orange flickering of the fire and the weak sunlight that filtered through the high windows. Several of the suits ran past Darren, perhaps trying to get back to the main door, perhaps just panicking and running in circles. Wherever they were going, they never got there. A flaming beam fell from the ceiling, crushing them and pinning them down as it burned their bodies. Darren heard their screams but was beyond caring. There was nothing but death and chaos all around him.

He saw Hector in the back of the barn, pulling his chauffeur, Reeve, from the half-dozen or so men that remained alive. "Get us the hell out of here!" Hector commanded. Reeve ran to the back of the room, seeing that the dogs were all busy eating other men, and grabbed a fire extinguisher. For a moment, Darren thought the man would try to fight the inferno raging all around him with nothing more than a household extinguisher, but instead he turned around and threw the extinguisher through one of the heavy plate glass windows.

The flames bent towards the window as the glass shattered, opening an enormous vortex of air. A beam of sunlight cut through the hazy smoke. Reeve guided the other men in stacking several boxes under the window, then ushered Hector up. Reeve pushed him up and over the sill, where he disappeared. The other men pushed towards their only means of escape, but Reeve cut ahead of them, climbing the boxes and leaping over the sill.

Darren ran for the window as the other men clambered over the broken glass. When he reached the boxes, he ran up them in an unbroken movement, leaping over the sill like an Olympic pole-vaulter. His leg dragged against a jagged shard of glass, opening an enormous gash that he was beyond caring about. As he cleared the sill, he saw that the ground on the other side was much further down than he had expected. His arms thrashed helplessly as he plummeted through the open air, landing bodily on a strip of grass with a hard thud. His breath instantly left his lungs, and his body was paralyzed with pain.

He lay in the grass for a long moment, watching the men who had escaped ahead of him struggle to pull themselves to their feet. None of them turned back to help him.

When Darren heard scratching on the sill above him, he was convinced the dogs had caught up with him. He flipped himself over, hoping to at least see his death coming, but instead saw the bouncer who had let them in, old what's-his-name, struggling to lift his enormous bulk over the frame, his face bloodied and smeared with soot.

"You have to help me!" he yelled, reaching out a hand. Darren reached up, hoping he could lower the man from the window. The bouncer struggled to climb over the sill, shards of glass sinking into his enormous belly, disappearing into spurts of blood. At first Darren thought that was why the man was screaming, then he saw him frantically beating his arms at something beyond the sill. Darren couldn't see what it was, nor did he need to, to know why the man was suddenly being pulled back into the darkness. Darren leaped for his disappearing arms, hoping to pull him back out, but the window was too far up for him to make the leap, especially on his injured leg.

As the bouncer disappeared over the window sill, Darren turned away, running for the parking lot with the man's screams still ringing in his ears. He heard several hard thuds behind him and didn't need to turn back to know they were the dogs leaping out the window. He ran as fast as his legs would carry him, ignoring the pain from the gash along his thigh. As he dashed through the narrow strip of grass between the building and the woods, he heard the thudding of dozens of sets of paws behind him.

As he rounded the corner of the building, he saw the half-dozen remaining men scattering across the dirt parking lot, dodging between the rows of vehicles to find their own. Darren wondered why they didn't all just head for the nearest car, but there was no time for communication or rational thought; they were all in panic mode, driven inexorably into their default patterns. Darren saw the rusted hulk of his van on the far side of the parking lot and ran towards it, dodging between cars whose owners must be dead and burning inside the building. Darren found himself wondering if their cars would simply sit here until they rusted away.

He had no time to think about that now. Behind him, he heard the scream of a man he had seen stopping at a Maserati parked a few rows back. From the sound of it, Darren guessed that a dog had hit the man hard enough to send his head through the driver's side window. His screams continued along with the tinkling of broken glass.

Unable to help himself, Darren turned back. A man in a pin-striped leisure suit was pulled down between two rows of cars, only the dogs' wagging tails and the man's horrible screams showing their struggle. An obese man in overalls and a John Deere trucker hat had just reached his rusted pick-up when an enormous rottweiler leaped onto the hood. The man turned back, but it was too late: the dog leapt and knocked him to the ground.

A cloud of dust rose up as they struggled. A grease-stained trucker hat flew across the parking lot as a man in a torn flannel ran for the woods, apparently having abandoned his truck. Several dogs closed on him like heat-seeking missiles, knocking him into the undergrowth, which swayed and shook with his screams.

A loud crash tore Darren from this scene of horror. The Xolo had landed on the hood of a Mercedes-Benz just to his left, denting the expensive metal under its weight. Darren thought its owner would be beyond caring, or he would have if terror left any room for thought in his brain. He turned and ran down an uneven aisle between two rows of parked cars, dodging between protruding hoods while the Xolo thumped on the ground behind him.

The rusted van stood alone just ahead of him. He pulled ahead of the Xolo and ran free of the cars, crossing the few feet of empty dirt that separated him from salvation. His hand was already on the door before he remembered that Billy had the keys. He tugged on the handle anyways, hoping that Billy had left it unlocked, unsure what he would even do once he was inside.

The handle thumped stupidly, the door refusing to give even an inch. "Damn it, Bil-" was all he got out before the Xolo slammed into his back. He felt the claws sinking into his back, felt the sudden weight pushing him forward. His face smashed into the window. The glass didn't break, but his nose did. He left a streak of blood down the window as he slid to the ground. Darren managed to flip himself over, but the Xolo was on him before he could even raise his arms to block it. Fangs slid into his neck. The possibility of breathing disappeared as his throat was ripped out. He felt the strangely peaceful release of warm blood being spilled across his chest. The Xolo sat on his lap, calmly chewing a chunk of his throat. His first instinct was to hit, to do anything to harm the beast that had already killed him, but as the thing looked into his eyes he felt calm wash over him.

His instinct to kill passed as he disappeared into the dog's eyes. He saw himself in the center of a stone structure, an ancient temple that he recognized as Aztec from a few documentaries he had seen on late-night TV. The dog stood over him, wearing a robe decked with jewels. As the creature leaned over him, he saw steam rising from his own mouth and being absorbed into the dog's. When he tried to raise a hand to stop the source of this steam, he discovered that his hands were bound to the stone altar he lay on. This knowledge did not panic him, but only increased his peacefulness at realizing that he was helpless to do anything about his situation.

He came back to reality for the last moment of his life. The Xolo was still crouched in his lap, breathing in the steam that really was pouring from his mouth and the wound in his throat. Its eyes seemed to be glowing brighter as it breathed in more of the steam. A limo sped by, kicking up a cloud of dust, probably Hector and his valet making their escape alone. That figured, the rich fucks making their escape while the lowly dogcatcher ended up the victim of the dog he had caught for them. He wanted to curse Hector, but his energy was gone, sucked up in the cloud whose last traces disappeared into the dog's nostrils as Darren's eyes grew dim.

Hector looked out the back window of the speeding limo, still in shock at the sight they were quickly leaving behind. Smoke poured from the windows of the lodge; the parking lot was littered with bodies which the dogs tore into. Hector saw the Xolo crouched over one of the men who had captured him; Hector had never bothered to learn their names. The Xolo seemed to be breathing in smoke or steam that emanated from the man as he died. Hector tried to look closer, but the man and the Xolo disappeared behind a row of parked cars.

Reeve piloted the limo onto the narrow dirt lane that led to the main road. Hopefully they would be able to escape before anyone on the road saw the smoke. Hector hoped even more that the fire would be able to destroy any evidence of his involvement in the lodge or its activities. The dogs had already taken care of any human witnesses.

But what about the dogs themselves? The only one that he could possibly be connected to was also the one that had started all of this destruction: the Xolo. He had known instantly it had been the one he had given to Derek. Even if there had been others of its species in this area, the cold intelligence in its eyes was unmistakable. But how had it become a man-eating killer? And why had Derek let it free in the woods? Hector knew only one man who had the answers.

The limo reached the deserted main road and sped down the mountain.

The Xolo let the other dogs eat until they had their fill. Although he hadn't eaten meat himself in days, he let the other dogs have most of the body of the man who had captured him. He was satisfied enough with the life energy he had taken from the human. This was the first time he had ever absorbed energy from a human, and the rush was almost overwhelming. Their intelligence, their advanced emotions, their capability for great love and great cruelty, all of it enhanced this energy and seemed to be conveyed to him by it. He felt more powerful than he ever had before.

With a series of short barks, he commanded the other dogs to gather around him. They left their meals reluctantly, but were still loyal enough to obey. Even if he hadn't had a chance to use his powers on them, their fear of those powers, combined with their gratitude for their escape, led them to recognize him as their leader. He inspected the pack gathered before him: a dozen or so rottweilers, a handful of pit bulls, and a few poodles and chihuahuas that had been meant as bait dogs. It wasn't much to start a new society with, but it would have to do.

He knew more humans would be here soon. The dogs had caused too much commotion, created too much noise. Inevitably more humans would gather and blame the dogs for acting in their own self-defense; he had learned that in the strange building the little Girl had brought him to. He would let the other dogs eat a little more, then lead them towards the woods.

While he waited, he began to chew through the leather band that wrapped around his neck and still dragged a long leash behind him, the last symbol of his oppression by the humans. After a moment, one of the rottweilers turned from its meal and came to help him, chewing through the band where his own jaws couldn't reach. After a moment's work, the band fell to the ground. The Xolo returned the favor and began to chew through the band around the rottweiler's neck. Soon, all of the dogs were gathered in a circle, chewing through the bands around each other's necks. After a few moments of concentrated, noisy gnawing, the bands fell almost as one to the ground, forming a circle of broken circles.

The Xolo led and the other dogs followed into the woods, leaving the burning building behind, which was already beginning to collapse as flames tore through its roof. The Xolo could hear in the distance the first high-pitched squeals which meant the approach of humans. He led the dogs into the woods, into what he hoped would be safety.

TEN

Night had fallen before the dogs stopped to rest. No humans could be heard following them, and this area of woods seemed clear of those ferocious orange predators or any other animals that could harm them. The Xolo found a thick grove of trees on the edge of a steep hill. There the dogs gathered together for warmth, lying with their backs towards the edge of the hill for safety, knowing no predators could make it up the steep slope without them hearing it.

As the others tried to sleep, the Xolo paced around them, unsettled by nervous energy. As he stared into the darkened woods, he heard a noise that made his ears stand up straight. In the distance, two dogs were mournfully howling, begging to be released from wherever they were imprisoned. He listened to the horrible sound for as long as he could bear, then looked back at the other dogs. They had obviously heard the sound, but were still huddled in their pile, more concerned about their warmth and safety than the sufferings of their fellow creatures.

If the Xolo had thought that way, they would be tearing each other to shreds right now while humans bayed and cheered. The Xolo barked at them, commanding a few to follow him to the edge of the hill. A few followed reluctantly, struggling to pull themselves free from the pile.

As they approached the edge of the hill, the Xolo saw a collection of human structures in a wide valley. One was a den like the Master's, but older and more run-down. Another was a long, red structure from which a repetitive whirring noise sounded now and then, along with occasional human shouts.

Amber light emanated from a wide entrance to this building, illuminating a fenced-in area full of large, docile, black-and-white animals. They looked content enough from this distance, but the Xolo couldn't help but feel his heart break at the sight of animals penned in by fences.

Still, they weren't the ones making the noise that had caught his attention. He looked around and saw a small cage on the end of the long red structure. The metal wiring was shaking in time with the barks as the dogs inside pounded against the walls, trying to get out.

The Xolo looked back at the other dogs, who looked ready to return to the safety of their warm pile and ignore the pleas of their fellow dogs. The Xolo growled at them to remain where they were, then returned to the pile. He barked at the other dogs until all of them were standing up. He heard the trapped dogs in the valley barking in return, sensing that their salvation was near at hand.

The Xolo howled in return and led his pack to the edge of the hill, but they were hesitant to follow. They wanted to sleep, to find something to eat, but most of all to do anything to avoid the attention of the humans. The Xolo knew that none of them could be safe while other dogs were still under the control of humans. Besides, their only safety was in numbers and the dogs in the cages sounded big and strong. He barked at the other dogs, nudging them with his snout, until all of them were up and standing.

He led them to the edge of the hill, looking down at the collection of human structures far below. A field of corn stretched from the edge of the long red structure to the base of the hill they were standing on. Nearby, the hill eased into a gentler slope, ending with a pile of broken rocks just at the edge of the field. The Xolo led the dogs down the hill, towards the field, where they could make their approach unnoticed.

"Ah, goddamitalltohell!!" Ernie Keeson shouted, all in one word, as the whirring engine sputtered and died and the spinning blades of the thresher slowed, then came to rest. He raised the wrench he had been using to try to fix the damn machine, now intending to simply smash the thing in frustration and hope that would convince the damn thing to work.

His farmhand, Ennis McCoy, stepped in as he usually did and stopped the blow by grabbing Ernie's arm. Normally this is where Ennis would have delivered some calming platitudes with a calm but empty look on his face, but now he was silent, cocking his head and looking out the open door of the barn. "You hear that?" he asked, fear straining his voice.

Now that the whirring of the ancient engine had died completely, Ernie could hear a familiar sound outside. "Ah, hell, it's those goddam dogs again." He tore his arm from Ennis' hand.

"Whaddya think they're barking at?" Ennis still sounded spooked, his eyes darting around the empty barn.

"Aw hell, let's go find out. Might take my mind off this pieceashit." He threw the wrench on the dirt-covered floor next to the thresher. The machine had been struggling for weeks now and had finally crapped out completely just when he needed to harvest his corn. He knew he should just break down and get a modern combine, but the expense hardly seemed worth it for his few rows of corn, especially when the cows that corn fed barely gave him enough milk to pay his bills as it was. Besides, Ernie was a man who always resisted change, and that thresher had been on the farm since his grandfather's time. Ernie had a feeling it would be around as long as he was alive.

Grabbing a massive portable floodlight off his work bench, Ernie stormed outside, not bothering to turn the light on yet. The glow of the barn's overhead lights flooded most of the yard outside the door, and the moonlight glowed bright beyond that. The cows stood in their pen just past the reach of the barn lights, stupidly chewing their cud as Ernie stomped towards the cage he had built at the end of the barn. Ernie gave the cows the finger as he walked by. They went on chewing and staring at him, unbothered by him or by the furious barking that was growing louder as Ernie tromped towards the edge of the barn.

The cage was little more than a lean-to on the edge of the barn facing the woods. A few boards and some chicken wire contained two German shepherds, who were currently slamming their bodies and raking their claws against the chicken wire, howling mournfully at nothing in the night air. "Shut the hell up, will ya?!" Ernie screamed, slamming a hand against the corner of the cage.

The dogs quieted to a whimper, but still scratched to be let out. "Whaddya think they hear out there?" Ennis asked, staring out at the darkness.

"The hell would I know? Probably just trying to drive me crazy like usual."

Ennis nodded and looked back towards the dogs. "Maybe it's a Chupacabra. Y'know, those little demons that suck the blood out of cattle? I heard on the History channel they've sucked the blood out of all the cattle in Mexico, so they've made their way up here."

Ernie rolled his eyes. "That's why there's no more cattle in Mexico, right?"

He enjoyed the puzzled look that snuck across Ennis' face. Although Ernie called Ennis his farmhand, Ennis was in reality only a few years younger than Ernie's own grizzled late-middle age. They had grown up together, and Ennis had been helping out on the farm since the days when Ernie's old man had run the place, although Ennis usually ended up breaking just as much as he fixed. Ernie liked him all the same, having gotten used to his steady, calming presence. Besides, he found that Ennis' optimistic attitude was about the only counterpoint to his own sullen outlook he could find on this farm.

It certainly wasn't going to come from these dogs. He kicked the cage as they started to bark again, then laughed and shook his head as he followed their gaze out to the darkened hills that surrounded his property. If the goddamn dogs weren't so good at herding cattle, he would have gotten rid of them years ago. "Goddamn Chupacabras," he muttered.

"Don't laugh!" Ennis wheezed, looking back at the cows to make sure they were safe. "They suck the blood out of people, too."

Ernie scoffed, but still turned on the floodlight and scanned the woods in the direction the dogs had been barking. The sight of the balding trees, whitened and starkly highlighted by the beam, was unquestionably eerie, though he had never been creeped out by the property before in all his years of living here. He shined the light across the line of trees, shuddering at the vast emptiness of the farm. Seeing nothing moving, he turned the light off and headed back towards the barn. "Come on, let's see if we can fix that pieceashit thresher."

With a final glance over the darkened hills, Ennis followed. They hadn't gotten more than a few feet when a rustling came from the corn field. Ernie stopped just as quickly as Ennis, fumbling with the flashlight to focus the beam on the rows of corn. The beam revealed nothing but endless stalks, swaying in a gentle breeze.

More rattled than he would have liked to admit, Ernie brought the beam across the yard between the corn and the barn. The beam froze on a bundle of gray, stick-like limbs, topped by a pair of glowing yellow eyes. Ernie told himself the glow was only the reflection of the flashlight.

"Shit, it's the Chupacabra!" Ennis yelled.

"Shit, nothing," Ernie scowled, "That's a dog." He grabbed Ennis by the shoulder, preventing him from bolting to the house, and stepped towards the dog, which he now saw was scrawny and hairless, without a collar or any other mark of human ownership. "Damn thing was probably lost in the woods, musta gotten mange or something." He crouched and held out a hand. "At least we finally know what's got my dogs so-"

He cut himself off when the corn rustled again. Ennis gasped, and Ernie swung his light towards the field faster than he was proud of. The unsteady beam focused on a section of stalks that rustled, then slowly parted. His light trembled as a form separated from the corn, revealing a toy poodle no bigger than a football.

Ernie and Ennis laughed in unison, feeling relief from a fear they didn't know they had. Like the hairless dog, the poodle was scarred and matted with mud. "Shit, somebody must have let the whole pound loose," Ennis chuckled, stepping towards the poodle with a hand outstretched.

As if in response, the corn began to rustle again, not just a few stalks this time, but the entire front row. Ernie nervously scanned the stalks, trying to illuminate all the corn that was moving, but it was impossible to take all of it in at once. The corn parted in more than a dozen places at once, revealing just as many dogs, not small poodles or starving mongrels this time, but heavy, muscular fighting dogs, pit bulls and rottweilers. Their faces were scarred, their bodies roped with muscle and coated with dirt, their faces smeared with what looked like fresh blood.

"What the fuck?" Ernie muttered slowly. Maybe Ennis was right, maybe an unscrupulous pound had dumped them all in the woods, but how had they all gotten into such rough condition, and what had inspired them all to come to his farm? For no reason he could think of, that question reminded Ernie of the hairless, mangy dog he had seen first. He swung the flashlight to the spot he had last seen it and found only empty ground.

A chorus of growls brought his attention back to the larger pack of dogs. They were slowly closing in, peeling their lips back to reveal sharp, blood-crusted fangs. Drool ran down their lips in long strings and pooled on the dirt. Ernie realized that he now had an answer to his last question: the dogs had come to his farm in search of food.

"Run, Ennis, run!" Ernie yelled, turning on his heels at the same time and bolting for the house. He hadn't gotten more than a few steps when he saw the hairless dog, sitting patiently on his front porch, blocking the main entrance to the house. The dog didn't move to chase him, just kept on sitting there, like it was biding its time. Ernie could swear the look on its face was one of malignant intelligence. Its eyes seemed to be glowing again, and this time Ernie knew that glow was not the reflection of the flashlight.

Ernie turned without thinking for the side yard, hoping he could get to the back door before the dogs. Several dogs came crashing out of the corn and filled the side yard in front of him, threatening him with their bare teeth. Ernie turned back and saw dogs closing in on him on three sides, the fourth blocked by the solid wall of the house. He realized with sickening horror that the dogs were herding him.

Ennis, who had tried to run across the open yard to his truck, had been rounded up by the same dogs and herded towards the house next to Ernie. He pointed to the open fields beyond Ernie's property. "That way. Maybe we can outrun 'em."

"Like hell we can. That's exactly where they want us. They'll tire us out, then run us down." He looked around and saw only one other place to escape. "The barn," he said, pointing to the open door.

"You kidding?" Ennis wheezed, "We'll never get the door shut in time."

"Who cares? If we can get up the ladder-"

Their plans were cut off by a loud bark from the dog on the porch. As if responding to an order from their general, the dogs moved as one, closing in on the men, who both ran for the barn. The time for argument was over.

As they ran, hearing the dogs' paws thundering behind them, Ennis looked back towards the house and saw that the dog on the porch had run to Ernie's dog cage. Nudging the cheap shitty latch with his nose, he managed to open the door and free the dogs. Ennis had told Ernie for years those latches were useless, but Ernie had insisted that the dogs were too stupid to figure it out. Apparently, this one wasn't.

Ennis felt an enormous weight slam into his back and realized that his curiosity had just cost him his life. "Ernie, help me!" he screamed as one of the enormous dogs knocked him to the ground, knowing it would do no good. Ernie never even slowed down as he dashed towards the barn, only looking back for a moment to see several dogs gathering around Ennis, each of them scrambling for a bite as Ennis thrashed helplessly.

Ernie looked forward again just in time to avoid colliding with the enormous thresher. Stopping himself, he turned back to the entrance to the barn and tried to push the ancient wooden door shut behind himself. Several dogs slammed into the door, forcing it back open as they dashed past, dazed by the impact. Taking advantage of their moment of confusion, Ernie bolted for the nearest of the two ladders to the loft.

Scrambling up the ladder so quickly he was sure he would miss a rung, Ernie climbed to the loft, pulling himself up and collapsing onto the wooden platform, lying on the floor as he struggled to catch his breath. Ennis's screams still echoed from outside, along with the tearing of fabric and the frantic yipping of the dogs as they competed for a bite. Ernie squeezed his calloused hands against his ears, squeezing his eyes shut as if that would stop the sound. He felt a single tear run down his leathery face.

He opened his eyes again at a thudding sound from nearby. He glanced over to see the top of the ladder banging rhythmically against the edge of the loft. Scrambling to the edge, he looked down to see one of his German shepherds crawling up the ladder, somehow using its spindly limbs to propel itself up. With a yell, Ernie grabbed the top of the ladder and pushed until the ladder fell back.

The dog tumbled from the falling ladder, impacting the thresher's control panel with a yelp. The collision was enough to flip the starter switch, bringing the ancient engine to creaky life. "*Of course, the pieceashit works now,*" Ernie found himself thinking. In the hopper just below him, the gigantic metal blades began to spin, quickly reaching full speed.

Ernie shied back as if the blades would be able to reach him here. Collapsing on the floor, he closed his eyes with relief, letting relaxation overtake his body. The straining whine of the engine was horrible, but at least it drowned out Ennis' screams and the yelping of the dogs outside. Ernie shuddered to think what it would have been like if that had been him.

The idea instantly brought to mind the second ladder to the loft. He was relieved to find the ladder clear of dogs and kicked it over with relish, enjoying the crash it made as it collided with the floor. Several dogs had gathered on the floor of the barn, looking up at him hungrily as they paced the barn. Several had fresh blood smeared around their mouths, which Ernie tried not to see.

Looking at them as he stood on the edge of the loft, Ernie felt a god-like sense of superiority, not just because of his immense height on the loft, which felt higher than ever as he stood upright. A moment ago, he had been running for his life from these mangy beasts, now he stood secure, where they were powerless to reach him.

Of course, that did leave the problem of what to do next. Ernie thought cell phones were an unnecessary distraction at his age, and the only landline was in the kitchen. He figured the dogs would eventually get bored and leave in search of other prey, then he could figure out a way to get down. The fall was too great to survive uninjured, though maybe he could get down by climbing onto the steel beam that held up the hopper on this end of the thresher, being careful to avoid the whirling blades. By the time the dogs left, the pieceashit machine would probably have sputtered back to death anyways.

A creak behind him interrupted these optimistic thoughts. Instead of turning, he stood completely still, both afraid and madly anxious to confirm what he had heard. As he stood motionless, another floor board behind him creaked, then another, accompanied by the soft clicking of leathery pads.

Ernie turned slowly. The mangy hairless thing, the strangely intelligent dog that seemed to be the leader of the others, must have climbed up the second ladder while he was distracted by the dog on the first, or maybe while he had stupidly taken that moment to rest instead of thinking about what to do next. Who knew, maybe the dog had even beaten him into the barn and been up here before he was.

As the dog stepped closer, he realized that didn't matter now. He took a step backwards and felt his heels hanging off the edge of the loft. He wondered again if he really could survive the fall from the loft and realized it didn't matter; the other dogs would be on him in a moment.

He looked around for a weapon but found nothing. He tried to scream, but the sound caught in his throat as the dog locked eyes with him. Even in the light of the barn, he could see that those eyes were glowing, and the glow was certainly no reflection. It was an organic but strangely unnatural light, one that seemed to have its ultimate source in the energy of another world, in some place where the laws of this world did not apply.

As he dissolved into that glow, Ernie seemed to experience a rush of memories, at first from his own life and then from what seemed to be past lives: as an animal, as a member of some ancient and primitive civilization that practiced human sacrifice, and even the blur of some incredibly strange impressions which Ernie's overwhelmed mind could only attribute to the memories of some past existence as a form of life on another planet, or even in another dimension.

Ernie's mind had never guessed at the possibility of such strange modes of experience, and his mind reeled at their overwhelming sensations. He felt his body grow light and limp, as if his energy were being drained. He returned to his own reality just as his body fell backwards, weakened and exhausted. The dog only watched as he plummeted over the edge of the loft.

His body flipped so he could see the whirling metal blades rushing towards him. In contrast to the dreamy sense-impressions of a moment before, his last moments were horribly vivid, as if every nerve had been raised to its maximum potential just before being shredded by the blades of the thresher, the eager metal consuming his body and repurposing it into his next existence, a transformation he was horribly aware of even as it happened.

His screams mingled with the whining struggle of the thresher's machinery until, with a final sickening push, the blades freed themselves of their temporary obstruction. A metal chute at the end of the machine rocked and trembled, as if in anticipation of the meal it was to disgorge, or perhaps in a struggle to hold it back, a struggle the machine ultimately lost.

A red pulp sprayed violently from the machine, coating the walls and floor with blood and chunks of gore. The dogs gathered around this unexpected feast, lapping up the spray even as the machine made more. The air misted red with the particulate spray of blood and finely diced flesh. The dogs fought amongst themselves for the juiciest bits, the occasional large chunks of muscle and organ that made it through the machine, ferociously lapping up blood from the floor, the walls, and the wooden beams that held up the roof. Occasionally, they had to settle for a blood-soaked piece of clothing, which they squeezed dry with their mouths when the fresh blood ran out. Eventually, the machine stopped producing more, the spray reducing to a fine mist, then a slow trickle that the dogs lapped up as it dripped onto the floor.

The Xolo watched all of this from his perch on the loft, his eyes glowing bright yellow as he observed his pack with glee. The dogs they had rescued gladly joined in on the feast of their previous master, fighting with the others for the chance to lick up the last drops of his blood. Deciding that the others had had enough, the Xolo leapt onto the metal hopper that had consumed the farmer, nimbly leaping off its edge to avoid the still-spinning blades and sliding down the long chute to the body of the machinery, where he was able to safely leap to the floor.

The pack had saved their leader a special treat, an especially tasty chunk of organ that contained the remnants of the farmer's last meal. Eating it strangely gave the Xolo even more of an impression of the human than the small amount of life energy he had been able to absorb before the man had fallen backwards into the machine. The life he had absorbed from it had been only a tease, and the pack had killed the other human too quickly for the Xolo to absorb him.

They would have their chance to absorb other humans, but they couldn't wait in this place for humans to find them. They could spend the night here, but at first light they would leave before more inevitably arrived and saw the trouble they had caused. In the meantime, the Xolo thought some of the dumb, braying animals in the yard would make a suitable replacement. The stupid energy of their life force could never match a human's, but at least the Xolo would have the satisfaction of the immense energy rush that came with absorbing a fresh life. For the other dogs, their immense and fatty meat would make a filling treat while they spent the next few days in the woods, searching for their next meal.

As the Xolo led the other dogs out of the barn towards the stupid, mindless animals, the machine behind them finally sputtered, coughed, and began to emit black smoke. Its noises grew louder and higher-pitched as it made its final struggle, then grew silent. As it died completely, the dogs closed in on the mindless animals, who only continued to chew their cud as the dogs drew near.

ELEVEN

SHERIFF GARTH CHAMBERS REMOVED HIS SUNGLASSES AND LOOKED OVER the still-smoking ruins of the old log cabin. The fire department had been at work most of the night putting out the blaze, ever since a trucker trying desperately to complete his route on time last evening by cutting through the small county road that passed through the mountains had seen the rising smoke and stopped just long enough to report it. Garth's own men had been searching and photographing the scene all night and into the morning.

At first, they hadn't even seen the bodies in the darkness. Without them, this would have seemed like a cut-and-dry case, maybe even one that wouldn't have required Garth to be there; just let the firefighters do their job and the state fire inspector (whenever he showed up) do his. Then one of those volunteer heroes had tripped while running a hose between the cars that filled the parking lot, trying to reach another corner of the blaze. When he had looked back to see what he had tripped over, he must have given himself quite a fright, his shoulder-mounted flashlight showing a body with a torn-open throat that had been leaning against a rusted-out van a moment before and was now leaning against his legs, blood spilling from the open mouth and pooling across his flame-retardant suit, the pale hands stretching blindly across his legs as if reaching out for help. Not the kind of thing you were used to seeing on their job.

And just like that went Garth's chances of a peaceful night's sleep. Not that he had much of one even on a good night, but even sitting at home nursing some bad memories and a bottle of Jack Daniels until the TV turned to infomercials was better than spending all night (and what was sure to become the next morning) supervising the dozens of men and hundreds of details that came with a major crime scene.

Some of those men had already finished their work. The fire had been reduced to a smolder, and the chief had at daybreak dismissed all but one ladder company. These men stayed behind to inspect the ruins, guide Garth's deputies safely through the scene, and wait for the fire inspector to finally arrive. Garth's own men had finished photographing the bodies in the parking lot, allowing the forensics team from the state crime laboratory to begin collecting evidence and hauling the bodies away.

Garth moved to the edge of the ruin, where his men were moving across what remained of the floor, the firefighters guiding them, being careful to stay clear of the ruins of the remaining walls, which stood like pillars made of solidified smoke. The deputies had already found enough evidence buried in the ashes to make the fire inspector's job easy once he did arrive.

Whoever had been occupying the building had created their own electrical and heating systems. The burned-out shell of a gas-powered generator filled the ruins of a shack just behind the main building, with frayed electrical wires running through what must have once been a rathole in the outer wall, where it branched from store-bought splitters into a tangled mess of lines, still visible by their trails of melted wire and rubber, to what looked like halogen work lights on metal stands and space heaters tucked in the corners of the rotting wood. To put such dangerous appliances anywhere indoors, let alone a log cabin nearly a century old, was so reckless that Garth was only surprised the place hadn't burned down earlier.

Garth stepped to what once been the outer wall of the building and was now the edge of a large pit, where the concrete floor had been laid several feet below the ground. When Garth had been a boy growing up on his father's farm, this building had been home to Al's Supper Club, the only thing even approaching fine dining in all of Puebla County. His father had taken him there once or twice when times had been good. His father liked to claim Al's had the best steak he had ever eaten, but Garth had never seen him eat any other. It was Al himself who had built the cow palace on the back of the restaurant to have cattle auctions. Of course, the best of them became the steaks he served, but the others ended up being sold between the local farmers or to a few larger beef concerns.

Al had died of a heart attack when he was about the age Garth was now, come to think of it, and his widow had sold the place to a group that tried unsuccessfully to turn the place into a sort of European-style ski chalet, sure that the then-booming sport would be coming to the Front Range any day now. But that business had failed to boom in Sunnydale just like every other kind had, and the place had been turned into a bed and breakfast which had struggled along for a few years before being sold as a private residence.

Garth had never found out who lived there, but that seemed to be when the trouble had begun. The few neighbors had made calls to the police about strange noises coming from the place at all hours of the night, and of cars taking off from the long road that served as its driveway and tearing down the county road, double digits over the speed limit. Garth, by then having left his old man's dying cattle farm to become a rookie patrol officer, had responded to a few of these calls, but had never found enough evidence to warrant searching the property. When he had occasionally driven by while on patrol, he sometimes saw the road blocked by one of several long black limos, men in equally black suits sitting on the hood, waiting to turn away intruders.

Sometime during the years when Garth was working his way up from patrol officer to chief deputy, the place had been abandoned, a situation that had officially continued until the current day. Even once Garth had been elected sheriff following the death of his old mentor Art Sharkey, he had still nursed his suspicions that the old log cabin was still being used for whatever nefarious purpose it had been used for before, no matter what the lease on the place said. However, in the enormous county he had to patrol and with the few men at his disposal, he had never had the resources to prove it. Secretly, he had long hoped that one of those greedy developers that had started encroaching on the town in recent years would buy this place instead of those pristine acres of forest and tear the damn building down, but apparently whatever had happened here had done the job before they could.

It was certainly easy enough to guess what had caused the fire: some good old boys had been brewing moonshine or cooking meth or whatever the fuck it was they did in here, and had knocked over one of their janky light stands or tripped over one of their snaking electrical wires while they were high or drunk, and the place had gone up like a Christmas tree over a candle. What was harder to say was what had killed the people in the parking lot. Even when the fire inspector did finally show up, he wouldn't be able to answer that. That would be up to Garth, and he shuddered at the thought of the task.

The bodies seemed to have been torn apart and partially eaten by what looked like wild animals, but whether that was the cause of death or had happened afterwards was impossible to say before an autopsy. Garth supposed it was just barely possible they had succumbed to smoke inhalation while escaping the building, collapsed outside, and had their bodies preyed upon by passing coyotes or bears, but he knew that idea was just his mind trying to force an explanation without having to deal with the difficult facts of the case. He had had to overcome that tendency while he was a rookie, and now that he was sailing right past the age where any reasonable lawman would have retired, he found it sneaking right back up. But until his nightmares settled down enough to let him retire or, more likely, he just dropped dead one day while on patrol, he still had a job to do, and he would be damned if he wasn't going to do it the best he could. That started with questioning his own assumptions, especially when they might be leading him away from the facts of the case.

For starters, it was pretty unlikely that all of these men had died simultaneously of smoke inhalation about the same distance from the building. The theory of their bodies being preyed upon by wild animals was plausible, but unlikely given how quickly the first firefighters had shown up on the scene. Anything feeding on the bodies would have to have moved in before they got there, and the firefighters didn't report any large animals fleeing the scene when they left.

That left the possibility that the men had been killed by whatever had then eaten them. That seemed difficult to believe on the face of it: animals rarely attacked humans at all, let alone a group of a half-dozen or more, and these men looked like some tough hombres, ones that wouldn't have gone down without a fight, which animals were rarely willing to give unless they had good reason.

And then there was the mystery of what had killed all the people inside the building. While searching the burned-out ruins, his deputies had discovered at least two dozen crispy, skeletal husks that had once been human beings, as well as one or two crispy critters that might have once been dogs. There may have been more of both, burned into the walls or fried into unrecognizable heaps of ash, but his men had already found enough to raise suspicion. Garth could see a few men perishing in a fire like this, but how had dozens been caught in this blaze? Many of them were curled up right next to what had once been doors or windows, as if they had given up just before they could have escaped.

The dead animals certainly raised suspicion too, as did the steel cages they found in what had once been the cow palace, their gates swinging open, their steel bars tarnished by flame. The cow palace had always been used to hold animals, of course, but these cages were far too small for cattle. Garth felt an idea beginning to form in his mind, a theory he forced himself to push away until he had collected more evidence.

A few of his deputies were returning from doing just that. His chief deputy, Andy Millam, a plain-faced man in his mid-thirties who looked a few years younger, was returning from the woods that ringed the property with a few other men. As he approached, he waved to the sheriff and held up the notepad he always had with him on a scene. "Found something you ought to take a look at, sheriff. Well, a couple a somethings actually."

Garth nodded and kicked a pile of cinders into the burned-out pit of the building. "Well, I ain't doing nothing else. Let's have a look."

Millam nodded and led him towards the woods. "We were searching the woods for any more bodies like you asked-"

"-I remember."

Millam grinned more widely and nervously than he usually did. "Right. And we found this." He pointed to a taped-off clump of scrub trees where several techs from the state crime lab were crouched in a circle, looked over by a nauseous deputy. "We found another body, even more torn up than the rest."

Garth nodded, glancing over the muddy, weed-choked ground that stood between him and the crime scene. "Well, I'll take your word for it. I guess it's safe to say he didn't die of smoke inhalation this far from the fire. And it's also safe to say these boys were trying to run from something."

"That's what I thought."

"See, that's why you'll be sheriff one day. Once you're done here, get him to the lab pronto. We need identity and cause of death on all of these guys ASAP as possible."

"Right, Sheriff. What do you think was the cause of death?"

Garth gave a sincere shrug. "What could have done it? Wolves, coyotes… . big dogs?" He gave a small laugh that Millam did not join in on.

"That reminds me of the other thing, Sheriff." He led them out of the thickest of the woods, onto a narrow strip of grass next to the dirt parking lot. "What do you make of these?"

Garth made his way around his chief deputy, more intrigued by the slight delay in seeing what he was brought here to see. He crouched over the spot of grass Millam had indicated, at first struggling to comprehend what he was seeing: a rough circle made out of smaller, broken circles. "Dog collars?" Garth said at last, enraged at how slowly his mind had matched the image with its meaning.

"Yup. Looks like they were ripped apart."

Garth looked at the frayed end of one, proud of himself for what he could still notice. "Or chewed. The end of this one still looks wet. Have these taken to the lab too. Might be fingerprints on 'em, and see if the crime lab can do a test on that drool to see if they can determine what kind of dog it is."

"Is that a thing?"

"Well, see if it is, and if it is, have them do it."

"Yessir, Sheriff. We already checked and the name tags on 'em are blank, so that doesn't help us in determining where they came from."

"Well, maybe not." Garth looked back towards the ruins of the old log cabin. "We've got an abandoned building where a lot of people were gathered, and the only physical evidence is some dog collars and a few steel cages. So, I would say there's only two possibilities: either they were running a dog-fighting ring, or they were gathered here for some good old-fashioned BDSM."

This time Millam joined in on the laugh, just as soon as understanding crossed his broad face. "You think it could be dogs that did this?"

"Well, I don't think the leather and chains set have that wide of a bite radius, and it certainly does fit all the evidence we have…" Garth could feel himself fighting off the certainty settling over him.

"But how could dogs have done all this?"

Garth shrugged, sweeping an arm over the wide parking lot. "Not sure. You see anybody we could ask?"

Millam shrugged, looking out over the parking lot and seeing only bodies.

"Ah, you see, that's why you're not sheriff yet. How about the driver of that car right there?" Garth pointed to a ragged pair of tire tracks in the soft dirt, which started as a deep rut in the center of the lot, then shallowed to a fine track that clearly showed the treads of the tires as they veered towards the narrow lane that served as the lot's only exit, deepening suddenly just before the lane as if the driver had slammed on the brakes to make the turn.

"Looks like he was in a mighty hurry on his way outta here. Sure would like to know why. Make sure the forensics team gets photos and a cast of that track. Maybe we'll get lucky and find a match."

"Maybe we'll get lucky and find the dog that drove it away," Millam said as he scribbled on his notepad. This time it was Garth's turn to laugh at his deputy's joke, a laugh that was interrupted by the radio on Garth's hip.

"Sheriff, we just got a call from a dairy farm on County Road H," his dispatcher's familiar voice squawked.

Garth scrambled for the radio, a sinking feeling of despair growing in his stomach. He travelled that little dirt lane on the edge of town often, and there was only one dairy farm he knew of on the whole stretch. "Not Ernie Kesson's farm, is it?" he said into the radio.

"I believe it is," Maria's reply came back.

"Then I don't need the address. I'm on my way." He tapped Andy on the shoulder. "And so are you. Come on."

Millam threw up his hands, nearly sending the pages of his notepad flying, but he followed Garth anyway, hastily shouting orders to the other deputies on his way to the sheriff's squad car.

"What'll we tell the fire inspector when he shows up?" one of the deputies yelled back.

"Tell him he'll have to wait," Garth shouted back with a laugh.

Garth had known Ernie since they were both kids growing up on neighboring farms. He had never known the man to be in any sort of trouble with the law, or to need to call the police himself. Even living on that big farm by himself, surrounded by endless forest and a little-used county road, Garth had been able to get by with just himself and his two dogs, and a little help from that mostly useless bumpkin, Ennis McCoy. If it weren't for Garth occasionally dropping in at the farm during his patrols for old time's sake, Garth would have probably long ago forgotten that the secluded property on County Road H was even occupied.

Maria had filled him in on the few details of the call on the drive over, just enough to get him worried. Bob Hudson, a mostly harmless and nearly senile old man who bought milk from all the local farms on behalf of a Denver-based dairy concern, had stopped by Ernie's farm early this morning for his usual pick-up and had come across a scene he had refused to describe over the phone, only imploring the police to get there as quick as they could.

As Garth piloted his cruiser down the otherwise empty dirt lane, he saw Bob's truck blocking the road, unable to pull off because of the steep ditches on either side. The sleek steel tanker looked like it should be transporting oil or liquid nitrogen, but the scrawny old man standing next to it would have looked at home nowhere else but on a farm. Bob's faded overalls barely hung on what remained of his thinning shoulders, and the rim of his straw hat was ripped into shreds as thin as the strand of wheat held between his teeth, which he had evidently plucked from a patch growing on the side of the road.

He nervously chewed the wheat until the sheriff parked his cruiser in the middle of the road so both he and Millam could climb out without tumbling into the swamp below. As he saw the police trekking the last few feet of dirt towards him, Bob took the wheat out of his mouth and walked towards them, quickly closing the gap. "'Bout time you badges got here; I got ten more pick-ups to make today; ain't got all day to wait for you guys." His words were defiant, but his voice was strangely nervous. The strand of wheat in his hand trembled with more than the shakiness of old age.

Garth laughed as he came face-to-face with the man. "Well, maybe you can speed things up by telling us what made you call today."

"Why bother? You guys can just go up there and see it for yourself."

"We need to get a statement either way. If you give it to us now, we can send you on your way," Millam said, his notepad at the ready.

Bob inhaled deeply, as if he was trying to get the entire story out in a single breath. "Well, I drove up this morning to see Ernie for my first pick-up of the day, which I'm still trying to make, by the way, and I didn't see Ernie, which is pretty odd, since he knows I come at the same time every week, and he's always there to meet me, so I walked up to the farm to look for him, and I noticed I couldn't hear anything, not even those awful god damn dogs of his, which is also pretty odd, since those things are always barking, and Ernie's always got some pieceashit machine running, and he's always yelling at it-"

"-I remember, Bob," Garth interrupted, "You wanna get to those pick-ups, remember? Just tell us what you saw and you can be on your way."

Bob lifted his narrow shoulders, almost knocking off the straps of his overalls. "Just walk around that barn and you'll see for yourself; you can't miss it. Now, I gotta make those pick-ups." He nodded down the dirt road. "You mind moving that cruiser so I can get out?" He sounded almost desperate to escape.

A few moments and a lot of vehicle wrangling later, Garth had his cruiser dug into the grass at the end of Ernie's yard, watching Bob's milk truck disappear down the road, the steel glinting in the morning sun as if he were about to disappear in a mirage. Garth watched him go and then motioned Millam to follow him towards the barn. "You think we need our weapons ready?" the deputy asked nervously.

Garth shrugged. "Bob didn't seem like he needed one." He tromped across the yard, listening to the mud squish beneath his boots. As he crossed the yard, he realized that was all he could hear. Bob had been right; there was no sound at all on the farm, except an occasional metallic clanging that made Garth uneasy for no reason he could describe.

As they rounded the corner of the barn, Garth saw the source of the noise. The cage Ernie had built for his dogs sat empty, its heavy door swinging in the breeze, clanging against the latch before blowing open again. For some reason, the sight made Garth think he did need his pistol after all. He kept his fingers on the grip as they walked around the barn.

As they came to the little patch of grass between the cow pen and the house, kept secret from the road by the broad back wall of the barn, everything at first seemed dismayingly normal. The cows were chewing their cud on the far side of the pen, arranged under a slightly storm-darkened sky to form an off-putting pastoral scene. Only after a moment did Garth realize that the scene was interrupted by a dead man.

He lay face down in the stretch of dirt between the cow pen and the entrance to the barn. His body was torn and bitten like those at the log cabin, but to a far worse degree. Evidently whatever had killed him had taken its time with him, long enough to hollow out his torso and remove the internal organs. The muscles on his arms and legs were mostly eaten away, and from what Garth could see poking up from the mud, most of his face was gone too.

"Was that Ernie?" Millam asked.

"Naw, that was Ennis McCoy, his farmhand." He pointed to one of the ragged, bloodied scraps of clothing still clinging to the body. "You can see those stupid overalls he always wears. Or wore."

Garth studied the body a moment longer, noting the confused tracks of half-formed prints that crossed each other in furious circles around the body. Garth supposed he had been killed early last night, but only an autopsy would reveal the time for sure.

"Well, Andy, you better get on the horn with the coroner. Tell him once he's done over at the log cabin, we got some more work for him over here." For some reason, Millam felt the need to write all of this down on his trusty notepad. "And call animal control as well, tell them we need an autopsy on a cow."

"What? Why?"

Garth pointed beyond the body, to the other thing that had disturbed his vision when first looking over the scene. On the near side of the pen, the grass was slick with blood and covered with a tangled pile of limbs and bones that must have come from two or three cows. The exact number was hard to tell because of how twisted the body parts were, and how much of them had been eaten away. Garth could see now why the other cows were huddled on the far end of the pen, superstitiously avoiding the scene of whatever had happened here. Garth looked at their dumb faces, wishing he could use them as witnesses.

"So where do you think Ernie is?" Millam asked.

Garth looked at the open barn doors, from which a pale-yellow light was faintly visible. "I think I got some idea," Garth said, already heading towards the building without another glance at the body on the ground.

As they entered the barn, the heavy smell of machine oil wafted over them, almost filling Garth's nose, nearly covering the faint, familiar metallic odor underneath. The source of the former was obviously the mass of rusted metal nearly filling the center of the barn. In the warm glow of the ancient incandescents overhead, it took Garth a moment to recognize the mass as the type of old-fashioned thresher abandoned by most farms years or even decades earlier. Ernie had always been the type to hold onto the old ways as long as possible, even staying on this farm long after it could have possibly turned much of a profit. Garth had the sinking feeling that it was that insistence on holding on to the old that had been Ernie's undoing.

The thresher's output chute, which would normally be aimed at a bin for collecting the freshly harvested grain, instead pointed into the darkest corner of the barn. Even amongst the shadows that collected there, Garth could see the pools and streaks of blood. The hopper on the other end was perched just below the barn's ancient loft, a few streaks of dried blood dripping down around the rim.

"Looks like someone fell in," Millam said, pointing at the hopper with his pencil.

"More like pushed," Garth scowled. He pointed at a ladder that lay across the floor and another on the far side of the barn. "Ernie must've been trying to hide from something up there," he pointed to the loft, tracing the path he imagined the ladders had once taken, "but somehow it followed him up and…" he trailed off as his hand traced an arc into the hopper.

Millam nodded and walked around the thresher, shining a flashlight into the darkened corner near the chute. "Christ, Sheriff, take a look at this."

Garth was still studying the loft, puzzling over what could have possibly climbed those ladders, and what would have made Ernie climb them. "I think I got a good idea of what I'm going to see, Andy: nothing but a lot of gore."

"Not as much as you might think."

Intrigued, Garth walked to the far corner, where Millam shined his flashlight into the darkness. Dried blood crossed the walls and floor, but only in long, thin streaks, with wide clean patches in between.

Garth made a deep noise of understanding. "Now, what does that tell you, deputy?"

Millam struggled to get the words out. "Something licked him up, sheriff," he said in a voice barely above a whisper, "A couple a somethings by the looks of it." He trained his beam on a spot of overlapping brush strokes in the dried blood. "You notice there's no big chunks? They fed his whole body through that thing and there's nothing left but blood? Whatever chased him here must have been hungry."

Garth gave him a wry smile. "And that is why you will be sheriff one day."

A moment later, the two men were outside, escaping the stench of blood and machine oil with the relatively fresh air outside, where the smell of blood was heavily diluted by the mountain wind. Garth stretched his back slowly, hoping to somehow clear away the sights and smells he had experienced in a single physical purge. "Alright, Andy, I need you to call everybody who's at the log cabin, tell 'em as soon as they're done there, we got another mess for them to clean up over here. I need you to hold the scene until they get here."

Andy instinctively chased after the sheriff, seeing that he was striding towards their only car. "Where are you gonna be, Sheriff?"

"I gotta hunch to follow up on. Remember, you're in charge. Don't touch anything until the techs get here."

Andy couldn't think of a single thing on this farm he would want to touch. He jogged a few more feet towards the car, dreading to be left alone. He stopped as Garth climbed into the car, realizing it was pointless.

He felt his boots sink into the soft mud and the cold mountain wind rip at his coat. The sky overhead was darkening. Andy hoped it wouldn't rain; if it did, he might have no choice but to take cover in that death barn, waiting for back-up while trying not to choke on the smell of blood. Even worse, what if the animals that had done this decided to come back?

"Remember, you're in charge!" Garth shouted through the rolled-down window, "Don't let those CSI fucks give you a hard time!" With that, he gunned the engine, spewing mud behind him as he turned onto the dirt road. Andy nodded, deciding his thoughts weren't the thoughts of a future sheriff. He would hold the scene as long as necessary, then take control when the others arrived. Still, he couldn't help but wish they would hurry up.

He watched the sheriff's cruiser disappear down the road, hoping at least that the rain wouldn't come.

Derek had been working intently for hours when he was brought out of his trance by the ring of the doorbell, nearly jumping out of his seat at the sudden noise. With the kids at school and Alison at work, there had been no noise in the house all morning except for the gentle pattering of rain on the windows. He hadn't even noticed the sound gently building over the last hour, he had been so engrossed in putting together a new presentation for William Metcalf and his other investors. He knew that he would have to impress them to make up for running out in the middle of his last presentation.

That would have to wait: the bell was ringing again, a few times in quick succession, each echo chasing the last around the empty house. Derek sighed and shut his laptop, looking out the window as he stood up from the desk. He was dismayed to see the sheriff's cruiser parked in the driveway, the black and white made even more ominous by the gray landscape it seemed to burst forth from.

Derek walked as slowly as he could to the front door, dreading what the sheriff might have to tell him. He wondered if the dog had been found in the woods, if it had bitten someone else, if he could be held responsible for that. Then he remembered that none of his wondering would help him figure out what the sheriff wanted. He took a deep breath and opened the door.

The rain seemed to have picked up as he was walking to the front door. It poured down in heavy sheets, almost erasing the squad car from view. Torrents poured off the small roof over the front stoop, slapping against the concrete and splattering the back of the sheriff's coat.

Derek stood in the entryway, feeling the cool air rush in around him. "Well, good morning, Derek," the sheriff began before Derek could.

"Morning, Sheriff, wasn't expecting to see you."

"Yeah, well, most people I see aren't."

Derek forced himself to laugh a little at that, leaving an awkward silence that was filled only by the sound of rain. Garth looked back at the pouring streams, removing his sunglasses and shaking off the water that had built up on them. "Say, Derek, maybe you wouldn't mind inviting me inside, it's a little rough out here."

Derek almost slapped himself, quickly standing back and waving the sheriff inside. "Of course, sheriff, I'm sorry, my mind is elsewhere." Garth nodded, stepping inside and casting a glance around the house that was obviously meant to be subtle.

Derek was secretly relieved by the implications of that sneaking glance. "If this is about the dog, sheriff, I got rid of him just like you said."

Garth nodded, still glancing around the house. "As a matter of fact, it is. I was just wondering where you might have gotten rid of him to." He gave Derek a long glance that Derek was afraid to break.

"To the pound. Where else?" Derek gave a little laugh that he hoped didn't feel forced.

Garth's face didn't change at all. "Which pound was that? There's a few in the area."

Derek made a show of searching his memory, trying to give himself enough time to think of what to say. "The nearest one, I suppose," was the best he could come up with. "Can't remember the name. It was just the first one that came up when I searched it on my phone."

Garth looked unimpressed. "Uh huh. Well, I'm guessing you were at home when you searched for it?"

"I guess so," Derek said, fearful he could already see where this was going.

When he said nothing, Garth shot him an icy grin. "Well, maybe you could pull your phone out right now and see which one pops up first."

Derek nodded, struggling to pull his phone from his pocket, which suddenly felt endlessly deep and tangled. The sheriff looked over his shoulder as he pulled up Apple Maps. His hands shook as he searched for animal shelters, hoping that more than one would pop up so he could mislead the sheriff. He held his breath as he waited for the results to appear.

He let out a small sigh when the lone result appeared. "Guess that must be the one, eh?" Garth said, still leaning over Derek's shoulder.

Derek didn't know what else to say. "I guess it must be."

The sheriff moved away from him, but only by a few steps. "Do you have any record of dropping the dog off? They give you any paperwork or anything?"

"They offered me something, but I didn't want any record of the dog around."

Garth seemed as impressed with Derek's creativity as Derek himself was. "I understand. Well, that's too bad, Mr. Rains. Now I'm gonna have to drive all the way up there to confirm your story."

"You can if you want to waste your time. The place seemed pretty skeezy to me. Wouldn't surprise me if they didn't keep good records."

The sheriff stared at him blankly for a moment. "Dr. Greene's been a competent professional in all the years I've known her. I'll swing by and see if that's changed." Derek swallowed, seeing his miscalculation. Garth put on the hat he had been holding in his hands and opened the door behind himself, facing the ever-increasing torrent of rain outside.

"Wait, Sheriff." Garth seemed more than happy to comply. "What's this all about?" Derek was desperate to know.

Garth turned back, leaving the door open to let the air rush in. "Well, we had a few animal attacks in the area last night, so I wanted to check with all the owners of problem animals in the county."

"How many of us are there?"

"Well, lately…." Garth made such a show of searching his memory that Derek was sure the sheriff was mocking him. He found his answer with a low sigh. "…Just you, Mr. Rains. Just you." Garth held Derek's gaze until Derek nodded, stepping back a little to excuse Garth from the room.

"These animal attacks," he asked, "were they… serious?"

"Fatal." Garth pronounced the word like a judge declaring a sentence. "Have a nice day, Mr. Rains." Derek gave an awkward wave and watched the sheriff head for his squad car, plunging into the waterfall of rain beyond the entryway and almost disappearing in the haze.

Derek shut the door behind him, locking it and then leaning against the door as if he were afraid the sheriff would try to burst back in and arrest him. He forced himself to breathe, holding his head in his hands as he leaned against the door. He told himself that the sheriff wouldn't really bother to investigate the pound, that he was only blustering in hopes of a confession. But a confession to what? Derek told himself that whatever had happened, it couldn't possibly have anything to do with the Xolo, but the thought couldn't chase away a nagging, incessant fear.

TWELVE

Dr. Angie Greene lifted a syringe and casually filled it with painkillers from an enormous bottle, not even bothering to check the dose before she injected it into the massive jet-black horse that lay on the steel table in front of her. From across that table, Kayla Porter watched in amazement, observing the massive form that lay between them grow even more relaxed. She loosened her grip on the enormous legs for the first time since they had given the animal its first dose outside. Eventually she felt confident enough to let go entirely.

"How do you always know how much to give them?" she asked the doctor in amazement. "Don't you ever worry about giving them too much?"

Dr. Greene gave a dry, humorless laugh, the only kind she ever gave. "You kidding? You ever heard the saying, 'Enough to knock out a horse?' That's not just a saying. It's practically impossible to overdose a horse on painkillers. You'll learn about that in vet school."

Kayla risked a small smile over the surgery table. She was working part-time as Dr. Greene's surgery tech while pursuing her biology degree at the University of Colorado in Denver. Certainly, there were closer vets' offices in Denver, but the hour-long drive was worth it for the chance to work with one of the longest-serving and most widely experienced vets in the state. Being on the border between the farm country of rural Colorado and the rapidly expanding suburbs around Denver, Dr. Greene dealt with both the common ailments of household pets and the more unusual injuries and animals that could only come from farm country.

The horse they were working on, for example, had twisted his ankle while his owner was riding him around his property, inspecting the fences on the furthest edges of his fields. Dr. Greene had sedated him and was now preparing to begin surgery, raising her scalpel without even having to mark the site of the incision. Kayla knew that some vets would find her methods reckless, and that even Dr. Greene herself would say she was more burnt out than confident, but Kayla couldn't help but be impressed.

Just as the scalpel began to press against flesh, Dr. Greene was interrupted by a noise from outside. Before either she or Kayla could figure out what the sound was, the dogs in the cage room next door began barking in unison, obscuring any noise from outside, or from inside, for that matter.

"What's got them so worked up?" Kayla asked.

Angie sighed and set the scalpel back in its tray. "Probably someone outside bringing in another emergency. Just what we need right now." Pulling off her surgical mask, she headed for the door. "You keep an eye on the patient." Kayla nodded and watched her go.

Angie Greene crossed the empty, shadowy lobby and entered the cage room. The dogs were furiously barking and howling in unison. They threw their weight against the doors of their cages, the biggest of them almost opening the cages by bending the bars back. Curiously, their howls all seemed to be aimed at the single large window in the room, but it was set far too high for Dr. Greene to see anything outside except the endless field of the night sky. With a shrug, she left the cage room. There was no point in trying to comfort the animals until she had dealt with what was bothering them in the first place.

Crossing the darkened lobby, she stepped out the front door and onto the sagging wooden porch that ran the width of the building. The halogen floodlight on the roof illuminated the dirt parking lot in a stark bone-white, but revealed nothing except her own van and Kayla's rusted-over Civic. The dirt showed no recent tire tracks and no movement was discernible even on the furthest edges of the pool of light.

She trained her eyes on the darkness, unable to make out anything beyond the parking lot except the vague suggestions of the mountains in the distance. Curious, she walked down the three steps to the parking lot, each of the boards creaking heavily beneath her feet. As she stepped onto the parking lot, the dirt crunching beneath her shoes, she entered the edge of the circle created by the floodlight.

Her shadow appeared to stretch across the parking lot ahead of her, like an arrow showing her intentions, its enormous height nearly bisecting the circle of light. She looked around the edge of the circle, but could still discern no movement. Behind her, she could still hear the barking of dogs through the door she had left open, growing even louder and wilder now. Certainly, it wasn't unusual for wild animals to pass through the nearly uninhabited land around her shelter, but no animals had ever gotten the dogs this excited.

She shuddered at the gothic landscape that was coming into view as she strained to see anything beyond the circle of light: the outlines of trees waved their limbs, increasingly bare as fall took a firm hold on the landscape, while beyond, mountains reached up and blocked the stars. Angie could swear the outlined peaks were more numerous than any she had seen during the day. She shivered at the sudden chill of the night wind and was about to turn back when she saw two yellow spots appear on the far edge of the circle of light. As she watched, they moved forward, a shadowy shape emerging from the darkness behind them and entering the circle of light, its long snout standing nearly head-to-head with her shadow, as if challenging her on some spiritual plane.

Dr. Greene almost ran before she recognized the animal. "Hey, I know you," she said softly, trying as much to calm the animal's fears as her own. "You're the Xolo that guy brought around a few weeks ago. I knew he wasn't trying to find a friend for you." She stepped softly across the parking lot, hoping the crunch of dirt beneath her feet was as calming to the dog as it was to her. She held out one hand in a gesture of friendship, inviting the dog to take a sniff. As she drew closer, she could see the scars and patches of pressed-in dirt that coated the bald thing's skin. She could even see marks where it must have chewed its own collar off.

"What did he do, just leave you in the woods?" she asked in the calmest tone she could muster. Dr. Greene had long ago grown accustomed to seeing the cruelty people could inflict on animals. After seeing so many examples of its aftermath on the animals she worked on, she had to admit that even she had done a few things to her patients that her younger self would have considered unforgivable, as if her standards for cruelty were being lowered by the barbarity she witnessed every day. Of course, in her more lucid moments she recognized that she was doing all she could, treating the animals as well as they needed to be treated in order to survive, and not expending energy she no longer had in doing anything more.

She knew that would come as a shock to a young idealist like Kayla, might even make her lose faith in the doctor she obviously looked up to so much, but it was the truth that Dr. Greene had come around to after so many decades in the field. Still, even for her, this treatment of a poor, defenseless dog was unforgiveable. The creature looked starved and miserable, and had obviously been sleeping outside for a few weeks at least. The bastard had probably dumped the thing in the woods the same night he had stopped here, realizing that giving it to the pound was just too much trouble. Didn't he realize the creature was liable to freeze to death in these cold fall nights? The dog was lucky it hadn't happened already.

She had to bring the thing inside. She stepped a little closer, being careful not to move too quickly for fear of scaring the thing off. After so many weeks in the wilderness, the thing probably wasn't used to any human activity. She wondered what had led the dog here. Maybe it remembered seeing the other dogs here and figured it would be taken in too. If so, the breed was just as smart as all of the kennel club books always said they were.

As she stepped closer, the dog remained just on the edge of the lake of light that filled the parking lot. It stared up at her, its eyes glowing yellow with what must have been the reflection of the halogen floodlight over her shoulder. She pushed away the thought that the floodlight was pure white and couldn't have been made yellow by the dog's pure black eyes, telling herself that was only her mind playing tricks on her, telling her to be afraid of the unknown dog.

She stepped within an arm's length of the dog and held out her hand. The dog stayed where it was, cautiously sniffing her hand. She reached out for its neck, encouraging it to move closer. Just as her fingers brushed the leathery skin, the dog lashed out, its jaws snapping together in an audible bite. She drew her hand back in fear and surprise, not even realizing she had been bitten until she felt the warm flow of blood running down her hand. She looked down and saw with stunned surprise that her first two fingers were gone to the knuckle. As she watched with shock, blood sprayed from the stumps in unison.

The dog stood up, growling and baring its blood-covered teeth. Overcome by rage and fear, Dr. Greene kicked the dog in the snout, using the bare teeth as a target. The impact was hard enough to knock the severed fingers from the dog's mouth, collecting dirt as they rolled across the parking lot. With a vague thought that she would have to return to collect the severed appendages so they could be reattached later, Dr. Greene turned and ran for the door, taking advantage of the slight daze her kick had put the dog into.

As she bounded up the steps to the porch, she could hear the dog on the dirt just behind her, but she had just enough of a head start to get inside and slam the door shut in the dog's face. The wooden frame rattled as the dog slammed into the wooden panels. She flipped the lock, unsure what good that would do, but too afraid to think clearly, struggling to work the bolt with her undamaged left hand.

She heard a scream behind her and realized that Kayla had seen the stumps of her fingers, smearing blood across the door as she struggled to hold it shut. Dr. Greene grimaced and pressed the stumps against the inside of her lab coat, blood quickly soaking through and showing a bright red bloom against the pure white fabric. "Kayla!" she yelled to the young vet tech. "Make sure all the doors and windows are shut, now!"

Kayla nodded and ran off without another word, disappearing through the door to the surgery she had just come from. Through the other door, Dr. Greene could hear the dogs still barking, louder than before. She realized with anger that she couldn't remember if the single large window in the room had been open or shut when she checked it. That had been just a moment before, but suddenly felt like a lifetime ago.

She entered the cage room to see the pane of glass angled inwards, the thin metal screen the only thing separating the room from whatever might be outside. Dodging past the cages full of barking dogs, Dr. Greene jumped on top of an empty cage to press the window shut. Just as the creaking pane lowered into place, the Xolo's head appeared on the other side, tearing through the metal screen in a single bite and nipping at her through the glass.

She stepped back in surprise, forgetting her footing for a moment and accidentally stepping to the edge of the cage she stood on. The cage tilted backwards under her weight, flipping out from underneath her and sending her tumbling towards the floor. She landed against one of the larger cages, the bars digging into her back and knocking the wind out of her.

Above her, the Xolo pressed its snout against the glass, smearing foam across the window as it tried to push its way inside. Dr. Greene was so transfixed by its glowing yellow eyes that she found herself unable to move. After a moment, she realized that the dogs in the room weren't moving either. For the first time since she had first heard them, the dogs were completely silent. They were all staring at the Xolo as one, completely transfixed by the sight of the dog. Dr. Greene was even more unsettled by the realization that the Xolo was staring at *them* in turn, looking each of the dogs in the eye for a moment before moving on to the next one.

With the Xolo looking away from her, Angie realized she could move again. She unsteadily pressed her arms against the floor and began to push herself up. As she did, the Xolo looked at the enormous pit bull in the cage behind her, holding its gaze for a long moment. As she pushed herself up, Dr. Greene felt the pit bull's snout press through the bars of the cage behind her and sink into her neck.

Kayla entered the room to find Dr. Greene screaming, pressed against the cage as if stuck to the bars. As she ran closer, she saw the greedy snout pressing through the bars, its teeth sunk into Dr. Greene's neck until blood welled up around them. Kayla struck what little was exposed of the nose with her foot, producing no effect. Grabbing the vet by the shoulders, she pulled down hard, only succeeding in dragging the dog's teeth through Dr. Greene's neck. Dr. Greene screamed as her skin stretched and tore in the dog's mouth, a chunk of flesh finally tearing free, an enormous amount of blood jetting and flowing from the wound. The dog swallowed the chunk as Dr. Greene fell from the bars, writhing in pain. Her flailing shoulder struck the latch that held the cage shut, flipping the thin strip of metal up and out of its eyehole.

The dog pressed forward, pushing the door open. Kayla pulled Dr. Greene away from the cage, worried that the dog would attack her again. An enormous amount of blood soaked the doctor's clothes and pooled on the floor. Kayla realized with horror that she must have torn the doctor's jugular when attempting to free her from the dog's bite. Dr. Greene groaned, trying in vain to cover the wound with her injured hand. More blood oozed over her stumps. Kayla pulled Dr. Greene to her feet and towards the door, kicking the cage door shut to keep the dog contained for another moment, all the time they needed to cross the room and escape.

In the hallway outside, Kayla pressed the door to the cage room shut, searching desperately for a lock, not sure why she would even need one. A groan from Dr. Greene brought her attention to nearer matters. The doctor was bleeding profusely, one entire side of her lab coat bright red and heavy with blood. The hand pressed limply over the hole in her neck was coated with blood, so thick it almost seemed to be a solid shell.

Kayla ran to the operating room and grabbed the first aid kit that hung on the wall, returning to find Dr. Greene unconscious, her blood-soaked hand hanging limply at her side. Praying that she wasn't too late already, Kayla removed the roll of gauze from the kit and began to wrap it around the doctor's neck. Blood continued to flow, immediately soaking the gauze until it began to shred under the stress of further movement.

The activity seemed to have awakened Dr. Greene, as she gasped and turned her head slightly towards Kayla. "No use..." she moaned. "We have to get... to the hospital." The last of her energy seemingly expended, she passed out again.

Kayla dropped the roll of gauze, knowing the doctor was right. She searched her pockets, already knowing she would find nothing. The doctor insisted on her staff keeping their cellphones out of sight and out of mind, which meant Kayla kept her phone in her backpack, which hung in a locker room on the far side of the cage room. The shelter's sole landline was in the office, which was also on the far side of the cage room. Kayla searched the doctor's pockets to make sure they were empty. She found nothing. The doctor's cellphone must have also been in one of those two places, if she even had one.

Kayla stood and looked through the single glass pane in the door to the cage room. The dog they had freed was moving purposefully through the room, ignoring the trail of blood the doctor had left behind as they escaped. It was moving to each cage one at a time, doing on purpose what she and the vet had done on accident, using its nose to turn up the thin metal latches and open the cages.

A strange hairless dog was perched at the window, its eyes glowing with what must have been reflected moonlight, its drool streaking down the pane, watching as the dog inside freed the others. That thing in the window must have been what attacked Dr. Greene outside. Kayla couldn't guess what it wanted, or why she had the feeling that it had somehow given the dog in the shelter the power to free the others. None of that mattered now; what mattered was getting Dr. Greene and herself to safety. At least the scene in the cage room, as terrifying as it was, meant that the thing outside was distracted enough for them to escape.

Kayla's car keys were in her backpack next to her cellphone, but the keys to the shelter's van hung as always on a hook next to the front door. Dr. Greene insisted they be there so she could grab them on the way out in case of an emergency. Why that logic didn't extend to cellphones, Kayla had been afraid to ask, and it seemed like that logic had come back to bite Dr. Greene in the ass, or in the neck, as it were. Without any way to call an ambulance, Kayla would have to drive the vet to Dr. Acharya's clinic on the far side of the valley by herself.

Hooking her arms under the unconscious vet's armpits, Kayla dragged Dr. Greene to the lobby, pushing the door from the hall open with her back. After a quick glance to make sure the way was clear, she dragged the vet across the lobby, the blood-soaked coat beneath her acting as a sort of sticky sled. Setting her down near the door, Kayla grabbed the keys off their hook and held them at the ready, the fob pressed between her thumb and first finger.

Sliding her arms under the still-unconscious vet, she struggled to lift the woman up, finding her lighter than she had expected. Perhaps Dr. Greene's imposing status and intellect had made a frail older woman seem physically more substantial than she really was, or perhaps all the blood she had lost had been enough to make a difference in her weight.

Kayla couldn't think like that. She had a responsibility to get the woman to safety and her negative thoughts wouldn't help her do that. Hoisting the doctor higher, she grabbed the doorknob with her free hand and opened the door slowly, not wanting to make too much noise. She stepped carefully onto the porch, scanning the parking lot for danger. She saw nothing.

Taking a deep breath, Kayla stepped off the porch, leaving the front door open behind her. The van was the nearer of the two vehicles in the parking lot and she moved towards it carefully, not wanting to make too much noise or risk dropping the doctor by running. As she neared the van, she raised the keys a little and pressed the button on the fob. She saw the red lights blink and heard the click of the doors unlocking. Letting out a sigh of relief, she hoisted the doctor over one shoulder and reached a newly free and bloodstained hand through the darkness before the van's passenger-side handle.

Several dogs burst from the darkness at the edge of the parking lot, wild-looking dogs she had never seen before. As they dashed towards her, they disappeared from her vision beneath the doctor, but she instantly felt the stab of pain as they bit into her legs. She tried not to scream, not wanting to attract the attention of any other dogs that may be hiding in the shadows, but soon the pain grew too intense. Kayla let out a low yell, struggling to kick the dogs away. She desperately held on to Dr. Greene, even when a mud-soaked German shepherd raised itself on its hind legs and sank its teeth into the doctor's arm.

She managed to keep hold of Dr. Greene, kicking the dogs away as she turned towards the van. More dogs leapt up, latching their fangs onto the vet, pulling her arms and legs away from Kayla. She held on tight to the doctor, pulling the vet's body away from the dogs even as they tore flesh from the older woman's limbs.

Kayla felt more needles of pain sinking into her legs, her nerves telling every muscle in her body to give up, to drop her burden and flee. She held on stubbornly to the doctor, twisting her fists under the limp body to swat the dogs away as best she could. She felt a warm, open mouth latch onto the back of her hand, fangs tearing through her skin and hooking into her tendons. The pain instinctively forced her hand to open, her fingers splaying wide. She heard the keys jangle against the ground before she felt that they had fallen from her hand. With the intense pain running through her body, she couldn't feel much of anything else.

Pushing the dogs away with her legs, she twisted the vet's body just enough to see the keys shining bright against the pavement. She bent her knees slightly, trying to keep the vet's body out of reach of the dogs while finding a way to grab the keys. She reached out one foot, hoping to drag the keys beneath her feet. A large rottweiler bit her ankle, twisting her leg away from the keys. Kayla hopped back on her free foot, dragging the dog across the dirt as it held her ankle in its jaws.

The dog's rear paws kicked the keys away. Kayla saw the flash of metal and heard the small clatter of the keys as they bounced across the parking lot, landing in the thickest part of the pack of dogs. Kayla saw the keys disappear behind a confusion of limbs and tails.

More dogs pressed in around her, pushing and biting each other as they fought for position, each pressing forward for the chance to take a bite out of her legs. She looked towards the van, which had seemed so close just a moment before. Now the field of dogs that filled the space between her and the van seemed to stretch for miles. She realized that even if she could reach the van and get inside without any dogs following her, she would be unable to do anything but wait for Dr. Greene to bleed out while the dogs surrounded them. Inside the building, she could at least treat Dr. Greene's wounds and hope for the dogs to lose interest and leave. Maybe she would even be able to reach a phone.

As she turned back to the shelter, a massive bulldog leapt at her arms, knocking Dr. Greene from her hands. Kayla screamed as she watched the vet hit the dirt, dogs crowding in around the woman. Dr. Greene woke up as they began to tear into her, fighting each other for the chance to burrow into her flesh. A few dogs were still attacking Kayla, preventing her from getting any closer to the vet. She tried not to listen to Dr. Greene's helpless screams as she ran for the front door, abandoning her mentor's life so she could save her own.

Kayla had been a champion track runner in high school; she knew she should have been able to cross the parking lot in just a few seconds. But when she ran track, she had never done so with bite wounds covering her legs and blood oozing out of her with every step. She took a few bounding uneasy steps, hating herself for feeling relieved at being free of the burden of the doctor's body. She could still hear the screams behind her, growing weaker as they were replaced by the sounds of tearing flesh and the gnashing of small teeth.

She crossed the parking lot in a few quick strides, her legs burning as the wounds opened further with each new step. She heard the padding of several sets of paws behind her, but managed to keep just ahead of them. When she reached the porch, she leapt over the steps, wincing as she landed on the sagging wood, feeling the impact travel through the wounds on her legs.

Kayla reached the door just ahead of the dogs and slammed it shut behind herself as she entered. She leaned against the frame, struggling to catch her breath. She felt the few dogs chasing her slam against the door, their impact enough to rattle the door, but nothing more. She smiled as she slid the bolt shut, knowing that she had escaped.

The screaming outside had stopped. The only sound was the ripping of flesh and the smacking of hungry mouths. Another, nearer sound joined this symphony. Kayla looked across the lobby and saw the far door slowly swinging open. A pack of dogs burst through. Every dog that had been in the cages in the next room was running free, all of them running directly towards her. Kayla screamed and threw up her hands, pressing herself against the door as if a few more inches of distance would keep her safe.

The impact of the pack of dogs all colliding with her at once was enough to break the door behind her, sending Kayla tumbling backwards onto the porch as several dogs bit into her. More dogs gathered around her, pressing in from outside for their own chance to take a bite of her flesh. All of them were pushed aside by a strange form. Through the haze of her pain, Kayla recognized the strange shape of the hairless dog she had seen outside the window, the one that must have first attacked the doctor. She wondered again how the hairless dog had led the others to do all this; what had made the dogs so vicious. Then the hairless dog looked into her eyes, absorbing her in a glow that she now knew could not be caused by natural light, and she wondered no more.

The Xolo watched as the others ate their fill. When they had taken all they could from the humans, they went inside, where they found more meat, ready for the taking. Once they were finished, he again locked eyes with each of the new dogs in turn. They were grateful for his freeing them from their prison, and for the meat he had helped procure. They needed no convincing to join his pack; they hated the humans as much as he did. That was good. They would need not only numbers for their revenge against the humans, but also hatred, the motivation to fight this fight until it was over.

They spent the night inside the human shelter, the new dogs returning reluctantly to their place of imprisonment. But it was warm and free from predators. It might be the last such place for them for a long time. Before first light, before the humans could find them, they would return to the woods and hide. Until then, they would rest, and plan, and dream of their revenge.

THIRTEEN

GARTH CHAMBERS NEVER FELT LIKE THE SHERIFF EARLY IN THE MORNING. It was hard to when your head was pounding, when your mouth was as dry as sandpaper, when you hadn't slept a wink the night before. Putting on his uniform always changed that. He adjusted his badge in the single small, dirty mirror that hung in his bedroom, seeing himself come together as the uniform fell into place. He tried not to look at the framed photos that gathered dust on the table under the mirror, memories of happier times and happier people.

A glimpse of a wedding dress brought his eye to a photo of himself on his wedding day, thirty years younger and more than twice that many pounds lighter. He slowly picked up the photo even as he commanded himself not to, not knowing why he lingered over the image, not sure why he even kept it. He was pulled from his reverie by the mechanical blaring of an alarm clock, the travel kind he used to take hunting and camping, when he had been young enough and stupid enough to do either one of those things. He crossed to the rumpled twin bed and pounded the alarm almost hard enough to break it, nearly sending the clock through the bottom of the overturned plastic bin that served as his night stand.

Cradling his head, he walked the few feet to the kitchen and searched the upper shelves. He didn't have to search long to find the bottle of whiskey he had told himself he hadn't been looking for. As he contemplated the bottle, a gentle knock came at his door. He sighed and hid the bottle. The knock came again, quick enough to interrupt anything he could be doing. "Yeah, hold on, I'm coming!" he yelled.

He searched the sink until he found his Thermos, then picked up a greasy pot half-full of coffee he couldn't remember brewing. He held the pot up to the light of the grimy window above the sink and slowly swirled the liquid inside, watching it leave streaks on the inside of the glass. He flipped the top open with his thumb and gave the liquid a sniff. Didn't smell too bad; couldn't have been older than a day or two. He poured it into a used cup from the sink and threw that in the dirty microwave. While he waited for a minute to count down, he ate a few slices of salami and a piece of cheese from the fridge. Enough to get him to the gas station for a breakfast sandwich, at least. He ripped the microwave open while he chewed the last of his breakfast, then poured the steaming coffee into his Thermos and headed for the door, mentally preparing himself for the day ahead.

Andy Millam paced the dirt patch that passed as a yard while he waited for the sheriff. He had stepped off the ramshackle front porch, afraid the sagging boards would collapse beneath his feet. He looked at the rundown shack of a house, still in disbelief that this was where their sheriff chose to live.

But when the sheriff emerged, he looked impeccable as always, his uniform fastidious and the Thermos of coffee in his hand steaming. He strode towards the waiting patrol car confidently. "Wait, Sheriff, ain't you gonna lock up?" Millam asked.

The sheriff gave the boisterous laugh he reserved only for his chief deputy. "Now, who would be dumb enough to rob the house of their local sheriff?" Millam shrugged at that and followed the sheriff to the car.

Millam jumped behind the wheel as the sheriff groaned and struggled into the passenger seat next to him. Once his passenger was situated, Millam took off down the narrow country lane, empty of any sign of human habitation except the sheriff's solitary home. The sheriff flipped through a small notepad, opening it to a hastily scrawled address somewhere in the mountains: *18 Valley View Road.*

"Now, if there aren't any more unexplained deaths for us to deal with, I'd like to stop over for a breakfast sandwich, then check out a lead I got yesterday," the sheriff said.

"Actually, Sheriff, there has been. Just got a call from an animal shelter in the mountains."

"Don't tell me – 18 Valley View Road?"

"That's the one."

"Shit." Garth tore the page off the notepad and crumpled it up. "Talk about killing two birds with one stone."

"You still wanna stop for that breakfast sandwich, Sheriff?"

Garth nodded, leaned his seat as far back as the cage behind him would allow, and pulled his hat over his eyes to block out the sun. "You know, Andy, I like the days when you drive." He opened the window with one finger on the switch and tossed the crumpled piece of paper out. In the rearview, Millam watched the yellow ball bounce across the asphalt and disappear into the brush.

Garth made sure to have his breakfast sandwich downed before Millam pulled up to the animal shelter. He saw Dr. Greene's battered practice van in the dirt parking lot near an even worse-for-wear Civic that he didn't recognize. A long horse trailer was parked across the entrance to the parking lot, headed by a shiny black pick-up whose driver was leaning against the perfectly polished hood, one immaculate leather cowboy boot balancing on the front tire. He pushed himself away from the truck as the squad car pulled up, standing with his hands on his hips as he impatiently waited for the sheriff to get out of the car.

Garth didn't recognize the man, but by the looks of his perfectly pressed shirt and stiff jeans, he was a wealthy hobbyist with a few horses on his property, rather than the rugged rancher he wanted to appear as. Garth hailed the man as he slowly walked from the cruiser. "What seems to be the trouble?"

The man whipped off his dark sunglasses as if he couldn't believe the sheriff didn't know already. "Man, there's two dead people in that ditch! That's the trouble!" He pointed to the ditch on the far end of the parking lot, which separated the lot from a thick stretch of woods. A heavy cloud of flies buzzed above one section of the ditch, turning the woods behind them into static. "I dropped my Betsy off last night for a twisted ankle," the faux-rancher continued, "came back this morning to pick 'er up, and I saw that!" He again pointed emphatically to the ditch. "No way was I going inside to get her with that out here, though. Who knows what could be in there."

Garth nodded. "Well, I guess we will in just a second. Let's take a look at that ditch, then we'll go in and find your Betsy."

That last sentence had been directed at Millam, but the rancher held up his hands as if to ward the statement away from himself. "Ah, hell no, you two go on by yourself, you're the police." He resumed his position against the truck. "I'm waiting the hell out here."

Garth smiled and tipped his hat at the man. "Thanks for the help. Maybe I oughtta add you to the force." Ignoring the man's offended look, Garth strode towards the ditch. Millam followed after him, both of them swatting away flies as they looked into the ditch.

There wasn't much left to see. Two bodies that were little more than skeletons were twisted at the bottom of the ditch, as if they had been hastily dumped there. Ragged scraps of clothing hung from the bones, alongside the last few scraps of meat which the flies were fighting over.

Millam nearly retched at the sight and the smell. "That Dr. Greene?" Millam asked, waving the flies away with his hat so he could point to the nearer of the two bodies.

"Sure looks like her coat," Garth agreed. "Other one must be one of her employees, we'll have to check her records to find a name." He stepped back from the ditch and looked at the building. From here, it looked perfectly peaceful, except for the front door hanging open on the porch. As his eyes adjusted to the early morning sunlight, he realized the door hadn't been accidentally left open, but was broken nearly off its hinges and hung on to the frame by only a thin strip of metal.

"You wanna see what happened inside?" Millam asked.

"Not really, but I suppose we oughtta." Garth motioned to the rancher. "We're gonna take a look inside, you just wait here like you have been."

"Shit, I ain't going nowhere," the man said, then half-followed them across the parking lot, staying just close enough to keep track of them.

As Garth stepped onto the porch, he glanced at the door, but said nothing. It had obviously been torn off its hinges by a single blow, the trace of the impact left in the lone crack that ran the height of the wood, nearly splitting it in two. Drops of blood were dried on the floor, continuing in a trail across the porch and down the steps. Garth guessed that if he followed them, he would end up back at the ditch with the dead bodies. He studied the door a moment, then moved inside.

The lobby was a mess. The chairs were knocked over, the two doors at the far end were left hanging open, and bloody tracks covered the floor in all directions. When he stooped to inspect them, Garth saw what he had secretly expected: paw prints. He followed the prints to a narrow hallway, where they were joined by more blood, the tracks eventually disappearing in a thick spray that covered the walls, the floor, and was even splattered across the ceiling. The blood was thickest near a narrow corner, beyond which was an open door. Garth looked back at Millam, then both pulled their revolvers from their holsters.

Garth used his fingers to silently count down from three. They moved around the corner in unison, Millam nearly slipping in the blood as he kicked the door out of the way. The door swung open to reveal a steel operating table covered entirely in blood, topped by an enormous pile of bones that Garth at first couldn't recognize.

"That's my Betsy!" a voice shouted from behind them. Garth whirled, raising his gun unconsciously, until he saw the faux-rancher rushing past them, his shiny leather boots sliding across the blood-soaked floor. He skidded to a stop just short of the operating table, obviously wanting to reach out for the skeletal remains of his horse, but afraid to touch the slimy bones that remained.

"Guess 'hungry enough to eat a horse' isn't just a saying, huh?" Garth said to Millam.

The faux-rancher whirled around, fury in his eyes. "You watch your tongue, Sheriff! That was my best animal." He took a step forward, like he intended to punch the sheriff out. Whatever he planned to do, he never got the chance. On his next step, his leather boots skidded on the blood, spilling him to the floor. He landed in the deepest pool of red-purple blood, staining his crisp new jeans and his perfectly pressed shirt.

Garth laughed a little and put away his gun, holding out a hand to help the man. "Alright, let my deputy here help you outside and take down your particulars; I'm gonna look around a bit more."

The man slapped a bloody hand into Garth's own, staining the sheriff's palm as he struggled to his feet. "Christ, Sheriff, what the hell could have done this?"

Garth looked down at the paw prints stamped in the blood. "I've got a little theory about that."

As Millam led the faux-rancher out, Garth followed the paw prints to a room filled with cages, which he wasn't too surprised to find were empty. Another trail of blood started near the largest of the cages and led to the lobby, its path interrupted by rows of crisscrossing paw prints. As Garth studied the scene, he heard the overpowered engine of a pick-up truck roar like a monster before heading off down the road.

A moment later, he heard Millam enter the lobby. Garth called out to him, then put a cigarette in his mouth, already looking forward to the break that smoking it would give him before the insanity of the day's work began. Right now, he was just relieved to be alone in the building with Millam.

"Andy, I need you to call the circus into town," he said through his unlit cigarette before the deputy had even entered the room. "The coroner, the forensics team, a few more deputies to control the scene, and animal control."

"Christ, Sheriff, you really think dogs did all this?"

"I don't know what else to think."

Millam looked around the room. "The cages are perfectly intact. The animals didn't break out, someone let them out."

Garth leaned closer to one, observing the slime dripping from the metal hook. "Someone with a slimy mouth," he grunted.

"You think another dog let them out?"

"Well, if I had a pack of dogs that was hungry enough to eat me, I sure as hell wouldn't let 'em out myself."

"Sure, but that's just crazy, Sheriff. You really think a pack of dogs planned a jailbreak?"

Garth shrugged and looked out the single window in the room. A drying film of drool covered the outside. "Maybe they had a little help from the outside."

By the end of the morning, the circus was in town. Endless rows of squad cars pulled into the dirt parking lot, spewing out deputies in seemingly impossible numbers. Dogcatchers ran across the scene, comically waving nets they hoped to use. Crime scene photographers set off flashbulbs like fireworks. Men in white suits piled out of tiny vans, spreading a large tent over the ditch where the bodies were found, while men in dark suits carried away heavy bags like trampolines meant to catch a falling trapeze artist. Playing the ringleader, Garth directed them around the site, watching the men scurry across the parking lot like they were rushing to put out fires or control a raging elephant. Garth could only hope this circus wouldn't have too many repeat performances.

Now he stood off to the side of the parking lot, having his third cigarette of the morning. The first two had been rushed, half-smoked to fit into the time between when Millam had called for back-up and when the first of the men had arrived, desperate for direction. As always, it had taken hours to get them set-up and running properly, but now their work was largely automatic; they had their orders and only had to carry them out, giving Garth a rare moment to relax. He took it, looking out over the mountains as he felt his lungs burn, trying to think through a theory he couldn't quite formulate even to himself.

A team of investigators from the state lab pushed a cart of equipment towards the building. Garth had ordered them to test the drool on the window to see if it matched the saliva on the chewed-up collars found at the log cabin. He nodded at them as they went by. "Getting a little too used to seeing you guys," he said flatly. The leader of the team shrugged and grinned and pushed his men on towards the building.

Coming outside at the same time, Millam dodged around the forensics team and made for the sheriff, waving a stack of files in one hand. "Some good news, sheriff; I found those records you wanted. Seems like the doc's office was untouched in all this, so I should be able to go through them right away."

Garth took a long drag to celebrate that. "Good. Go through the employee records to see who that second body might be. When you're done with that, pull the records of every dog dropped off here in the past month, in particular if it's an unusual breed."

"What do you consider unusual, Sheriff?"

"I'm looking for some Mexican breed, called a 'cholo' or something."

"I think you mean 'Xolo,' Sheriff," said a smooth female voice behind them. The cops turned to see Heloise Lopez, the head of the county's animal control department. Heloise was in her early thirties, and, Garth thought, amazingly capable for her young age. He had to admit to himself that she impressed him even more because she was one of the few female department heads in the county, and the first he knew of in the county's history who was Hispanic or Latino or whichever term Garth was supposed to use. After so many years, and so many changes to the terminology, he found it hard to remember.

"X-O-L-O. Xoloitzcuintli, in full," Heloise pronounced flawlessly in the accent she had picked up from her immigrant parents, with just a hint of the snark she could have only picked up in the American public school system. The smile she flashed afterwards was bright, beautiful, and mischievous.

"Well, Loise, took you long enough to get here," Garth said, using the nickname she had only allowed him to use after a long working history had warmed her initial iciness towards him.

She flashed him another smile, this one with a slight edge meant to warn him off his growing friendliness. "Sorry, Sheriff, had a bear running loose up near Denver. Didn't do any harm, but sure gave the residents a fright until we bear-sprayed him a bit and rounded him up. Now, is this the same Xolo that bit that kid at the elementary school a few weeks ago?"

"That's what I want to find out." The sheriff turned to Millam. "Search those records and see if they had one of these 'Xolo' things dropped off here recently."

Millam pulled out his trusty pen and paper. "Sure thing, Sheriff. How do you spell the full name again?"

Garth rolled his eyes and violently yanked the cigarette from his mouth. "Christ, Andy, it starts with an X. You know any other dog breeds that start with an X?" he asked Heloise. She shook her head with a barely suppressed smirk. "Good. Then just look for any dog breed that starts with an X, and let me know when you find one."

"Right away, Sheriff." Millam bounded back towards the building, almost colliding with the cart of equipment the techs were bringing outside.

Watching him stumble apologetically towards the building, Garth turned back to Loise as they shared a laugh. "Now, tell me all about this Xolo," he said, lighting a fresh cigarette off the butt of the old one.

Heloise shrugged. "They're a rare breed in America. My parents said they were the national dog in Mexico, but I've never actually seen one. I've heard they're smart."

"As smart as a man?" Garth asked.

Heloise laughed a little at that. Garth followed her gaze to Millam as he almost collided with the crime scene photographers coming out the front door. Papers spilled from the folders in his hand and fanned out across the front porch.

"Depends on which man, Sheriff. But smarter than a woman.... Definitely not."

They shared a laugh as Heloise looked over the crime scene. "Sheriff, do you really think a dog was behind all this?"

Garth took a slow drag on his fresh cigarette, being careful to throw the old one away from the crime scene. "I don't know, but I know that incident at the elementary school was the only serious dog attack we've had in this county in years, and just a month later, we get three fatal attacks that sure as hell look like they were done by dogs. And this shelter is where the owner supposedly took that Xolo. That's his story anyways."

"Seems like a little more than a coincidence," Loise agreed. "But I've never heard of dogs doing anything like this."

"Well, tell me this," the sheriff asked, "do dog packs have any kind of planning ability? Do they have leaders?"

Heloise only looked at him strangely.

"Alright, tell me this: are these Xolos usually aggressive?"

"Not usually, but they've been trained to be fighters in the past. Dogs are like people: their attitude depends on what they're exposed to."

"Yeah, I know a little about that. Thanks for coming by, Loise."

"Anytime, Sheriff. Let me know when you've got a suspect I can hunt."

"If my hunch is right, it might be sooner than you think."

He threw his cigarette out and headed for his squad car, watching the circus unfold as he left.

FOURTEEN

Emily burst from the mouth of the cave into the fresh sunlight, greedily inhaling the scent of the flowers and grass that bloomed all around her. She was at the mouth of a wide valley, the cave behind her ending near the bottom of the tallest mountain. Other mountains, less tall but no less imposing, ringed the sky, standing like sentinels over the silent valley. If the sun had been on the other side of the sky, their shadows would have been long enough to encase the entire valley in darkness. Thankfully, the sun shone full and high overhead. She raised her face towards the light for a moment, basking in the glow, enjoying the sunlight after the months spent in the gloom of the castle, and what had felt like years crawling through the darkness of the tunnels and caves through which she had escaped.

For a moment, she even forgot the creatures that were pursuing her. The feeling of relaxation that came with forgetting instantly reminded her of the danger. She must not let her guard down, even for a second. Looking back towards the cave, she wondered if sunlight would stop the creatures. As she looked, she heard a strangely human roar emerge from the depths of the cave, a sound like Michael's scream of rage and despair mixed with the baying of a dejected wolf. After that, she heard the clicking of pads along the cave floor, several pairs of paws quickly closing in on her.

Emily looked towards the valley below and realized that the way down was steeper than she had initially realized. A rocky hill that quickly turned into something resembling a sheer cliff surrounded her on three sides, leading to a drop that was much too far to survive without injury. Behind her was only the sheer wall of the mountain, offering nowhere to climb and no other openings besides the one from which the terrible clicking of the pads emerged. Emily stepped to the edge of the cliff, wondering what she could do.

Alison Rains paused with her fingers hovering over the keyboard, wondering much the same thing. Once again, she had written herself into a corner, only this time it was nearly literal. Alison reread her last few pages, quickly growing more frustrated. Not only was she stuck in terms of story, her prose wasn't even good today. From the first sentence, she hated the overused verb "burst," and how could sunlight possibly be "fresh"? She wondered why Emily would possibly think that sunlight would stop werewolves; everyone knew that was vampires. Alison was unsure about the plausibility of the geography she had described, but she knew it made it nearly impossible to continue the plot.

She stood up from the desk, pacing the room to work off her frustration. She hadn't been writing enough lately, she decided. Every time she took a day off, it was harder and harder to get back into the habit. It wasn't as if she could blame that on work. The illustrious firm of Myers, Harim, and Donaldson had decided to let her go. They claimed it was because of her "inability to complete scheduled shifts," as if it were her fault that she had to leave work to attend to her injured son, but she knew it was really her writing during work hours that had been the issue. Alison had always hoped for more time to focus on her writing; now she had just that and she couldn't produce a decent page to save her life.

Part of that was stress, she knew. She should be spending this time looking for a job, not fiddling around with a novel that would probably never be published. Even though Derek insisted they were fine, that they would have all the money they needed once the next phase of the development got its investors, she couldn't help but worry hearing statements like that. She knew everything could go south and they would need some source of income. But in a small town like this, there were few jobs available, and even fewer (she hated to admit) that she was interested in.

Derek insisted that her job was to take care of the kids, though she suspected that included him. Besides, the kids hardly seemed to be around much anymore. Max had gone back to school, and his free time was usually spent with the small group of friends she had been relieved he had found, though they never came over here. He spent long hours at their houses after school, often sleeping over, and seemed to purposefully avoid his family when he did come home, giving evasive answers when asked what they had done together. On the rare occasions that he did see the family, Max seemed angry and sullen.

Alison could almost understand that after they had taken in the dog that bit him, but more than a month had passed since the incident and his behavior was still getting no better. She knew from his teachers that his grades were slipping, and he seemed constantly tired when he was at home. Alison would almost suspect he was doing drugs, but she had no idea where he would get them at his age.

Gracie was little better. She had been angry and despondent with Alison since she had asked Derek to get rid of the Xolo. The golden retriever Derek had bought for her (without asking Alison) had at least helped her mood a little, but had done nothing to improve the rift that had developed between her and Alison.

Derek himself seemed little better than his children. She knew how little sleep he got, but it didn't entirely explain the nervous, agitated state he seemed to be in constantly, especially the last few days, as if he were harboring a guilty secret. If he weren't spending all of his time at work, she would suspect an affair, but she knew how much of his energy he was pouring into the new development.

What she hated to see was how little of that energy was paying off. He seemed to be making no forward momentum on convincing investors to come aboard the new development, and she knew how that must be preying on Derek's mind. Even worse were the constant phone calls from his potential business partner, who was still hounding Derek to sell the land in Mexico. Alison knew how much he hated the man's plans for the land, but she also knew that the money could easily pay for the new development, or save the family if that development never came through.

Still, Alison wanted to support her husband and was proud of him for making a stand. She just wished this potential business partner would stop calling at all hours of the day and night. She could see Derek cringe every time the phone rang, as if being reminded of an unpleasant memory.

No wonder she couldn't write. With all that going on, there was no room in her head for her own creativity. She felt selfish for even thinking that, when her family had so many problems, but writing was something she had to do, a need as essential as food or water, and lately it had felt impossible.

The doorbell rang. She was startled by the noise but glad for the distraction. Looking out the window, she saw no vehicle in the driveway, but a long black limo idling on the street below. Equal parts intrigued and suspicious, Alison made her way to the door.

The man on the doorstep was strange, nervous, and wore an ill-fitting suit that made him look even more overweight than he was. Alison had never seen him before, but instantly disliked him. The man took off his hat in what seemed to Alison a parody of civility, bowing slightly as he did so. "Good morning, Mrs. Rains, I'm wondering if your husband might be at home?" He met her gaze with a faint smile but in a moment, his eyes were already travelling past her, probing the interior of the house as if searching for Derek.

"Can I ask who wants to know?"

The smile of fake civility forced itself wider and the eyes returned to her. Alison could swear he slightly crushed the hat against his chest. "Aw, pardon me, miss. I am Mr. Hector Ramirez, your husband's business partner in… foreign affairs." He bowed again slightly and put his hat back on as if completing an image for her.

Alison cringed slightly, involuntarily pulling back from the hand he offered. "You mean his *potential* business partner, right? You're the one who wants to buy that land in Mexico?'

The fake smile grew even wider. "Yes, that's right."

Alison wouldn't have thought it possible, but she liked the man even less now. He was the one who had called her husband away for a week when she needed him, who was constantly pestering Derek with calls at all hours of the night, who had given him a moral dilemma that Derek obviously couldn't handle.

But worst of all, he was the one who had given Derek that dog. That had been when all the trouble had started, as if a single dog bite had infected their entire family. Now the fiend who had brought that animal into their home was standing on her doorstep, trying to invite himself in, grinning his grin of fake civility, hoping he could deceive her.

"I'm sorry, Mr. Ramirez, but my husband is not at home."

Over his shoulder, she saw again the black limo idling in the street. She could see a man in the driver's seat, through the distance made it impossible to make out anything about him. She already felt her words echo through the empty house behind her. She wished that her answer hadn't been honest, even if it meant that Derek would have to deal with this strange, nervous man. Alison felt that some of his nervous energy was transferring to her.

He was again looking past her, as if checking the house to make sure she was telling the truth. "Aw, well, that is too bad, Mrs. Rains. As you may know, I am the one who gifted your husband that lovely dog…"

"I'm aware," she said curtly.

"Yes," he said, grinning as if he didn't pick up on her tone. "Well, I just came by to check on the animal. Do you have it here?" He stepped forward slightly, as if to move into the house and investigate for himself.

Alison stepped to the lip of the door to block him. "You must not have heard. The animal was aggressive and bit my son. We had to give it away."

Hector gave a look of shock that seemed even faker than his look of civility. When he had obviously felt that this look had lasted long enough to be convincing, he remembered to be angry. "You know, Mrs. Rains, that animal was a very expensive gift; you had no right to give it away."

"You'll have to talk to my husband about that," she said, hating herself for giving him the encouragement.

"I intend to. Do you know who your husband might have given the dog away to?" He was still looking around the house as if he didn't believe her. She wondered where he thought she would have the dog hidden away, and why.

"I really wouldn't know, Mr. Ramirez, you would have to ask my husband about that."

"And when might I have the ability to do that?" Both his tone and his phrasing made it seem as if he intended to wait at the house until Derek returned, along with the puppy-dog way he returned his hat to his hands, looking up at her as she stood on the lip of the door.

"Unfortunately, Mr. Ramirez, my husband is away on business and will be gone for the night." She was momentarily proud of her deception, until she realized its potential consequences. She looked back to the man in the limo, who still hadn't moved. "But I will be sure to tell him to call you when I talk to him tonight," she said quickly, already starting to shut the door.

Hector stared blankly at her for a moment. Alison continued closing the door, afraid of what he might do. He only put his hat back on and said softly,

"Very good, Mrs. Rains. I look forward to hearing from your husband." He took a final look around the house, as if still looking for the dog, then turned back to the limo.

Alison instantly closed and locked the door, then headed for the study. Through the window, she saw Hector approaching the limo. Talking to the driver for a moment, he pointed back to the house. Alison saw the shape of the driver turn its head towards the window and she realized she was exposed. With a gasp, she pulled the curtains shut, her hands trembling until she heard the limo's engine start. After a moment's thought, Alison rushed to the back door, then to every other door and window in the house, making sure they were all locked.

She knew this made no sense, that the man was already gone, and that even when he had been here, he had never done anything overtly threatening. Still, she couldn't shake the eerie feeling the man had given her. She wandered the empty halls of the house, telling herself she was just pacing to clear her head, but knowing she was secretly searching for an intruder in wait, as if the man had somehow gotten inside.

Alison desperately wished she weren't home alone. The kids wouldn't be back from school for hours, and Derek not until much later. She needed to take her mind off the strange man and decided writing would be just the thing. But when she sat back down at the keyboard, she realized that the man had followed her into her writing. Emily seemed to have no escape. No matter what Alison wrote, every choice Emily made led her to doom, like one of those choose your own adventure books Alison had loved in elementary school.

After what might have been minutes or hours, Alison was interrupted by another knock on the door. Jumping out of her seat, she tentatively parted the curtains and saw a vehicle in the driveway that might have been called there by her mind. Running to the front door, she looked out the small window to make sure and saw a face that at any other time would have been highly unwelcome.

Sheriff Garth Chambers stood on the doorstep, not holding his hat in his hands or begging with his eyes to be let in. After a stiff greeting, he asked directly if Alison's husband was at home. She didn't feel the need to lie this time. After being told that Derek was at work, Garth was about to leave, until Alison stopped him.

She told him all about the strange man who had appeared at her doorstep and the unsettling impression he had given her. Garth listened carefully, nodding at the key details. "Well, Mrs. Rains, did he actually threaten you? Try to push his way in the house, anything like that?"

"Well, not exactly."

"Then I'm afraid there's nothing the law can do. It's not a crime to make you feel uncomfortable."

Alison nodded, feeling foolish for even bringing it up.

"Now, Mrs. Rains, when might I be able to expect your husband back?"

As Derek drove home, he felt good for the first time in weeks. His visit from the sheriff the other day had gone without a follow-up, and he assumed that Garth had either forgotten about the vet or never followed up with her. Now, Derek was on a phone call with a group of investors whose vision perfectly matched his own.

"Derek, I think you're right about the property," said the first investor, a capital manager named Sarah Highmore, who was in her late twenties and always spoke with the breathless tones of a teenager. "The more we keep the land intact, the higher the value of each lot will be."

That was exactly what Derek wanted to hear, but he felt superstitious about letting them know that. Derek was just glad they couldn't hear his grin. "I'm glad you came around to it. Do you think we have a deal?"

A second voice crackled through his car speakers. This one was Dave Hortiz, Sarah's boss and the owner of Cañon City Capital. "I think so, Derek. We just need to go over a few final details. Would you be able to swing by our office tomorrow?"

Derek smiled as he turned onto his street. The smile faded when he looked up at his driveway and saw the sheriff's squad car parked there. Without knowing why he was doing it, Derek slammed on his brakes, bringing his car to a stop in the middle of the street with a loud squeal.

"Derek? Everything alright over there?" For a moment, Derek was confused where the voice was coming from. Then he remembered his phone call and realized the squeal of brakes had been audible on their end.

"Yeah, yeah, everything's fine. I'll, um, stop by tomorrow."

"That sounds good, Derek," Dave said.

Derek hung up without another word. It was only when he was pulling into his driveway that he realized he had hung up without agreeing on a time for tomorrow, like a character in a movie. He felt even more like a movie character as he pulled his car into the driveway and got out without locking it, stumbling in a daze around the cruiser that blocked the garage, his mind preoccupied on what he would find inside.

Nothing could have prepared him for the oddly calm, domestic scene he found. The sheriff's hat sat on the kitchen island next to a half-empty glass of water. The sheriff himself was tucked into one of the barstools at the island, his massive belly bulging over the counter as he laughed at something just said by Alison, who stood across the island from him, leaning against the kitchen counter while sipping a glass of wine. If the sheriff had been anyone else, Derek would have instinctively suspected an affair.

The two of them seemed calm enough, but the very presence of the lawman made Derek uneasy. Derek closed the door behind himself, feeling more like a movie character then ever as he entered his own house through the door normally reserved for visitors. The sheriff, who had previously seemed not to notice him, suddenly turned as far as his girth would allow and said, without looking directly at him, "Evening, Derek; you seem to be in fine spirits."

Derek wondered what made him think that, but decided not to ask. "Yeah, just closed a deal on a new development."

Alison beamed at him over her wine glass. The sheriff gave a shark-like grin and said, "Oh? Good for you. I thought it might be because you thought you were able to pull a fast one on me."

Alison looked suddenly bewildered.

"I'm not sure what you mean, Sheriff," Derek said.

Garth cocked an eyebrow. "I assume you heard about what happened up at the animal shelter? It was all over the news."

"I only pay attention to sports. Which animal shelter was that?"

"The one in the mountains. You know, the one you told me about when I came to visit the other day."

Derek ignored Alison's confused look. "Oh yes, of course."

"Funny thing, Derek, they didn't have any record of your cholo being dropped off there. Naturally, I had to check after finding Dr. Greene and her assistant dead."

Derek swallowed the sinking feeling that threatened to overwhelm him. "Dead? What happened to them?"

"Eaten alive, by the looks of it."

"I suppose that's one hazard of working with wild animals," Derek instantly wished he hadn't said.

Garth stared blankly at him. "You know, Derek, I've seen a lot of wild things in my time, but nuthin' half so wild as two people's flesh stripped to the bone by a pack of domestic dogs."

Alison put down her glass of wine and threw her hands over her mouth. Derek said nothing; there was nothing he could say.

The sheriff took the opportunity and continued. "In fact, the only other animal attack I've seen around here lately was when your dog went wild on that boy."

Derek summoned all the anger he could muster. "*That* boy happened to be my son, Sheriff. And I told you, I got rid of the dog."

"And I told *you*, I ain't got no record of that."

"Didn't I say the place seemed skeezy? Poorly run? The vet was so overworked, she probably sent the dog straight to the gas chamber or whatever without making any record."

Garth turned around fully, his massive bulk leaning out of the chair. "And didn't I tell YOU that Dr. Greene was always a competent professional in the twenty years I knew her?" The Sheriff's tone was now harsh enough to rattle the china in the cabinets. "And now she's dead. So, I want you to start being honest with me."

"What do you want me to tell you, Sheriff? That my dog is a murderer? What does this attack at the vet prove?"

"You haven't heard the details of the other two cases, have you?"

"Sorry, Sheriff. Like I said, I don't watch the news much."

"There was an attack on a farm outside town. An old friend of mine was killed. His two dogs went missing, but forensics on the body we had showed bites from more than a dozen different dogs."

"I'm sorry to hear about that, Sheriff, but was one of them my Xolo?"

"Well, since you never got him registered, we have no way of knowing that. Now, the other case was even worse. The old supper club up in the mountains, you remember the place, don'tchya? What am I saying, of course you don't, you're a newcomer, and you would have been just a kid then anyways. Well, turns out a group of thugs were running a dog fighting ring outta the place. Some of their dogs must've gotten loose and killed everybody there."

"And all this shortly after the Xolo bit my son, huh?"

"That's right."

"And do you have any evidence connecting my Xolo to all of this?"

"Not yet."

Derek sighed as heavily as he could. "I didn't think so. Sheriff, if you want to accuse me of selling my dog to criminals or teaching it to commit murder or whatever it is you're saying, why don't you come back when you have some evidence?"

Garth said nothing. Derek took a little pride in how taken aback the sheriff seemed. With only a small nod towards Alison, the lawman scooped up his hat and headed for the door. Derek moved out of his way as the sheriff's frame filled the entryway. With one hand on the door, the sheriff turned back to Derek. "Alright, Mr. Rains, I'll see you real soon, then. In the meantime, if you do remember anything I oughtta know, don't hesitate to call."

"I won't," Derek said firmly. The sheriff nodded again and headed out. Derek made sure the door was locked behind him. Derek took a moment to compose himself before turning back to Alison. "Christ, did you know he was going to ambush me like that?"

Alison was already clutching her wine glass again. She raised her shoulders in confusion, struggling to keep the wine glass level between her hands. "He just said he wanted to talk to you. I didn't know what about; thought it would look suspicious if I tried to give you a heads up. I mean, you did drop that dog off at the pound, didn't you?"

Derek turned on her sharply. "How can you even ask me that? Don't you believe anything I say anymore?"

"I was just asking." She took a small sip of wine and walked out of the kitchen. Derek at first thought she was storming out of the fight, but she was only walking to the study, where he followed.

Gracie's new golden retriever was huddled in the corner, shaking. "Did the sheriff scare him?" Derek asked, not expecting a reply.

"He said he came straight from the crime scene at the pound." It took Derek a moment to realize she meant the sheriff. She waved to the dog. "He must have smelt all the other dogs on the sheriff. It really shook him up." Derek at first thought she was giving in to the sheriff's crazy idea about killer dogs, then realized she simply meant the dogs at the pound.

"He's not the only one who's shaken up."

"What's got you so excited?" Alison was sitting behind her desk, her gaze drifting towards her laptop.

"Nothing. I think I'm just nervous about this deal. It'll finally get that asshole Hector off my back."

Alison snapped her fingers. "How could I forget? He stopped by today."

"Who? Hector? What did he want?"

"Nothing that I could figure out. He was just asking about the dog. He seemed offended that we got rid of it; said it was expensive."

Derek waved the thought away. "Aw, that's nothing for a crook like him…" He trailed off as his thoughts raced into a supposition so crazy, he couldn't even believe it himself. "What did he want with the dog?"

Alison shrugged. "He didn't say. Just seemed like he was looking for it. Honey, I don't want him around here anymore."

"Don't worry, he won't be. I'll give him a call after my meeting tomorrow. Once this deal for the new expansion comes through, I'll be able to sit on the land in Mexico for a while. I can finally afford to tell him off."

"And when can we afford to move back to Illinois?"

"Not this again. I already told you, land isn't selling for anything out there."

"Well, maybe you can find something wonderful to do with all that cheap land. And maybe we can make enough that I can afford to write full-time."

Derek followed her gaze to her laptop, which seemed to be gathering dust. "How is the novel going?"

"It's not. Between the job search, the kids, and all of your social visitors…"

"Wait, where are the kids?" Derek suddenly realized he hadn't heard a peep from them since he got home.

"Oh, Gracie's up in her room doing homework. Max is at his friend's house, having a sleepover."

Derek felt irrationally alarmed. He had already convinced himself that the sheriff was wrong, that whatever was going on could have nothing to do with his Xolo, that the animal must have died in the woods long before now. Yet he still felt nervous at the thought of his son unsupervised, at the possibility of him being outside alone when there was a dangerous animal on the loose.

He tried to hide the fear in his voice from Alison. "Which friend?"

FIFTEEN

Max knew he was being hunted. As he glanced down the long hallway, he could sense something coming for him. He blocked out the distracting motion from the edge of his vision and focused solely on the abandoned corridor in front of him. When he saw movement among the shadows, he raised his gun, looking down the sights and preparing to fire.

The next burst of motion came from the edge of his vision, but this time it wasn't from one of the other three player screens that quartered the TV. He realized too late that this was the movement he should have been paying attention to. It streaked from the side of his screen and was upon him in a minute, the form slashing him with its power sword as his screen flashed red.

Max leaned forward, desperately mashing buttons to escape the thing, but it was far too late. Steve jumped to his feet and cheered as Max's screen went dark, giving Steve enough points to win the deathmatch. Max was about to suggest another round when he heard his phone vibrating on the table in front of him.

The screen lit up, displaying the name "Dad" below the goofy selfie that his father had insisted on setting as his contact photo when he had bought Max the phone. Max grimaced. He should have known his dad had only bought him the thing in order to stalk and pester him. Deciding he should answer the call before his friends saw it, Max scooped up the phone. "Sorry, gotta take this," he said, getting up and walking away from the couch. At the same time, Jeremy picked up the nearly empty chip bowl and headed upstairs to "replenish the food supply," as he put it.

Stepping away from the carpeted area around the couches, Max crossed to the other half of the Soto's basement, an unfinished storage area full of cardboard boxes. When he was sure he was out of earshot, Max reluctantly answered the phone.

"Max, everything alright?" his dad asked.

Max turned back to the TV, which Steve was yelling at as he sprayed machine gun fire into Trevor's character. Max stepped behind a wall of boxes in hopes of blocking the noise. "Yeah, we're just playing a video game."

"Are you over at your friend Trevor's?"

"Yeah, just like I told Mom I would be."

"Okay, good. Did you hear about the animal attacks the last few days?'

"Just a little at school, but not much."

Max peeked out from behind the boxes, watching as Trevor's character disintegrated into chunks of gore under Steve's relentless fire. Max covered the speaker as Steve burst into a profanity-laden cheer.

"Well, they were pretty bad," his father was saying. "I don't want you to go outside tonight, no matter what your friends do."

"Don't worry, Dad. We'll just be here chilling all night."

"Okay, good. Have fun. I'll see you in the morning."

"Yeah. See you tomorrow." Max hung up before his friends could wonder what was taking him so long.

Steve was continuing his profanity-laden cheer. "Fuck yeah, suck my nuts!" he yelled at Trevor, as the kid about half his age simply stared blankly at him.

Jeremy was returning from upstairs with a bowl full of chips and a box of cookies under his arm. "Hey, not so loud man, my parents just went to sleep."

Steve threw down the controller, suddenly losing all interest in the game. "Good, then we can finally get the hell out of here."

Max and Trevor exchanged a look. "Where are you guys going?" Max was the first to ask.

Jeremy smiled at him. "Not we, us."

"Okay, where are *we* going?" Trevor asked his older brother with a sneer.

"Everywhere and nowhere," Jeremy replied with a grin that made Max nervous. He had been slightly suspicious when Trevor had invited him over for a sleepover with his older brother and his brother's best friend. Max had been trying to figure out why two teenagers would want to hang out with a pair of fifth graders. Now he suspected they were setting him and Trevor up for a prank or plotting to get them in trouble.

Trevor asked again where they were going, a little more forcefully this time. This only raised more sneers from the teenagers. "You'll find out when we get there," Jeremy assured them, "it's this really cool place we found, we want to show you."

Trevor and Max exchanged another look. "What about our rematch?" Max asked desperately. "We're tied right now."

"We'll do a tie-breaker when we get back," Steve said, "but none of that ADD bullshit you kids like; we need an old-school game of strategy and wits."

"What, like Final Fantasy?" Trevor asked, eyebrow raised.

"I was thinking Mortal Kombat," Steve replied.

He jerked a thumb towards the mini-computer he had plugged into the TV, which had files for thousands of pirated games uploaded onto it, a wealth of video game knowledge the teens thoroughly enjoyed lording over the younger kids. Since it didn't have a power switch, Jeremy pulled the plug from its back, the whirring of the motor slowing and dying as the thing turned off.

Grabbing the coats they had thrown on the floor behind one couch, Jeremy tossed one to Steve and started pulling the other on himself. "Come on, let's go before it's too late."

"But it's already after curfew," Max instantly wished he hadn't said, "how will we get out?"

Jeremy mimed stroking his chin like a Confucian sage. "Hmm, now that is a problem." Continuing to mime stroking his chin, Jeremy crossed the basement to the sliding glass door in the back wall, which he unlocked and opened with one hand while still mock-stroking his chin. "But I thought we would just use the door. We'll turn the lights off on our way out so if my parents wake up, they'll think we're asleep."

"That'll be the day," Trevor said, pulling on his own coat.

Max stared nervously at the blackness on the other side of the glass door, his father's warnings suddenly coming back to him with far more force than they had contained when he had at first ignored them. "Do you guys sneak out like this often?" he asked.

"Only every night," Trevor answered, tossing Max his own coat.

Max clutched the coat to his chest, not caring how babyish the gesture made him look. He cast a final look around the basement as the others gathered near the door. He had never found Trevor's house as comforting as his own, with its spare pieces of carpet tossed haphazardly across the concrete and the run-down furniture gathered too close to the TV to form the basement living room, but right now it was the most comfortable place in the world compared to the mysteries that awaited them outside.

"Come on, dude, don't be a nutsack," Jeremy complained, "we're all going."

Max pondered telling them about his father's warning, about the series of mysterious animal attacks, or even about his own sighting of the Xolo the last time they had snuck out when they weren't supposed to, but he knew the others would dismiss that as his imagination, and point out that the animal attacks were miles from here, on the other side of the county. Max decided they would probably be right, that there was nothing to fear, they were just going to take a short walk and come back, but he still found his feet unable to move.

"Come on, man, hurry up," Trevor said.

Something still held Max up, made him want to stay in the basement where it was safe, but then the others were moving towards the door, and Max was moving with them, he couldn't help himself, and-

"-And leave your phone here," Steve said.

Max's suspicions about the teens flared up again. "What? Why?"

Jeremy nodded at Steve. "He's right. We all heard your dad calling to tuck you in tonight. He probably has a tracking app on your phone, too."

Max pulled the phone from his pocket and decided that Jeremy was probably right. It was hard to imagine his dad operating any technology correctly, but he had gotten Max the phone exclusively for emergencies. Tossing the phone on the couch, he joined the others near the door, where their shoes were still carelessly piled on the rug where they had tossed them earlier after playing frisbee in the backyard.

Max still lingered behind the others as they pulled on their shoes and stepped outside. Jeremy reached back in and turned off the lights, leaving Max alone in the darkness. He was surprised to see that it was brighter outside, the glow of the moon and stars creeping through the windows and highlighting the darkened shapes of the furniture in the basement. Max didn't want to stare too long at those shapes, imagining what they could transform into. More by reflex than by choice, Max followed the others outside, casting a final glance back to make sure the screen of his phone hadn't lit up with a missed call.

As Max stepped outside, Jeremy closed the door behind him, testing to make sure the door was unlocked for their return. Signaling to the others to be quiet, he pointed to his parent's windows above them. All seemed quiet and still.

Max looked to each side, at a row of evenly spaced houses which, from behind and in the darkness, looked nearly identical. Their backyards formed a continuous sea of grass that seemed to shimmer silver in the moonlight, flowing in the wind like white-capped surf. This narrow sea was all that separated the houses from a dark wall of trees.

This neighborhood had been built about two decades before Sylvan Springs, at the base of the same mountains and backed up to the same forest. Max shuddered to think what could be hiding in those woods. He couldn't see the mountains, but in the darkness, he could feel their presence looming over him.

Instead of walking around the house to the street like Max had expected, the others made directly for the woods, crossing the sea of grass like intrepid sailors. Not wanting to make any noise, Max held back the urge to ask where they were going and just followed them.

Beyond a sandbox that hadn't been used in years and a tool shed that threatened to be overtaken by vines, the others closed in on a narrow gap in the trees barely visible until they were already disappearing inside it. Trevor and Jeremy had obviously been working on this path for years, gradually beating back the underbrush, trampling the grass, and training the tree branches to allow them access.

Max stepped onto the rotting wood frame of the sandbox, which served as a sort of marker to this entryway. No doubt the brothers had gotten bored with their childhood play area and started exploring these woods when they were young. Max walked through the sand, crushing the weeds that sprouted across its length, and stepped off the far side of the sandbox into the woods.

They were immediately swallowed by the darkness, the trees pressing in on every side and cutting off all but the faintest glimmer of moonlight. Max moved quickly, keeping the others in sight just ahead of him. The path was surprisingly easy to walk, the grass having been levelled off by years of exploration. Max imagined that other neighborhood kids had been introduced to this path and had taken to crossing the silver sea of grass on their own at night.

Branches closed in on them from all sides, forcing the kids to walk single file. Max almost screamed when one branch reached out to grab his arm. He pulled his arm free and hurried to keep up with the others.

Eventually, the path widened and Jeremy brought the others to a halt. Steve sparked his lighter, revealing that they were in a little clearing littered with trash. Two ratty lawn chairs that looked like they had been saved from a dumpster were the only decoration. Beer cans, candy wrappers, and clamshell hamburger boxes littered the ground and stuck to the weeds at the edge of the woods. A small pit had been dug on one side that was obviously meant to be for bonfires, but seemed to be filled only with more trash and a pile of weed ash.

"This is what you came out here to show us?" Trevor whined. "The lame spot where you guys come to smoke your weed?"

Steve was in the middle of raising his lighter to the bowl pressed between his lips. "Hey, I take offense at that."

Jeremy rolled his eyes. "This is just a stopping point. We've got something way cooler to show ya. This path connects Steve's neighborhood and ours, so this is our usual meeting spot."

"Wouldn't it have been faster to just use the road?" Max asked, knowing that by faster, he really meant safer.

Jeremy glared at him as if he knew what Max meant, too. "Only if you want to get busted. Like you said, it's after curfew, and the cops patrol that road all the time."

Steve took another few hits from his bowl, then passed it to Jeremy, who offered it to Max and Trevor. They both refused. He shrugged, finished the bowl, and ashed it into the fire pit before leading them on.

After a few more minutes in the dark woods, they emerged into a neighborhood that Max had never seen before. It looked newer than the one the Soto's lived in, but not quite as upscale as Sylvan Springs, full instead of the chic but generic pop-up homes that Max's father despised.

The entrance to this neighborhood lay just behind a steel road barrier installed at the end of an empty cul-de-sac. The houses lining the streets ahead seemed uniformly dark and empty, as if the curfew applied to everyone inside, not just minors outside. Max followed the others hesitantly as they crossed the street and picked up the sidewalk near the first homes.

"Aren't you guys afraid the cops will see you here?" Max asked as he caught up with the others.

"Relax," Steve cooed. "The cops have agreements with neighborhoods like this. They don't come nosing around in here unless somebody calls them. So, we just have to stay quiet and not attract suspicion."

Max thought that might be true, but it seemed like Steve said it awfully loud. Worse still, he lit a joint as they walked down the street, while Trevor and Jeremy continued to have a too loud conversation about some video game they wanted to play when they got back.

Max hung behind the others, observing the unfamiliar streets. Even if he had known them, they would have been unrecognizable in the spare illumination afforded by the amber streetlights, which drowned out the moonlight and cut the streets into alternating pockets of light and shadow, broken only by occasional glowing islands around the fronts of homes. It seemed almost every home in this neighborhood left their outside lights on at night, as if standing guard against intruders.

Looking at the houses, Max imagined he saw figures moving in the windows, shapes that disappeared as soon as he caught sight of them, crawling away to report on what they saw outside. Max forced himself to look away from the homes, but the spaces between them made him even more nervous: dark slivers where the woods beyond were visible, slices of darkness where he could imagine even worse shapes moving.

Trevor called him from his fears, far too loudly for Max's liking, and encouraged him to join whatever stupid conversation they were having about video games or something else Max didn't understand. He moved closer to them, more in a primitive hope of protection than because they wanted him to. Steve was still smoking his joint and the others were still talking far too loudly. Max couldn't help but glance back and forth at the houses, praying no one would be looking out their window.

But in neighborhoods like this, no one ever seemed to be looking out the window. The beautiful house fronts and well-manicured lawns seemed designed only for one initial rush of appreciation, for some private sense of superiority. Trevor called Max from his reverie again, telling him not to fall behind.

They made their way through the neighborhood without incident and reached a street where the houses suddenly gave way to thick trees on both sides. A bridge over a shallow creek seemed to mark the edge of the neighborhood. As the teens moved close, instinctively closing in on a narrow path through the grass, Max shuddered as he remembered the last time they had snuck under a bridge.

He wanted to ask the teens what their obsession with bridges was all about, but they were already disappearing over the bank. Max couldn't help looking back to make sure there were no cars on the road before following Trevor to the bank. A steep trail was roughly trampled in the grass, indicating this was another spot that neighborhood kids had discovered and made their own. Max wondered how he had missed out on so much of the hidden world around him created by kids his own age.

The kids scrambled down the bank, struggling to remain upright as they slid to the bottom. When they reached the river bank, Max found himself lost in darkness, unable to tell even which way the teenagers had gone. A flash of light, accompanied by the flicking sound of a lighter, showed him the way. Jeremy and Steve were beneath the bridge, sharing another bowl. Max waited for them just beyond the edge of the bridge, keeping a lookout on the banks above.

He grew nervous when he realized that the river banks here looked exactly like those he had seen the Xolo on. In the darkness, he could imagine the outline of the dog appearing above him. Waving the thought away, Max entered the cloud of smoke beneath the bridge. "You know," Jeremy said, "if you keep looking for trouble, you're gonna find it." Max thought Jeremy must have seen the worried look on his face, but Max didn't know how that was possible in the darkness.

Without waiting for a reply, Jeremy crouched and flicked his lighter again, this time holding the flame steady to reveal a line of rocks placed through the water, forming a rough bridge. "We realized you couldn't climb down the banks on the other side of the bridge," Jeremy explained, "too rough and overgrown. But some little kids started this bridge so we finished it. Now you can walk along the river bank on the other side and get really deep into the woods."

"How far do the woods go?" Trevor asked.

Jeremy shrugged. "To the edge of the county, I guess."

"I hope we're not going that far," Max muttered.

Steve smiled and blew his ash into the creek. He patted Max on the back in a way that was both patronizing and fear-inducing. He still wondered where the teens could possibly be taking them, but by now he knew better than to ask.

Holding his lighter out in front of him, Jeremy crossed the rough rock bridge, looking more like an explorer than ever, except for the baggy jeans he had to pull up to avoid getting them wet. When he reached the far bank, he crouched and cast the light back on the rocks, illuminating the way for the others. While Max waited his turn behind Steve and Trevor, he nervously looked up the bank of the river into the shadowy country beyond. He wondered where they were going, and what else might be out there.

He saw in his memory, not his imagination, the shape of the Xolo peering over the edge of the river bank, and felt again its bite sinking into his hand. His left hand instinctively reached over to the right, squeezing where the bandages once had been, feeling the scar tissue in the shape of its bite. For the first time he thought of the incident with remorse, not anger. After all, the dog hadn't been aggressive towards him first, he had pulled the thing's tail, for God's sake. It had only been a stupid prank, one of the millions of stupid impulses that crossed Max's brain every day and usually instantly disappeared, but this one had been egged on by Trevor, and resentment towards his sister. She was always the center of attention, but Max shouldn't resent her for that; maybe if Max applied himself the same way she did, he would get the same level of attention.

And maybe if he didn't let his friends talk him into such stupid decisions, he wouldn't get in trouble so much. Trevor was just stepping off the rocks, leaving Max alone on his side of the creek. He instinctively reached for his cell phone, and after a moment of panic, remembered he had left it behind. He wondered why he let his friends talk him into such obviously stupid decisions. But it was too late to turn back now; he didn't know the way back, and even if he did reach the Soto's home on his own, he could only wait in the woods until the others returned from whatever they were doing now. He decided it was safer to follow them.

By the time Max had scrambled most of the way across the rock bridge, Jeremy was already moving down the creek bank with the others, holding the lighter out ahead of him, leaving Max to finish the crossing in the dark. He stepped onto what he thought was the edge of the bank and sank ankle-deep in water. He held back a cry of disgust and anger and simply pulled his foot free, hurrying after the others with alternately squishing steps.

As he let go of the rough denim, the scars on his hand itched and burned. The burning seemed to intensify as he followed the others up the bank. Max told himself that was only remorse working its way under his skin. At least the burning distracted his mind from the cold and damp in his shoe.

Trying to ignore both the burning and the freezing, Max hurried after the others as they made their way along the broken, rocky river bank, hemmed in by thick weeds and close-spaced trees on one side and the lapping, unpredictable shore on the other. The ancient dogwoods on both sides leaned over the river in an arch, as if trying to keep the water secret.

They were certainly keeping the boys' progress a secret. Another residential street followed the creek on their right side, separated from the water by only a single line of trees. In the summer, that would have been enough to conceal them completely, but now that they were well into October, the branches had been stripped of their leaves, revealing a row of identical townhomes that Max's dad would have hated. He kept his eye on the openings in the leaves, sneaking past them as quickly as possible, always watching the darkened eyes of the houses that peered through the veil of leaves.

Up ahead, they heard loud voices that Max at first thought emanated from the endless stretch of woods on their left side. As they got closer, he realized the bassy voices were slapping off the fuller stand of trees on the left, but ultimately emanating from a hole in the branches on their right side, where the entire back deck of one townhome was exposed to view. A group of men in sleeveless tank tops were talking loudly, smoking cigarettes, and drinking beer while music blared. A string of Christmas lights along the railings of their deck framed them in an oddly off-season scene. As they neared the opening, the boys saw two of the men leaning over the railing nearest the woods, practically blowing their cigarette smoke into the hole through the forest canopy. The glare of their Christmas lights shone a spotlight into the woods, illuminating the creek bank from the edge of the trees to the shore.

Jeremy stopped just before the light, motioning for the others to do the same. They all knew that if they were spotted, that would be the end of their excursion. The woods above the creek bank were too thick to allow any entrance, so there was only one way around. Jeremy crouched on the river bank, the hems of his jeans dipping into the water, and lowered himself until he was just beneath the edge of the light.

Practically crawling along the riverbank, he moved beneath the beam of light, struggled to his feet on the other side, then motioned for the others to do the same. Once again, Max waited his turn, watching the darkened woods behind them as Steve and Trevor crawled beneath the light. Once they were done, Max inhaled a deep breath and followed them, struggling to keep his body just below the light without falling into the creek.

Sooner than he would have thought, he was beyond the light and being helped to his feet by Jeremy and Trevor while Steve lit another joint. Once Steve had finished his celebration, tempting fate by blowing a cloud of smoke into the beam of light, where the harsh multi-colored light made it look like a ghost rising from the river bank, the group continued on their way.

Eventually, they reached a spot where the creek bent sharply to the right, the residential neighborhood on the right coming to an end, while only dark, unbroken woods stretched on to the left and ahead of them. Finally leaving the creek behind, Jeremy walked up the banks to a ridge, where he found a break in the trees and beckoned for the others to follow.

Max looked back at the houses across the creek, a few of which were still visible through the trees. He wondered if anybody inside would be able to hear them scream for help if they had to. Jeremy yelled at him to hurry up, as if wondering the same thing. Scrambling up the bank as quickly as he could, Max cast a final look back at the houses. All was still, as if the houses themselves were sleeping. Max realized that no one had heard Jeremy's yell. He was unsure if that was a comforting or terrifying thought. Ahead, the others had nearly vanished into the darkness. Swallowing his fear, he followed them into the woods.

When he reached the top of the ridge, the others were gone from sight. They had probably left him behind again, moving on alone to the open expanse of swamp grass ahead. He reached out for the waist-high wall of grass and weeds that rose up ahead of him. Just before he touched the first weed, something shot from the darkness and wrapped around his wrist. Max screamed before he saw Jeremy's face, made terrifying by the lighter he held just beneath it. "Relax," the disembodied face said as Max felt his wrist being released in the darkness, "we don't want to make any noise."

Instead of telling Jeremy that he was going to say the same thing, Max asked why Jeremy thought he was about to make noise. As his eyes adjusted to the deeper darkness of the woods, he saw Trevor and Steve deeper in the woods, looking for breaks in the wall of matted grass, which seemed to be solid and straight across the entire forest.

"Because," the disembodied face said, disappearing as Jeremy raised the lighter to the wall of grass, "you would have definitely made a noise when you touched that." He carefully raised a hand to the matted grass and pulled a clump aside, revealing an ancient barbed wire fence beneath. The wooden posts were rotted and mossy but still solid, while the wire itself was coated in rust, but still looked sharp and painful.

As Jeremy pulled more grass from the fence, Steve and Trevor returned from their scouting trip. "Thing looks solid all the way across," Steve reported, "Damn thing must be over a hundred years old."

"Probably is," Max said. "I think this is the edge of the property my dad owns. He likes to keep all the old farm stuff up, says it makes the landscape more rustic."

The others were silent. Max saw Jeremy roll his eyes and instantly wished he hadn't said anything. "That explains what we found up ahead," Steve said, puffing his joint as he watched Jeremy rip more grass from the fence. "Something that probably even your dad doesn't know about."

"Don't ruin it, dude," Jeremy said as he tested one of the leaning wooden posts. When it held steady beneath his foot, he reached and pulled himself up by the thickest tree branch overhead. After tottering for a moment on top of the post, Jeremy leaped to the other side and landed in soft grass. "Just a little further," he said as he reached back to help the others over the fence. When they had all struggled over the post, they continued down the ridge.

Before them opened a wide grassy plain, a swamp broken only by occasional stands of trees. As the boys began to make their way across, being careful to step only on the large clumps of more solid earth between the open stretches of swampy water, the moon suddenly emerged from the clouds it had been hiding behind, bathing the swamp in silver light.

The boys were as visible as if it had been full daylight. As Max scanned the swamp, the only man-made structure in sight was the distant ridge of a curving county road, which emerged briefly from the woods on their left before curving back and disappearing among the trees again, where it would eventually cross the bridge they had passed under. Max wasn't sure whether to be comforted by this loneliness or horrified. Now that the landscape around them was fully visible, Max could see the wells of darkness within the stands of trees even more clearly. His mind raced at the thought of what could be hiding there.

He followed Trevor and the teenagers across a wide plain of grass, watching their long, hard-edged shadows stretch across the swamp, as if their every step were being matched by a group of stalkers. The air grew colder as they crossed the swamp, freezing their ragged breaths into clouds of crystal that sparkled in the moonlight. Steve couldn't help but add to it with a few puffs of his weed, which seemed to sparkle even more.

Suddenly, a beam of light even harsher than the moonlight passed across the trees. Max froze as the headlights closed in on him, dropping to the ground just seconds before they reached him. Looking through the grass, Max saw a single car on the road, its shape and details impossible to distinguish behind the blinding glare of the headlights. The lights flared in his eyes as the vehicle rounded the curve furthest into the swamp and sped off towards the woods, disappearing in the direction of the bridge they had started from.

As the sound of the engine died away, Max slowly pulled himself to his feet and saw that Steve and Jeremy were still standing, unmoved by the threat of being seen. Steve defiantly puffed his joint, tossing it into the water as he drew the last puff. The teens laughed at the younger boys as Trevor pulled himself from the grass next to Max. "You weren't worried about being spotted?" Max said, brushing weeds and leaves off his clothes.

"You kidding?" Jeremy asked, "You see how fast they were going? They didn't even have time to see us."

Max certainly hoped so. He followed the others towards the largest group of trees. With each step, he waited to hear the wail of a police siren or the hum of the car's engine returning, but there was only the crunch of grass and the occasional splash of water beneath their feet.

As they drew nearer to the largest stand of trees, the swamp seemed to grow even more tangled and treacherous, the water forming pools that the boys had to step around carefully for fear of sinking to their waists. The teens berated them for slowing down, keeping up their harassment until the entire group had gathered around the foreboding grove. Steve lit a fresh joint, then held the lighter out like a flashlight as he searched the base of the stand, looking for a way into the wall of intertwined branches that prevented entrance to the fortress of trees.

"Don't you guys know the way?" Max asked. "You led us here."

Steve looked back, the joint still dangling from his mouth. The cherry flashed like a Christmas light and a puff of smoke emerged from his nose. Pushing himself to his knees, he pulled the joint from his mouth with a dirty hand. "We know the way. Just looking for the sign we left at the entrance." He put the joint back in his mouth and continued his search, holding the lighter so close to the dead branches that Max was nervous they would start on fire.

Eventually, Steve found the sign he had left behind: a Mountain Dew Flamin' Hot bottle stuck upside down in the dirt. Raising his hand from the spot where the bottle's knobbed base pointed the way, he parted a few branches and peeled back a wall of vines, holding them open like an opera attendant peeling back a velvet curtain. Jeremy waved the boys into the shadowy opening beyond.

Ducking beneath the branches, Max stepped into the opening, still nervously anticipating the older boys' plans. As he reluctantly stepped into the darkness, he found himself in a different world: a bower enclosed in shadow, the moonlight blocked by the thick, intertwined branches. As the teens entered behind them, they let the curtain of vines fall, blocking out the last wedge of light behind them. Total darkness surrounded them, leaving Max alone in a world of smell and sound. A musty, strangely familiar odor came to Max's nostrils, setting off a dim sense of panic. The feeling was drowned out by the overwhelming impressions of his senses as Steve flicked his lighter again, revealing the full extent of the strange world they were in.

The tangled tree branches formed an almost perfect dome, except at the top where they opened to the sky. These innumerable bare branches laid the carpet for this bower, a covering of leaves that crunched beneath every step. In the center of the bower was what they had obviously come for: an imposing, run-down nineteenth-century farmhouse. The paint was gone, the windows were shattered, but its high gothic shape was still undeniably impressive. Max's imagination reeled at the thought of this ancient edifice existing so long undetected in this secret forest. "This must have been the house of the farmer who originally owned the property," he told anyone who would listen. "They planted all these trees to block the wind. When he left, the property must have been left to the trees, and they swallowed it."

Trevor was less impressed. "You took us all this way for this?" he whined. "Just to see some old house?"

"Not just any old house," Jeremy corrected. "Our new clubhouse."

As the younger boys reluctantly followed him towards the clubhouse, the moon came out from behind the clouds and peeked in through the open roof of the bower. Max thought the silver face that emerged looked like a child's peeking in through the open roof of a dollhouse.

The moonlight was met by the glow of Steve's lighter and the harsh beam of the cellphone that Jeremy produced now that he was sure they could not be seen. Still, the light was never enough to reveal more than a fraction of the property at one time, turning the rest into only a vague outline where Max could project his fears. He tried to take a final look around the domed world they were leaving behind, but the moonlight revealed only glimpses of branches and trees.

Not wanting to be left alone in the darkness, Max hurried to catch up with the others. Steve pushed aside the heavy front door, which hung loosely on its ancient hinges. It swung open slowly, disappearing into the black maw of the house with a massive creak that filled the dome of trees with sound. Max winced, wondering who might have heard that, then remembered there was no one around to hear. The thought was hardly comforting.

They stepped in single file through the door. As Max entered, last as usual, the musty, strangely familiar smell came to him again, almost overpowering in the darkness. Max grew nervous, trying to remember where he had smelled this scent before, but the others didn't seem to notice anything; they were too engrossed in the wonders of the old house around them.

Jeremy was shining his light around the empty and decaying first floor: wallpaper hung from the walls in long strips, muddy hardwood floors showed through a floor of decaying leaves, and those windows that remained hung partly open.

Max turned at a loud creak to see Steve on the rotting stairs to the second floor, which stood in the middle of the house. Under Jeremy's light, Max could see the boards of the steps sag beneath his weight. "I wouldn't go up there if I were you," Max warned.

Steve snorted, but stopped on the middle step, as if waiting for an explanation. "Yeah? Well, if you were me, you wouldn't be a huge pussy either."

Max sighed and pushed Jeremy's arm towards the ceiling. The light revealed a crumbling, water-damaged ceiling with large chunks of plaster fallen away. "Who knows how old this place is. The floor could collapse beneath you."

Steve snorted again, but returned to the main floor. "Whatever. The cool shit's in the basement anyways." As he passed in front of the group, he shook his head at Jeremy in a way that was obviously meant to be seen. "Man, I don't know why we even bothered bringing these babies."

Without a response, the group followed him through what had once been the kitchen, to a door beneath the stairs. Steve forced the weather-warped door open with a struggle, then shined his lighter in to reveal a flight of stairs leading down into darkness. Trevor and Max looked at each other, then back at that doorway. If they hadn't been with the younger brother of one of those teens, Max's suspicion of their motives would have gone from a simple prank to outright murder. The dark pit of the basement beckoned terribly. The uneven, rotting steps seemed to continue down forever.

The teens plunged onto them intrepidly, laughing and shoving each other as they pushed their way down into the dark. The younger boys, realizing that their only light sources were disappearing alongside the older boys, followed nervously. Max walked behind Trevor, taking each creaking, uneven step carefully. As the wall opened on his left, Max gripped the loose, rotted handrail that hung from the wall on the right, being careful not to lean on it too hard for fear of pulling it out of the wall and plunging into the endless darkness on the other side. Looking too deeply into that darkness, Max bumped into Trevor, almost toppling both of them down the stairs.

They recovered and took a few more steps. Before they realized it, their feet were slapping against cement. Max looked around what he could see of the basement and spotted the glow from Jeremy's light shining on Steve, who was removing his backpack and taking out several candles, which he lit with his lighter and placed at intervals around the room.

As their light began to grow, the small cellar slowly came into view. It was a single open space with bare concrete walls and a plain ceiling of rotten floor joists. The stairs took up most of one wall, with all the others bare of doors or even windows, giving the space a secret, private feel. Now Max could see why the teenagers wanted to make this place into their clubhouse.

They had already started to decorate with a few items that had apparently been taken from home, plucked out of the swamp, or found on the other floors of this house. There was a large wooden spool to serve as a table, surrounded by a few broken lawn chairs like the ones at their smoke pit behind the house, a nudie calendar hung on the wall that was decades out of date (both in years and the amount of pubic hair displayed by the yellowing model) and an old clay jug that was already beginning to fill with cigarette butts and ashed weed. Apparently in a race to fill the jug completely, Steve and Jeremy lit up again, puffing joints that quickly began to fill the basement with smoke. At the far reaches of the candlelight, Max saw curls of smoke drifting out the open door.

"Maybe this isn't so bad," Trevor said, surveying the place agreeably. "We could definitely do whatever we want here."

"Oh, yeah, nobody will ever find us out here," Jeremy said. Max could only hear something ominous in that statement. The dread it incurred was blown away as Steve produced a portable speaker from his backpack. Jeremy started playing music from his phone and soon the basement was filled with blasting, thumping dance music.

Max was just beginning to relax when he heard a noise cutting through the beat: a slow creaking that he at first thought was part of the annoying trap music, but soon realized was moving in an entirely different rhythm: the slow, stealthy padding of footsteps.

"Hey, what was that?" he asked the others.

They gave him a long, slow look from where they had gathered around the wooden spool. Steve was pouring out weed for a fresh joint while Jeremy was drinking a beer he had taken from Steve's back pack. "Oh, it's nothing, just your imagination," Jeremy laughed. His laughs cut off as the sounds came again: a series of quick, sharp creaks that cut through the music and could not be ignored. Scrambling from his seat at the makeshift table, Jeremy dashed to his phone and cut off the music.

As the room fell silent, they all listened intently. As if toying with them, the sounds were not heard for a long moment, then came again: a series of rhythmic footsteps, like someone going down stairs. Max looked at the stairs to the basement, which stood empty, the door at the top still hanging open to the darkened main floor.

"Someone's coming down from the second floor," Max said. "There must have been someone hiding up there."

Jeremy raised a hand to shush him. "Those steps are too quick to be someone. It must be an animal that got inside the house."

"What the fuck kinda animal would be out here?" Trevor groaned. Max thought of one possibility, and clutched the burning scars on his right hand. He wondered why he had ever ignored his father's warnings.

"Relax," Jeremy implored, "it's probably just a deer or something, at worst a fox looking for somewhere to spend the night." The stealthy sound of paws padded across the floor above, lending credence to the theory. "I'll go check it out."

"You stay here," Steve said, seeing Trevor instinctively reach for his older brother's shirt sleeve. "I'll check it out while you keep the kiddies calm. Just gimme your phone."

Jeremy handed him the phone and Steve turned the light back on, using it to navigate the uneven steps. The beam briefly illuminated the kitchen at the top of the stairs, then disappeared around a corner. From the basement floor, the others could see only occasional glints of light on the walls. Steve's footsteps sounded through the floor, the floorboards sagging and dropping clouds of dust in time with his steps, distinct enough for the others to track his path from below.

Max listened as the quieter footsteps of the animal (*DOG*) drew close to Steve's, then stopped. Steve's own footsteps stopped too. They heard a sharp gasp, followed by a laugh. "It's just a dog!" they heard him call down.

Max saw the others grow more relaxed, but he only grew more tense. "What kind of dog?" he called back, not minding the strange looks the others gave him.

"Um, I'm not really sure," was the reply. From above, they heard the patter of several more sets of paws. Dust fell from across the ceiling as all the floor boards rocked in unison. "Actually, it's a couple of dogs," Steve called down. "Like, a lot, a whole pack of them, all different kinds." The footfalls closed in on the spot Steve's voice was coming from, then stopped.

Suddenly, they heard a chorus of growls. Steve's voice came again, softer and more nervous this time. "Uh, they seem kind of mad..." he said unsteadily.

Whatever he was about to say next was cut off by a chorus of mad barks, followed by a loud thump that shook the floorboards. Dust rained from the ceiling as his screams grew more intense, almost drowned out by crashing pawfalls and the sounds of struggle.

Max and Trevor looked at Jeremy, wondering what they should do. For a long moment, he only looked back, fear twisting his face as the flickering candlelight distorted his features. Just as he was about to speak, a bright red stain appeared on his cheek and dripped into his mouth. He wiped it away in disbelief, letting the sticky liquid run between his fingers as he studied it in the candlelight. As more red dripped onto his face, he reached for one of the candles on the table nearby. Holding it up high, the flickering flame revealed a pool of blood gathering in the corner between two floor joists, seeming to defy the laws of physics as a droplet gathered in the center, slowly bending downwards before separating from the pool and dropping. The droplet landed on top of the candle, snuffing out the flame with a sickening sizzle. As darkness gathered around the boys, a nauseatingly sweet smell filled Max's nostrils.

Jeremy set the extinguished candle next to another that was still lit. In the flickering half-light, the extinguished candle looked like it was dripping cooling red wax over the hardened yellow. Jeremy grabbed the still-lit candle and, being careful to avoid the dripping blood, led the way towards the stairs. "Come on, we have to help him!" he yelled to the boys, waving them upstairs.

Finding each other's eyes in the darkness, the younger boys shared a look of terror, but were led on by the older boy's enthusiasm and the desire to do whatever they could about the terrible screams that continued from above. Even if there was nothing they could do to help, they had to at least escape from this basement. The younger boys grabbed candles off the table and ran up the stairs after Jeremy, bumping into each other on the way up, almost knocking each other off the stairs in their desire to be the first one out of the basement.

As they reached the main floor, the younger boys followed Jeremy around a corner into what had once been the living room. The glow of their candles was enough to reveal glimpses of a pack of dogs gathered around a struggling human form, which writhed and screamed as the dogs ripped at his flesh. Jeremy's cell phone lay on the ground next to Steve, its beam still shining up, revealing glimpses of his pained, blood-stained face as he begged for mercy.

A glimpse was all Max needed. He turned away, knowing there was nothing the three of them could do to help their friend. Trevor followed and, after some hesitation, so did Jeremy, though they made no sound for fear of attracting the dogs to them next. They moved quickly towards a back door off the kitchen, which hung limply on long-rusted hinges. As they approached the rectangle of moonlight, its lower half was suddenly distorted by a shadowy outline that appeared from outside.

Max recognized it from its shape, even before it stepped into the candle light. The bite on his hand burned anew as the dog moved towards them. Its eyes seemed to glow in the dark, occasionally catching the flickering candlelight to add to the glow. Max had recognized the Xolo immediately, and even worse, it seemed to recognize him. He remembered Jeremy warning him that if he kept looking for trouble, he would find it. Max thought now that he had been telling the truth, that the Xolo in front of him was nothing less than the projection of his own fears, a mental image brought to life by his focus on it.

The Xolo let out a sharp bark, at which the sound of the other dogs chewing stopped at once. Max turned back to see them let go of Steve's body like a toy they had grown bored with. His body fell limp. No more screams emanated from him. Moving into the kitchen, the dogs lined up like soldiers in the war movies Max enjoyed watching with his dad. Max had an impression, which must have been crazy, that the Xolo actually was their leader, that the other dogs had to obey him. But the sight of the other dogs gathering around them, growling and baring their teeth in unison after a bark from the Xolo, made the impression seem not so crazy.

At another bark from the Xolo, the dogs rushed at them. The Xolo ran directly towards Max. Grabbing Trevor by the sleeve, Max bolted for the stairs to the second floor, not caring anymore if they might collapse beneath him. When he was halfway up the stairs, Max risked a glance back to see Jeremy, who had been separated from them by the incoming rush of dogs, running out the back door, several dogs in pursuit.

Only the Xolo was pursuing them up the stairs, with its thin, spindly legs struggling to make it up the high, uneven steps. Taking advantage of the slight delay, Max and Trevor bounded up the last few steps and reached the second floor. They still held their candles, and thrust them into the unknown darkness. Without speaking to each other, they chose separate paths and, both too frightened to turn back, kept on them, quickly losing each other in the maze of rooms.

Feeling like he was in a nightmare, Max plunged from one darkened room to the next, dodging through a small, windowless bathroom with mildewed tiles, into a series of bedrooms with moldering beds and decaying curtains, his candle playing over these ghostly skeletons of the former occupant's life, the flickering shadows seeming to call new ghosts from the corners of the rooms. Finally, he found himself in a corner bedroom with no further escape. Setting the candle on a rotting end table, he shut the door behind himself.

Across the house, Trevor had done largely the same, dodging through a few small chambers until he found himself in a wide master bedroom with a series of tall windows on the far wall. Hearing the pattering of the strange hairless dog's paws just behind him, he ran straight towards the windows, knowing his only hope of escape was to dive straight through them and try to make an escape from the roof. Not even stopping to close the door behind him, he ran for the windows, not wanting to lose speed or courage.

Trevor had almost reached the windows when they began to slide upwards and away from him. At first, he thought he was passing out from terror, but then he felt the air moving quickly across his face and heard the floor giving way beneath him and he realized that Max had been right. He threw his arms out as the rotted floor collapsed beneath his weight, just barely managing to catch onto a complete floor joist before he could fall completely through.

His legs dangled above the lower floor, desperately kicking in hopes of finding something stable to push himself up with. They found only the hungry mouths of the dogs waiting below, which bit at his legs as if they were dangling treats. Still desperately holding on to the floor above, Trevor kicked them away, but felt more painfully latch on to his legs, trying to pull him through the hole in the floor.

Grimacing in pain, Trevor sunk his fingers into the moldering carpet, which began to peel back beneath his nails as the dogs pulled him down. Trevor reached his hands out further, digging his bloodied nails into a fresh section of carpet. As he began to pull himself back up, the hairless dog appeared next to him, staring him straight in the eyes. For a moment, Trevor was strangely calm, relaxing his grip on the carpet as the pain of the dogs tearing his flesh began to fade away.

Then, the Xolo leapt at his face and all calm disappeared. Trevor couldn't raise his hands from the carpet to fight the dog away for fear of falling through the hole, but he was unsure which was worse: falling to the hungry pack below or sitting here and having his face torn apart by the hairless dog.

After a moment, the choice was no longer up to him. As the Xolo ripped flesh from his face, his energy began to ebb along with his blood. The Xolo stood back, as if admiring its handiwork. As the dog locked its glowing eyes with his, Trevor felt strangely peaceful.

His grip relaxed on the carpet. He felt himself falling to the dogs below, but he was beyond caring. As he landed on the floor, he saw the hairless dog looking down at him through the hole in the ceiling, its gaze keeping him calm until the other dogs crowded around him, blocking out everything in his sight but their slobbering jaws as they tore into him.

His screams echoed through the house, reaching Max in the bedroom he had barricaded himself in. He stopped in his work of pushing a nightstand against the door, debating if he should leave to help Trevor. As much as he wanted to, he knew it would do no good. The empty room provided no weapons; he would have no better chance of survival than the others. His only hope was to make an escape for himself.

Looking out the single small window in the room, Max saw a tiny outcropping of roof. It seemed to extend at least far enough for him to stand on, but the window was not the kind that opened. He felt around the moldering frame. The glass was secure and firm; he had no chance of pushing it out.

Walking back to the night stand, he picked up an antique lamp which looked heavy enough to break the glass. Following the thick cord with his candle, he traced it to an outlet behind the night stand, the old-fashioned kind that had been built long after the house, with a shielded electric cord running up the outside of the wall. If he had been in any other situation, Max would have laughed at the irony of this use of ancient technology to find a modern one.

Leaning over the nightstand to reach the plug, Max had to balance himself on top of the piece of furniture, which swayed unsteadily beneath his weight. It would have been easier to move the night stand, but Max had nothing else to block the door and was afraid to leave it unguarded. Just as he grasped the plug, the door swayed inwards with a loud thump, as if to confirm his fears. Max rolled off the night stand, pulling the cord out as he fell to the ground.

The nightstand swayed above him, threatening to tip over. Max reached up an arm and managed to keep the stand pinned against the door as the frame rattled. Both the lamp and the candle fell from the stand. Max managed to grab the lamp before it fell on top of him, but the candle fell to the ground. Max worried for an insane instant that the dried wood of the floor would burst instantly into flames, but the wet, moldy floor only smothered the flame, setting out the blaze with a small hiss and leaving him in darkness.

He heard the Xolo land on the floor outside and whimper with almost human disappointment. After a moment, he heard its footsteps retreating down the hall and knew that it had decided to give up. Max breathed a sigh of relief. Clutching the heavy metal lamp against his chest, he made his way back to the window in the darkness, not bothering to gather the extinguished candle, which he had no way of re-lighting anyways.

In the darkness, he could distinctly hear the dogs below drop Trevor's body, the same way they had dropped Steve's. His screams had stopped and Max knew that Trevor was dead. In the next instant, he heard the Xolo bark, then the other dogs running in unison towards the stairs and he knew just as certainly that they were coming for him. A moment later, the door rattled again, louder and longer this time, and he heard the nightstand scrape against the floor as it moved forward. Several of the dogs he had seen below were big enough to move the thing by themselves. Max knew he had no hope of keeping them back.

His only hope was to escape; and it would have to be quickly. Turning the base of the lamp towards the window, he thrust the heavy piece of metal directly into the center of the glass, hearing a satisfying smash as he turned his face away for safety. He dragged the base of the lamp around the frame to clear out the remaining shards of glass, then dragged a small desk beneath the window so he would have something to stand on.

Hearing the door slide further open as the barks and scrabbling of the dogs increased, Max pulled himself up and through the frame, grimacing as the few shards of glass he had missed dug into his fingers. He ignored the pain and the warmth of blood oozing over his palms, raising himself until he was balancing on the window frame, then kicked the desk out from under his feet so the dogs couldn't climb after him. As he heard the door bursting open behind him, he desperately pushed himself forward and plummeted outside, unable to see where he was going.

Landing on a stretch of shingles with a hard thump, he heard the clatter of something falling and prayed it wasn't the roof collapsing beneath him. He saw the lamp, which he had managed to pull outside with him, tumbling off the corner of the roof. He reached out to grab the cord, but the sudden shift in his weight sent him tumbling after it.

He rolled off the edge of the roof, just barely managing to grab the ancient gutters before he plummeted to the ground. The rusted metal dug into his fingers, but the gutters somehow managed to hold on to the sagging roof. He heard the lamp crash into the earth below him, followed immediately by the wild barking of gathering dogs.

Max could already feel them biting into his ankles, but after a moment he realized his feet were still swinging free; only the sound of their jaws snapping was making his mind think they were biting him. When he looked down, he saw the ground was much further away than he had thought; the rottweiler and the Doberman pacing below looked like puppies. Max wasn't sure he was comforted by that, and turned his eyes away from the sloping ground before he could be nauseated by the height.

His fingers dug painfully into the metal as he pulled himself up, blood welling from the inside bend of his joints and pooling in the filth-filled trenches at the bottom of the gutters. He felt the gutter peeling back beneath his weight and saw the long nails pulling out of the roof. With a massive push that he prayed wouldn't dislodge the gutter, Max threw his weight over the gutter and thrust one arm across the roof, desperately searching for any kind of hand hold. He managed to find the very top of the narrow peak he had fallen from and began to pull himself up, the rusted gutter slicing into his belly as he dragged his weight over it.

When he was up high enough, he reached with his other hand and grabbed the peak of the roof. Now pulling with both arms, he braced his feet on the gutter and pushed himself up. There was a moment of panic as the gutter finally tore from the roof beneath him, taking his feet out from under him, but he managed to hold on.

Perched on the peak like some absurd bird, Max heard one of the dogs below yelp as the fallen gutter smashed into it with a loud crash. Max couldn't help but laugh, burying his face in the shingles to muffle the sound. Ancient tar filled his mouth. A loud bark from somewhere very close silenced his laughs. Flipping himself over, Max saw the tips of snouts briefly appear, then disappear below the frame of the window he had just escaped from. He laughed again as he realized the dogs were desperately trying to follow him through the window, though they couldn't reach anywhere close.

Leaning back on the roof and laughing, realizing that he was at last safe, if only temporarily, Max felt like Snoopy on the roof of his doghouse. After a few minutes the peak of the roof began to stab into his back and he forced himself to sit up, careful not to tip himself over the edge of the roof again. The dogs had already stopped barking inside, probably realizing they had no way to get him, more likely chasing after another target. That made him think of Jeremy, who he had completely lost track of inside the house. Max leaned as far as he dared over the edge of the roof, but saw no sign of him. Most likely he had escaped the grove of trees and was running to get help, but Max couldn't count on that.

He saw only a few dogs down below, lazily patrolling the yard as if waiting for him. The others, led by the Xolo, burst from the house in a single mass, making a beeline for an opening in the trees. Max was now sure that Jeremy had escaped, and that the dogs were after him. Max had to warn him, to help him somehow, but first, he had to escape. The drop from the roof to the ground was far too long to escape uninjured, and the dogs below, although they were calm now, would be on him in a moment. Going back through the house was too risky; if even one of the dogs were still hiding in there it could catch him by surprise.

Looking up at the hole in the roof of the bower, Max saw the moon balancing on the tips of the branches. Max followed its beam, his only source of light, across the silvery branches. A few of them hung over the highest part of the roof, dropping tantalizing vines down to the shingles. Max climbed to the highest part of the roof and tested the branches. They were low enough for him to grab, and when he tested them, they seemed to hold his weight.

Taking a deep breath, Max pulled himself up, grimacing as moss and flecks of bark sunk into the wounds on his hands. Rappelling hand over hand, Max moved beyond the edge of the roof, willing himself not to look down at the ground which suddenly seemed so far below. He focused on the branch, which grew thicker and sturdier as he drew nearer to the trunk. When he reached the trunk, he swung his lower body forward, catching the tree with his legs.

After a moment's scrambling, he managed to step on a branch that seemed sturdy enough to hold his weight.

He twisted his body closer to the tree, nearly dislocating his shoulders in the process, but it was still a long while before he felt safe releasing the branch overhead. When he did so, he instantly threw himself forward, hugging the trunk like a child at its mother's knee. When he was finally brave enough to turn away and open his eyes again, he found himself nearly lost in the canopy of trees. The overgrown yard of the house was barely visible through the branches. Far below, he saw the dogs still ignorantly patrolling the yard, apparently waiting for him to fall off the roof or walk out the front door. He laughed a little at getting the best of them, but was again reminded of soldiers in a movie. Who had told the dogs to patrol the house, and how had they known to do it?

More importantly right now, how was he going to escape them? The branches seemed to be spaced just close enough for him to climb down, but he would have to make his way to the other side of the tree before he reached the bottom; it would do him no good to evade the dogs only to land in the yard directly in front of them. If he climbed down on the other side of the tree, he would be in the thick of the grove and might have a chance of escaping unnoticed.

Swallowing his fear, Max forced himself to look away from the view below him. If he tilted his head down any longer, he was afraid the nausea would overpower him and he would fall from the tree. He preferred a slower method of getting down.

When he was younger, Max had spent most of his time at the old house in Illinois exploring the woods and fields around the farm house they had lived in. He had spent hours climbing trees, and had gotten quite good at it, although for some reason in the last few years he had stopped entirely. He had never realized until now how much he had missed it, although he had never been up this high, or had such enormous stakes attached to his success.

Pushing these considerations from his mind, Max forced himself to focus on one branch at a time, starting with the next one down. He narrowed his vision to that single branch, lowering himself to a sitting position on the current one and stretching his legs until his feet hit the next limb. Holding onto a thinner branch for support, he stood up and off the branch, finding himself standing unsteadily but securely on the next one. Taking a deep breath and congratulating himself for getting that one right, he turned his attention to the next branch down.

Moving through the maze of interweaving branches, Max moved slowly but steadily downwards. His mind occasionally drifted to thoughts of what would happen once he got there, but he forced himself not to think of that. He would find a way to escape. After all, he had heard no screams from Jeremy, so he must have been able to outrun the dogs.

Jeremy dashed through the swamp, not daring to look back. He could hear the dogs crashing through the weeds and splashing in the swamp; he didn't need to see them too. He thought he had gotten enough of a lead when he had dashed out of the house, but now it sounded like most of the dogs were just behind him, their low bodies crashing through the dry, tangled grass, which thankfully seemed to be slowing them down.

Unfortunately, it was slowing him down too, the ancient weeds tangling on his feet and seeming to reach up to loop around his ankles. The candle dropped from his hand as he tripped over an especially thick clump of weeds. For a moment, he thought that the dry weeds would light on fire, that it might signal for help or even burn the dogs to death, but the flame simply disappeared into the water and was extinguished with a soft hiss.

He wasted a moment stopping to reach for the candle before he remembered he had no way to relight it; the lighter had been in Steve's pocket when he died. Jeremy's cellphone had been in his hand, its beam still shining on Steve's face as it was torn apart by dogs, or otherwise Jeremy would be able to call for help. As it was, his only hope was to outrun the dogs. He wished he had been able to take his little brother and his friend with him, but they had disappeared too quickly inside the house. If he had tried to follow them, he would have only been killed by the dogs. He could only hope that they had been able to find safety on the second floor.

A scream from the darkness let him know that wasn't true. For the first time since leaving the house, he stopped and turned back. He had somehow gotten outside the bower of trees, crashing through the outer layer of branches in his flight without even noticing. Now the house was out of sight, but the scream, which he now recognized as his little brother's, rang out clearly.

He paused at the base of a small ridge, trying to decide whether to turn back. The screams intensified, then suddenly cut off, and he knew it was already too late. The sound of the dogs, however, was still coming. He turned to run up the ridge, hoping it would be easier to move over dry land.

He ducked under branches that reached from the darkness, whipping his face and tearing his skin. Pushing the branches aside, he winced at the sound the dry sticks made as they cracked. He could hear the dogs crashing through the woods behind him, unimpeded by the darkness, and now unimpeded by the swamp grass. Only he was held back by the branches that seemed impossible to avoid.

Using his speed on the solid ground as his only advantage, Jeremy ducked between the trees, occasionally colliding with their trunks before stumbling on in a new direction, unsure if he was any longer heading towards the creek. The bed of dried leaves crunched beneath his feet, making him wince with every step, knowing that the dogs could track him by the sound.

He heard several of them closing in on him, their paws making smaller but quicker versions of the crunching noises his own plodding steps conjured up. They seemed to be closing in on him from all sides, although the darkness made their exact position impossible to tell.

Desperately plunging into the darkness, Jeremy ran ahead at full speed, his arms outstretched in case he ran into another tree. As he heard the dogs gaining on him, he ran faster. He spotted a sliver of light ahead of him and ran towards it, imbuing it with all the hope he had left.

The light was a glint of moonlight off the top of a ridge of grass. Jeremy ran towards the ridge, the sound of the dogs closing in behind him. As he moved closer, he saw the ridge was a layer of tangled grass, about waist high, just tall enough to jump over with the momentum he had built up. When the ridge was only a few feet away, Jeremy sprung off the ground and saw the ridge slide beneath his vision. It didn't take long for him to realize that either the darkness or his own bravado had led him to misjudge the height. His body sunk towards the ground again, the ridge of grass moving up towards him.

His body slammed into the ridge, instantly stopping his forward movement. At first, he thought the dogs had caught up with him and were pulling him back. Then he felt the stinging pain creeping stealthily through his lower body and realized what had happened. He looked down and, in the moonlight, barely glimpsed a rusted length of barbed-wire poking out of the grass. His lower body had sunk into the grass just enough to get tangled in the barbed wire fence. The wires were dug deep into his groin and wrapped around his legs.

Jeremy tried to move, but that only made the wires dig deeper into him, dragging painfully across his groin, cutting paths in his flesh that weltered with fresh blood. He heard the dogs howling in the darkness, undoubtedly excited by the smell of blood. They crashed through the undergrowth, no longer mindlessly pursuing, but closing in on him with the accuracy of heat-seeking missiles.

Desperate to free himself before the dogs found him, Jeremy grabbed the wire with his bare hands, ignoring the pain as the barbs tore his fingers to the bone. He held back a scream, not sure why he even bothered; the dogs already knew where he was. When he had managed to pull the wire from his leg, he tried to pull the limb free, only to find it even more tangled in another stretch of wire around his ankle. He finally let out the scream as he felt the teeth of the barbed wire sink into his flesh, scraping the knob of bone. His fingers let the wire slip, the barbs again digging into his thigh.

Jeremy again let out his scream, not caring if the dogs heard him. He screamed even louder when he saw a light turn on from the corner of his eye. Realizing that he had reached the edge of the swamp and that the first houses were just on the other side of the creek bed, he turned his head up and bellowed as loud as he could, hoping for the first time in his life that someone would call the cops on him.

His screams were cut off as a dog latched on to his exposed throat, bending his head back with its powerful jaws. Jeremy's hands closed on a hairy, powerful body, but were unable to push it off. He tried to bend his head down, to at least see what was attacking him, but his neck was unable to move against the force of the bite. He felt warm blood spurt from his throat as the teeth began to sink into flesh. He tried to scream again, but all that came out was a hoarse choke.

Wrapping his hands around the muscular neck, Jeremy tried to push the head away, but only succeeded in tearing more flesh from his own throat. As he sunk his nails into the dog's skin, another set of jaws sank into his arm. As he fought to push it away, another mouth latched on to his other arm. Both mouths pulled back simultaneously, as if spreading his limbs so the other dogs could make an easy feast of him.

Soon, what felt like a dozen more dogs were biting into his torso. He tried to scream again as he felt the pain of them tearing his flesh in all directions. A harsh gurgle emerged from his throat, along with a spray of bloody foam that dripped back into his eyes. Trying to struggle away from the dogs only got him more tangled in the wire, the jagged teeth digging painfully into his limbs, slicing chunks of flesh that the dogs tore off and swallowed and drawing blood that he felt them eagerly lapping up.

Despite knowing he had no hope of escaping, the pain was too intense for Jeremy not to try. As he slid along the wires, the loop around his thigh moved up and dragged painfully against his penis. He felt the dogs fighting over the blood that the slice raised and even more pain as their teeth burrowed for more. Even the dog on his throat was finally compelled to let go, its powerful jaws latching onto him again a moment later, sucking blood from his fresher wounds.

Finally, his head was free, although he no longer desired to look down at his attackers. All he could do was scream, despite the damage to his throat. At first there was only a spray of red foam. Then, as if a blockage had been removed, his scream suddenly appeared, followed by a large burst of vomit.

With his throat cleared, Jeremy did the only thing he could, screaming as loudly as he could, for as long as he was able.

The screaming started just as Max reached the lowest of the branches. He turned too quickly trying to find the source of the sound and accidentally overbalanced himself. Feeling himself tipping forward, he desperately reached for another branch to grab onto, but felt only air rushing between his fingers. The ground rushed up towards him, enveloping his vision in a darkness so complete that he at first thought he had been knocked unconscious. When Max noticed he was having this thought, he realized it couldn't be true and opened his eyes.

Seeing no movement, he dared to look around. He was in a clearing in the otherwise tangled line of trees that separated the secret world of the bower from the swamp outside. There were no dogs as far as he could see, and if they were approaching through the thick brush, Max was sure he would have been able to hear them.

The screams rang out again, louder and more desperate this time, quickly devolving into a choking gargle. As they died away, he could only hear an unpleasant ripping sound. He had to be careful; the dogs were close enough for him to hear their activities in detail, but he couldn't see where they were.

Not daring to make a noise, he moved quietly through the underbrush, gently moving branches and leaves aside with one hand. As he reached the thickest, outermost layer of intertwined branches, he realized the best way to avoid making noise was to crawl beneath them, where the leaves thinned out just before the forest floor.

Pressing himself as flat as he could go, Max crawled blindly under the branches. He pressed his face into the dirt, even holding in his breath to avoid disturbing the leaves. He reached his hands outside the bower, where even the air felt different against his skin, praying that there were no dogs waiting just outside, watching his hands like they were a tasty morsel.

He almost screamed when his fingers slid into something soft and wet. As he held the scream in, he noticed his fingers felt cold and slimy, not the warmth he would expect from a dog's mouth. He realized that his hand had found the edge of the swamp water outside. He dug his hands into the muck until he had a solid handhold and pulled the rest of his body forward.

As the scars on his hand slid beneath the water, they began to burn as if they were infected. He paused for a moment, remembering that they had burned when he was first entering the woods. It almost seemed as if the scars were reacting to the presence of the animal that had created them. The thought almost filled his brain with panic, urging him to get up and run blindly across the swamp, but he forced himself to remain calm. If the dogs knew where he was, he reasoned, they would already be on him.

Pulling himself to his feet, Max saw lights in the distance. The sight almost made him want to take off running again, but the sound of the dogs nearby made him more cautious. Stepping softly into the muck, he made his way for a ridge of trees on the far side of the swamp, where he saw the beams of flashlights swinging through the branches. Max forced himself to take one slow, cautious step after another, barely making a noise as the lights moved infinitesimally closer.

Hearing voices calling out in the distance, Max fought the urge to call back. After a moment, he heard more noises: the slow, stealthy dragging of paws against dry grass. Max's muscles tensed even tighter, his breath remaining frozen in his chest. Then he heard the sounds picking up and multiplying in all directions and realized the dogs were closing in.

Max took off running without a second thought, screaming to the distant voices for help. His screams were cut off as he tripped in a pool of stagnant water, his arms disappearing to the elbow as he caught himself. His scars began to burn even more, as if they knew the Xolo was closing in. Picking himself up, he navigated by the faint moonlight towards the brighter lights bouncing off the branches. As he neared the trees they were emerging from, he could hear the dogs just behind him. He ran faster, sparing just enough breath to continue screaming, waving his arms as if the men holding the flashlights could see him through the trees.

Ahead, Max could see the beams converging and the voices shouting over one another. He shouted in return, begging them for help. When he heard a powerful voice shout an indistinct reply, he closed in on it, dodging between the trees that surrounded the creek as he heard an enormous dog crash through the growth behind him. Almost too late, he remembered the barbed-wire fence. With an agility he didn't know he had, Max leapt for the broken fence post that Jeremy had helped him over in another age.

The ancient wood gave way in the muddy earth beneath the sudden onset of his weight. Max tumbled forward, landing just clear of the razor teeth of the wire. He felt his ankle twist painfully and the hem of his jeans tangle in the barbed wire, the cuff tearing as he fell to the ground. One angular tooth of metal sliced his ankle as he fell, carving a thin line of pain across the lower half of his leg. Finding his tattered pant leg caught in the barbed wire, Max reached back and tore the shredded cuff off his jeans, leaving a blood-soaked scrap of denim caught in the wire as he dashed for the creek.

Behind him, he heard a dog crash into the fence, yipping as the barbed wire tore into its skin. Max was too terrified to feel pity, or even turn around, especially as he heard the fence post crash into the ground and the enormous bulk of the dog hit the ground behind him. Max pushed himself forward, dragging his injured foot, feeling fresh blood ooze from his wound with every step.

Ducking around the last few trees, Max saw the drunken men who had nearly spotted them from their balcony, along with a few other people, some waving flashlights, some clutching cellphones, all looking worried and confused. Max screamed and waved his arms as they came in view, believing superstitiously that the dogs couldn't kill him in sight of other people.

The flashlights converged on Max, nearly blinding him. The people holding them were separated from him only by the few feet of murky water in the creek, but to Max this final obstacle seemed the most impossible of all. He plunged into the icy water, desperately shouting warnings to the people gathered on the opposite bank.

Max had never been a strong swimmer, but as he reached the center of the creek and found the water reaching his neck, he did his best to paddle through the water, kicking painfully with his injured leg. Behind him, he heard an enormous splash and for the first time dared to look back. An enormous German shepherd was paddling expertly across the water, keeping its mouth above the water so it could snarl, foam oozing from its mouth and forming a trail in the water behind it. Max paddled as quickly as he could, but the dog was moving faster than he possibly could.

Reaching an arm towards shore, Max suddenly felt something grab him. He writhed and struggled until he looked back up and saw the drunken neighbors, waist-deep in the water, pulling him by the shoulder. Max went limp as another arm hooked beneath his other shoulder, their combined force pulling him towards the bank, but when Max looked back, the dog was still closing in on them, its hungry mouth opening as he tried to scramble onto the bank. Max squeezed his eyes shut as the dog burst from the water.

He could feel the front paws scratching his wounded leg when an explosion of sound suddenly drowned out all his other senses. Max opened his eyes to see a spurt of blood eject from a hole in the dog's torso. Max could feel the creek grow warmer as the water filled with the dog's blood.

Despite its injury, the dog continued struggling towards Max, not even minding its attacker. A second shot rang out, ending the dog's struggles as the dome of its skull exploded in a spray of red, white, and gray that showered the creek, the larger pieces floating on the water's surface. The dog's body went limp and sank below the water, its snout remaining above the surface for a moment like a submarine's periscope, slowly descending, then disappearing in a flume of bubbles as the last air escaped its body.

Max's own body went limp with relief as the men pulled him on shore. He heard no more dogs, and he felt safe now that the neighbors were gathering around him. Among them, he saw the sheriff who had been at school the day he was bitten. The sheriff pointed a revolver towards the trees, its barrel still smoking. "You okay, son?" he asked.

Max wasn't sure. "The dogs," he tried to warn them, "there's dozens more in the woods." A chorus of howls emerged from the swamp, as if confirming his story. Max sat up in alarm, the sound sending a chill through his heart, but the howls were growing more distant now. The dogs had probably been scared off by the sound of the gunshots.

Above them all, Max could hear the low, plaintive howl of the Xolo. Even as one of the drunken men from the balcony threw a blanket over him, Max began to shiver, but not because of the cold water soaking him.

SIXTEEN

"Your son sustained several injuries while escaping, but none life-threatening." The young doctor checked her chart as she led the family through the maze-like corridors of Hell's Pass Hospital. "A sprained ankle, some cuts and abrasions, one along his leg that needed stitches-"

Alison shifted Gracie in her arms impatiently. "I'm sorry, but escaping from what?"

"Dogs," said a gruff male voice before the doctor could look up from her chart. "Lots of dogs," Sheriff Chambers said as he heaved himself from a chair outside a patient room, taking his hat from the chair beside him.

Seeing a question cross Allison's face that he wasn't sure he wanted answered, Derek squeezed her by the shoulder. "Why don't you and Gracie go visit Max while I talk to the sheriff?"

She nodded and carried Gracie into the room. The doctor shut the door behind them, then hurried off to her next case, leaving Derek and the sheriff alone in the hallway. There was a long silence which Derek realized the sheriff wanted him to fill.

"I heard you saved my boy, Sheriff. Thank you."

Garth bowed his head slightly. "Three other boys weren't so lucky. Two teenagers and one your boy's age." Derek hung his head, as if these facts were an accusation directed at him.

"My son's friends. What happened to the dogs?"

"I shot one of 'em," the sheriff said nonchalantly. "The rest scattered at the sound. Got my deputies looking for 'em now, but you know better than us how many miles of woods and swamps there are out there. They could be anywhere."

"Where do you think they came from?"

The sheriff gave Derek a look that instantly made him regret his question. "Yeah, I've been thinking about that myself," he said as if Derek would know. "The one I shot was one of Ernie Kesson's German shepherds, but he only had two, and there were a helluva lot more than two out there. Your boy said nearly a hundred, and I would be inclined to write that off as boyish imagination, 'cept I heard the howling myself. Quite a few kinds I've never heard before too."

Derek sighed, figuring where the sheriff was going with this. "And you think my Xolo's part of that pack, right?"

Garth shrugged. "Well, you said you dropped him off at Dr. Greene's place, and every dog in there escaped, so if your dog *was* at the vet's, he must be part of the pack now. I figure they're the core of this pack, along with the beasts that broke out of that dog fighting ring. If they're not, I'll just about eat my badge."

For the first time, Derek was glad he hadn't really left the dog at the pound, though of course he couldn't say that to the sheriff. "Unless, of course, she euthanized him right away like I thought she would," he offered.

Garth laughed in a way that showed he didn't believe that. "Well, let's just hope she did."

They both turned at the sound of the door opening. Garth turned away when he saw Alison. Her eyes were red and swollen with fresh tears, and she clutched Gracie to her chest, hiding the girl's face.

"Max wants to see you, Derek," Alison managed to say hoarsely.

Derek looked to the sheriff, as if asking his permission. Garth stood aside and waved Derek inside with his hat. Giving Alison a small squeeze on her shoulder, Derek headed for the room, wondering vaguely what the sheriff would say to his wife while he was gone.

Closing the door behind himself, Derek waited in the small hallway between a supply closet and a shower stall before the main room. He could see the foot of a hospital bed around the corner, a lump underneath the sheets that must have been his son's foot.

Derek swallowed hard, pressing his back against the door until the storm of contrasting thoughts in his mind could settle. He felt guilty, of course, but mostly in the vague, illogical way a parent always felt guilty when harm came to their child, but also because he had known about the old farm house where the attack had happened.

Ever since the sheriff's dispatcher had woken him from bed with the frantic story of what had happened, waves of remorse had been crashing in his mind. The house had belonged to the old farmer he had bought the property from, who had cleared out in such a hurry with the check Derek gave him that he had never even bothered to remove his belongings. Derek had considered tearing the house down, but somehow he had liked its secret, rustic flavor, and the expense of demolition, he had thought, was better spent on construction. Derek had limited his expenses to removing the single winding dirt lane that led to the house and planting more trees to hide the property. He had never thought that anyone, even teenagers, would venture far enough out in the swamp to find it.

The barbed wire fences, however, he couldn't forgive himself for. He should have known they would be dangerous, that some young kid would eventually wander out and hurt himself on them, but he had never imagined a circumstance as horrible as what the dispatcher had described in the second teenager's death.

Mostly, he felt guilty about setting the Xolo free, though he wasn't sure why; there was no proof that the Xolo was involved in this. It was just an idea that the sheriff had put in his mind because he needed someone to blame for a case he could not solve.

The lump under the sheet moved slightly and a hoarse, creaky voice emerged which Derek almost didn't recognize as his own son's. "Dad, is that you?" the voice rasped, sounding like it was using the last of its energy to form the words.

Wondering how long he had been standing there lost in thought, Derek pushed himself off the door. "Yeah, it's me, Max." As he stepped around the corner, he had to make an effort not to look shocked at his son's appearance. Although there were no visible injuries, Max's entire frame seemed shrunken and withered, as if he were battling cancer instead of shock and a sprained ankle. Derek realized, almost for the first time, that his son had seen and experienced horrible things tonight, things even few adults ever experienced and that no young boy ever should.

"Dad, I'm sorry," Max croaked, looking away from Derek as he spoke.

Derek felt the urge to kneel down next to his son's bed, but was for some reason afraid of moving too close to him. "It's okay, son," Derek said softly, unsure what he was supposed to be absolving his son for. He supposed he could be mad at Max for sneaking out when he told him not to, but the fact that he had almost died made that seem like a moot point. Mostly he was just glad Max was okay. He wanted to find a way to express that, but he couldn't find the words.

Max turned away from him, as if trying to keep a secret. A heavy silence hung in the air, broken only by the whirs and beeps of machinery. "I don't care that you snuck out," Derek said, doing anything to fill the silence.

Max turned on his back, keeping his gaze focused on the ceiling. "It's not that, Dad." There was a long pause, then, "I saw the Xolo."

It took Derek a moment to recognize the full import of that simple statement. "What, like our Xolo? The one that bit you?"

"Yeah. I recognized it right away. And it seemed to recognize me; that was the creepy part. It came right for me, like it was hunting me. And it ordered the other dogs to hunt us too; I swear it was communicating with them."

Derek was silent for a long moment. He was terrified to suddenly hear so exact a description of the strange, unnamed fears that the sheriff seemed to be guessing at so accurately.

His mind stayed on the sheriff, who he assumed was still waiting outside. "Did you tell the police?" he asked Max.

"I wanted to," Max said, sounding more like a boy half his age as his head sank into the pillow, "but they would think I was crazy."

Derek felt a guilty wave of relief wash over him at knowing that the sheriff didn't know. "I'll talk to him," he told Max.

"Should we tell him I saw the Xolo once before?" Max asked, sounding even more like a younger boy.

"What, you mean when it bit you at school?"

Max shook his head. "After that. After you dropped it off at the pound. It must have escaped."

Derek felt his cheeks turn hot. "Yeah, I guess it must have. Where did you see it?"

Max somehow sunk even further into his bed. "Under the bridge at the end of the county." He turned away from his father, facing the opposite wall. "My friends like to hang out there after school. Well, liked to, I guess."

Derek let the silence hang in the air. "When was this?" he asked.

Max shrugged, his shoulders dragging against the stiff, papery bedsheets. The bed creaked as he turned towards Derek. "A few weeks ago, I guess. I only saw it for a second. I thought it was just a hallucination, but now that I've seen it again, I'm not so sure." He turned his head away again, this time to hide the tears that were beginning to soak his pillow. "I should have told you then," he said, struggling to choke the words out between his sobs.

"It's okay, son," Derek said, moving to the bedside and putting a hand on his shoulder, "it wasn't your fault, it's nobody's fault," *except the Xolo's*, his mind added automatically. *And whose fault is it that the Xolo is running free?* argued another part of his mind. Derek pushed the warring voices away.

He saw Max slump back against his pillow, struggling to stay awake. "Why don't you get some rest, son? I'll talk to the police." Max nodded, his eyes already closing. On his way out, Derek shut off the light and closed the door as gently as he could.

Derek expected to see Garth still waiting for him in the hall, but he found Alison in the sheriff's place, cradling Gracie in her arms. With a nod, Derek motioned her to follow him and led them through the maze of hallways.

When they reached the glass-walled lobby, he saw the sight he had been dreading. Through the wall of glass at the front of the building, he saw the sheriff just outside the doors, smoking a cigarette much closer to the exit than the law allowed.

Derek held up a hand, motioning Alison to a row of seats in the corner of the lobby. "Why don't you guys wait here a minute? I need to have a word with the sheriff."

Alison looked confused and concerned, but she took Gracie to the waiting area, trying to interest her in a toy with brightly-colored balls on a series of curving tracks. Derek took a deep breath and headed outside through the automatic doors, the glass sliding apart to reveal a world of hazy smoke. He stepped through the cloud, approaching the sheriff with a nod.

"How's your boy?" Garth said as a greeting.

Derek shrugged. "Seems to be doing alright. As alright as can be expected under the circumstances."

Garth nodded slowly. "Well, that's always the qualifier in my line of work." He took another slow drag of his cigarette. "Did he tell you anything we oughtta know? I don't want to subject him to a full interview until he's had a chance to recover, but seeing as how I've got a whole crew of deputies out there now, I wondered if there was anything we oughtta know right away." The sheriff took a long, slow drag on his cigarette, as if patiently waiting for an answer he already knew was coming.

Derek sighed, looking back through the glass at his family. Alison was desperately trying to get Gracie to sit in one of the uncomfortable plastic chairs, holding out a stack of magazines that Gracie was rejecting one by one. Both of them were bundled in their heavy fall coats, already beginning to sweat in the steam heat of the lobby. Alison shot Derek a pleading look through the glass. He held up one finger to her and then turned back to the sheriff. "Yeah, Sheriff, I think there is."

Garth let out a cloud of smoke, as if he had been holding his breath in anticipation. "Well, I'm all ears." He took another drag as he waited for a response.

Derek took a deep breath, accidentally breathing in some of the sheriff's cigarette smoke. He wasn't sure if it was the smoke or the anxiety that made his lungs feel like they were burning. "You were right, Sheriff. My boy saw the Xolo in the woods. He said it seemed to be leading the other dogs. He told me he saw it a few weeks ago too, like the dog was following him."

"Yeah? And how was this cholo following him a few weeks ago if he was locked up at the pound until just the other day?"

Derek sighed, knowing the sheriff was simply waiting to hear answers he had already figured out on his own. "Because I never dropped the dog off at the pound, as I'm sure you suspected."

Garth took another deep drag, his face betraying no emotion. "So, what'd you do, just leave him in the woods?"

"Pretty much. I figured that without food, and with the cold weather coming, he would die in a few months."

"And that was better than sending him to the pound?"

"It was better than letting him live in a cage before they just killed him anyways. He was completely unruly; no one would have adopted him."

"Well, I think you're right about that. Especially since he's a killer."

"How was I supposed to know that?! I mean, how the hell did you know what was going on?"

"I didn't. Not until now." The sheriff looked quite pleased with himself as he took another long drag. "But your cholo was the last animal attack we had in the area for a long time, so when we suddenly started having more, I thought it might not be a coincidence. Besides, when I asked you about it, your face told me right away you were lying."

Derek kicked a chunk of loose pavement. "Yeah, guess I've never been a great liar."

"Well, now that you are telling the truth, maybe you can help us."

The sheriff's tone made it clear this was more than a suggestion. Derek looked back at Alison, who was busy trying to keep Gracie from running outside, and sighed. "Yeah. You need me to come with you?"

"That would be nice," the sheriff said with a smirk. "I can give you a ride home when we're done." He gestured toward a patrol car parked nearby.

Derek took a deep breath and looked back towards his family. "Alright. Just let me tell my wife."

Derek expected the sheriff to follow him inside, to lead him by a pair of handcuffs strapped around both their wrists, but the sheriff only calmly waited outside, lighting another cigarette from the dying embers of his old one. Derek rushed inside, quickly explaining to an unamused Alison that the sheriff needed his help and that he wouldn't be back until late that night, or even the next morning. Derek secretly wondered if he would be back at all. He slapped the keys into Alison's hand and told her and Gracie he would see them in the morning.

Without another word, Derek went back outside and followed Garth to the waiting patrol car. As the car started across the parking lot, Derek looked back, catching a final glimpse of Alison and Gracie framed in the windows. The forward movement of the car made them look like sailors drifting away into a sea of darkness. As his family disappeared into the night, Derek looked at the darkness ahead, wondering for no reason he could name if he would see them again.

SEVENTEEN

THE NARROW TWO-LANE ROAD LEADING OUT OF THE LITTLE NEIGHBORHOOD at the base of the mountains had once been one of the most non-descript in the entire county. The small cluster of houses built a decade or two before Sylvan Springs didn't even have a name, and the single bridge leading away from it was similarly unadorned: a plain metal structure spanning a narrow creek between thick forest and an endless stretch of swamp.

But that once-quiet road was now filled with a flurry of activity. Squad cars and ambulances filled the shoulder on both sides, their lights spinning and turning the leaves into disordered streaks of red and blue. A massive mobile crime lab filled most of the road, making the barriers set across the bridge unnecessary.

The sheriff found some room on the shoulder and parked his cruiser. Pulling the keys from the ignition, he looked down at the loafers Derek had pulled on in his rush to leave the house. "Ain't gonna be a walk in the park; might get your shoes wet."

Knowing it was too late for that kind of concern, Derek shrugged and followed him out of the car. The sheriff led him to a narrow gap in the trees which the police cars seemed to be clustered around. Ducking through the trees, they found themselves at the edge of a stretch of swamp that reached to the edge of Derek's vision. The police had already laid down a track of plywood that led to a large stand of trees. As Garth stepped onto the plywood, it sank beneath his weight, mud and water oozing over the edges of the wood.

Derek followed warily, keeping the plywood pinned down after the sheriff stepped off.

Ahead, the trail of plywood led through a path cut into a line of trees. As they passed through a tunnel of branches, the sheriff pointed out their ragged, broken ends. "Had to clear this shit out with a machete," he said. "Just like in those old jungle movies." Derek grinned a little at that. "Only way to get the equipment in, and the bodies out." Derek's grin faded.

On the other side of the trees, the path of plywood continued, a curving line eventually visible only as a flattened track through the waist-high weeds and grasses, leading to a menacing bower in the center of the swamp.

At every fifth sheet of plywood or so, a second sheet was placed alongside the main track with a battery-powered light on it, illuminating the weeds in odd directions. Derek shuddered at the pools of shadow between the weeds, dreading what might be lurking there. When the path finally reached the bower, there was another opening cleared by machetes, a low archway hacked through the branches through which an incongruous white light poured, as if they were about to step into some fairy's glen.

As Derek's eyes adjusted to the bright light inside, he found anything but a fairytale world. Instead of elves or fairies, he saw grim-faced policemen and crime scene investigators shuffling through the scene. The entire bower was lit by halogen spotlights, throwing both the bower and the house into an off-putting artificial sunlight. Derek had never actually seen the house before, only heard about it when he had bought the property. He was stunned by how overpowering the tall, gothic structure was, even more so in the harsh white light, which was no longer charming and fanciful, as it had seemed from outside the bower.

He followed the sheriff into the house through a rotted door left barely hanging on its hinges. Inside, they were immediately greeted by a huddle of crime scene technicians, their backs to the door, blocking the view of whatever they were furiously working over. Derek got only a glimpse between their shoulders as they moved to hand equipment to one another. A glimpse was all he wanted. When one of the technicians raised a camera to photograph the corpse, Derek got a longer look at the torn, bloody face through the viewfinder. He turned away with a shudder, barely suppressing his need to vomit.

"Jesus, Sheriff, you sure you need me to see all this? I'm just a real estate guy; I'm no cop."

Garth nodded as if he hadn't been listening. "I know it's rough, but I want you to see what we're up against before you agree to help us."

"I already agreed to help, Sheriff." Derek thought the sheriff was really trying to guilt him by showing him the horrific consequences of his actions, but Derek already felt guilty enough. "But you haven't explained what you need me to do." Garth slowly turned his head toward him and Derek knew instantly that he had overstepped his bounds.

The sheriff continued on his grisly tour as if he hadn't heard Derek, pointing to a hole in the ceiling, through which Derek could see more investigators working upstairs. "Seems like the boy fell through the ceiling here. Or the floor, as he would have thought of it. Seems he was running for the window when he broke through. There's quite a few scratches on the floor upstairs, so I expect he broke through, caught himself on the floor, then was dragged down by the dogs." Derek shuddered imagining that. "I would take you up there, but the floor's obviously unsafe."

"That's alright, Sheriff, I think I've seen enough." Derek turned back towards the exit only to find his way blocked by more crime scene technicians. There were dozens of them, scraping samples off every conceivable surface.

Garth followed his astounded gaze and laughed. "A lotta dogs here. Trying to see if we can figure out how many."

"You have any idea what would have driven them to do something like this?"

"No idea," answered a female voice from the next room. "I've never seen this type of behavior from a dog, let alone a pack of them."

Derek turned to see a woman about his own age in a tactical uniform with a badge that identified her as the lead county animal control officer. "My only thought is they could have been making a den out here when the boys stumbled upon them," she said. "Maybe they were just defending their territory."

Garth followed Derek's look with a knowing wink. "Derek, I'd like you to meet our head of animal control, Heloise Lopez. I see you already saw her credentials," he said with a smirk, prompting Derek to raise his eyes from where they had been resting on her badge.

"Now," the sheriff said to Heloise, "that doesn't explain the other attacks. Or the fact that they seem to have chased the boys upstairs, like they were trying to trap them." He motioned to Derek. "His boy only escaped by running upstairs, same as this young man here," he motioned to the object the crime scene technicians were working over. Derek forced himself not to follow the sheriff's gaze. "Only he didn't run into any weak spots in the floor, so he was able to tell us that this crazy cholo that his family had for a while was apparently the ring leader of all this."

Derek felt acutely the shame that the sheriff was trying to pile upon him, but Heloise only laughed. "I think you mean pack leader, Sheriff."

"Well, the boy said the cholo seemed to be giving orders to the other dogs by barking at them, so whatever the term is for that."

Heloise furrowed her brow. "I don't think there is a word for that. I've never heard of that kind of behavior, especially between different breeds. Seems very odd."

"Yeah, well, everything about this case seems very fucking odd to me." The sheriff reached in his shirt pocket for a cigarette, then, remembering where he was, tucked the pack away.

Heloise was forced to agree with the sheriff's conclusion. "What else did the boy say?"

Since she had seemed to be asking both of them and the sheriff was still fiddling with his pack of cigarettes, Derek spoke up. "He said the dog seemed to be following him."

Heloise didn't seem as surprised by that as Derek would have thought. "The dog might remember him by smell; it's possible the dog's own scent might still be embedded in the boy's bite wound."

The sheriff looked at Derek excitedly. "That's exactly what I figured."

Made uncomfortable by the sheriff's strange looks, Derek finally snapped. "So, you, what, brought me out here so the dogs could sniff me out? Trying to prove my guilt?"

Garth gave a laugh that made Derek even more uncomfortable. "Not quite. You see, all you did was dump a dog in the wild. That's no crime." He glanced over at Heloise, who was giving him a sharp look. "Well, technically, it is, but I'm willing to look past that if you're willing to help us. You see, my job is to protect the people of Puebla County, and right now, there's a pack a wild dogs out there that can harm those people."

"You don't need to remind me, Sheriff."

"And I'm sure I also don't need to remind you that those dogs have about a thousand square miles of forest to hide in, and even more to escape to if they can cross a few roads and bridges?"

"You do not."

"Good. Because I don't intend to let them escape and harm anyone else. Not in my town. I intend to track them down and destroy them before they can."

"I'm with you, Sheriff, just not sure how exactly I can help."

Garth laughed and looked to Heloise, who only gave Derek the briefest of glances before looking away. "Well," said Garth, slowly turning back to Derek, "in order to have a hope of finding these dogs in all this wilderness, I'm going to need something to lure them out."

Derek still didn't understand, but followed the sheriff's gaze to the bite marks on his hand, which suddenly burned and itched. Understanding came in a terrible flash. "You're planning to use me as bait?"

Garth laughed again, the most uncomfortable and incongruous one yet. "Don't be thick, boy; bait always gets eaten. I'm gonna do my best to make sure that doesn't happen."

"Very reassuring, Sheriff."

Whatever the sheriff was about to say in response was cut off by the blaring of his radio. "Sheriff, we found the other boy," said a nervous voice on the other end.

"Do I have to ask if he's alive?" Garth scowled into his radio.

"You can ask, but it won't do any good. I'm sending Bernie back to get you right now."

Garth smiled as he put the radio away. "Sound like something you oughtta see," he said to Derek.

"I don't think I want to, sheriff."

"I don't think that was a question." The sheriff's tone and countenance suddenly showed a streak of cruelty that Derek had never seen before. Seeing that he had no choice, Derek followed the sheriff outside, where they were met by a pale, horror-stricken deputy who was just returning from the swamp, his waders dripping with slimy water. He pointed towards a path through the swamp to a ridge of trees, where more deputies were rushing to build a path out of plywood.

Impatient with their progress, Garth trudged through the swamp ahead of them, not seeming to mind his boots sinking in the water. Derek looked back at Heloise, then at his loafers. Getting only a shrug from Heloise, he trudged after the sheriff, who showed no sign of waiting for him. Derek felt his feet sink to the ankle, groaning as cold, slimy water soaked through his socks.

As they neared the ridge of trees, Derek saw unearthly glimmers and an occasional flash light the trees ahead. As they pulled themselves free from the water and trudged uphill, Derek saw more deputies moving through the scene, their forms only silhouettes in the powerful glare of the portable lights, which illuminated the woods more than Derek would have liked. A photographer moved through the scene, the occasional flashes of his camera revealing mercifully quick details: strips of flesh wrapped around strands of wire, a severed hand tangled in one coil, the mass of the skeletal body discarded in a pile of broken weeds. All of these were terrible, but for Derek, the most pathetic sight of all was the blood-stained scrap of sweatshirt hanging from the top of one fence post, its ragged ends blowing in the breeze, the skate company logo still mostly visible through the blood. Derek wasn't sure whether to cry or vomit.

Garth, on the other hand, knew exactly what he should do. As he assigned the men to their tasks, he pulled a few deputies aside and told them to get ready for a trek. "You ready?" he asked Derek.

Derek looked back at the path towards the house, which the deputies had nearly completed. He felt the cold water soaking his socks, the wind ripping at his jacket. Then he looked at what remained of the body on the barbed wire fence and slowly nodded in agreement.

"Good," said Garth. "Heloise is putting her team together back at the house. We'll meet up with them, then head out to the woods. I want to move on these puppies before they have a chance to get themselves too entrenched."

Derek looked around at the men who were following Garth back towards the house. "Quite a crew we'll have," he said, "police, animal control, and a real estate developer."

The other men did not share Derek's laugh.

EIGHTEEN

OFFICER PRESTON ROMAN TUGGED HARD ON THE LEASH, BRINGING HIS dog to a halt. For hours they had been searching the woods and so far, their dogs had turned up only a few vague clues: some patches of fur which could have come from almost any animal, some matted-down spots in the weeds, and now a burrow that looked more likely to be used by foxes than the mythical killer dogs this country bumpkin of a sheriff had them chasing after.

"Come on, get outta there," Roman told the dog, pulling harder on its leash, "don't need you getting your nose bit." The German shepherd cocked its head at him as if it had understood that. Pushing the dog out of the way, Roman shined his flashlight into the hole, which turned out to be empty. "Well, what do you know, another wild goose chase. Or wild dog chase, I guess," he muttered to himself. "Hey, Benny!" he called out to his partner, "you finding anything over there?!"

After a moment's rustling, Benny Corbett's German shepherd appeared from the brush, followed a moment later by Benny himself, looking somehow even more animalistic than his partner. "Naw, man, I haven't seen shit."

"Figures. This would be a helluva lot easier in the daylight."

Benny's tired look suddenly turned to one of fierce determination. "Hey, you heard the sheriff," he grumbled, "we can't let the dogs get away."

"Eh, he ain't my sheriff," Roman grumbled. The little strip of mountains that called itself Puebla County was such a damn podunk place, they barely had enough officers to search the local bar. When a big crime like this happened, (and, to Roman's knowledge, this was the first time that anything that happened in Puebla County could be described as big) the damn podunk sheriff had to call in deputies and officers from neighboring counties, along with officers and crime scene techs from the state police.

Benny and himself had been called in from the Castle Rock PD, along with a dozen others. Roman had complained about being called here in the middle of the night the whole ride here, but Benny kept assuring him that the Puebla County Sheriff's office would do the same for them if they needed it. Roman had laughed at that, wondering what a few hillbilly deputies could possibly do for Castle Rock. They were big enough to have their own police department, unlike this podunk shithole. The only reason this shithole city had any police presence in the first place was because their county sheriff just so happened to have his little shack on the outskirts of town.

"Man, you really believe this sheriff's crazy shit about killer dogs?" Roman asked, leading his dog away from a dead squirrel.

"If that's what they say it is," Benny answered, guiding his dog to keep up with Roman. "You got any better ideas?"

"Wolves, maybe, or some other kinda wild animal, but just domesticated dogs running wild, tearing people up? I don't buy it. But they got us out here in the middle of the night, searching for something this sheriff probably dreamt up while he was swilling moonshine or some shit."

"Relax, Roman, you're getting overtime for being out here, same as the rest of us." The thought seemed to give him another and he brought his dog to a halt, tilting his head up as curiously as the dog's. "Wait a minute, you hear something?"

"Of course not, what's there to hear in the woods?"

"Well, the other deputies, for one. We were supposed to stay within earshot, remember?"

Roman rolled his eyes. The country bumpkin sheriff had assigned each pair of deputies a spot along a line of trees, with instructions to travel as deep into the woods as they could, in as straight a line as they could, without getting out of hearing range of the next pair of deputies. Now they seemed to be out of hearing range of everything but crickets, frogs, and a distant owl.

"Hey, guys, can you hear us!?" Benny called, a hint of desperation sneaking into his voice. The only response was his own words, echoing off the endless trees and ringing in a distant canyon. No human voice replied. Even the flashlights of the other deputies were out of sight. Benny called again. This time there was a response: a soft, stealthy rustling in the woods behind them.

Benny whirled around, pulling his gun from its holster. Roman laughed at his quick, panicked glances into the brush. "Will you relax, Tex? It was probably just a deer that got startled by your bellowing."

Motioning for Roman to shut up, Benny let his dog move closer to the spot where the brush was now visibly rustling. When Roman started to say something else, Benny gave him a hard look, the barrel of his gun pressed to his lips. Roman held up his hands in apology, stepping back to the center of a large clearing. His dog sat by his side, anxiously looking up at him.

The rustling was coming from a large hole in a deep patch of brush. Benny's dog pulled at its leash, eager to get at whatever was doing the rustling. Benny held him back, not wanting the dog to encounter whatever was in there all alone. He slowly stepped closer, his gun at the ready.

His dog reached the edge of the brush, then suddenly stopped, intensely interested but not willing to move any closer. It stared into the darkness inside the foxhole, transfixed by something only it could see.

Suddenly, a pair of yellow eyes opened in the darkness, seeming to glow with their own internal light. Benny's dog was fixed on them, as if he were hypnotized. His low growling stopped, and drool ran from the corners of his snout. Giving a small shout, Benny raised his weapon, horrified by the sight of those unearthly eyes, and aimed the barrel over his dog's head, lining up a shot just between the horrible glowing eyes.

As he pulled the hammer back, his dog turned and leaped at him, its own eyes glowing like the pair it had been staring into. The German shepherd's powerful jaws sank into Benny's exposed forearm, twisting his arm down. Benny's hand squeezed involuntarily, firing a shot into his right foot. The patent leather toe exploded, spraying blood and chunks of flesh. Benny screamed as he lost balance on the injured foot, tumbling beneath the weight of the attacking dog.

He tried to pull back the hammer for another shot, but his dog's teeth were tearing into his muscle, preventing any command from reaching his hand. He raised the flashlight in his other hand, intending to beat his dog until it let him go. Before he could land a blow, more dogs burst from the thicket on all sides, crowding around him as they sank their jaws into his flesh.

Roman watched in shock as more dogs poured out of the woods, surrounding Benny until he disappeared, each of them dipping their heads into the fray and emerging with a mouthful of ripped muscle, Benny's own dog fighting the most viciously for his flesh.

The pitiful screams emerging from the middle of the pile snapped Roman back to reality. He reached for his gun, fumbling and flailing with the holster. His dog pulled on its leash, tugging his hands away from the holster. Whether the dog wanted to fight the others or have its own bite of Benny, Roman couldn't be sure. As he pulled his gun from his holster, the dog suddenly pulled forward, jostling him hard enough to knock the revolver from his hand. As Roman bent over to pick it up, he heard the crashing of several sets of paws. He looked up just in time to see several dogs charging at him, his own dog letting them pass as it charged towards the glowing eyes in the foxhole.

Roman had no time to do anything but scream.

"Alright, listen up, people, we've got more than a thousand acres of unexplored wilderness these puppies could be hiding out in, and the longer we wait, the better they're gonna hide themselves."

Derek looked around the gathering of deputies and animal control officers who were listening to Garth's grand speech, which he delivered from the front porch of the abandoned house. "Now, the only way we're gonna find them is by drawing them out, and that man-" he pointed to Derek, who wanted to hide from the attention, "is the key to that. If my thinking's right, they're gonna be coming after him."

"Does that mean I get a gun?" Derek asked.

He was a little disconcerted by the chorus of laughs from the deputies. "Just stick to the center of the group," Garth said through a chuckle, "you'll be fine. Now, we all ready to go?"

As if in answer, a gunshot sounded from the woods, followed a moment later by distant screams. Garth jumped down from the porch and signaled the group towards the path out of the bower. Along the way, he pulled out his radio.

"All units, this is Sheriff Chambers, who was firing?" He heard no response as he led the group out of the bower. Cursing to himself, he pulled the radio out again. "All units, if you can hear this, move towards the entry point. Main team is moving in, we are going to strike the dogs as one."

Garth led them towards a ridge of grass, beyond which stretched only endless trees. Derek nervously scanned the deputies, all of them waving pistols and flashlights. Along with them were Heloise and several of her animal control officers, all of them armed with dart guns full of tranquilizer, with what looked like electric cattle prods swinging at their hips. Derek tried his best to stick to the middle of the group.

The sheriff ran ahead of the others, frantically calling on his radio for the injured deputies and receiving no response. He led the group to an entrance to the woods, following a path that only he could see. The other men and women weaved between the trees, which seemed to press in and instantly surround them.

Garth froze at a rustling from the woods ahead. Holding up a hand to signal to the others, he pulled his gun from its holster. The deputies behind him did the same. Their hammers clicked in unison as a large dog burst from the woods. Derek saw their fingers pressing against the triggers until another deputy emerged from the branches just behind the dog, holding the other end of its leash. The thin man looked over his strapped-on glasses at the guns pointed at him and almost reached for his own in response. The sheriff waved the weapons down, scowling at the hapless deputy.

"Goddamit, O'Brien, you almost got yourself shot."

The man's look made it perfectly clear he was aware of that. "I'm sorry, Sheriff, I was just following your orders." He held up a radio with his free hand.

Garth grimaced, slamming his gun into his holster. "Oh, never mind all that, just fall in and keep up." The deputy did as he was told, he and his dog following along as the group made their way deeper into the woods.

The dog ran ahead of the group, straining its leash when it heard the sound of several animals crashing through the undergrowth ahead. There was no mistaking the sound now; it was the wild rushing of a pack of frightened animals, not the deliberate tread of another human. The deputy's dog rushed at the receding noises, straining at its leash to follow them.

The dog led them to a clearing where the deputies' flashlights revealed glimpses of half-eaten bodies and severed limbs. One detached hand was still holding the chewed-up remnants of a leash. A middle-aged female officer, who Derek noticed for the first time was wearing the badge of the Castle Rock PD, crouched beside the remains when she saw the same badge on the shredded scraps of uniform that still clung to the bodies. "Damn, this was Roman and Benny," she said breathlessly, reading the names on the blood-stained badges.

As horror spread across her face, the sheriff pulled her to her feet. "Come on, if we lose the dogs, they'll be able to do this to even more people." They could still hear the faint crashing ahead, but the sounds seemed to have scattered in many different directions.

"Maybe we should split up, cover more ground," another deputy suggested.

Garth shook his head so violently Derek was worried it might come off. "That's how the damn dogs got the jump on these guys," he said, waving his guns at the remains. "Besides, we only need to get the cholo, he's the ring leader, or whatever the fuck you call him," he said, glancing at Heloise, "and it's gonna come for him." For a long, panicked moment, Derek was sure the sheriff was going to shoot him, to let him bleed out so the dogs would catch the scent and come running, but he was only using the gun to point at Derek.

"So, let's stay in a group and stay around him. We stay together, we fight together, right?" The deputies and animal control officers all nodded at that, quietly muttering their assent. "Our priority is capturing or killing the hairless dog," the sheriff continued, "the others are a bonus if we get them. You all got that?" This time, there was a louder chorus of agreement from the deputies.

At the sheriff's command, the officers tightened into a bunch, squeezing Derek into the middle, leaving him unable to do anything but follow the pack as the sheriff led them deeper into the woods.

NINETEEN

As the group moved through the woods, they collected more deputies and their dogs, like some gigantic snowball collecting men and animals. Derek was glad for their presence; the woods were now eerily silent except for their own too loud trampling. Derek had no idea where they were going and he suspected none of the other men did either, but their dogs led them on, finally reaching a clearing where the sheriff ordered everyone to stop, even though the dogs were straining at their leashes to continue.

"This looks like a good place to set up," the sheriff said.

"What, are we camping here?" Derek asked the nearest deputy, a kindly-looking man about his own age who had introduced himself as Millam, Garth's chief deputy.

Millam gave a small smile at Derek's question, which turned into a vicious grin as he answered. "Hell, no! We're gonna lay a trap for these little fuckers."

Derek looked past the deputy to Heloise and her animal control officers, who were pulling a steel cable over the thickest branch of a large tree in the center of the clearing. At the other end of the cable was a steel cage with an open bottom, large enough to trap a dog. As Derek walked closer, another animal control officer placed a steel plate on the ground, hooking the other end of the cable into the plate. Derek guessed that when a dog stepped onto the plate, the cable would disengage, dropping the cage on top of him.

The purpose of their next trap was equally obvious: a series of steel cables tied into nooses the size of a dog's legs, hung over tree branches and small, bent-over saplings, the nooses fixed to the ground by metal hooks so that an animal who stepped into one would be pulled off the ground.

"Not exactly humane," Heloise said when Derek caught her eye, "but it will get the job done."

Derek paced around the clearing, feeling useless among the bustle of activity. As Heloise's team finished setting up their traps, the deputies took up positions along the edge of the clearing, their dogs at their sides.

After an hour or so of no activity, two or three of the police dogs started to bark and whine at once, all of them looking out at the same spot in the woods. The deputies raised their guns as the leaves began to rustle. They raised their guns as a low form emerged from the woods. "Hold your fire!" Garth yelled as the shape came into view. "It's one of ours."

Flashlights revealed the shape of a German shepherd, its collar still around its neck, the tattered remnants of its leash dragging behind it. "Shit, that's Roman's dog," said one of the deputies with a Castle Rock badge, stepping forward to comfort the animal.

Derek grew nervous as he watched the deputy crouch beside the animal, but couldn't explain exactly why. "Can you shine your light on the dog?" he asked Millam, who looked at him strangely, but did it anyways. As the Castle Rock deputy coaxed the dog closer, the beam revealed a streak of drying blood ringed around its mouth. The light caught the dog's eyes, revealing their yellow glow. Derek tried to warn the deputy, but it was already too late.

The dog leapt at the deputy, knocking her to the ground and tearing at her throat. As other deputies rushed forward to help, more dogs burst from the woods and charged towards them. The officers opened fire in a confused volley, downing a few dogs who were quickly replaced by more.

Derek cowered behind the others, crouching to avoid being hit by a stray bullet. He watched as the deputies fired in all directions, occasionally being run down by the wall of incoming dogs when they stopped to reload, but mostly managing to hold their positions. The police dogs barked at their feet, held back on their leashes but eager to join the fray, until one by one they began to stop barking and stared quietly into the same spot in the woods. The deputies, busy defending themselves, did not notice, but Derek followed their gaze to the edge of the clearing, where he saw the Xolo, its eyes glowing yellow as it looked each of the police dogs in the eye in turn.

Derek called out to Millam, who was reloading his gun nearby. "That little shit!" Millam cried when he saw the hairless dog. Snapping the chamber shut on his revolver, he opened fire on the dog, who immediately disappeared into the woods, unharmed. Derek looked back to the police dogs, who also seemed to be unaffected. For a moment, he believed they had acted in time to save the dogs from the Xolo's influence. Then the police dogs turned back in unison, turning on their masters before the humans had a chance to react.

Men were thrown to the ground and had their throats torn out, others were accidentally shot as the deputies turned their fire inwards, confused by the sudden violence. Taking advantage of the confusion, more dogs burst from the woods, overwhelming the deputies. Derek watched helplessly as one of the police dogs ran circles around its former master, wrapping his leash around the man's legs until he fell to the ground. The dog ran into the woods, dragging the man behind him. His screams echoed from the woods as more dogs descended on him.

Derek pulled himself to his feet, scanning the scene around him. Deputies were overwhelmed as they ran out of ammo. Heloise and her team fired tranquilizer darts, but the few dogs they hit still had time to maul the animal control officers before they went down. Desperate and running out of ammo, the remaining animal control officers tried to fight off the dogs with their electric prods. The dogs ran wild over the clearing, knocking down the remaining officers.

Millam slapped open his revolver and dumped out the empty shells. He patted his pockets, searching desperately for more ammo and finding nothing. Grabbing Derek by the shoulder, he pulled him towards the edge of the clearing. "Come on, we gotta get outta here!"

Derek ran ahead of him, not knowing where exactly they would go in these endless woods, not even knowing how they would find their way back without the sheriff, who he had lost track of in the confusion, not knowing anything other than the primal need to escape from the dogs.

Over his shoulder he heard a scream and turned to see Millam being pulled backwards, seeming to levitate as he turned upside down. Derek saw a sapling snap upwards and the flash of a steel wire in the moonlight, the noose digging into Millam's ankle. Derek rushed back to help Millam as he hung helplessly in the leg trap, but the dogs were already on him, tearing at his face and body as he tried desperately to pull them away. Derek wished more than ever that the sheriff had given him a gun, even though they hadn't done much good for the others.

Seeing more dogs approaching, Derek turned back towards the edge of the clearing. The Xolo was waiting for him, watching the carnage with delight. Derek froze, looking for another way to escape. Dogs surrounded him on all sides, but stayed away from him, as if leaving Derek for their master. The Xolo stepped forward to accept their offering.

The other dogs started to move away, herding the remaining deputies and animal control officers to the far side of the clearing. Derek thought of running into the woods, but remembering how fast the Xolo could run, Derek knew it was pointless. Looking around the clearing, he saw the sturdy oak tree with the cage hanging from its branches. The trigger for the cage was just below, only about thirty feet from Derek.

He moved slowly, not wanting to provoke the Xolo. The animal moved forward at the same speed, as if it were playing with him. Derek stepped backwards, occasionally looking over his shoulder, moving until he had the trigger positioned between the Xolo and himself.

As the Xolo moved in, Derek turned and took off at a run. Risking a look over his shoulder, Derek saw its front paws miss the trigger by only an inch. Derek involuntarily paused, turning to watch the Xolo. He screamed as it readied itself to jump at him. As the dog prepared to push itself off the ground, its rear paws just barely brushed the trigger. It was enough for the cable attached to the trigger to loosen and pull away. Derek heard the cage swaying and creaking overhead as its massive bulk began to fall.

The Xolo leapt off the ground, its jaws open and its paws reaching towards Derek. He screamed and covered his face, sensing the cage would fall too slowly to stop the dog. As Derek squeezed his eyes shut, he heard a massive crash and the small, confused whine of the Xolo. Opening his eyes, he saw the Xolo trapped in the cage, its head pressed against the bars.

The Xolo let out a low, mournful howl, realizing it had no way to escape from the cage. The other dogs stopped at hearing their master's cries. The brief pause in the assault gave the remaining deputies and animal control officers enough time to fight back. They shot and tranquilized several dogs, but the remaining animals continued to attack. The Xolo continued howling, as if calling its compatriots. Dogs closed in on all sides, giving Derek no way to escape.

"Derek!" a voice called from nearby. He turned to see Heloise, surrounded by several dogs. She held up her dart gun and tossed it to Derek. He clumsily caught the gun, accidentally grabbing it with the barrel pointed towards his face. Once he turned it around, he looked up to see Heloise holding the dogs at bay with her electric prod. He held the gun up in confusion, wondering what she expected him to do to save her.

She must have seen the confused look on his face, since she turned to wave an arm at the Xolo. "Tranq him! He's the leader, remember?"

Derek nodded, then turned towards the Xolo, whose high-pitched howls still pierced the night. When Derek shoved the dart gun between the bars of the cage, the dog bared its teeth, as if intending to bite the barrel in half. As the dog lunged towards the gun, Derek pulled the trigger. The snarling and howling stopped immediately. The dog struggled to stay on its feet a moment longer, then passed out, slumping against the bars of the cage.

Remembering the other dogs, Derek quickly turned, raising the dart gun against the approaching horde. He found the dogs stopped in their tracks, looking at each other as if in confusion. The deputies took their chance and shot a few more of the dogs. The remaining dogs, frightened by the sound, scattered and ran in all directions. One deputy gave chase, slamming more bullets into his revolver. "Don't let 'em get away, let's finish this!"

A few other deputies followed, but were stopped by the sheriff, who held up one hand and pressed the other to a bleeding cut on his face. "That's enough for now." He motioned to the cage with his free hand. "We got their leader, that's enough."

The sheriff walked towards the cage, holding out a hand to Derek. "That was quick thinking with the cage."

Derek shrugged, feeling unable to take any credit in a situation he had unintentionally caused. "I just wish we could have got them sooner, Sheriff."

"So do I."

He nodded towards Millam, whose body hung upside down in the leg trap, his face mostly eaten away, his torn throat pouring out the last of his blood.

TWENTY

THE WOODS SEEMED TO STRETCH ON FOREVER, BOBBING AND WEAVING in front of Derek's eyes. Paramedics carried out body bags and injured officers on stretchers, while Heloise and her team carried out the still-unconscious Xolo in a full cage. The entire scene drifted in and out of focus, the view skewing wildly across the vast expanse of forest. Words scrolled across the bottom of the screen, too fast for Derek to read. A bright red logo burned from the corner, giving him a headache.

Sinking back into the couch, Derek forced himself to keep watching the newscast. It was the last thing he wanted to do after living through the real thing, but Alison thought it would be a good way for the kids to process their trauma.

Thankfully, the low-rent local news anchor was doing all the explaining for him. His monotone baritone droned over the footage, making the angles even more disorienting. "This was the scene outside Johnson's woods early this morning," he intoned, "where a series of brutal murders that have rocked the community came to an apparent end with the revelation that the culprits were a pack of wild dogs."

His drone cut off as the angle switched from the shaky helicopter footage to an even shakier handheld shot of the police leaving the woods at dawn. The camera chased a perky young reporter as she thrust a microphone at Sheriff Chambers. "Sheriff, can the people of the community rest easy knowing that the danger is over?"

Garth sighed, pulling a bloody cloth from the cuts on his cheek as he turned to the microphone. "Let me just say this," he said sternly, "as long as I am sheriff, there will never be another dog attack in this county."

Garth moved on without another word. Holding out her microphone to beg for an interview, the reporter moved past the sullen deputies and animal control officers, who purposefully turned their gaze away. Only the one person in civilian clothes was dumb enough to make eye contact. The reporter moved in like a shark sensing blood.

"Sir, could you tell me your role in all this?"

"No comment," Derek on the TV said.

Derek on the couch groaned. Seeing himself on TV made the entire scene even more surreal; it was more than he could handle. He tried to sink into the couch, as if trying to make himself invisible. He saw his children looking at him, Gracie lying on the floor, nervously petting the golden retriever, while Max lay back on the easy chair, as if he were also trying to sink into the furniture.

"You should have said your role was the hero," Alison said, moving closer to Derek on the couch.

Derek slumped lower. "More like the villain. It was my fault the Xolo was loose in the first place."

Alison pulled his head up. "Hey, you could have never guessed what would happen. No one could have. But it's over now and that's because of you." She pulled him closer and kissed his head.

Max rolled his eyes. "Oh, barf, I'm outta here." Although he looked even more exhausted than Derek, Max pulled himself out of the chair, limping slightly as he crossed the room.

"Oh, man, you just got home from the hospital and you already want to leave?!" Alison cooed, watching him hobble out to the hallway.

Derek groaned as the local news anchors started to repeat themselves, recapping the story while showing the same footage again. "Isn't there anything else on?"

Derek's phone began to ring, distracting him as Alison flipped through channels, each of which showed another news story about the dogs. Scooping his phone off the table, Derek groaned even louder when he saw the name on his screen. He glanced over at Alison, who looked at him sharply. "This will be the last time he calls; I promise."

Alison's look did not soften. "Are you telling me or yourself?"

Without answering, Derek stepped over Gracie and out of the room. He entered the study and shut the doors behind himself before answering the phone. "What the hell do you want?" he demanded.

"Oh, come now," Hector chided him, "what way is that to greet an old friend? Especially one who brought you such a lovely gift?"

"You're no friend of mine, Hector. And your gift was responsible for the deaths of a lot of people." Derek paced the study, trying not to let his anger get the best of him.

"Yes, I just saw the news," Hector's voice belied a sympathy that was obviously false. "I wanted to call and check in on you; I hope the publicity over this incident hasn't affected your interests."

Derek hoped that Hector could hear his eyes rolling over the phone. He had known immediately the purpose of this call, but hadn't expected Hector to be so blunt about it. "Well, the family and I are fine, Hector; thank you for asking."

"And what about your business? I heard you were close to striking a deal on a new development."

"Yeah, that. Turns out the attacks last night were on part of the property that the investors wanted to redevelop." He looked towards the computer that had brought him the news early that morning. "They decided to pull out until the publicity had died down."

Hector tutted in obviously fake sympathy. "Oh, that's too bad. I thought that might be the case, so I wanted to help you out in your time of need. I'd like to double my offer for the land in Mexico."

Derek sighed heavily. "Forget it, Hector. I'm giving that land back to the locals. It's too valuable to them; I'm not letting you tear it apart so your rich buddies have another place to golf."

The faux-sympathy disappeared from Hector's voice. "Now listen, Derek-"

"-No, you listen, Hector; I'm done dealing with you. So, if you ever call me again, or stop by my house, we're going to have problems. You understand?"

Before Hector could respond, Derek hung up the phone.

Hector set his cell phone on the small glass side table and smiled to himself. "Well, how do you like that? I offer him a deal, and he hangs up on me."

Reeve looked up from the gun he was cleaning on the pool deck. "I don't like it, boss. I don't like it at all." He set down the slide of a handgun he had just finished polishing and began to reassemble the body. Hector sipped a margarita while he watched Reeve work, then set the drink down on the glass-topped table next to his cell phone.

An idea began to formulate in his mind. After the incident at the log cabin, Hector and Reeve had realized that the dog responsible for the killings was the one Hector had so generously given to Derek. They had also realized that, despite his wife's insistence that he had given the animal to the pound, Derek must have dumped the unruly beast in the woods, where it had been allowed to go on its killing spree. Hector had planned to capture the animal to use as a bargaining chip: if Derek couldn't see reason in their negotiations, Hector would threaten to show the animal to the county sheriff.

But now that knowledge had come out publicly and Hector's plans were shot. Even his last-ditch effort to capitalize on Derek's sudden bad publicity had failed. Hector was desperate for that land, had to have it if he were going to keep his promises to the cartel back in Mexico, and he didn't want to find out what would happen if he didn't. But now that he saw Reeve packing up the equipment he had gathered for their initial expedition: rope, duct tape, taser, nets, and a few guns in case things went south, another plan formed in his mind.

He looked out over the pool and smiled. The rented mansion was built in a faux-Spanish style, and nestled at the foot of one of the larger mountains. Beyond the pool and the courtyard, he had a stunning view of the forest, but it was nothing compared to the view from Derek's land. From *his* land, Hector corrected himself, Derek just didn't know he would be giving it to Hector yet.

Hector held up a hand. "Hold on a moment." Reeve looked up from the clip he was sliding bullets out of. "Let's gather this stuff up again. I've got a new plan." Reeve leaned forward, obviously interested. "Let's keep an eye on Derek, wait for the right moment to drop in and pay him a visit. Then make him an offer he can't refuse."

Reeve smiled and began to slide bullets back into the clip. "Fuck yeah." He finished loading the clip and slapped it back into the handgun.

TWENTY-ONE

THE NIGHTS WERE GROWING COLDER. EACH NIGHT, MORE WIND BLEW through the trees, which were growing increasingly bare, leaving the dogs no place to take shelter. Those that had survived the assault by the humans had eventually regrouped deeper in the woods, the task of finding each other made more difficult without their leader. Some had been injured by the humans, just barely managing to escape with their lives. Most of those had died the next night, or in the days after, slowly succumbing to the wounds the human's weapons had pierced in their sides.

Others had been unable to keep up with the pack, their legs broken and injured by the humans. The dogs already knew that the humans were hunting them; the pack could not afford to slow down for the injured, or else they would risk losing every member, and thus losing their cause against the humans for good. To abandon these few members to the whims of the humans seemed cruel, abhorrent, antithetical to everything the Xolo had taught them, so the German shepherd had led the other dogs in killing them, biting into their necks as quickly as they could in order to kill them mercifully. For both the dogs they killed and the dogs that had been killed by the humans, the German shepherd led the crowd in eating them, making use of their bodies for the good of the pack.

Some of the dogs were reluctant to eat their own kind, but their hunger and the smell of the fresh blood quickly overcame their objections. As they ate the raw flesh, the German shepherd thought of the Xolo, who he was sure was eating even less well than them. The humans had taken him alive, the German shepherd was sure of that, but he was unsure why. Maybe they were planning to eat him, or maybe they were going to put him back in the place with the cages where he had freed most of the other dogs in the pack. But they had only captured the Xolo, as if specifically targeting him, and the German shepherd could only think they had figured out he was the leader.

Maybe they were doing it to punish and disorient the rest of the group, or maybe they had captured the Xolo in hopes he would lead them back to the others. In any case, the dogs would have purely selfish reasons for wanting to rescue their leader. But for the German shepherd, there was more. In his old life at the farm, he had slept in a small cage, exposed to the cold at night and the winds in winter, his master never heeding his howls to be let inside, his only companion the other German shepherd, with whom he had huddled together on many cold and sleepless nights.

The Xolo had rescued him from that life, had come down from the mountains when he didn't have to, had risked his own life simply because he had heard the howls of two desperate, trapped animals and had wanted to help. Now, the German shepherd could hear the Xolo's howls and had to respond. They were quiet, muffled by distance and by the walls of whatever prison the humans had put him in, but they were there, echoing inside the shepherd's soul, crying out to him for rescue. He simply could not stand by and let his leader die at the hands of the humans. To do so would be the death of the pack, either by the elements as winter approached, or at the hands of the humans when they returned to finish what they had started on that terrible night.

More than that, it would be a moral abandonment, an abandonment of all that had made them break the other dogs out of that strange prison, that had made them kill the boys who had invaded their territory, that had led them to fight so desperately against the humans and the traitor dogs who had hunted them. All of those had been German shepherds like himself, but most of them had been turned to their own side by the powers of the Xolo. None of them could be replacements for the companion he had lost, the warm companion of those long-gone winter nights in the farmer's cage, who had rushed out alone after the last of the intruders and had been killed by the humans who hunted them.

The German shepherd had heard the strange sound of the humans' weapons, followed by the whimpering of his companion, which had been silenced by another sound from their weapons. The German shepherd had waited for his companion for hours, until the other dogs were almost lost in the woods. That had given him a personal reason for wanting revenge on the humans, but in order to do that they would need to find their leader.

The German shepherd rallied the others: tired, injured, cold, and dispirited. He barked at them until they gathered in a clearing. They would rest here for the night; in the morning they would start their trek through the woods, moving in the direction the humans had taken the Xolo, not stopping until they picked up his scent again, then moving as one to rescue him, just as the Xolo had rescued all of them. If the humans tried to stop them, the dogs would have their revenge.

TWENTY-TWO

The imposing, gray brick building looked more like a prison than a pound. Heloise had always hated the ancient structure the county used to house the animal control department. The towering, windowless front wall looked like a medieval fortress, or a prison for the hapless animals trapped inside. The impression of a prison was made even stronger today by the unmarked black vans lined up in front of the building.

"What now?" Heloise muttered to herself as she walked from her truck to the entrance. For the past two weeks, the pressure on her had been enormous, as the sheriff, the media, and everyone else in town pressured her to find answers about the Xolo. They wanted to know what made it so aggressive, what led it to kill, how it seemed to be able to command an entire pack of dogs, and to confirm anecdotal reports that the Xolo had been able to hypnotize other dogs simply by looking them in the eye.

But Heloise had no idea how she was supposed to be able to do all that with her limited resources. In a perfect world, she would have done the testing at Dr. Greene's clinic, with her experience and expertise to guide the examinations, not to mention her more advanced lab and equipment. But Dr. Greene had been cremated late last week and her lab was still a crime scene, its ultimate fate uncertain once the police were done.

In its place, Heloise had only the ancient building in front of her, its weathered front a perfect metaphor for the aging, worn-out labs inside. Heloise shuddered as she stopped into the entryway, dreading the work ahead of her. For two weeks she had done every test she could think of on the Xolo, with no results. She supposed that was why the men in the black suits were here, though they said nothing to her as they rushed between the building and the unmarked vans, hauling in strange pieces of equipment she had never seen before.

"Excuse me, can I ask who you gentlemen are working for?" she asked one of the men as he returned from the building empty-handed.

"No, you may not, ma'am," the man said, tilting his mirrored sunglasses down at her in a look that only reflected her own astonishment. "That's classified information."

"Well, I don't allow anything to be '*classified*' in my own lab," she said, unsure whether producing her badge in front of the building she had managed for two years would be a sign of strength or weakness.

The man nodded in a way that showed no sympathy, only the most technical sense of understanding. "Our boss is right inside," he said, waving a hand as if she didn't know the way. She was going to ask who gave his boss permission to go inside, but she thought it was better to find out directly, leaving the man to return to his van.

As she stepped into the dark interior, she felt even more than usual like she was entering a cave, the room made damp and cool by the windowless stone walls. Her assistants and lab techs dropped their eyes as they hurried by in their regular work, trying to stay out of the way of the men in black suits who roamed the corridors.

Following two of these men into the main lab, Heloise searched for anyone who was obviously in charge, but saw only men in black suits or white coats clustered around various instruments. Heloise loudly dropped a briefcase full of papers she had been studying last night on a metal table, enjoying the look of surprise the men gave as they turned to her.

"Morning, gentlemen, do any of you mind telling me what's going on in my lab?"

One man turned slower than the rest, perhaps because of his more advanced age, which by his weathered face and shock of white hair, Heloise guessed to be somewhere around seventy. Perhaps because of his age, the man scrunched his face to squint at Heloise, an expression she didn't like regardless of its cause. "Aw, you must be Ms. Lopez," he said. "I've heard much about you. Unfortunately, however, this is no longer your lab." He immediately turned back to his work as if the conversation were finished.

"Oh? Then whose is it?" Heloise asked.

The man glanced up from his work and gave a small, distracted smile. "My apologies. I forgot to introduce myself." He pulled out a badge and read off the most prominent words on it. "Dr. Herman Pretorius, FBI."

He held out a gloved hand, which Heloise would have refused even if she weren't trying to process what he had just told her. "What does the FBI care about a few wild dog attacks?" she asked in disbelief.

Pretorius smiled and put his badge away. "About the attacks themselves, nothing. About the source of those attacks, a lot. We want to find out what made these animals so aggressive; we believe that some virulent new disease might be involved."

"Well, our tests have already eliminated rabies."

Pretorius smiled slowly. "Well, that's not exactly a new disease, is it?"

Heloise ignored him and opened her briefcase, holding out the stack of papers for his review. "Here's the results of our tests so far, you can see for yourself."

Holding the papers by one corner, Pretorius looked around at his men. "Thank you, Ms. Lopez, this should be most amusing." His men let out a round of laughter which Heloise tried to ignore. "Tell me, why do you choose to study this fascinating specimen in this…." He swept his arms to indicate the dark, cavernous space. "Well, let's just say you don't have the latest equipment."

Heloise held in a sigh. "Well, we'd certainly like to transfer the… fascinating specimen, as you say, to a more advanced facility, but we're worried about it dying in transport."

She looked at the Xolo, which lay on a steel operating table with IVs running through its side. "It's been on a hunger strike since we captured it, so we've been feeding it through a tube. But it doesn't like that, so we have to sedate it first. We're not sure if we could transfer the specimen while maintaining all that."

"I'm sure the federal government can handle it. But tell me, why are you so concerned about the specimen dying? Surely, he wouldn't care if you died."

"I know he wouldn't. But I want to find out what made him so aggressive; what gave him the ability to lead the other dogs."

"And you think that can only be done while he is alive?"

"Well, if it's a virus, it won't last much longer after his death, and we'd have a hard time studying it then."

"Uh huh. And what if it isn't a virus?"

"What else would it be?"

Pretorius didn't answer, but looked into the distance as if contemplating her question. "Well, perhaps it is better if we study the animal on its own turf…"

Heloise didn't know what he meant by this strange remark, just as she didn't know what he meant by this entire line of questioning. Right now, she had only one question of her own on her mind. "Since you say it's your lab now, what do you expect me and my people to do?"

"I still expect you to assist me in my researches," Pretorius said casually, as if he could expect nothing less.

Heloise had to physically swallow her pride. "And how do you want us to do that?"

Pretorius crossed the room and studied the Xolo for a long moment. "We'll need live animals to study the Xolo," he said distractedly.

"And how can I help with that?"

He turned slowly from the cage. "Well, your facility is full of them, is it not?"

Heloise didn't like at all the grin that slowly spread across his face.

"I wanna know who the hell gave these assholes permission to take over my lab!"

Garth winced as Heloise pounded her fist on his desk. He held his head, which throbbed with last night's hangover and the still-healing scars of the dog bites. "They gave themselves permission!" he roared, his head pounding with each word, "If the feds claim jurisdiction, there's not a damn thing I can do about it."

Heloise sighed and sat in the chair across Garth's desk. "I don't know what kind of jurisdiction the feds have over animal attacks," she sighed.

Garth shrugged, holding his head in his hands. He was still exhausted from the dog hunt and all the media attention that had come with it. On top of that, he and his men had been busy preparing for the car accidents, overdoses, and lost trick-or-treaters that were sure to overrun the town tonight. The last thing he wanted to do was field complaints about a federal agency he could do nothing about.

He groaned slowly, dragging his hands across his face. "People are saying it could be some kind of new virus that makes the dogs crazy; cooked up by the Chinese, just like they did a few years ago."

"Well, it looks to me like they're testing for black magic or some shit." Heloise shuddered, thinking of all she had seen in the last few days. "That Pretorius is a weirdo. He keeps asking for live animals and won't tell me what he's using them for."

Garth raised his hands, as if physically waving the words away. He had heard this kind of thing too much and had no more patience for it. "Listen, Heloise, I don't like these outsiders any more than you do, but the more you cooperate with them, the sooner they'll be gone."

Heloise jumped out of her chair. "I've been cooperating with these assholes, and they're still no closer to being gone. Part of me wishes they would just chop the damn thing's head off and be done with it."

"Yeah, well that makes two of us."

Storming out of the lobby, Heloise blew past deputies transporting stacks of paperwork, an occasional cuffed criminal, or trays of doughnuts and coffee. Halloween decorations festooned the walls; ghosts and zombies hung between posters warning parents about the dangers of razor blades in candy and the higher risk of traffic deaths this night.

As Heloise moved through the breezeway, she passed Derek on his way in. "Hey, Loise, long time, no see." Heloise thought it had not been so long, until she realized that all the times she had seen Derek lately had been on the news. She quickly returned the greeting as they shook hands.

"You here to see the sheriff?" she asked him.

Derek nodded. "I want to make sure he's doing everything he can to protect the community. There will be lots of kids wandering the streets tonight. If the dogs did decide to come back…"

"I don't think you have to worry about that. We've still got the Xolo safely locked away."

"Well, I've been thinking; what if the pack can function without him?"

"Then they haven't been functioning too much lately. Besides, I'm sure Dr. Frankenstein will get to the bottom of that mystery soon." Heloise's phone began to ring. She grumbled as she fished it out. "Speaking of which…." The screen on her phone read simply PRETORIUS.

"Good luck with the sheriff," Heloise said as she leaned on the outside door. "I don't think you'll find him in the most accepting of moods."

She saw Derek nod his thanks as she pushed her way outside and answered her phone. "What is it?" she demanded of Pretorius. Any pretense of cordiality had disappeared long ago.

"I need you at the laboratory right away," Pretorius demanded. "I have a job for you."

"Gee, doc, can't one of your G-boys pick up your laundry? I was planning to get home, hand out candy, and watch the monster movie marathon on channel five."

"I promise I have something far more frightening than any movie."

Heloise wasn't sure if the dry hint of menace in his voice was meant to be cruelly ironic or was wholly unintentional. Either way, the last place Heloise wanted to be was in the lab Pretorius had made his own. But, remembering Garth's advice about cooperating with the G-men until they were gone, she sighed heavily, told Pretorius she would be right over, and headed for her van.

When Heloise arrived at the lab, she at first thought everyone else had left. The black vans were still parked outside, but the main entrance and corridor seemed abandoned. Hearing voices from the main lab, Heloise entered, only to be greeted by a long sheet of plastic hanging across the room, obscuring most of the lab from view. Outlined by harsh work lights, Heloise could see the silhouettes of the government team working on the other side, but couldn't tell what they were doing. Her own team had all left over the last few days, either disgusted with Pretorius' actions or fired by him when they refused to carry out his orders.

Peeling back the curtain, Heloise stepped to the other side to see what was happening. Pretorius was still dressed in the same gray suit he had been wearing every day since he had first taken over the lab, but now he was wearing a lab coat instead of his usual trench coat. When he heard Heloise enter, he turned back and beckoned to her with one leather glove-clad hand.

"Heloise, I've been waiting," he said without a hint of impatience. "We need more live animals for our experiments."

"The entire building is full of live animals, what's wrong with them?"

Pretorius looked around at his men, as if silently sharing a laugh. "They, uh, did not meet our requirements for this particular experiment."

"Forget it, Pretorius. I'm not helping you anymore until I know what the hell you're up to."

Pretorius stared blankly at her for a long moment. "Very well."

Beckoning her to follow, he led her to a surgical table, where the Xolo was splayed out, fully awake but stuck with IVs and tubes on every side. The other agents moved quickly around the dog, reading data from instruments Heloise had never seen before. "What the hell is all this?" Heloise asked.

Before Pretorius could answer, another G-man entered, dragging a golden retriever on a leash. "Got that stray you were asking for-" the man said, cutting himself off when he saw Heloise. Pretorius gave him a hard look, then motioned to a spot in front of the table, just next to the Xolo's head.

"What the fuck is this, Pretorius? You have your men just kidnapping dogs off the street?!" Heloise yelled, looking at the dog's collar. The dog pulled at its leash as the G-man drew it closer to the Xolo, as if actively cowering away from the unconscious dog.

In response to Heloise's question, Pretorius only shrugged. "We ran out of specimens here."

"How the fuck did you run out of specimens? There are dozens of dogs in this facility."

"There were."

"And what did you do to them? Kill them?"

Pretorius looked down his nose at her as if the answer should be obvious.

"That's it; I don't give a fuck what you guys are trying to do; I'm calling the cops."

Pretorius and his men shared another laugh. Heloise immediately realized the irony of threatening to call the police on what were essentially the federal police, but she didn't care. There had to be something Garth could do about these intruders.

As she made her way for the exit, Heloise realized another, more immediate problem with her plan. The G-men had arranged themselves in a loose circle, blocking every possible way of escape. One of the men stepped forward, pulling out a gun that Heloise was sure would be the last thing she would ever see. She stepped backwards, knowing any direction she took would only bring her into the path of more G-men. As the man raised the gun and aimed, Heloise squeezed her eyes shut for a long moment, so long that she eventually realized the shot was not coming.

When she opened her eyes, the G-man had his gun trained on the Xolo, which one of Pretorius' research assistants was partially freeing from its bonds. As the G-man holding the leash dragged the golden retriever in front of the table, the Xolo began to slowly awaken, sniffing the air as its eyes gradually opened. One research assistant rushed to point something that looked like the barrel of a ray gun from an old sci-fi movie at the Xolo's head while other assistants rushed to check readouts.

The G-man held the retriever in place while it struggled to escape. The Xolo slowly awakened and sat up as much as its remaining bonds would allow, locking eyes with the retriever, which suddenly grew calm and still. As the Xolo stared deeper into the retriever's eyes, the researchers gathered closer around the monitors, which began to display wildly increasing readings. Heloise heard alarms going off and saw the look of excitement in the researcher's faces.

The retriever began to go as wild as the readings on the monitor, whining and growling as its entire body began to shake. Finally, the Xolo let out a single sharp bark, like a drill sergeant's command. Instantly, the retriever turned to the nearest research assistant and bared his fangs, a growl building up as he prepared to strike. The G-man holding the leash held him back, but the animal still pushed forward, the research assistant stepping back in turn and almost knocking over the machinery.

Just as the dog drew within range of the man, a shot rang out. The retriever fell to the ground, blood pooling from a hole in its neck. The G-man stood motionless, smoke emanating from his gun, no expression on his face.

Heloise stared in disbelief at his boss. "Pretorius, God damn you-"

"Quiet," he demanded softly, "the good part is just beginning."

The Xolo stood up, pulling at its bonds in order to look over the edge of the table at the dying dog. As the dogs locked eyes again, the retriever once again grew still and calm, its death thrashings coming to an end. Even its heartbeat slowed, judging by the slowing of the blood flowing from its neck. Heloise stared in disbelief as the Xolo's eyes began to glow.

Pretorius motioned for his assistants to get in place, but there was no need: they were already furiously moving instruments into place like news photographers desperate not to miss a shot. Steam began to rise from the dying retriever's nose and mouth and from the hole in its neck. Heloise's eyes widened in disbelief as the Xolo breathed in the steam, its own eyes glowing brighter the more it breathed in. The scientists stared in horror at their monitors as the readings went off the chart. As the Xolo breathed in the last of the steam, the retriever died.

"What the hell is this?" Heloise asked.

Pretorius did not answer. "Clean it up," he said simply to his assistants, one of whom dragged away the dog's body while others printed out readings from their machinery or took notes in lab notebooks. The Xolo watched them all impassively, its eyes glowing.

Heloise tried again. "You mind telling me what the hell all this is, Pretorius?"

"That's what we're trying to find out. It seems the Xolo is capable of taking control of other dogs. And of absorbing their life force."

Heloise eyed him suspiciously. "Is that a scientific term?"

Pretorius looked into the Xolo's glowing eyes, as if hoping he could also be hypnotized. "There is no scientific term for the phenomena we are studying. At least, not yet."

"So, it's not some new virus?"

"It is the answer to questions that man has puzzled over for ages: what is the nature of our spirit? What happens to us when we die?"

Heloise looked around at Pretorius' men, all of whom calmly carried on with their work during this speech. "And the FBI is interested in the answers to those questions?"

Pretorius laughed scornfully. "The FBI is interested in anything that will give the American government a new weapon: mind control, life force absorption, psychic healing, all of these could be used in combat. But I am only interested in knowledge, the knowledge of worlds beyond ours, the knowledge of how to control life and death, the knowledge of the principle of life, and you can have the honor of helping me discover that knowledge."

"How?" Heloise was only interested in having the honor of sending this psycho to jail, but she had a feeling he was about to reveal some critical piece of information that would help her do that.

Pretorius did not disappoint. "You can help by bringing me fresh souls. More dogs, to use in my experiments. And dying animals of all types."

"Something tells me you would use humans if you could."

Pretorius shrugged. "We need all the data we can. Especially now, when our tests will be most effective."

"What do you mean?"

Pretorius looked at her as if he couldn't believe her ignorance. "You surprise me, Loise. You wanted to rush home and celebrate this holiday, I assumed you would know its history."

"Halloween? What does that have to do with your little science experiment?"

Pretorius' grin of disbelief turned into a sneer of active malice. "Don't you know the significance of the date? The ancient Celts believed it was the time when the veil between the worlds of the living and the dead was at its thinnest. Since the Xolo takes its powers from the dead, I believe this night is also when his power will be at its strongest."

Heloise's mind went back to her meeting with Derek, how he had worried about whether the pack was still active. She wondered if tonight they would be active again. "Forget it, Pretorius, I'm not going along with this. You want to do your crazy experiments, you do them on your own."

As Heloise turned towards the exit, several of the G-men stood to block her way. "I'm afraid I can't let you do that," she heard Pretorius say, followed by the snap of his fingers.

The G-man with the gun held it up just enough to show he meant business, then grabbed Heloise rudely by the shoulder. As he tried to pull her across the room, she stood her ground, casting her glance downwards at a metal rack near the exit lined with cans labelled BEAR SPRAY. Holding back a smile, she waited for the man to step past her and begin to pull her towards the doctor.

Allowing herself to be pulled back, Heloise used the motion of her body to disguise the action of reaching for the bear spray. As she felt her hand close around the enormous metal can, she let herself tumble backwards into the G-man, giving in to the force he exerted on her arm. The sudden application of her weight, combined with the force of his own pull, sent him tumbling backwards, colliding with a metal rack of equipment.

As the man struggled to regain his footing, Heloise spun out of his grasp, raising the can of bear spray as she did so. As the man lunged towards her, Heloise squeezed and sprayed directly into his eyes. The G-man fell back screaming, dropping his gun as both hands instinctively raised to defend his eyes from further attack.

As the other G-men closed in on her, Heloise picked up his gun, holding up the gun in one hand, the can of bear spray in the other. "Back off, fuckers."

The G-men stopped in their tracks, casting confused looks at Pretorius. The doctor only looked bored. "She won't shoot." He cast a cold glance at Heloise. "She doesn't have the heart of a killer."

His stare was so intense and his confidence so certain that for a moment she was sure he was right. Feeling her confidence waver, she pointed the gun at the Xolo on the table. "Any of you take one step closer, and I'll kill your little science experiment. You know I'll do it, Pretorius, I hate that fucking thing even more than I hate you."

Pretorius almost looked impressed. "Very well," he sighed, "let her go." He waved a hand dismissively at his G-men, who backed away from the exit.

For a moment, Heloise stood where she was, unsure if this was another trick. "You all better be gone when I get back," she rasped, slowly backing towards the door. Although none of the men moved, she kept her weapons on them until she had ducked under the sheet of plastic.

Once she was out of sight of the G-men, she turned and ran for the door, then dashed through the night air, not stopping until she was in her van and on her way to safety and freedom.

TWENTY-THREE

AFTER THE ANIMAL CONTROL OFFICER FLED THE LAB, THE RESEARCHERS and special agents in the room stayed silent for a long moment. When they heard the outer door slam and knew that she was gone, they let out a collective sigh of relief that echoed against the stone walls. First-year research assistant Charles "Chuck" Rosen was the first to break the silence. "What do we do now, boss?" he asked Pretorius.

Pretorius shrugged, not even bothering to look his subordinate in the eye. "Like she said, we get out of here. I'm sure she's on her way to fetch that country bumpkin sheriff. We don't need that sort of trouble getting in the way of our experiments." He turned to the men and women still gathered around the equipment. "Pack up the Xolo and let's go."

Peggy Castillo, a research supervisor a few years older than Chuck, looked up from her monitor with a look of concern. "I don't think that's wise. The Xolo's not responding to the IVs anymore. If we take him off for too long, he could die."

For the first time, Pretorius betrayed emotion, a sudden spark of anger that made Chuck scared on Peggy's behalf. "How is that possible?" he bellowed, "the Xolo just fed!"

Peggy straightened her glasses, trying to hide the hurt that snuck across her face. "You see, sir, he hadn't absorbed in so long that the extra energy only drove his system into overdrive." She looked over at the Xolo, who was again lying down on the steel table, the glow in his eyes fading. "His body is burning through energy so quickly now, he'll need another dose soon to stabilize him."

Pretorius nodded grimly, looking out over the gathered research assistants and agents. "Well then, let's give it to him."

Knowing what was coming, Chuck willed himself to be invisible, afraid that any movement would only attract more attention to himself. Pretorius raised a finger that travelled slowly across the gathered men and women. Perhaps angered at him for being the first to speak up, Pretorius' finger settled on Chuck. "You," he addressed Chuck bluntly, pointing the same finger towards the door. "Go fetch me another life to feed the Xolo."

Chuck froze, looking around at the other men, who backed away as if he were diseased. "Me, sir?" Chuck said stupidly, unsure of what else to say.

Pretorius stared at him impatiently. "Well, Jerry can't very well do it." He pointed to the agent who the animal control officer had hit with bear spray. He still lay on the floor, holding his eyes and moaning as he rocked back and forth.

Chuck still felt the unexplainable need to stall, no matter how much it pissed off Pretorius. "But the pound is empty," he stammered, unable to think of any other explanation for his inability to produce a fresh life for this madman's experiments.

Pretorius only stared impatiently. "But the woods aren't. Find me anything: a turtle, a rabbit, a fucking squirrel, and bring it back quickly." He turned to the others. "The rest of you, start packing up."

Chuck let out a low sigh, feeling relief from a worry that he didn't even know he had and still couldn't explain. As the others scrambled to disassemble their equipment, Chuck headed for the door, waiting for further instructions that never came.

As his assistant left the building, Pretorius approached the table, standing over the nearly comatose Xolo. "As for you, my dear…" he whispered, "You're going to have to learn how to live only on what you can get for yourself." He yanked the IV out of the dog's side, drawing a spray of blood. The dog sat up a little, letting out a terrible howl.

The German shepherd's ears pricked up at a sudden, familiar sound: a mournful wail echoing through the woods ahead. A moment later, he also caught a familiar scent, which was almost immediately blown away by a breeze.

Still, it was enough to give the other dogs hope. For weeks he had led them through the woods, using only the faintest scent of their old leader to guide them. Often the scent had seemed to grow weaker the further they travelled. The other dogs had begun to lose hope; even the German shepherd had begun to lose faith in his own abilities, but now there was evidence that they had come the right way, that their goal was just ahead of them.

The German shepherd sniffed the air, gulping up the chilly night wind, feeling like he could inhale the moonlight that turned the woods around him into a sea of silver. He felt as if his sense of smell was stronger tonight than it had ever been before, as if his connection to the old leader was more immediate, more powerful than ever.

Smelling out the correct path, the German shepherd led the other dogs forward, his mouth salivating in excitement.

Chuck stepped into the chilly Halloween air with a low grumble. Buttoning his coat, he stepped off the low concrete steps of the side entrance and walked past the metal picnic table and circle of flattened grass that served for these backwoods hicks as their smoking area. Chuck almost sneered at the plastic bin surrounded by rain-soaked butts as he passed through the circle to the woods beyond. This run-down lab and the desolate countryside surrounding it were exactly the kind of scene Chuck had wanted to escape when he had left the suburbs of Green Bay for college and eventually graduate school at Stanford. Chuck had thought that a post-graduate opportunity with the FBI in their secretive Biological Weapons Research division would have brought him to many exciting places, but instead he was right back in the endless country sprawl he had tried to escape.

Chuck shuddered as he reached the edge of the woods. He cast a final look back at the lab behind him. Even the shabby brick wall was more appealing than the wilderness. Chuck had always hated nature, too unpredictable. He preferred the certainty and security of working in a lab. As he stepped into the woods and out of the reach of the halogen lights on the side of the building, he realized he had forgotten to even bring a flashlight. Pretorius forbade them from bringing their cellphones to work, so his was still sitting in the locker room in the lab, and he didn't dare incur Pretorius' wrath by going back inside.

Thankfully, the moon was full and bright, and enough of its beams pierced the forest canopy to light his way over the uneven ground. But light his way to what? Chuck realized he had also forgotten to bring anything to catch an animal with: a net, a box, anything. But hopefully even a small life would be enough to satisfy what Pretorius insisted on calling the Xolo's "life energy," no matter how unscientific that term sounded to Chuck. In fact, most of the things Pretorius said sounded downright crazy to Chuck, as if Pretorius were a medieval wizard instead of a modern doctor.

Chuck wasn't even sure if his central theory about the Xolo leading a pack of killer dogs was scientifically feasible, no matter what hypotheses the incompetent county sheriff and sensationalist local news tried to foist on a gullible and unsuspecting public. Chuck knew the doctor had a reputation for being brilliant, which was why the FBI had put him in charge of their organic weapons projects, but-

A rustling from the woods interrupted his chain of thought. Chuck suddenly realized he had travelled much deeper into the forest than he had intended to; the building behind him was now entirely lost behind the foliage. He found himself in a large clearing. As he looked around, he saw no signs of life, not even the frogs or toads he had intended to catch. But something was making the noise he had heard. As he stopped to listen, it came again.

Chuck stood in the center of the clearing, holding his breath as the rustling grew closer. Whatever was making the noise, it was a lot bigger than a toad. A large bush began to shake in time with the rustling, then parted as a shadowy form emerged from the woods. Chuck almost screamed until he realized the animal was nothing more than a German shepherd. The beast had probably wandered off from its owner at some terrible crumbling farmhouse on the edge of the woods. The stupid animal emerged from the brush and stood staring up at him.

"Well, I guess you'll work for our experiments," Chuck mumbled. "Would you like to come with me? C'mon, boy!"

To Chuck's surprise, the dog drew closer, sniffing the air cautiously as it stepped forward. Chuck crouched slowly, holding out a hand that the dog sniffed slowly. "That's it, good boy. You wanna come inside?" The dog barked once, as if in answer. More rustling immediately came from the woods all around him.

Chuck turned to see dogs entering the clearing from all directions. He stared in confusion as they circled around him, staring at him eagerly. "What, did you guys all run away from the pound together?" The dogs moved in on him, smelling his clothes and hands. "Come on, guys, I don't have anything to eat…"

As the dogs slowly closed in on him, Chuck began to recall some of the stories he had heard when he was first deployed to this backwater burg. He began to think that some of the sheriff's stories weren't so crazy after all. Slowly he began to put two and two together. The bark from the German shepherd hadn't been an answer, but a summons to the rest of his pack. The smell that the dogs were so eagerly sniffing was the smell of the Xolo he had been working on in the lab. These dogs must be the remainder of his pack, come to rescue their old master.

As if angry at him for discovering their secret, the dogs began to growl at him, baring their fangs in unison. Chuck's mind reeled through the knowledge acquired during his years of education, but found nothing that could help him. All he could think to do was hold up his hands, as if they could defend him. Instead, they lured the dogs onwards, who leaped at the waving appendages as if they were hanging pieces of meat. Chuck could only scream as the dogs piled on him.

Peggy Castillo looked up from the monitors she was carefully unplugging, trying to determine if she had really heard what she thought she had. The sound's second coming a moment later confirmed it, even if it was quickly cut off. "That sounded like Chuck," she said to anyone who would listen, which at the moment was hardly anyone. The other researchers were tending to the Xolo or packing up their equipment while the agents were mostly tending to Jerry, one helping him to his feet, one trying to wipe the spray from his eyes, and several standing around not helping. Pretorius, for his part, was watching all of this with an angry scowl. He pretended to ignore Peggy, but turned when she repeated her observation.

"What sounded like Chuck?" he asked drily.

"That scream; I think he might be in trouble."

"Well, I guess you better go check on him, shouldn't you?" Pretorius asked as if this were a challenge.

Trying to ignore Pretorius' sneer, Peggy turned towards the side exit she had seen Chuck leave through. She had always been one to face a challenge, from completing the rigorous Synthetic Biology program at MIT, to being accepted at the secretive biological weapons program at the FBI, then rising to become the head of a research team. She had been the first Hispanic woman, and often the first woman at all, to achieve most of these honors, but Peggy put more pride in the honors than the firsts; her accomplishments were hers alone. Still, she thought as she opened the side door onto endless darkness, dealing with Pretorius might have been her greatest challenge yet. The man was brilliant, yes, but secretive even for a government scientist, as is he were afraid of what she might tell his superiors.

Her thoughts were cut off by a massive bulk that leaped from the darkness and smashed into her chest, knocking her off her feet. Her head smashed into the concrete, silencing her thoughts completely. The German shepherd landed on her chest and immediately tore into her throat, bringing Peggy's thoughts, and her brilliant academic career, to a sudden and premature end in a spectacular fountain of blood.

One of the G-men attending to Jerry, his attention attracted by the noise, turned and saw the fountain of blood, as well as the furiously snarling beast that produced it. Letting out a shout, he ran towards the dog and the open door beyond it, trying to pull his gun from his holster as he ran.

The researchers, seeing the dog eating their friend, mostly froze in terror, though one ran towards the door as she saw more dogs dashing up the concrete steps. She tried to push the door shut just as the G-man raised his gun at the German shepherd. The shepherd turned from the body it was consuming in a flash, biting down hard on the G-man's forearm. He screamed as his arm twisted back, his muscles squeezing involuntarily and pulling off a shot, which landed in the stomach of another of the G-men attending to Jerry. "What's going on?!" the still-blinded man yelled as he heard his friend land on the ground next to him.

At the same moment, the researcher at the door succeeded in pushing the heavy metal door shut, only for it to immediately burst open under the combined onslaught of the dogs colliding with it, knocking her slender frame backwards as it swung open. She tripped over the mutilated body of Peggy Castillo and landed hard on her back, knocking the wind out of her and stunning her just long enough for dogs to swarm around her. She screamed as they began to tear into her, but her fellow researchers were heedless of her screams. The remaining dogs came pouring in through the open door, each of them seeming to pick a target and immediately honing in on them.

The remaining G-men tried to raise their guns against the dogs, but they were too slow, the dogs biting at the arms they had learned to see as a threat from the horrible men who had kidnapped their leader and killed their brethren in the woods. Perched on his metal table, the Xolo watched impassively as his pack took down the men with guns.

Panicked researchers scrambled as the dogs chased them down, tackling them into the equipment they had once held so dear, their blood covering the monitors and keyboards as the dogs tore into them, the equipment sparking and shorting out as the red liquid leaked inside.

Jerry, still blind, lay on the floor where he had fallen, trying to crawl to his comrade who had fallen next to him. Blood coated the floor, making forward movement nearly impossible as his hands could only slide across the liquid. "What's happening?!" he yelled, his voice nearly drowned out by the screams and commotion coming from every corner of the room.

After a great struggle, Jerry reached his fallen comrade, one sticky, blood-soaked hand slapping across his friend's torso. "What's happening?!" he yelled again, shaking his comrade to get him to answer. Hearing no response, he moved his hand up the body to check for breathing. As he reached the spot where his neck should be, he found only a wet, ragged mass whose flappy edges slid gelatinously between his fingers.

A burst of air on his fingers was made warmer by the cold blood on his hands. A moment later, he felt drops of saliva dripping on his fingers, then the crush of the sharp fangs that had a moment earlier been tearing into the neck of his dead comrade. Before he could pull back his fingers, he felt those fangs close in around them, swallowing his fingers to the first knuckle.

His hand pulled back automatically. He could feel his blood spewing from the stumps and mixing with that of his dead friend, the dog's mouth lapping it up as the fangs followed the bleeding stumps towards his own body. Jerry tried to hide the bleeding hand under his torso, desperately hoping that would be enough to block the smell, but it was too late. He screamed as he felt the fangs slide into the back of his shoulder, followed a moment later by more fangs sliding into every inch of his back. Jerry screamed as they all tore in separate directions, ripping his flesh in large strips as they burrowed their way around his ribs and towards his organs.

Pretorius watched all of this with clinical fascination. Even if he hadn't been surrounded by dogs on all sides, he was too intrigued by this display of the dogs' hunger and cunning to even think of running away. Only when one of the enormous Rottweilers approached him, its teeth dripping with blood, did he wake up to the reality of the situation.

He looked around for a way out, but realized that the dogs had surrounded him. He thought his best bet was to fight, or perhaps to hold the Xolo that lay on the table behind him hostage, but when the Rottweiler let out a furious bark, blood-soaked spit spraying from its mouth, the rational part of his mind was consumed by fear. He turned to run, but was almost immediately overtaken by the Rottweiler, whose weight knocked him over, splaying him across a stool in front of the Xolo.

Pretorius screamed as he felt more dogs joining the fray, their needle-sharp teeth sinking into his back and tearing away the flesh. The Xolo sat up, even more fascinated by this carnage than Pretorius himself had been just a moment before. As the other dogs tore into him, the Xolo's eyes began glowing yellow, its gaze narrowing on Pretorius' eyes. The doctor observed with merely clinical interest as steam flowed from his own nose and mouth, which the Xolo breathed in with evident satisfaction. It dawned on Pretorius that he was experiencing first-hand the phenomena he had been studying for years: the transmutation of life energy from one being into another.

He surrendered to it, making clinical observations of all that he felt and experienced. His own vision faded away, his body growing still as he left the sensations of pain behind. He felt his consciousness meld with that of the Xolo. He saw visions of ancient temples and sacred ceremonies, over which the Xolo, bedecked in ceremonial robes, stood lord and master. Pretorius marveled at the horrible beauty of these scenes until he realized his own position in them. He was not a high priest or even the objective observer he was used to being, but the helpless victim strapped to the stone altar.

In that moment, he felt, more than logically realized, that through the process of absorbing his life energy, his consciousness would not be permanently melded with that of the beast, or even mercifully destroyed. His consciousness, and all the essence of what he had once been, would be *enslaved*, made subject to the will and passions of the Xolo, his mind only an instrument for the consumption of more souls, his consciousness made witness and unwilling participant in a thousand unnamable horrors, and a million unmentionable degradations.

He fought to resist this indignity, his consciousness instantly returning to his physical body. With his body returned the pain. He felt every bite and tear as the dogs ripped into him, and he was by now too weak and injured to fight back. The steam still rose from his mouth and nose, and from other openings beyond his field of vision which the dogs had opened up, and the Xolo breathed it all in greedily, its eyes glowing brighter than ever. The dog stood up as it absorbed the last of the steam, breaking through its bonds with newfound strength. Pretorius was still scientist enough to feel vindicated in his theory that the Xolo had needed only a single life to reclaim its former strength, but his victory was short-lived with the remembrance that that life was his.

He felt himself slipping into darkness, and realized with relief that he had escaped an eternity of servitude in the mind of the Xolo. He closed his eyes, letting himself sink into that darkness, letting even the pain of the dogs consuming him slip away. As he settled into the darkness, he felt himself supported and comforted.

He opened his eyes and found himself in a cool, dark cave. Too late, he realized the cave was the same one from his vision, where the Xolo presided over weird, ancient rites. The dog's face appeared above his own, opening its mouth to absorb his life energy, and this time, there was nothing he could do to stop it; he was bound to a horrible stone altar, unable to struggle or escape.

As his consciousness was enslaved by that of the dog, his mind received its final sense impressions as an independent entity, though already they were from the point of view of the dog, tinted by the yellow glow of its eyes. Just before his mind was utterly absorbed and permanently enslaved in the greater mind of the Xolo, Pretorius' final earthly visions were those of his own body, being torn to shreds and eaten by the pack of ravenous dogs. He could only make a final clinical observation as the dogs ripped open his belly, fighting over the rights to consume his intestines.

TWENTY-FOUR

Demons and ghosts haunted the streets, occasionally emerging from the shadows to approach the dimly lit homes. Derek looked nervously out the kitchen window, clutching the curtains to his side as if trying to disguise himself as one of those evil spirits. He sensed danger, and not of the supernatural kind which the children's costumes had originally been designed to ward off. He feared for the safety of the children who wandered the neighborhood, many alone and unsupervised. The endless woods were just at the edge of the community, threatening to spill out the remaining dogs if a hapless child wandered too close.

"There's nothing to worry about, honey."

Even the soothing sound of Alison's voice almost made Derek jump out the window. He hadn't realized how tense he had been. He released the tension now, letting out a long sigh. He turned around, dropping the curtain he hadn't realized he had been holding around himself. "Did you hear that?" he asked, almost apologetically.

"Hear what, honey?"

"It sounded like a howl."

Alison put her hands on her hips. "Well, it is Halloween night, maybe it was just a werewolf." She put up a hand as he started to object. She had heard all of his theories about how the pack might have survived, how they might regroup without their leader. "Honey, it's okay. It's over." She took him by the shoulders. "Everything's gonna be alright."

He turned back towards the window, not wanting to push her away. "I know, honey, I'm just worried about the kids." Max and Gracie had been trick-or-treating around the neighborhood for about an hour now, and at their insistence (as well as Alison's) had gone without him. It was the first time either of the kids had been out since the night of the attack in the woods, and Derek couldn't help but imagine horrible things happening. As he watched through the window, every shape that strode towards the house became a policeman coming to tell Derek that his children would never come home again, while the costumes of the children passing on the street morphed them into even worse monsters. The ninja and the princess shambling up the driveway at first seemed like vague, twisted figures, undead versions of themselves crawling up from the dark spot in the woods where they had died. As they stepped into the amber glow of the porch light, Derek finally recognized the forms of his own children and rushed to the front door.

As Derek opened the door, Max was pulling off the black hood of his ninja outfit. Maybe it was just the effect of the Halloween costume, but to Derek his son suddenly looked shockingly young, like the child he had been just a few years earlier. The shock and exhaustion of the attack suddenly seemed gone from his face, along with the weeks of trauma that Derek knew his son had been silently processing, despite his attempts to hide it from Derek and his mother. Max had told Derek that he chose the costume because it would prevent anyone in the neighborhood from seeing his face, avoiding the risk of them recognizing him from the news, but Derek thought the reason ran deeper, that it was a chance to hide himself completely, for the first time since the attack, to truly put his identity and his recent experiences away and to fully submerge himself in one of the great rituals of childhood. Whatever it was, it had obviously worked: Max looked the happiest Derek had seen him in weeks.

The Max of a few weeks ago returned instantly when Derek asked if the kids still wanted to go to the Halloween party at their school. "Yeah, any chance to spend more time at school," Max said, rolling his eyes. Derek laughed and tousled his hair in a way he knew Max hated.

"Do you mind driving them?" Alison asked Derek, taking a seat on the couch with her laptop.

Derek was already heading for the drawer with his car keys. "You gonna get some writing done?" he asked, eyeing her laptop.

Alison sat back and put her feet up on the coffee table, dragging the remote to herself with her foot as she did so. "Yup. Over the channel five monster movie marathon. You care to join me when you get back?"

As he pulled on his coat, Derek could see Max pretending to gag himself in the corner of his vision. "I think I'll pass. I've had enough scares to last a lifetime."

Derek grabbed his keys and led the kids towards the car, making sure to lock the door behind himself.

Because the various neighborhoods of Sunnydale were either spread out across acres of farm land or densely packed in small mountain developments like Derek's, the elementary school was kind enough to throw a Halloween party for their students on the school grounds. So, once the farm kid's parents had driven them as far as they cared to in their trucks and tractors between the neighboring farms, and once the mountain kids had walked to as many houses as they could before they reached the edge of the forest, the face of a steep cliff or the winding path of an unwalkable county road, they would all pile into their parents' cars and spend (mostly unwillingly) another few hours of their week at school while their parents cuddled up at home with scary movies and the remaining candy they had been unable to hand out.

Derek had agreed to give Max and Gracie a ride to this party mostly so he would have a chance to look over the neighborhood. While the kids fought in the backseat, Derek scanned the nearly empty streets, looking for the danger he knew was still out there.

As he drove down the road that led to the bottom of the mountain and eventually to the elementary school, Gracie began loudly shrieking about Max taking some of her candy. Secretly relieved that Max seemed to be back to his old self, Derek turned back in his seat, fulfilling his role in establishing order. Just as he was getting into a prepared lecture about Max's responsibility as an older brother, Gracie's eyes suddenly bulged in terror. "Look out, Dad!" Derek slammed on the brakes even as he turned in his seat.

As the car came to a halt, Derek saw a skeleton crossing the road. As it entered the glare of the headlights, the skeleton casually looked at Derek through the windshield, then continued on towards the other side of the street, seemingly unaware of how close it had come to death.

The man in the skeleton costume finished crossing the street, striding across a wide lawn to an ancient Victorian farmhouse set far back from the street. They had reached the bottom of the mountain, and this ancient house lay between the steep face of the mountain and the edge of the thick woods that surrounded the range and continued across the county.

Derek had passed the old house many times without realizing anyone even lived there, but now the house was blazing with light and crawling with demons, ghosts, and witches, who spilled out over the wide front porch and the narrow balcony on the second floor, while still more were gathered in clusters across the wide lawn. Derek watched the partiers for a moment, until the sound of his children resuming their fight in the backseat reminded him he had more pressing obligations. Releasing the brake with a pent-up sigh, he continued down the road.

When they reached the elementary school, Derek at first didn't recognize the building. He realized he had never seen it at night before, but that didn't entirely explain its twisted, warped appearance. As he drove up the circle of asphalt that was normally the exclusive domain of school buses, he remembered that the last time he had been here was the day Max had been bitten by the xolo. Since then, the building had lost its natural sheen of innocence. In fact, Derek now almost feared the place. If his own reaction was that bad, he could only imagine how his son must feel, especially when he had to come back to the place every day.

Derek tried to study his face in the rearview, but Max was already climbing out of the car, followed quickly by Gracie. Whether to face his fear of the place or to keep an eye on his children, Derek climbed out and followed them across the wide front lawn. Max walked a few feet ahead of him, pulling on his ninja hood as if trying to hide from his father.

As they followed a small cluster of other parents and students to the front door, Derek saw Gracie's teacher, Ms. Lightheart, and the principal, whose last name he now remembered was Brown, standing in front of the door greeting students as they arrived. Ms. Lightheart was dressed in the most conservative witch costume Derek had ever seen, while Principal Brown was dressed, as usual, in a suit that matched his name, unable to give up his authority as principal, even for an after-school party.

"Greetings, children!" Ms. Lightheart said enthusiastically as Max and Gracie approached. "Happy Halloween! Don't you two look cute?!" Principal Brown rolled his eyes as Ms. Lightheart straightened Gracie's tiara and adjusted Max's hood. Derek found the principal's eyes and held out a hand, as if in apology.

"Thanks for taking them both back, after the, uh, incident."

The principal returned the handshake for only as long as politeness required, then dropped his hand so quickly that Derek's remained in the air. "Yes, well, from what I see on the news, seems like we got off easy."

Returning his hand to his side, Derek dropped his eyes and nodded. "Yeah, well, um, happy Halloween, Bob." The principal only nodded in reply.

Turning his attention to the kids, Derek urged them to be good. "We will," Gracie said sweetly. Max only waved as he headed inside. With only a slight nod to Ms. Lightheart, Derek turned back towards his car.

"I think it's time for the festivities to begin!" he heard the teacher say excitedly as he recrossed the wide lawn.

The principal only grunted in exchange. "Yeah, let's get this over with," he said. Derek smiled and got back into his car, forgetting for a moment the vague fears that had driven him here.

They came back to him as he drove home through the darkness. As he passed the farmhouse at the base of the mountain, he told himself he was only looking out for drunken teens crossing the road, but he knew the real reason he was peering so long into the darkness; he was looking for danger, which he instinctively sensed was near.

Seeing nothing, he drove on. Derek tried to tell himself there was nothing to worry about, that his anxiety was a lasting side effect of his experiences in the woods and that there was nothing new to fear. The thought helped calm him down a little. As he started up the mountain road towards home, he had almost started to believe it.

Finally making his way out of the structure the humans had confined him in for weeks, the Xolo inhaled the mountain air, the first fresh air he had smelled since the night of his capture. The other dogs had helped chew through his straps and now they were feeding on the corpses of the humans who had tortured him during his captivity. For his own part, the Xolo needed no food: he was more nourished than he had been in a long time, his body overflowing with the energy of the souls he had absorbed.

With that energy, his senses had returned to their full strength. On the fresh mountain breeze, he smelled the man who had been responsible for his capture, and the boy who had first brought the wrath of the humans upon him. The scent of the bites he had left inside them was faint, but unmistakable. Once he had tracked them down and absorbed their souls, his revenge would be complete. Once the others had eaten their fill, he would lead them on into the night. Besides the two humans he had bitten before, he could smell many others on the wind, young and fresh ones, enough for the entire pack to enjoy.

Tonight, they would feast.

TWENTY-FIVE

"I am telling you, Sheriff, it's beyond animal cruelty, it's just... cruelty."

Garth sighed and put his feet on his desk, interlocking his fingers behind his head. He felt as if he were struggling to keep all his thoughts inside his head. He had already been swamped with calls all night, totally overwhelming his mind, and that was before his desk sergeant had dragged in Heloise Lopez, telling him the animal control supervisor had burst into the station, a handgun in one hand and a can of bear spray in the other, demanding to see the sheriff. Once Garth had finally gotten her to calm down, she had told him an insane story about how these items had come to be in her possession.

Garth nodded at the weapons, which still lay on his desk. "So, when these G-men were trying to detain you, you didn't happen to shoot any of 'em, did you?"

Heloise shrugged. "Only with the bear spray."

Garth's eyes widened as he imagined that. "Jesus."

Heloise finally sat down in the chair across his desk. "Sheriff, those men tried to kill me. And they're going to get away."

Garth leaned back in his chair and sighed. It wasn't that he didn't want to drive away the outsiders who had taken over a once-quiet county building and kept alive the worst chapter in the town's history, (while simultaneously creating some bizarre rumors of their own) but it was Halloween night and he was already short of men. He had extra patrols out to watch the kids and respond quickly to any accidents, and his reserves were all out on calls throughout the county.

But, like Derek, he was nervous and secretly worried that something terrible would happen tonight. At the same time, he knew how much it took to get Loise shaken, and right now she was the most upset he had ever seen her. Since he couldn't afford to spare a man, there was only one option.

Sighing heavily, Garth pushed himself up from his desk. "Alright, just let me leave some instructions with O'Leary, then I'll drive us both out there."

Heloise looked relieved as she stood up from her chair. "Thank you, Sheriff."

"Don't thank me yet." He pointed to the gun and bear spray on his desk. "I'll have to have O'Leary lock up the weapons too. Who knows, they might want to file a report on you."

Heloise gave him a look as she followed him out of the office.

As Garth piloted his cruiser down the dark, empty road towards the county animal control center, Loise leaned back in his passenger seat, a million images of what they might see forming in her mind. She could already see the empty parking lot, the G-men's vehicles gone as if they had never been there. The lab would be empty, their equipment and test subjects gone, or perhaps the entire building would have disappeared, replaced by an unbroken lawn of grass, as if they were trying to remove all trace of them ever being there.

The only image she wasn't expecting was the one she finally saw. The small parking lot was still crowded with the black government vans, all in the same place they had been when Loise left. As they climbed out of the car, she could see that one van's back doors had been left hanging open, the cargo area half-filled with hastily stacked equipment. Loise looked towards the entryway, but could see no one. "I don't like the looks of this," she told the sheriff.

Garth drew his gun. "That makes two of us. You wait out here."

"No way. How do you know it's any safer out here? Besides, my weapons are just inside." Garth gave her a harsh look, which Heloise responded to with a shrug. "Hey, if you hadn't confiscated my gun and bear spray, I'd be armed right now."

Garth rolled his eyes, turning towards the building as he did so. "Alright," he growled, "just stay behind me."

The entryway was deserted. Heloise softly shut the door behind them as Garth stood listening just beyond the breezeway. "Quiet," Garth whispered. Loise wasn't sure if that was a command or an observation, but either way, wasn't about to disagree. "Which way's the lab?" Garth growled.

Loise pointed the way and Garth took a few steps towards the door. "But," Loise said as Garth turned back with a grimace, "my locker is this way."

Garth scowled but stood guard as she crossed the hallway and opened her locker, quickly retrieving her dart gun, a case of tranquilizer darts, and an electric prod. The clicks of the darts sliding into the chamber echoed on the tile floor and the steel lockers that lined the walls. Hanging the prod from her belt, she raised the fully-loaded dart gun and nodded at Garth.

Approaching the entrance to the lab, they heard no noise, saw no shadows interrupting the sliver of light that came from the half-open door. Garth stopped just ahead of the door, looked back at Loise, and nodded. They both raised their weapons as Garth kicked the door open. Jutting his revolver into the room, he stepped into the doorway, filling the frame with his bulk.

Still standing in the hallway, Heloise could see his eyes sweep the room, his expression gradually changing from apprehension to shock to horror. His grip on the revolver tightened, then relaxed, then succumbed completely as he put the gun back into its holster. Loise tapped his shoulder to remind him she was there. He jumped slightly, then nodded as if answering a question. "What is it, Sheriff?" she whispered.

He responded at his usual volume. "Well, I've got good news, and I've got bad news."

"What's the bad news?"

Garth buttoned the strap on his holster with a sharp snap. "Looks like the dogs are loose again. But they've left here, it seems."

"Is that the good news?"

She saw Garth's eyes slowly scan the room again, as if he couldn't believe what he was seeing. "...Nope. Good news is, we don't have to worry about getting rid of those G-men, after all."

He swung the door open the rest of the way and stepped aside. Without being sure she wanted to, Loise stepped towards the doorway. Each step felt like an eternity as a million more images of what she might see flowed through her mind, each so vivid and horrible that it took her a moment to process what she finally saw. Blood covered the walls and floors, pooled between the torn, mutilated bodies of the G-men and the scientists. The far door hung open, revealing a dark rectangle of the outdoors. The body of a woman that Heloise thought was Peggy Castillo lay at the base of the door, overlapping tracks of paw prints stamped in her blood leading deeper into the lab. In the center of the room was the table the Xolo had been on, its straps roughly torn and chewed. A body that had probably once been Pretorius lay on the floor beneath it, its body cavity ripped open and emptied out, the face eaten down to the bone.

As Loise and Garth approached the table, they stepped over the body of the G-man that Loise had maced. His body cavity was also hollowed out, but this time from behind. His eyes were still swollen and purple from the bear spray, the puffy flesh partially torn, as if the dogs had bitten at his eyes only once before tasting the bear spray and being persuaded to move on to an easier meal.

"Damn, this is all starting to look a little too familiar," Garth growled.

Loise could only agree. "We need to get all the trick or treaters off the streets right now; the dogs could be anywhere."

Garth looked like he hadn't even thought of that. "Yeah. I'll call O'Leary, tell him not to bother with this mess until we take care of the dogs. We need every unit we have on the streets." He marched towards the front door, pulling out his radio as he walked. "I'm gonna call for backup."

Loise followed him, fishing out her phone as she walked. "So am I."

Derek was just passing the sign for Sylvan Springs when his cell phone began to ring. Searching for it in his cupholders, a thousand nightmarish images of who might be calling him and why began to play in his mind. As his fingers raked through the loose change and balled-up straw wrappers without finding his phone, he imagined it was Miss Lightheart, calling to inform him of an attack at the Halloween party. As he scraped the leather in the passenger seat, finding nothing but crumpled napkins, he imagined the continuing rings were from his wife, telling him about some strange noises that were gathering outside the door. As his fingertips walked across the glovebox, he had a mental image of Sheriff Chambers, holding his cellphone to his ear and his hat over his heart.

When he finally found the phone on his dashboard, he was expecting to see anything on his screen besides the random string of numbers that appeared there. The unknown number at first eased his mind, until he considered the myriad other explanations there could be for the call. Realizing he was only forming excuses to put off answering, he pulled over and answered.

"Hi Derek, it's me."

The voice rang a bell, but Derek found himself unable to place its speaker, only the frantic, clipped tone it spoke in, which infected him with its nervous energy. "I'm sorry?" was all he could manage.

"Derek?" the voice on the phone pleaded. "It's Heloise."

Derek realized for the first time that he had never asked Heloise for her number, and had no idea how she had found his, but her desperate tone drove that out of his mind. "Heloise? What's up?"

"The dogs," she said simply. Derek was already turning his car around when she needlessly informed him, "they're back. Can you meet us at county animal control in ten minutes?"

Derek was already speeding out of the neighborhood. "I'll be there in five." He hung up without another word. As he turned onto the county road, he was already starting another call.

"Up next on our marathon of fear: HORRORS OF SPIDER ISLAND, followed by THE WASP WOMAN."

As the TV announcer's echoing voice faded into the tinny opening strains of the first film, Alison found her attention drifting away from the troubles of Emily on her computer screen and more towards the adventures of the strangely familiar-looking actor on the TV screen. As he negotiated with a room full of models and loaded them onto a plane in glorious black-and-white, Alison found herself closing the laptop and setting it on the coffee table as she settled back on the couch. She didn't normally like these types of movies, but she had thought it would be good background noise for her writing. Now she found the movie distracting her from her writing and wasn't particularly upset about it.

As the familiar-looking actor and his plane full of models found themselves stranded in the ocean after a spectacularly cheap plane crash, Alison found herself sighing when her phone began to ring. Forcing herself off the couch, she saw it was Derek calling and answered the phone.

Alison had never heard his voice so serious and intense. "Honey, the dogs are loose again." He rushed on before she could interject. "I'm going to meet the sheriff right now. Stay inside and make sure the doors are locked."

"I'll call the school and make sure the kids are all inside."

"Good idea. I'll be in touch."

He hung up before she could say goodbye. Instantly, she was dialing the number for Sunnydale Elementary. As a long trill of rings echoed endlessly, Alison for the first time regretted not getting her children cell phones. That thought led her to dial Ms. Lightheart's cell number, which also gave her only an endless series of rings. Alison could see in her mind's eye the phone ringing on the teacher's desk while through a nearby window children played happily, unaware of the approaching danger.

Before she could even consciously decide to do it, Alison was pulling on her coat and retrieving her car keys. If she was unable to warn the children any other way, she would have to drive to the school herself. As she searched through the drawer for her keys, her thoughts were interrupted by the ringing of the doorbell, the first trick-or-treaters in nearly an hour. Alison ran for the door. If the dogs were in the neighborhood, the kids would need a ride home.

As she opened the door, Alison was greeted by a face she did not at first consciously recognize. As the two men on the porch slowly grinned at her, she recognized the shorter, heavier man in the back as her husband's would-be business partner, Hector Ramirez. The taller, stockier man in front also looked vaguely familiar, though it was a long moment before she recognized him as the chauffeur that had dropped Derek off on the day he had brought home the dog.

"You…" was all she could choke out, though she wasn't sure which one she meant. Anything else she would have said was forgotten when the chauffeur raised a fist crowned with a heavy set of brass knuckles. Alison tried to slam the door shut, but the chauffeur pushed it open with his other hand, knocking Alison back even before the brass knuckles collided with her face, knocking her unconscious and sending her flying to the ground.

Reeve stepped through the door and began to drag Alison deeper into the house. Hector followed, carrying a length of rope, a briefcase, and a roll of duct tape. "Do not worry, Mrs. Rains," he said as he studied the concerned expression still stamped on her unconscious face. "We will not harm you, as long as your husband cooperates."

Reeve studied her face, which was beginning to swell and bleed where he had hit her. "Well, we won't harm her any more then we already have, right, boss?" The two men shared a cackle as they dragged the unconscious woman up the stairs, the door behind them swaying in the breeze.

TWENTY-SIX

EDNA LIGHTHEART LOOKED OVER THE PLAYGROUND WITH CONTENT. At a station near the school, a few kids were playing carnival games rented from a local fair. Although they could no longer bob for apples (due to the threat of disease spreading in the water) or play pin the tail on the donkey (because of a few kids who had had the tail pinned in their backs or in their stomachs) as they would have in Edna's ideal image of this fair, the kids seemed happy enough trying to toss rings over plastic cones or drop pucks through rows of pegs. A few others were following clues for a scavenger hunt around the playground, though most were busying themselves with the playground equipment itself, idly tossing themselves on the swings or chasing each other across the platforms and swinging metal bridges as they did every afternoon at recess, the experience made novel by the darkness and the costumes that trailed behind them or the masks that threatened to blow off as they ran.

Although sensitivity to the dog attacks in the woods beyond the edge of town that had taken the life of one of their fellow students and almost killed another had forced Edna to cancel her original plans for a more ambitious scavenger hunt that would have brought the students through the stretch of forest behind the school, she was still delighted with how everything had turned out. The playground at Sunnydale Elementary was ideal for this fair, with its wide lawn that stretched from the one-story brick building to the edge of a steeply sloping hill overlooking a dramatic view of the mountains beyond. Because the school had been renovated in the last few years, the chain-link fence that separated this slope from the edge of the plateau the school was built on was still fresh and intact, free of the vines that would inevitably tangle around it and the tears that little hands would rip in it over the next few years.

The playground equipment, a tangled maze of brightly colored plastic platforms, tunnels, bridges, and towers, lay in a sandpit among a stand of ancient oak trees at the furthest point of the grassy plateau, just inside a corner of the chain-link fence. The playground was made of three distinct structures, each connected to the others by monkey bars, walkways of spinning platforms, or metal-tracked devices that looked to Edna like metal ziplines. The highest towers and slides on these structures reached above the height of the chain-link fence, making Edna nervous when she thought of their proximity to the steep slope and the wilderness beyond, but in her calmer moments the towers seemed almost majestic, like some whimsical wizard's mad dream of a medieval castle, rendered in neon-colored plastic instead of brick and stone.

To Edna, Sunnydale Elementary was the ideal image of an elementary school, exactly the kind of place she had fantasized about teaching at when she was earning her degree at the University of Colorado, Boulder. Teaching reminded her of her own carefree school days, when life had been ordered and logical, free from the chaos and uncertainty of the adult world. For her, it was a privilege to teach because it gave her a chance to connect to those long-gone days while creating them for the next generation.

But she also knew there were many in her profession who did not feel the same enthusiasm, and there could be no clearer reminder of that than the man who was more obligated than excited to chaperone this event with her, since none of his other staff had volunteered to help Edna. Principal Brown was dressed in his usual suit, so dark that he nearly blended in with the night as he stood on the very edge of the grassy field, just at the furthest reaches of the few lights on the side of the school building. The playground had never been meant to be used at night, but thankfully the halogen lights on the side of the school were still new, their cases fresh and clean enough to let out all the light the fresh bulbs could emit, and they were helped by the bright light of the full moon.

"Perfect night for this, isn't it?" Lightheart said to Brown as soon as she could find him in the darkness.

She heard more than saw him shrug. "It's Halloween night, Edna. It's not like you had much of a choice."

Edna held in a sigh, as she had held in so much else in the few months she had been teaching at Sunnydale. As he always did, Principal Brown had taken even the slightest hint of positivity and optimism and taken it as a sign that she was bragging, an offense he always felt the need to crack down on immediately.

She supposed that forty years in the public education system would do that to a person, but she would have hoped that an assignment like this, as principal of a small school in a well-off county, with remodeled facilities and good pay for his staff and himself, would have made him appreciative of the position the school board had granted him for the last few years before his retirement and perhaps softened his attitude towards his staff, but instead it seemed to have hardened him, whether because he resented the rather small and obscure position he had been granted in exchange for his decades of teaching service in the struggling schools of Denver's inner city, or because his first taste of unquestioned power, in a school far from the cares of the school board or the district superintendent, had brought out the petty tyrant that had always existed within him, Edna could not be sure, but either way, she resented the man for his inability to appreciate the position he had been given and the people who worked beneath him.

But, as she often had to remind herself, she was stuck with the man for the rest of the year at least. She didn't have to like him, but she had to at least get along with him if she was going to make the experience of working at her dream school worthwhile. She was about to ask him if he cared to join her as she circled through the fair, asking the students if they were having a good time, when she saw him surreptitiously slip a flask from his suit pocket and take a large swig while facing away into the darkness.

When he turned back and saw her staring, he calmly held out the flask. "Something to warm you up?"

"I think I'll walk a lap instead."

As she walked towards the students, Edna instantly regretted leaving Principal Brown behind. She should have at least taken a sip of his flask, even if it was against district policy to consume alcohol on school grounds. That was exactly the kind of attitude her mother was always warning her about, she chided herself, that fussy schoolmarmish tone that instantly turned both potential boyfriends and potential employers away, as her mother never failed to remind her. Principal Brown held the future of her dream job in his hands and she had just missed a chance to connect with him in a more personal way. She was thinking about turning back to tell him she had changed her mind, but her first student had just crossed her path and it was too late.

Gracie Rains was the most precocious and intelligent student in Edna's class, and because of that, often her most annoying. Edna could sympathize with the girl who was always the first to raise her hand in class, who always had the right answer, who always had to correct another student (or even the teacher) when they were wrong; Edna had been that girl at Gracie's age, and now she saw why her teachers and other students had so often avoided her. She had a feeling that Gracie's mother might soon be telling her she was turning potential boyfriends away.

"How are you enjoying the fair?" she asked Gracie as enthusiastically as she could.

The girl straightened her plastic tiara and beamed at her teacher. "I love it! I found this on the scavenger hunt!" she said as enthusiastically as she always did, holding up a stuffed teddy bear. Edna had to admit, the girl was nothing if not positive, and even everything that had happened with her old dog hadn't seemed to dampen her spirits in the slightest.

That thought led her to others even darker. "Where's your brother?" she asked quietly, as if begging for confidential information.

Gracie's smile finally darkened. In answer, she only pointed to the swing set at the end of the playground, where a shadowy shape was listlessly rocking back and forth on the last swing. At first, Edna thought the shape was only a shadow in the shape of a boy, until she remembered the ninja suit that Max had worn to the party. Thanking Gracie, Edna crossed the wide stretch of blacktop to the playground, resisting the urge to jump through the hopscotch squares that lined the pavement. She glanced over at Principal Brown, hoping he wouldn't notice her willing him to notice her, but he had his back to the playground, probably concealing another swig from his flask.

Forcing herself not to care about that, Edna reminded herself that she had gotten into education to make life better for her students, even those of her students who made her own life more difficult. She kept that in mind as she approached Max. As she stepped over the wooden lip of the playground and felt her heels crunch into the sand, she saw that Max's face wasn't simply lost in shadow; he was still wearing the full hood of the ninja suit, completely concealing his face, as if he wanted to hide even from his fellow students. As Edna approached, the hooded head did not move at all.

Edna ground one heel into the sand, unsure of what to say. "Had enough of the festivities?" she said finally.

The hooded head raised slightly, as if noticing her for the first time. "No offense, Ms. Lightheart," a muffled voice mumbled, "but school is the last place I want to be on Halloween." As he spoke, the center of his hood bubbled and inverted with each word.

Ms. Lightheart laughed a little at that. "I understand. You'd probably rather be at home watching the channel five horror movie marathon."

That at least got Max to raise his head. Before he tried to speak again, he pulled off the hood. In the faint moonlight, Edna could see that his face was more animated and excited than she had expected. "Yeah! They're showing HORRORS OF SPIDER ISLAND. I hear that one's got a ton of hot babes in it."

Embarrassment quickly crossed Max's face as he remembered who he was talking to. Ms. Lightheart cleared her throat awkwardly and turned slightly away. To spare Max any further embarrassment, she pretended to be looking for Principal Brown in the darkness, an excuse that quickly became real when she realized she couldn't see him anywhere. "Uh, sorry," she heard Max say, pulling her back to her current location.

Surprised to see the principal completely gone, Edna had already forgotten what Max was apologizing for. When she saw the embarrassed look on his face again, she instantly remembered and chuckled. "That's alright, Max. I think you're very nice to come and look after your sister. I'm sure you'd much rather be out with your friends tonight."

Even the faint moonlight revealed the look of hurt that Max tried to conceal. As Edna remembered what had happened to the trouble-making boy who had disappeared from Max's class and the two teens she had read about in the papers, she realized how callous her remark had been. "I guess it's my turn to apologize, Max."

"It's okay, Ms. Lightheart," Max said, casting his eyes downwards. Edna thought she saw the faint glimmer of a tear catch the moonlight and turned her head away to give Max his privacy, searching again for Principal Brown. She just barely saw him, a slightly lighter patch of darkness against the night, moving towards the fence that separated the playground from the wide front yard of the school. The gate that normally allowed the groundskeepers to drive the riding mower between the two yards hung open, swaying in the breeze and Principal Brown was moving towards the gate to close it. A large dog, which appeared to be a German shepherd, was entering the yard through the gate.

The dog from down the street must have wandered over here again, Edna thought to herself, turning back to Max. His face was deadly pale. At first, she thought it was only the silvery sheen of the moonlight on his skin, until she realized she could actually *see him growing paler* right before her eyes. Max's eyes were locked on the dog, his mouth hanging open in horror.

When she put an arm on his shoulder to comfort him, she could feel that he was trembling. "Max, it's okay, it's just the neighbor's dog, it's nothing to worry about."

At first, she thought she had overstepped her bounds when Max shoved her hand off his shoulder, until she realized he was only trying to climb to his feet. As he struggled out of the swing, he pointed towards the gate, struggling to choke out words that came out only as sharp gasps. Edna followed his gaze.

More dogs were streaming in through the gate, among them one that looked like the hairless dog she had seen on TV. When Max saw the beast, he began to back away, looking frantically around the playground for a means of escape. Principal Brown was still crouched near the German shepherd, looking for its collar, apparently unaware of the pack approaching.

"Bob!" Edna yelled, running towards him, kicking up clods of sand behind her.

Max watched her go, then looked at the other students, who were still idly playing games and chasing each other around the playground. "Look out!!!" he yelled, waving his arms in a vain attempt to get their attention.

Principal Brown turned at the sound, giving Max a look of frustrated impatience. As he strained his neck to see what the trouble was, the German shepherd leaped for his exposed throat, knocking him to the ground as it tore into him. The other students finally looked up at the sound of his screams, taking in the horror of what was happening to their principal. The other dogs were quickly approaching, moving between the students and the only entrance to the school.

"Get over here, get up high!" Max yelled, jumping onto a ramp leading up to the play structures. Several kids ran towards him, but Gracie still stood near the ring toss, frozen in terror. Max ran after her, dodging around the stream of students flowing towards him. Max yelled at them to climb as high as they possibly could. When he reached Gracie and grabbed her shoulder, she jumped and looked at him in shock. Several dogs were already closing in on them, moving between them and the playground.

Deeper in the darkness, they heard a muffled groan as the German shepherd tore open Principal Brown's throat, loosing a spray of blood that was visible even in the darkness. The man groaned as he slumped and died. The German shepherd began to eat him before he had even let out his final breath. Ms. Lightheart froze on the edge of the asphalt, her entire reason for running into danger now expired. She looked around for a moment, unsure where to go, seeing dogs surrounding her on all sides.

"This way, Ms. Lightheart!" Max called, waving her towards the playground. Seeing more dogs in that direction, the teacher took a cautious step, then turned towards the nearest door of the school, which was further away, but had fewer dogs blocking the way. As she began to run, the dogs closed in on her, quickly outrunning her over the vast distance. Still more than twenty feet from the door, several dogs collided with her legs, instantly knocking her off her feet. She let out a cry as her head collided with the pavement in a sharp crack. She was still too stunned to move as the dogs gathered around her, each vying with the others to get the first bite. Even the dogs that had been guarding Max and Gracie moved in, shoving into the pack as Ms. Lightheart desperately tried to push them back, her efforts too little to do any good.

Seeing an opening with the dogs distracted, Max silently pushed Gracie towards the playground, where the other kids were climbing onto the roofs of the play structures or scaling the nearby trees. As they ran across the asphalt, Max saw the Xolo from the corner of his eye, breaking away from the pack and running after them. He urged Gracie to run faster as he heard its paws slapping on the asphalt just behind them.

As they reached the edge of the play structures, Max and Gracie clambered up a sheet of interlocking metal rings that led to a raised platform. As they crossed the platform to a long ramp leading even higher, Max risked a look back to confirm what he had suspected: the Xolo had followed their path exactly, using its long, spindly legs to clamber up the metal rings, slower but no less nimbly than they had. The delay gave them just enough time to cross to the next platform, where a swinging metal bridge led to another platform crowned by a high tower.

Several kids were perched on the plastic roof, urging them across. The bridge swayed horribly as they ran across, nearly tossing them over the chain handrails as it bounced. When they were halfway across, the bridge bounced in a new direction, then swayed in a series of quicker, smaller bounces. Max didn't need to look back to know the Xolo was just behind them.

They were almost across the bridge and several kids were leaning off the edge of the roof, extending their hands to pull them up. Max pushed Gracie onto the railing at the end of the bridge, bringing her just high enough for several other kids to grab her and pull her up. As he climbed onto the railing after her, he felt the metal slats beneath bouncing rhythmically, each bounce getting slightly larger as the Xolo pulled up just behind him. Max thrust his hand up blindly, knowing that the Xolo would get him before the other kids could reach him. He felt a hand wrap around his own, then another grab his wrist. He pushed himself off the railing, using his free hand and his feet to clamber up the side of the play structure.

He heard the Xolo leaping towards him just as several more students reached out for him, grabbing his arms and the front of his costume, pulling him onto the roof and dumping him hard on the plastic just beside them. He heard the mass of the Xolo rush past him midair, then the crash as it collided with the ground. Carefully turning himself around on the small roof, Max peered over the edge and saw the Xolo lying flat on the sand far below, whining as it clambered to its feet.

As he breathed a sigh of relief, the Xolo leaped straight into the air, coming much closer to Max than he would have thought possible. He leaped back, almost throwing himself off the far side of the plastic roof before the other students caught him. Safe in their arms, Max began to relax, realizing that the Xolo was still trying to leap towards them, but could not come within reach of the roof. As he looked around the playground, he saw several other groups of students clustered on the top of the roofs of other play structures or hiding in the tallest branches of trees. Dogs were gathered beneath them, desperately leaping towards the hanging children or trying to scale the obstacles that led to them, but without success. They were all safe, at least for now.

"Did everyone make it up?" Max yelled.

"Yeah," another kid yelled back, "everyone except the teachers."

In the desperate struggle to escape, Max had forgotten for a moment about the principal and Ms. Lightheart. Looking towards the edge of the playground, he could just barely make out their fallen forms on the very edge of the light, their only movements now caused by the dogs that tore into their bodies.

Max forced himself to look away and focus on what he could do about their current situation. "Does anybody have a cell phone?" he called out.

Several kids shook their heads no. "My mom won't let me have one," a chubby boy on the roof next to Max grumbled, almost complaining. "I left mine inside," another boy, a rich-looking kid whose polo had been dirtied and torn by the tree he had been forced to climb, said for anyone who cared to listen.

Max shook his head and looked down at the Xolo, which had given up its futile leaping and now sat on its haunches, staring up at them and whining. "Well, I guess we're stuck here for a while then," Max muttered.

As if it had heard him, the Xolo suddenly stopped whining and began to furiously sniff the air. After a moment, it stood up, raising its head higher and sniffing even more deeply. Running to the other dogs, the Xolo barked wildly, as if handing out orders. Max thought of the night in the abandoned house and shuddered. He wondered what orders the Xolo was handing out now.

Most of the dogs followed the Xolo out of the gate they had entered from, while a few remained beneath the children, at least one for each group. "They left a guard for us," one kid observed.

Max nodded, watching the Xolo disappear into the darkness. "Where do you think they're going, Max?" Gracie asked.

He shrugged. "I dunno, but I'm guessing they smell something good."

Donald was surrounded by demons. They surrounded him in the hallways and swarmed around him in the living room as he searched desperately for a way out of the house. Ever since he had eaten the mushrooms Brian had given him, the house had turned into an endless maze. Even worse, the need to vomit was growing worse, the pressure building in his stomach from the beers he had foolishly chugged while waiting for the 'shrooms to kick in. The rooms were spinning around him, each hallway seeming to lead back to where he had started, the bathroom that he had seen when he was sober having been replaced by a coat closet. After considering throwing up there anyway, he decided not to risk his friendship with Melanie and to try to keep it in until he could get outside.

Finally, he saw the front door and ran for it before it could disappear. He found the porch crowded with even more demons, some of them in appealing outfits, but all of them deformed and monstrous. He pushed his way through them, avoiding the twisted claws they reached out to rake him with.

Shoving his way off the porch, Donald took a single step into the dry bushes that circled the house and let his vomit loose, not even bothering to push back the long, curly hair that hung in his face. A voice echoed and wavered from the distance, the words seeming to hang visibly in the air. "Hey Donald, you okay, man?" Turning away from the dried bush that he had ruined, Donald saw a skeleton step from the group of demons on the front porch. The skeleton went down the two steps to the ground, reaching out its long, bony fingers at him. Donald thought of fighting back, of swinging a fist through the skeleton's femur and seeing if it collapsed, until the skeleton reached up and pulled off its own skull, revealing a familiar face beneath.

Holding his skeleton mask in one hand, Brian Johnson held out the other to steady his friend Donald Williams, who seemed to be on the verge of passing out. Looking around the porch, Brian couldn't see their friend Melanie Richards, who was hosting the party.

Her grandparents had left her the decaying old house when they had died a few years ago, back when Sunnydale was a small, dying town with a shrinking population. Melanie had lived here for a few years while she worked as a travelling cosmetic sales consultant, but now the surrounding area was picking up and the property taxes had grown so high that Melanie had figured she might as well make the move to Denver that she had always planned.

Thankfully, a real estate developer had offered to buy the wide, flat plain of grass that stretched before the base of the mountains, including the property on which Melanie's house stood. So, the rotting Victorian gothic mansion would soon be coming down, but before that, she wanted to have one final wild bash in the house, and what better night than Halloween for a wild party in a creepy old house?

Brian and Donald had known Melanie since they had all gone to college at the University of Colorado, Denver, where Melanie had earned the business degree that had led to her current sales job, where Brian had earned the sports medicine degree that he had hoped would lead him to a career in the health department of a major-league baseball team, but had only led him to a job as a personal coach in the Denver LA Fitness, and where Donald had earned the Political Science degree that had led to him throwing up in the bushes outside Melanie's house.

Brian again searched the porch for Melanie, but saw only the disgusted looks of the partygoers staring at Donald. Brian had thought that he and Melanie had been close in college, otherwise he wouldn't have driven over an hour on Halloween night just to be here, but he didn't recognize any of the people at this party. Maybe Melanie's social circle in college had been wider than he had realized, or maybe her travelling sales job somehow brought her into contact with more local people than Brian would have thought possible, but either way, the entire house, and even the porch, were packed with people Brian did not recognize, and none of them seemed particularly interested in helping Donald.

Brian helped his friend to his feet, wincing at the long hair that came swinging at him, smelling of puke and covered in chunks that threatened to fly towards Brian's face as the blonde curls swung back and forth. Donald turned away from the house, putting his hands on his knees as he looked out into the endless night. "Hey, am I tripping or is that a pack of dogs?" Donald said weakly.

Brian looked out at the wide plain of grass that usually served as Melanie's front yard and tonight had served as a parking lot, the guests not worried about tearing up the grass that would soon be razed to make way for dug-out basements and flattened roads. Beyond the cluster of cars was the narrow country road where Brian had almost been run over by some nerdy-looking guy in a sleek sedan, too distracted by his two kids fighting in the backseat to pay attention to the road. The front yard had been so crowded with the strangers who now filled the party that Brian had been forced to park his truck on a patch of dirt across the road which would soon become the second part of the new neighborhood.

Across the grass and between the cars, Brian could see nothing moving. He was about to tell Donald he was just tripping, no matter how unhelpful that might be in his current situation, when he saw the first flash of movement: a strange, spindly form crawling out from under one of the cars, its long, bald body dragging across the ground. More dogs crawled out from beneath the cars or flooded in from the spaces between them, an enormous pack that quickly joined together with the bald dog at its head.

"Uh, I don't know if you're tripping or not, Donald, but that definitely is a pack of dogs out there."

Both of them stared for a long moment, watching the dogs as they ran closer, crossing the wide yard in far less time than Brian would have thought possible. The bald dog leading the charge bared its fangs as it drew closer. Brian noticed that many of the dogs following were doing the same. He turned to Donald. "Uh, maybe we should go inside?" Donald turned to him and nodded, puke chunks flying from his curls as they bounced.

Turning back to the porch, Brian realized that everyone else was oblivious to the dogs, still drinking and talking as if nothing were happening. The mass of people on the porch was too solid for him to move through. Even when he asked politely to move in, the crowd went on drinking and talking. Looking back over his shoulder, he saw the dogs far closer than he had expected and still moving in quickly. "Hey, there's a pack of wild dogs out here, maybe we should get inside?!" he yelled, his voice squeaking with suppressed terror, still unsure if the danger was as real as he imagined it to be.

When he turned back again, he was sure. The dogs were closing in, only yards away now, their mouths hanging open to reveal wicked, blood-soaked fangs, foam dripping from their lips in anticipation. Brian hoped it was only the light from the full moon, but the bald dog's eyes seemed to be glowing.

Brian turned back to the crowd on the porch, renewing his plea. "Come on, we have to get inside! There's wild dogs out there!" The people on the porch continued their drinks and their conversation, a few looking at him as if he were crazy, others laughing as if he were trying to pull a joke on them, but most completely indifferent.

Seeing that Brian was getting no results, Donald tried a different tactic. "Come on, people, I'm gonna hurl!" he yelled, shoving himself into the crowd. Most of them jumped back at the smell of the puke in his hair, twisting themselves away to avoid being touched by it, inadvertently opening a path for him as they moved aside. Brian tried to follow, but the crowd rejoined as quickly as they had parted, leaving him with no way in and no ability to use the same tactic that Donald had.

"Okay, don't say I didn't warn you!" he yelled as he jumped off the stairs to the porch. He ran for the side of the house, hoping the dogs would go for the larger target instead of the easier one. As he rounded the corner of the house, he got his answer as he heard the screams of those gathered on the porch. Risking a look back around the corner, he saw the dogs tearing into the crowd, pulling a man in a Dracula costume off the porch and throwing him to the ground, the rest of the crowd screaming and trying to back away as the dogs tore him apart. The panicked partiers moved towards the door, all of them forming a chokepoint at the narrow doorway. As the crowd packed together on the porch, the dogs picked off the partiers at their leisure.

Moving down the outside wall to the nearest window, Brian saw Donald burst into the house like a champagne cork released from its bottle, waving his arms and screaming warnings that were audible even through the thick, ancient glass. Few of the revelers seemed to notice him, even when several other bloodied, bruised partiers shoved their way in behind him, shouting similar warnings. Only when the dogs burst in did they pay attention, and by then it was too late.

The hairless dog leaped at the throat of a man who only a moment before had been calmly smoking a joint in an easy chair. As the dog's jaws ripped into his throat, a cloud of smoke and a spray of blood erupted from his mouth. Other partiers leaped from their chairs and ran for the stairs, the dogs following them to the second floor. Brian saw Donald among the crowd escaping to the second floor.

Unable to do anything else, Brian ran for the next window, where he saw the dogs attack a group of people doing cocaine off a card table. The flimsy table flew onto its side as the dogs collided with it, a cloud of white powder filling the air and coating a man in dark sunglasses as he fell to the ground. At first glance, it looked as if the dogs that surrounded him were trying to lick the white powder off of him, until Brian saw the jets of blood that squirted up between the dogs as they jockeyed for position.

Looking around the empty yard, Brian realized he just might be able to make it to his truck; the dogs had flooded into the house, leaving the sea of grass open and clear. He made his way cautiously to the edge of the house, then began to run when he saw the open field between him and his truck. As he moved towards the parked vehicles, a large pit bull emerged from between two parked cars. The dog immediately sighted him and began to bark, like a sentry warning its comrades of an escaped prisoner. Realizing he could never outrun the dog over the open grass, Brian did the unthinkable and ran back towards the now-empty porch. His only hope was that, while the dogs were busy chasing the other partiers upstairs, he would be able to find a place to hide inside.

The first part of his plan turned out to be correct. Running inside and shutting the door behind himself, Brian realized that the main floor was still and quiet; the shouts and screams all came from the second floor. This brief moment of peace was interrupted when the door rattled on Brian's back as the pit bull collided with the frame. Brian jumped away from the door, as if afraid the dog could bite him through the wood. He heard the dog's claws scratching at the wood and its pained, mournful howls as it called for its fellow pack members. The dogs upstairs sounded as if they were too busy killing the other partiers to have time for him right now, but Brian knew that could change at any moment.

Looking around for a place to hide, Brian found only a coat closet in the front hall that someone had evidently decided to piss in earlier in the night. Grimacing at the smell, Brian locked himself in, moving behind the heavy coats for protection like a child hiding beneath the covers. Even through the coats and the ceiling above him, he could hear screams and shouts and footsteps crossing the floor in every direction, followed by the smaller sounds of paws.

When the latter inevitably caught up with the former, there would be a heavy thud, then more screams, followed by noises that made Brian wish he could hear nothing at all. He wondered vaguely how something so terrible could have happened, what could have inspired the dogs to rise up against humans, what could have made them so violent. But as he listened to the screams coming from the second floor, he mostly wondered if Donald was okay.

―――――――――
―――――――――

Donald was again surrounded by demons. These were not the fantasy demons of earlier, fashioned as ghosts and skeletons and baring ghastly grins as they downed their drinks; those demons were being taken down all around him by the real demons, the beasts that looked like ordinary dogs but could not have been because of their extraordinary power and speed. Even if Donald hadn't seen the glowing eyes of their leader, he knew that these beasts fought too ferociously to be the animals that he knew and loved. Their blood lust was extraordinary, ripping into the helpless demons all around him and lapping up their blood even as the victims still screamed.

There were plenty of victims to choose from: the seething mass of humanity that had crowded the porch and filled the lower floor had now all seethed upstairs, knocking over Melanie's unbelievably bougie PLEASE STAY DOWNSTAIRS sign that had blocked the narrow staircase. The crowd filled the hallways and flooded the bedrooms, searching desperately for a place to hide and finding none. By the time someone entered a room and tried to shut the door behind themselves, the dogs had already flooded in behind them.

Donald saw the only other option: it stretched out before him across the wall of a bedroom that Melanie had turned into a sitting room. The farthest wall was completely covered by a trio of wide picture windows showing an expanse of darkened lawn and the woods beyond. Donald couldn't remember if there were an overhang of roof invisible beneath those windows, but right now it didn't matter. The only possible escape from the dogs was through the window. As Donald ran for them, he saw the other people at the party being run down by the dogs as they ran in circles, unable to find any other way out. He saw Melanie among them, her lovely face contorting with screams as the dogs tore at her. Donald wished he could help, but knew that it was too late. Slowing down would only cost him his own life too.

His only hope was out the window. He dove forward as he approached the window, executing a perfect dive pose that he didn't know he was capable of. His hands shattered the ancient glass with surprising ease, but the shards cut into his knuckles and sliced through his arms. He turned his face away to avoid even worse cuts, but the shards still sliced through his cheek, the blood mixing with the vomit in his hair as it matted his face.

Even through the tangled, bloodied mess that now clung to his face, Donald could see that he had underestimated the jump. No lip of roof or top of porch stretched beneath the window to break his fall, and the hard, flat ground was much further down than he would have thought. He waved his arms as if that would slow his fall or that he would somehow break into flight, but it only prevented him from using his arms for whatever meager effect they would have had on breaking his fall. Instead, his knees took the brunt of the impact, shattering as he slammed into the ground.

Donald let out a groan that only escaped into the dirt his face was buried in, the earth pressing hair and blood and vomit into his eyes, blinding him. But he didn't need eyes to hear the dogs streaming out of the house after him, or to feel their fangs sinking into his flesh. Donald tried to crawl away, but there was only so far that his arms could take him, and he was unable to stand on his broken legs. He collapsed to the ground, hoping that if he didn't fight back the dogs would at least take him quickly.

He forced his eyes open, desperately trying to take in one last glimpse of the world he knew he was leaving behind, even if that glimpse was horrible and terrifying. Through his vomit-matted hair, he saw the strange hairless dog that had led the pack in their initial charge. It stood at the edge of the yard some distance from the house, surrounded by several other dogs. The hairless dog was scanning the scene, as if taking pride in the chaos it had created. Donald could hear more screams from inside, but they were quickly dying down. More dogs gathered around the hairless one as it barked repeatedly, as if it were a squad leader gathering his troops. Donald even felt a few of the dogs that were biting him release their grip. A moment later, they entered his field of vision and trotted towards the pack. He supposed the remaining few that were still biting him would join the others once they had finished with him, then the entire pack would move on, spreading their terror elsewhere.

Donald forced himself to look at the dogs that were eating him. Even through his fading vision, he could see a few. Donald was surrounded by demons, tearing into his flesh and eating his organs. Soon they would be finished with him and he would know peace at last.

Carl Schloss sighed as his daughter, Luna, pulled him down the street, straining to get to the last few houses before the eight o'clock curfew he had imposed. For the first time since he and Eric had adopted her, Carl was regretting their decision (well, let's be honest, Eric's decision, he thought and immediately pushed away) to home-school her. If she had been going to Sunnydale Elementary, he would have been able to drop her off for a night of fun and games with other kids her own age instead of having to drag her through the neighborhood to trick or treat. Carl had never realized there were so many houses in the few tangled streets that made up Sylvan Springs, and they seemed to be walking uphill to get to every one of them.

But it was hard to be mad at Luna when she was beaming up at him in her Sailor Moon outfit, so he pushed away the thought that he could be at home right now, relaxing with Eric on the couch, watching the channel five horror movie marathon, and instead walked Luna towards the last house on the block. The crumbling Craftsman-style American Foursquare was one of the last remnants of the scattered homes that had stood watch over the mountainside before the modern planned community had come in. Most of the older homes had been torn down by the developer, but some, like Ms. Glick's decaying eyesore, had been subsumed into the neighborhood, with wide, paved streets replacing the narrow dirt lanes, and modern, cookie-cutter homes being built next to her family home in what had long been open land.

As the porch stairs creaked beneath their feet, Carl saw a flash of movement out of the corner of his eye. He turned to see a boy in a ghost costume running down the street, the flaps of his costume trailing comically behind him. Carl laughed and rang the rusted door bell, thinking that a real ghost was coming to answer. He had gotten the impression that Ms. Glick didn't like him during one of her contentious visits to the monthly meeting of the local homeowner's association, where she had made a few offhanded comments about his and Eric's "choice of lifestyle."

Carl was surprised the old bat didn't just turn out her porch lights on Halloween, but she came to the door with a cracked porcelain bowl full of candy, the edges of the wrappers hanging over the faded jack o'lanterns barely visible on the rim. Seeing Luna's costume, she bent over with the candy bowl, squealing with delight as she reached out to ruffle a few of the delicate bows. "Oh, a cute little sailor, how wonderful," she said with charming ignorance. As his daughter reached for the bowl, too focused on her prize to correct the old woman, Carl's attention was again broken by movement on the street. This time it was two teens, one dressed as a pirate, the other in a costume so lazy it was impossible to distinguish at this distance, both running as fast as they could from the direction of a nearby park, yelling something that Carl couldn't understand over the constant cooing from Ms. Glick. "Oh, how lovely your little bows are," she said, slipping the girl another candy bar.

Carl urged Luna to thank the woman, then turned towards the street, scanning the darkness for the two teens. They must have been running faster than he thought, since they had already disappeared into the darkness. As he and Luna stepped off the creaking porch, Luna tugged on his hand, raising her plastic jack o'lantern to point at another streak of movement emerging from the darkness. "Look, Daddy, dogs."

At first Carl thought she was only referring to a group of pets on a walk or maybe some trick-or-treaters in costume. The girl was obsessed with animals and he paid no mind, just dreaming of the couch and the movie marathon and Eric's arms that awaited him now that they had reached the final house in the neighborhood, but his progress toward home was stopped by Luna's surprisingly insistent grip, pulling him back to look where her shaking candy bucket was pointed.

As he squinted into the shadows, Carl at first saw only another teenager, running in the same direction as the others and just as quickly. But as his eyes adjusted to the darkness, Carl quickly saw the low forms that followed her: scurrying four-legged animals that must have been dogs, if it weren't for the glowing eyes of their leader and the ravenous way they nipped at the fleeing girl. Carl pulled Luna closer to him, unsure what was going to happen. He got his answer when the girl suddenly tripped, the scurrying animals quickly gathering around her. She reached out an arm to the pair of people she could see in the distance, but the animals caught that too, nearly ripping her arm off as they pulled it back. Her screams were quickly drowned out by the sounds of tearing flesh and clothes.

Carl scooped up Luna and ran for Ms. Glick's house. The candy bucket dropped from the terrified girl's arm, hitting the pavement with a noisy clatter. Some of the animals turned towards them, apparently already finished with the teenager. As Carl took the creaking steps two at a time to Ms. Glick's porch, he heard the animals dashing after them, their paws clicking wildly on the pavement. He reached the door and smashed the ancient door bell, almost tearing the rusted bronze plate from the frame. Not hearing any answer but the approaching paws, he began to pound on the door with his fist, yelling at Ms. Glick to let them in.

The old woman cracked the door open carefully, eyeing him with suspicion through the crack between the door and the frame. No doubt she was wondering what kind of tricks he was up to now, but he had no time to convince her of his good intentions. Already he could hear the paws landing on the first step to the porch. He ran for the door and shoved it open. The old woman tried to hold it shut, but she was no match for him. The candy bowl fell from her hand as the door pushed her back, the porcelain shattering into shards that mixed with the candy on the floor.

Ms. Glick stared stupidly at the remains of the bowl as Carl pushed past her, dropping Luna on the floor as he turned back to shut the door. He immediately regretted even that slight delay when a single snout pushed its way between the frame and the closing door. The blood-matted fur peeled back from the snout as it tried to push its way inside, while Carl attempted to squeeze the door shut, as if the edge of the door could slice through flesh and bone. The small nostrils flared and sniffed, while a lolling tongue searched the air for prey. "What is that thing?!" Ms. Glick shouted, as if the terror of the scene had made her forgot what a dog's snout looked like.

Carl felt more dogs pushing at the door. If he didn't get it shut soon, he wouldn't be able to keep them out. Raising his foot, he shouted at Ms. Glick to cover Luna's eyes. She had always been an animal lover and he didn't want her to see this. Bringing his foot down hard, he stomped on the snout until it began to spew blood. A few more stomps disfigured the snout enough to persuade it to pull back, and Carl took the opportunity to slam the door shut, locking it immediately, as if the dogs would be able to open to turn the knob.

Leaning against the frame for extra security, he felt the dogs still slamming against the door, but knew that their force wouldn't be enough to open it. Looking at Luna, whose tears flowed into the old woman's chest, and at Ms. Glick, who glared at him while cradling the hip he had injured while pushing her down, he wanted to apologize to them both, but found he could only laugh. He was just too glad to have survived, to have brought Luna out of danger, to do anything else. Even when the old woman's glare became angrier, even when Luna's tears flowed more heavily, even when the screams of those still trapped outside made the laugh even more inappropriate, Carl couldn't help it. All he could do was laugh.

Rob Stackpole slowly exhaled a thin cloud of smoke, coughing weakly as he leaned back on the edge of the playground equipment, struggling to hold on to the monkey bars with his free hand as he took another shallow drag. His lungs bristled at the burning vapors, but he held in the inevitable cough when he saw movement approaching from the darkness. He held in the smoke still in his mouth until he could feel it growing stale, meanwhile hiding the still-burning cigarette behind his back.

Ever since his mother, Linda Stackpole (Rob laughed at her desperately holding on to his father's last name, when it had been her who had asked for the divorce) had dragged both of them to this dull, cookie-cutter neighborhood, Rob had found that this tiny neighborhood park, just down the street from the dull, cookie-cutter house they shared, was the perfect hiding place for his nocturnal activities. Since the dope who had planned this neighborhood didn't want anyone to use the park after nightfall, no doubt to prevent any nefarious nocturnal activity that might interrupt the dull, cookie-cutter lives of the people who lived nearby, he naturally hadn't put a streetlight anywhere near the park. The purpose had been to prevent people from using the park after dark, but the inevitable result was, of course, to encourage it.

Rob loved coming here after dark, smoking cigarettes or sometimes joints, and even more rarely stronger substances, that he got from the kids at school who had older siblings, or taking Mary Sue along to forget all they learned during the day in Catholic school, all under the perfect cover of darkness. With no streetlights to illuminate it, the little park seemed to sail away from the world after sunset, the neighborhood outside the huddled collection of swings, slides, and metal platforms replaced by an ocean of darkness.

Rob had often sat on the highest tower of the playground, looking out like a captain at his mast while some neighborhood dope walked by on the sidewalk, completely unaware that he was being watched. Sometimes a patrol car would pass by, delightfully ignorant of the illegal activities he was just barely missing. Rob would simply keep the burning cherry of his joint behind the metal wall of the mast-like structure on top of the playground, ducking behind the wall just before the headlights reached the play structure, smiling to himself as he watched the headlights dance off the metal structures around him, taking a self-congratulatory puff as they faded away.

The darkened playground fortress also served as the perfect headquarters for what had become Rob's annual Halloween tradition ever since he had become too old to trick-or-treat himself, which for Rob had been right after his mom had stopped forcing him to just so she could show off his costume to all her friends. Rob had thrown aside that childish stuff. Now his annual tradition was to steal candy from the younger kids, sparing him the embarrassment of having to beg for it at his neighbors' doors while giving the kids the scare they really wanted.

The last few years Rob had done this by himself, but this year he had recruited a few of his friends from St. Nicholas Academy. Their parents had given them rides from the tiny clusters of homes they lived in, believing that they were only coming to trick-or-treat in this larger neighborhood. They had all worn costumes, both to complete the illusion for their parents and to blend in with the kids they were stealing from. Rob gave them a cover story and offered his ship of shadows as a hiding place. In exchange, they were doing most of the work this year, going out to steal the candy, while he held down the fortress, keeping it safe from the few kids who wandered near the playground by pretending to be the voice of a ghost emanating from the darkness, smiling to himself as he watched them run screaming into the night.

In between, he would smoke self-congratulatory cigarettes, thinking of how perfectly suited he was for the career in politics he envisioned for himself. Unlike his father, he wouldn't be some lame strategist, toiling behind the scenes for other people's glory. He would be a candidate, an office-holder, using his father's connections to run as a Republican, since he agreed with them that crime needed to be punished, and that people needed to be controlled in order to accomplish anything. Tonight was a test run for that theory.

There was only one problem with his plan. When small children approached, it was easy enough to recognize their tiny forms, but when anyone older approached, the natural darkness of the playground worked against him, showing only a shadowy shape like the one that now approached. Rob held his breath, unsure if the approaching shape was one of his friends or a stranger investigating the strange voices his children had heard. Rob wasn't sure what he would do if it was the latter. Thankfully, the shape stopped just shy of the playground and called out his name in a familiar voice. He responded by taking a deep puff on his cigarette, hoping the flare of the cherry would be enough to illuminate his face. It must have worked, since the shape waved an arm of shadow and started climbing a set of uneven metal rungs that led to the mast Rob stood on. Rob extended a hand and helped her up, delighting in the soft warmth of her delicate touch.

Mary Sue set a bucket of candy, disappointingly filled only halfway, on the platform with her free hand, then pulled herself up. Taking the cigarette Rob offered, she drew in a deep breath, the flare lighting up her face, which was strong and beautiful, even when distorted by the shadows and covered by the odd makeup which made her eyes look sunken and dead, and which drew a stitched-up smile across her cheeks, ending just beneath her small, elven ears. As she passed the cigarette back, the flare revealed a glimpse of her tattered, torn dress.

"You scare many kids in that?" Rob asked as he took the cigarette back, letting his fingers linger on hers.

He heard more than saw her shrug. "Not many. The streets were pretty empty. I think all the kids went to that party at the elementary school."

Although he would have never admitted it, Rob had a brief moment of jealousy that his mother wouldn't let him go to public school. At least there they could celebrate Halloween; at the stuffy Catholic academy, the nuns who ran the place acted like Halloween didn't even exist, when it was clearly the best holiday of the year, far superior to the false sentimentality of Christmas and the empty promises of Easter. Pushing those thoughts away, Rob reminded himself that he was too old for that party anyways.

He had to push those childish thoughts away. There were a lot of good things about being a little older, and one of those things was right in front of him, waiting for his attention. Luring her down with the cigarette, Rob sat with his back to the metal wall of the mast, so they could inspect their loot without fear of being seen. Pulling a lighter from his pocket, Rob cast the flame over the bowl like a witch waving her wand over a boiling cauldron. He wished he had magic powers when he saw the meager contents of the bowl: a few fun-size candy bars, a handful of individually wrapped peanut butter cups, and a box of raisins.

Even with the flame held away from his face, Rob got the impression that Mary Sue could see the disappointment on his face. "Sorry," she said sheepishly, "I got what I could, but like I said, there weren't too many kids out there."

Rob raised the flame so she could see the forgiving smile on his face, then brought the lighter closer to her. Mary Sue's name was as innocent as she wasn't. The Van Thornes had given her the name in an obvious attempt to keep their only daughter as virtuous as the reputation of their ancient New England family demanded, even when they had uprooted that family from their native soil to follow her father's career designing missile guidance systems to Buckley Space Force Base on the outskirts of Denver. The stiff Old-World manners of New England hadn't followed them to the West, and the family's attempts to control the morals of their oldest daughter had predictably backfired, leading her to rebel against them and the conventions of the academy they had stuck her in.

In the flickering flame, he saw her mischievous smile, made even more mysterious by her makeup and the shifting shadows. Rob slowly brought the flame closer to his face, hoping her own would follow. He wasn't disappointed when her eerie death mask swooped out of the darkness, descending on him like a vampire bat in search of prey. He sank into darkness as she kissed him, feeling the heat of the flame die away.

"Interrupting anything?" a voice said from the darkness as it did so. They both jumped a little, Rob probably more than Mary Sue, though he still instinctively reached out to comfort her. Reigniting the flame, he saw Keith Leon perched on the edge of the metal platform, gripping the uneven rungs as if he had been hanging there for a long time.

Mary Sue swiped at Keith as if she could knock the obnoxious smirk from his face. "You pervert!" she cried. "How long have you been there?"

Keith's grin widened as he cracked the gum he was chewing. "Long enough. You were waving that lighter around so much I thought you were signaling me up."

Before Rob could object, Keith raised the overflowing candy bucket he had been hiding beneath the platform, making a show of pushing Mary Sue's comparatively meager haul aside as he overturned the contents on the metal platform. Keith was always doing that, going out of his way to do something obnoxious and then overwhelming his target with kindness before they could react. Rob often thought that if Keith weren't charming enough to always get what he wanted from people, he would undoubtedly be the school bully. Like Linda Stackpole, Keith's family was not strictly Catholic, and had only stuck Keith in the academy after he had proven too undisciplined for St. Thomas, the private military school where Mary Sue probably would have gone if she were a boy.

Rob thanked her genetics that she wasn't as he held her close, admiring the enormous pile of candy in front of them. "You must have scared a lot of kids to get all this."

Keith's grin was growing wider than even he had probably intended. "That's just the thing, I didn't have to! These stupid kids were running down the street and they left this bucket of candy behind."

"Running? What were they running from?" Mary Sue asked. Rob noted with disdain the hint of terror creeping into her voice.

"Who knows? It's Halloween night; maybe they were running from a ghost. I didn't get a chance to ask. I just saw them running, they were out of sight before I got there. Come to think of it," he said, chewing thoughtfully on a Butterfinger, "I didn't see anyone else on the street."

"Probably just that party at the elementary school, like I said," Mary Sue reassured herself, nervously snatching a Snickers from the pile.

Keith rolled his eyes, upset as always that someone had tried to correct him. "Well, how was I supposed to know you said that?" he whined, "I wasn't watching you that long."

"Yeah, right, pervert!" Mary Sue shouted, playfully shoving him. Keith tumbled backwards, throwing himself back to exaggerate the blow, and rolled towards the edge of the metal platform, where he nearly collided with a thin, shadowy form that was just poking its head over the edge. This form had a narrow face dwarfed by large glasses and recoiled horribly when Keith almost rolled into it. Neil Cameron was perched awkwardly on the topmost of the metal rungs, his thin hands splayed out over the metal floor, the tips of his long fingers somehow shoved into the tiny holes lining the platform, apparently enough to keep him balanced there. To Rob, he looked like some gigantic, awkward bird perched on its nest. Keith held out a piece of candy, as if he were luring an animal, then helped Neil climb up, almost ripping the boy's skinny arm off as he pulled him up.

Keith noted his empty hands with dismay. "Didn't you steal from any kids like you were supposed to?"

Neil sat down, adjusting his glasses. "I'm sorry, I couldn't find any. The streets were totally deserted."

Rob snorted. He should have known: out of all the kids at the academy, Neil was probably the only one who actually believed the stuff the nuns were trying to cram down their throats. For that reason, he claimed to hate Halloween for being an evil holiday, and had agreed to join in on Rob's scheme only in order to punish the kids who did choose to participate in this pagan holiday, as he called it, though Rob noted he seemed to have no problem eating the candy the others had stolen. Rob should have known he would never be able to steal. Probably for the same reason, his parents hadn't allowed him to wear a costume, and he was still dressed in the same checked shirt and neatly pressed pants he had worn to school that day.

"It was creepy," Neil said, downing his third piece of candy since he had sat down just a moment before, "there was absolutely no one on the streets."

"See, that's what I just said!" Keith yelled, looking around for the validation no one cared to give.

"But I did hear something," Neil continued without responding to Keith. He looked around for a moment, chewing thoughtfully on a Moon Pie, as if trying to build the suspense. When no one ventured a guess, he simply blurted out what he had heard. "Dogs. Dogs howling in the woods. That was the only thing I heard out there."

When this didn't get the reaction he was hoping for, Neil gave his usual nasally sigh. "Don't you guys remember? All those stories about the killer dogs?"

Mary Sue sighed and reached for another piece of candy. "Yeah, but the cops got them all. You probably just heard some regular neighborhood dogs barking at all the trick-or-treaters."

Neil sighed. "But there were no trick-or-treaters! I just told you that..."

"There's one now!" Keith shouted over him. Standing up on the mast, he cupped his hands over his mouth. "Hey! Where are you running to?" he shouted. Rob tried to pull him down, afraid that his shouts would draw the wrong kind of attention, but Keith only waved him away. "Aw, she's leaving anyway. Apparently, she didn't want to talk to me."

"Can't imagine why," Mary Sue snorted.

Peering over the edge of the mast, Rob saw a teenage girl in a Bride of Frankenstein costume running down the street. She occasionally looked back over her shoulder as if looking for someone following her, but did not turn back when Keith called again. As she passed through the last circle of streetlight, she dropped something that landed just out of sight in the shadows.

"She must have dropped her candy!" Keith said, pushing away the pile of candy already in front of him as he clambered for the metal rungs. Rob reached out a hand to stop him, but he was already gone. He had an uneasy feeling as he watched Keith cross the shadowy playground, ducking around the swings and slides. He told himself that the girl had only been running to keep up with her friends, occasionally looking over her shoulder to watch out for traffic, but he had a hard time convincing himself. He didn't know what else would explain her behavior, but he still couldn't shake his uneasy feeling as he watched Keith cross the wide plain of darkness before the street.

Casting a glance down the street, Rob saw no movement. When he looked back to Keith, he found him decapitated by the edge of the streetlight. As Keith crouched and retrieved whatever the girl had dropped, parts of his body seemed to come in and out of existence, as if he had reached the edge of the known universe. He seemed to be crouching for an unusually long time, as if the candy the girl had dropped had scattered across the street. Rob told himself that was all it was, unable to stop himself from looking up and down the empty street, chiding himself for the childish fears that threatened to overwhelm him.

Rob was about to call out to Keith when the younger boy suddenly stood up, his entire body coming back into existence at once. He turned and held up a single unrecognizable object which gleamed white in the streetlight. Rob squinted, but the object refused to come into focus. Even when Keith waved it to get their attention, the object remained only a blur, as if his mind refused to take in the thing's true form; even when Keith called out, Rob's mind still chose to at first misinterpret what he said.

"It's a hand!" Keith yelled again, almost excited, waving the severed appendage like a prize won at a carnival game. Rob's eyes followed the waving object, trying to tell his mind that it was a prop, a Halloween decoration the girl had been carrying for some unknown reason, even though he could see the articulated fingers stiffly wagging back and forth as Keith waved the hand. A few drops of drying, clotted blood fell from the ragged wrist, which was wrapped by the cuff of a dark suit sleeve, a contrast to the pallid, white flesh.

"Hey, you think she was like a serial killer or something?" Keith asked. "Like, should we call the cops?"

"Just wait there, Keith, I'm coming down," Mary Sue said with her usual bravery. Rob again reached out, trying to stop her, but it was again too late. He watched helplessly as she clambered down the bars and disappeared into the darkness beneath the tangle of equipment. Rob thought of chasing after her, but the darkness loomed ahead of him like a solid wall, preventing him from moving off the platform. He moved to the outer wall of the mast and held his breath until she appeared again in the faint arc of light at the end of the playground.

After a moment, she joined Keith in the center of the circle of streetlight. She studied the object in the light for a moment, the skeptical look on her face quickly turning to horror. "It's real!" she said, backing away as if the thing could reach out to her. "It's a real hand!" she yelled, too loudly. Rob looked at the houses across the street, but saw no lights turning on, no movement in the windows. He was unsure whether to be comforted by that or not. "We should call the cops," she yelled to anyone who would listen, maybe hoping to be overheard.

"And tell them what?" Keith said, still waving the severed appendage to make a point. "That we were out here smoking weed and stealing candy?" he yelled, also too loudly.

"Who gives a fuck about that?" Mary Sue yelled. She made a motion as if to slap the hand away, but stopped, not wanting to touch it. "This could be a murder!"

"It's a sign," a thin voice said from behind Rob. He jumped, having forgotten for a moment that Neil was even there. When he turned back, the boy was almost invisible in the darkness, huddled on the far end of the mast, rocking back and forth and holding his knees.

"A sign of what?" Rob asked.

"A sign that we've been sinful and God will punish us," Neil said. "His wrath is coming."

Rob turned away from him, not sure what he could say to someone so delusional. But he couldn't deny the nervous feeling that now seemed to be emptying him out, not helped by Neil's nervous declarations. He found himself scanning the street again, but told himself he was only looking for traffic that might hit Keith and Mary Sue, who still stood in the center of the street, arguing. Their words had faded away to static, the fear in his mind seeming to turn into audible noise that drowned out all else. He found himself clutching the plastic ship's wheel built into the wall of the mast, as if he were trying to steer the playground structure through its sea of sand to rescue them, and realized he had no idea how long he had been holding on to it. As he let go, he realized that enough sweat had collected between his hands and the wheel to fall away with an audible plop as it hit the metal floor.

Wiping his hands on his jeans, he called out to Keith and Mary Sue against his better judgment. "Maybe we should go inside. We can decide what to do later." For the first time, he was grateful for the cookie-cutter house with his mother, and was desperate for the security being there would bring.

Keith waved him away with the severed hand. "Aw, c'mon, it's Halloween night. We need a good scare. Let's follow that chick and see where she went. I bet she's our mad killer."

"Come on, Keith," Mary Sue scolded, "put that thing down."

"Why should I? Don't you want it for evidence when you call the cops? Besides," he intoned, holding out the severed appendage like a lantern as he stumbled towards the girl in a crouching, shambling gait. "Maybe it will point out its killer for us."

Mary Sue shrieked as he thrust the severed appendage towards her. Turning away from the boy and the severed hand, she turned and ran, stopping suddenly at the edge of the circle of streetlight. The effect was uncannily like a stage actor trying not to get outside their spotlight. Watching from his mast as if he had a balcony seat, Rob had an overwhelming moment of disassociation, as if he really were only a spectator and all of this was some fictitious drama. He shook his head, trying to push those thoughts away, knowing it was only his mind trying to make the horror of his situation more palatable.

He forced himself to focus on Mary Sue, and whatever was making her look so terrified. As she backed away from the edge of the streetlight, Keith seemed to see it too, for he grew as pale as the hand he still clutched by his side. As both of them stood frozen, the object of their terror came suddenly into view. It was a dog, blood streaking the fur around its mouth and paws. Rob thought it was a German shepherd, but he had never been a dog person and certainly didn't want to waste brain power identifying the animal. He wanted to call out to Keith and Mary Sue, but told himself it would only agitate the animal, knowing he was really only scared of giving away his own position.

As more dogs entered the circle of streetlight, Keith stepped forward, pushing Mary Sue behind him. He raised the severed hand, wagging it in front of the dogs as if offering a treat. When he saw their eyes following the hand, he tossed it away into the darkness, using the skills he had learned before the football team had cut him for skipping practice. The dogs leaped at the hand, but not the dead one: several sets of jaws clamped around Keith's wrist, twisting his strong arm down and pulling the boy to his knees. More dogs emerged from the darkness, quickly gathering around him and knocking him to the ground as they began to tear his flesh.

Mary Sue turned away and screamed, abandoning her would-be savior for the imagined safety of the playground fortress. As she disappeared into the darkness closer to the playground, Rob clutched the plastic steering wheel tighter, as if it could guide him to Mary Sue. As she ducked between the outlying structures of the playground, shadowy forms emerged from beneath the metal platforms. Before Rob could shout a warning, the shadows converged on her, forming a larger shadowy shape whose struggle was indicated only by her screams.

Rob stepped away from the edge of the mast, hoping that not seeing the scene would block out the horrible screams of his friends. As his mind tried to focus elsewhere, he realized he could hear whispering in the darkness near him. It was Neil, softly muttering a prayer that Rob felt he should have recognized. "They're demons," he whispered to Rob, "demons in the shape of dogs, sent to punish us for our sins."

"It's okay, Neil. We'll be safe up here," Rob whispered back, as if Neil had suggested they risk their own lives to save the others. Rob knew that was impossible.

Returning to the edge of the mast, he squeezed the steering wheel as he watched the struggling shapes in the darkness below. He knew it was too late to rescue Mary Sue; nothing could have saved her from those beasts, and he knew she wouldn't want him sacrificing his own life to try.

Looking out to the street, Rob could see Keith perfectly centered in the circle of streetlight, every detail of what the dogs were doing to him perfectly illuminated. Rob cast his eyes beyond that, to the distant houses. Finally, some of their lights were turning on, and he saw a few people at the windows.

"Come on, Neil," he said, pulling the younger boy by his shoulder. "We'll be safe if we can get to the houses across the street."

The small boy pulled away from him with surprising strength. "The only safety is in repentance," he said in a stronger tone than Rob had ever heard from him before, as if he had been suddenly possessed by the spirit of one of the saints they had learned about in school.

Both of them turned at a sound from the base of the play structure. Even in the darkness, Rob could see a few dim shapes climbing the ramp from the ground, sniffing the air ahead of them as they moved towards the boys. Rob ran for higher ground, but Neil stood confidently, striding towards the ramp with his arms spread like a saint.

As Rob climbed for the only higher point on the playground, a small platform containing the entrance to the largest slide, he saw Neil walk confidently towards the dogs and kneel in the center of the ramp, bowing his head and putting his hands together in prayer. "Dear Lord, forgive me my sins," Rob heard him say as the dogs drew near. The animals gathered around him, sniffed him for a long moment, then sank their fangs into his neck, replacing his prayers with a series of choking gasps.

As the dogs began to tear into Neil, Rob knew he didn't have much longer. Once the dogs had finished with the younger boy, they would come for him. Looking out across the street, he saw more lights turning on and heard the shouts of neighbors. He even saw a few forms dash out into the street, attempting to rescue Keith. They were greeted by more dogs, who quickly overran them. Still, more people were gathered outside and their front doors were open. If Rob could reach them, he would be safe.

His only way down was the slide. To move back down the ramps would bring him directly into contact with the dogs. Swallowing his fear, he plunged himself into the twisting darkness of the tunnel, trying not to scream as the slide brought him around one blind turn after another. As he came around the final turn, even the dim light of the moon shone bright after the darkness of the slide. As the exit widened ahead of him, that relative brightness was suddenly obscured by shadows. Several dogs were gathered around the bottom of the slide, waiting for him to reach them so they could feast. One in the center almost made Rob believe Neil's story of devils. It was completely hairless, and as he looked, its eyes began to glow a horrible yellow that couldn't be simply the reflection of the moon.

Rob pressed his hands and feet against the walls of the slide as if that could stop him. The plastic scraped painfully against his skin. Static electricity built, burst, and charged through his limbs, but all of it only delayed the inevitable; he was still moving towards the dogs. Rob felt like he was trapped in a nightmare as he tried to crawl back up the slide, making no progress against the slippery plastic. That strange sense of disassociation came over him again as he watched himself struggle while remaining in place. One of the dogs now crawled into the slide and scrambled up towards him.

The feeling of being outside himself, of being only a spectator, immediately faded as he felt the dog's fangs slide into his ankle. He still tried to struggle, to stop himself from being pulled out, but as he heard the screams of his friends die out and the screams of their would-be rescuers start up, he knew it was no use. His sweat-coated hands slid across the plastic of the tunnel, his exhausted muscles giving up their fight, as the dog pulled him towards the exit and the inevitable, towards the waiting, hungry mouths, towards the glowing eyes that would be his doom, and towards the endless darkness that he knew was all that would follow.

The duct tape glinted in the moonlight as Hector unfurled another roll. Alison sat in an antique wooden chair in the sitting area of her bedroom, near the windows overlooking the street. She had regained consciousness a few minutes earlier and instinctively began to scream and struggle, but found the thugs had already bound her wrists and ankles to the chair with sturdy rope and covered her mouth with duct tape. Now they were preparing to wrap more duct tape around her torso, preventing her from struggling at all. As Hector drew near with the roll, Alison tried to twist her torso, hoping she could at least loosen their bond on her.

"Quit struggling, Mrs. Rains, or I'll put a piece over your nose and see how much you struggle then!" Hector snarled.

Allison knew he wouldn't; he couldn't afford to kill her. If she had understood the conversation she had overheard correctly, they were only holding her hostage to get Derek's land. Even if that was the case, there was no need to draw their wrath; Alison trusted Derek to do the right thing. She just hoped she could trust him to get here in time.

There was another member of the family who didn't seem to have the same patience. Gracie's golden retriever ran into the bedroom, growling at the intruders and leaping at Hector, knocking the roll of duct tape from his hands. When the dog tried to leap again, Hector knocked the animal to the ground. "God damn it, Reeve, take care of this beast!" he bellowed.

The valet, whose name Alison hadn't known until now, grunted and set down the coil of rope he was unfurling, trudging to the dog with heavy steps. "Come on, mutt, let's get out of here," he said, pulling the struggling animal by its collar.

As his valet pulled the dog out of sight, Hector straightened out his suit, trying to compose himself. "Now, don't you worry, Mrs. Rains," he whispered, leaning over her, "everything will be alright, just as long as your husband cooperates."

Alison could only stare daggers at him.

Downstairs in the kitchen, Reeve pulled the struggling dog towards the sliding glass door that led to the backyard. Reeve wasn't sure if Hector had wanted him to kill the poor animal, but that would be impossible to do without alerting the neighbors. A gunshot would surely attract their attention, and even a knife would raise enough noise from the animal to make them suspicious. Besides, Reeve was an animal lover, no matter how much he despised most members of his own species, and looking into the dog's face, he knew he wouldn't be able to harm the thing. Sliding open the glass door with one hand, he shoved the dog into the backyard. "Out you go, mutt," he muttered, slamming the door shut before the dog could get back in.

The retriever pressed its nose and front paws against the glass, watching the man through the window until he disappeared into the shadows. It sat there for a long time afterward, stupidly hoping the man would come back. When the fog from his breath began to obscure his view, and the condensation made it hard for his paws to stay on the glass, the dog finally let itself drop to the ground. Pacing around the patio, the dog wondered what it could do to get inside. The strangers were hurting his master's family, of that, he was sure. He was only unsure what he could do about it.

An unfamiliar bark from across the yard gave him his answer. He turned to see a dog he had never seen before, standing just beyond the gate to the front yard. Its shape and size were roughly similar to his own, but its skin was completely bare, without even a trace of hair. As he watched, the strange dog stood on its rear paws, leaning against the gate with its front paws, using it nose to push open the latch that kept the gate sealed from the other side. As the gate swung open, the dog fell forward, its front paws landing on the ground. It sat patiently in front of the gate, as if waiting for him. Although the retriever was made nervous by this dog's strange looks and sudden appearance, he didn't know any other way to get out of the back yard, so he trotted towards the dog and sat before it, staring into its strange, hypnotic eyes.

As he stared, he suddenly grew calm. The strange, hairless dog seemed to be speaking to him through its eyes, telling him how to get even with the humans who were hurting his family. It seemed as if that wasn't all the dog wanted him to do, but that didn't matter right now. What mattered was getting even with the men who were hurting his family, and this dog could give him the power to do that. All he had to do was surrender to its control. Through him, the hairless dog would have part of its revenge on all humans, but the retriever would have the power to focus that revenge on those he hated most.

The retriever lost himself in the strange dog's eyes and surrendered to that power.

Garth's siren blared as his cruiser blazed into the neighborhood. The spinning lights turned the familiar houses into strobing, distorted funhouse-mirror versions of themselves. Trapped in the backseat, Derek felt like a prisoner, but instead of being dragged away from the scene of the crime, he was being taken towards it. The cruiser was pulling him towards the scene of the next massacre perpetrated by the force he had unleashed.

He hadn't seen what had happened inside the county animal shelter. By the time he had arrived, Heloise and Garth were too agitated to wait any longer, but by their brief, horrified descriptions he had known it was bad, even worse than the attacks in the woods. They had quickly piled into Garth's cruiser, Heloise in the passenger seat, Derek in the back like a criminal, and made towards Sylvan Springs, where the first reports of attacks by wild animals were already coming in. Garth had sped through the night, leaning over the steering wheel as if that would help him move quicker.

As they entered the neighborhood, all seemed calm and still at first. The distorting effect of the sheriff's lights seemed perfectly natural on the homes, where ghosts and skeletons flapped slowly in the gentle wind. Animatronic witches and mummies waved slowly in their endless motions, while demons projected on LCD screens peered out of windows, beckoning to the absent trick-or-treaters. "There's no one here," Derek said.

As if to prove him wrong, a young boy in a ghost costume dashed into the street just ahead of the cruiser. Garth slammed on the brakes to avoid him. As the boy sprinted across the street, the tails of his costume blew behind him in the wind. A large Doberman followed after, foam dripping from its jaws as it chased him. Garth slammed on the gas again when the boy was just past him. The Doberman never stopped until the cruiser collided with it, the front bumper ringing as it sent the dog's body flying. The dog hit the pavement at the furthest reach of the headlights and moved no more. A yell from a nearby house brought Derek's attention to an opening door, where a woman welcomed the boy with open arms. As he dashed inside, she slammed the door shut so quickly she almost caught the tails of his costume in the door.

Heloise brought their attention back to the streets ahead. "Christ, Sheriff, they're everywhere."

She was right. In the glow of the streetlights at the next corner, they could see the silhouettes of dogs chasing both kids and adults. The wildly fleeing forms looked like figures in some grotesque shadow show. Garth slammed on the gas, deftly avoiding the Doberman's corpse as he sped down the street, clutching the wheel with one hand while the other operated the controls for the siren, rapidly changing the pitch and volume of the sound, creating a wailing, unpredictable cry that pierced Derek's ears and rattled his teeth.

The sound had the desired effect, however, for as the cruiser pulled up on the pack of attacking dogs, its brakes squealing as it stopped just a few feet short of the first people, the animals began to scatter, scared off by the loud noises and bright lights. Garth started the spotlight on his roof and turned it towards a shadowy park on the corner nearest him. The light revealed a teen-aged couple in matching zombie costumes standing on a picnic table, two dogs nipping at their ankles. Garth rolled his window down and pulled out his revolver. Derek covered his ears as two shots drowned out the already loud noise of the siren. The two dogs went down a few seconds apart and the teens ran for the nearest home.

Garth rolled up his window and surveyed the scene. The people and dogs had scattered, leaving behind only a few dead bodies in the street, but there was nothing he could do for them now. His radio blared to life, the dispatcher bringing news of people he could help.

"Sheriff, we got a call from a house full of partiers, say the dogs have them trapped inside." Garth pulled his cruiser around while the dispatcher read off the address, but Derek could have told him where they were going; the address was the house he had seen on the way back from dropping Max and Gracie off at the party. That memory made him want to call Alison and check what she had heard from the school, but he didn't want to appear unfocused on what they were doing right now.

What he could contribute to the fight, however, was unclear. "Do you think you'll need me to draw them out again?" he asked the sheriff.

Heloise answered for him. "Doesn't seem like they need drawing out this time. Looks more like they're on a mission of destruction. I'm not sure they would even respond to you anymore."

Derek slumped back in the seat, feeling even more useless than before. As they sped through the empty streets, Garth pulled out the handset of his intercom and spoke urgently to the empty world through the speaker on his roof: "Attention! This is Sheriff Garth Chambers. For your own safety, remain in your homes until an all-clear has been sounded!"

They turned out of the neighborhood and rocketed down the county road that led to the house at the bottom of the hill. Derek watched the trees being lit up by the cruiser's lights, wondering what he could possibly do to help. He was relieved to feel his phone vibrating in his pocket, glad just to have something to distract him, and even more relieved when he saw it was a video call from Alison.

His relief vanished when he answered the call and saw the last face he expected. The face was so out of place in its environment that for a long moment, he didn't consciously recognize it, even though he had seen it a thousand times before. "Hector, what the hell are you doing in my house?" he asked when he could finally speak.

Hector's grin widened enough to fill the screen. The phone moved and his face disappeared, replaced by a sight that made Derek's heart sink and leap simultaneously: Alison, her face bleeding and bruised, tied to a chair in their bedroom, her hands and feet bound with rope. Her mouth was covered with duct tape, but her eyes pleaded silently with Derek. In the next moment, Hector's face filled the screen again, his grin even wider than before.

"Hector, you son of a bitch, what the hell have you done?"

The businessman's grin burst into open laughter. "Don't worry, Derek, I haven't done anything yet. And I won't do anything, as long as you and I can come to terms on your land."

"Whatever you want, Hector; just don't hurt her."

"That's exactly what I wanted to hear. Come meet me to discuss terms. Alone."

The call ended and Derek was left staring at a blank screen. When he looked up, Garth was bringing the cruiser to a halt while answering another radio call. "What the hell was that all about, Derek?" he asked as he hung up the headset.

"It was my old business partner," Derek heard himself say, "He's holding my wife hostage."

Even in the dark, Derek could see Garth scowl. "Damn it," he muttered, looking across the street to the old house. A crowd of revelers filled the second-floor balcony, desperately waving for rescue. Dogs paced the yard below them. "Bad timing. All my men are tied up with the dogs."

"That's alright, sheriff, you can do more good here. I know my old business partner; he just wants to negotiate. He won't do anything to hurt her. I'll go back and talk to him alone."

Garth nodded, impressed, then looked back at the house. "We won't get all of them out of here in this tiny thing, anyways." He nodded at Heloise in the passenger seat. "Whaddya say? We go fight off those dogs, rescue those people, and use their vehicles to get everybody out?"

Heloise raised her dart gun and nodded. "Hell yeah."

The sheriff turned back to Derek. "Alright, then the cruiser is all yours."

Derek felt strangely like a teenager being given the car for the night by his parents, especially when Garth had to climb out and open the door for him to get out. Derek climbed out and stood next to Garth, who held the shotgun he had taken from the cruiser, and Heloise, who still brandished her dart gun. "Thank you, Garth."

"Don't mention it. Your wife is a fine woman. I'm sorry I can't help you myself, but I trust you'll see to it that she's released safely."

"I will."

"Well, take this, just in case you and your old partner can't quite come to terms."

Garth undid his leather belt and handed it to Derek, including the revolver in its holster. Derek stared at the instrument of death for a long moment, then grabbed it before he could change his mind. "Isn't this illegal for a civilian, Sheriff?" he asked nervously as he fumbled putting the belt on.

Garth winked at him. "Consider yourself deputized."

Derek thanked him again, checked that the belt was secure, and climbed back into the cruiser, taking the vehicle in a wide uncertain loop and setting off for Sylvan Springs. Garth watched until he was gone, then turned back to the house. He could hear pleas for help coming from the people trapped on the upper floor. More dogs seemed to have gathered below, as if they were begging at their master's table, waiting for tasty morsels to fall to them.

Garth glanced at Loise and raised his weapon. "You ready for this?"

Loise exhaled slowly, tapping the steel barrel of her dart gun with the fingers of one hand. "As ready as I'm gonna be."

That was good enough for Garth. He nodded and they set off towards the house, weapons in hand.

TWENTY-SEVEN

THE NIGHT HAD BEEN LONG AND FULL OF STRANGE NOISES.

Alison had sat patiently (not that she had much of a choice) in the old wooden chair, feeling her hands and feet fall asleep from the tape that bound them, while cold sweat poured down her face. She had hoped that the sweat would melt the glue on the tape, but so far, no such luck. Maybe it had to be hot sweat in order to melt the glue, she thought, desperately trying to distract herself. Even through her pain and terror, or maybe because of it, she laughed a little at her strange joke. The sound emerged as a splattery burst of air that barely managed to escape the edge of the duct tape over her mouth.

Reeve turned at the spluttering sound, scowling at his charge. Ever since he had returned from whatever he had done with Gracie's dog, he had been pacing the room and muttering to himself, a sour look on his face. Alison hoped his foul mood wasn't a sign that he had killed the dog. Shortly after he had returned, she had tried pleading with him with her eyes, looking for some reassurance that the dog was still alive, but he had misinterpreted her expression as a different kind of pleading and had leaned over her, whispering horrible things in her ear until Hector, probably jealous, had yelled at him to stop. The older man had sat by the window all night, silently counting the hours or minutes that had gone by since they had tied Alison to the chair, leaving her in her own bedroom without any way of telling the time.

As those hours or minutes had passed, increasingly strange noises had come from the streets outside. They had heard children running and screaming, not the usual excited cries of kids cutting loose on Halloween, but terrified yelps and rushing slaps on the pavement, as if the kids were fleeing from some horrible menace. Every few minutes a police car would whiz by, its sirens drowning out all other noise, its lights bouncing through the bedroom windows and briefly illuminating the room in a swirl of flashing reds and blues. Each time, Hector and Reeve would rush to the window, reaching for their weapons like gangsters in an old black-and-white movie, then gently release them as the lights disappeared, the sirens dopplering away down the street. In the silences that followed, Alison often thought she heard the barking of dogs, but couldn't be sure it wasn't her imagination.

"Man, what the fuck do you think's going on out there?" Reeve asked after they had waited a minute or an hour. "It sounds like all hell's breaking loose. The cops are running all over."

"Good," Hector replied from his spot at the window, never taking his eyes from the street outside, "Just so long as they're not running over here."

As if to prove him wrong, the room suddenly filled with swirling red and blue. Alison had to squeeze her eyes shut as the lights flooded in. This time, they did not move on. Judging from their angle, Alison guessed the squad car was parked directly in the driveway.

"That idiot," Hector groaned, struggling to see through the blinding lights, "I told him not to get the police involved."

Again as if in defiance to Hector's will, an amplified voice boomed through the house. But the voice from the police intercom was not the authoritative voice of an officer; it was nervous, shaky, and familiar. Alison smiled through the duct tape at that voice. "It's Derek, Hector. I come alone. I only want Alison back safely. Let's just talk and I'll give you whatever you want."

Hector nodded and grinned. "I'm sure you will. Reeve, go check him out."

The valet nodded and Alison watched him disappear through the open door of the bedroom, digging his handgun out of his belt as he went. A moment later, she saw the doorway growing smaller and felt her chair being dragged backwards. The dragging stopped when she was near the windows, still facing the door. She couldn't see Hector behind her, but she felt the barrel of his gun press against her cheek and heard the click of the hammer as he pulled it back. She felt his great sweaty bulk lean over her as he whispered, "And now, Mrs. Rains, we will see just how reasonable of a man your husband is."

Alison tried to force herself to smile against the tape that bound her mouth.

Derek felt anything but confident as he piloted the cruiser into his driveway. He had always imagined that driving a police cruiser would instantly fill its driver with a feeling of surety, but as he had piloted the empty streets, Derek had only felt awkward, not wanting to attract the attention of anyone who might run to the vehicle for help. At least the sirens were off, but he was unable to figure out which of the many switches on the panel operated the lights and had been forced to drive with them on, the strobing lights passing over the empty houses, revealing glimpses of their warped, twisting facades.

Only after he had pulled into the driveway did he realize that the lights would grab Hector's attention. If Hector thought the police were closing in on him, he was liable to do something crazy. Thankfully Derek had seen Garth operate the speaker on the outside of the car and thought he remembered how to do it. Grabbing the handset, he spoke as slowly and calmly as he could, hoping the fear he felt in his voice wouldn't be projected through the loudspeaker. When he was done, he hung up the handset and climbed out of the car, leaving the driver's side door open in case he needed to make a quick exit.

As he crossed the driveway, he scanned the yard for dogs and saw nothing. Reaching beneath the hem of his coat, he felt for the gun in its holster. He didn't want to enter holding it in case that gave Hector the wrong idea, but he was reassured to find it still there.

Scanning the darkened windows, Derek wondered where Hector could be. On his call, he and Alison had been in the bedroom, but Derek couldn't see any movement or lights at the bedroom windows. The entire situation made him nervous, as if Hector was laying a trap for him. Still, Derek didn't have any choice but to enter that trap. Alison was in danger and he couldn't put any other concern above that.

Stepping onto the stoop, Derek realized the front door was already hanging open. The hinges creaked loudly as he pushed it open the rest of the way, making him wince as he poked his head into the darkness inside. Seeing no movement as his eyes adjusted to the dark, Derek entered, calling Hector's name. He received no answer from the echoing darkness, but thought he heard a slight rustling from upstairs.

Leaving the front door open to give himself a little more light, Derek crossed the entryway towards the stairs, peering into the shadowed entrances of the kitchen and the living room, seeing nothing on either side. As the first stair creaked beneath his foot, he immediately heard a rushing noise behind him. Before he could turn, a strong hand was on his shoulder, and he felt something cold and hard pressing into the center of his spine. The click of a hammer being pulled back removed all doubt of what the thing was.

"Just wait right there," a familiar voice whispered as Derek was pulled back off the steps. The rough hand left his shoulder and began to pat him down, but the gun never moved. Derek held his breath as the hand reached beneath the hem of his coat. He could feel the excitement as the fingers wrapped around the sheriff's revolver. They excitedly pushed up his coat, unsnapped his holster, and pulled out the gun. A moment later, Derek could feel two barrels pressed against his back. "You always bring a gun to negotiate?" the voice sneered, its owners' face pressing against Derek's cheek. Derek recognized Hector's valet, the one who had said that his boss could do Derek great harm, or many favors. Derek had never imagined a favor like this.

Seeing he would get no response from his hostage, the valet pressed both barrels into Derek's spine, shoving him towards the stairs. "Get moving," he barked. Derek trudged up the stairs in time with his captor, trying not to give him a reason to shoot by moving too quickly. They moved in an odd sort of dance, perfectly in time with each other as Derek climbed to what he knew would be his doom.

Brian Johnson had been huddled in the coat closet for what felt like hours. The screams and cries from upstairs had finally subsided hours or minutes ago, but he could still hear the dogs scratching at the closet door. Brian thought if they kept at it long enough, they might be able to scratch all the way through the wooden panels. Holding the knob until his hand began to sweat, Brian held the door in place, fearful that they would knock the door open if he let go.

Suddenly, the rattling stopped and Brian realized how hard he had been holding on to the knob. Without the pressure from the other side, he found himself leaning so hard on the door that his sweat-slicked hands slipped off the metal. His body tumbled to the floor so quickly he almost hit his head on the frame. Picking himself up off the floor, he scrambled for the knob again, struggling to grasp the dripping metal. He was surprised to find the door not pressing in without him holding it shut.

Even the sounds of the scratching had stopped. As Brian listened, he realized that all the sounds in the house had changed. The dogs that he had heard pacing the upper floor all night were now bounding down the stairs overhead, the sounds of their paws congregating into a terrible thunderstorm. They all seemed to be heading towards the front door, which Brian heard creaking open on its hinges. A moment later, there was an incredibly loud blast, like the sound of thunder, only much closer and much more intense. Brian had to press his hands against his ears as the sound came again and again. After each blast, he heard dogs yelp and howl, then fall silent. More blasts tore through the house, silencing more dogs.

Eventually, Brian realized what was happening: the cavalry had finally arrived! The police had stormed in to come to everyone's rescue. Already the dogs and the blasts had fallen silent and he could hear the heavy-booted footsteps of the law just outside. He swung open the door, desperate to be rescued. A paunchy, middle-aged lawman turned from the nearby kitchen and raised his shotgun at the noise. Too late, Brian realized his mistake. He squeezed his eyes shut, waiting for the final blast.

Instead, he heard only a sharp, delirious cackle. "Boy, you almost got yourself shot running out like that," a soft voice drawled. Brian slowly opened his eyes, taking in the lawman who held his still-smoking shotgun at his side. Next to him was a Hispanic woman wearing a tactical suit with a badge that read ANIMAL CONTROL and holding a steel gun made for firing darts.

On the floor around them, between the torn human corpses, were piled several dogs, some of them blown apart by the shotgun's blasts, their heads missing or their sides split open, spilling their organs, while others lay unconscious with darts stuck in their necks or sides, their sides heaving as they struggled to breath. The linoleum floor was so slick with blood that Brian struggled to walk across the kitchen to the lawman. The feet of his costume slid across the floor, almost spilling him among the corpses. He felt the blood soaking through the fabric of his costume.

"How many more are upstairs?" the lawman asked him, pushing more shells into his shotgun.

"People? Or dogs?"

"Both."

"A lot… Of both."

The lawman sighed, looking towards the ceiling, where they could still hear the padding of dozens of sets of paws from the second floor.

"You'll never make it up there," Brian told them, "There's way too many of them."

Garth nodded, slamming another shell into his shotgun. "We gotta get those people out somehow."

Brian thought for a moment. "We could use my truck."

The animal control officer tilted her head towards him. "Where's it parked?"

A moment later, Brian was running across the open yard towards the street, followed by Garth and Heloise, as they had hastily introduced themselves. Halfway across the field, Garth told them he would hold down the fort until they brought the truck back. Sweat poured down his face and he struggled to catch his breath. Brian moved on without him, scanning the area around the parked vehicles for dogs. He saw none, as if they had all been ordered to guard the house by their commander.

As he climbed the step-rail into his lifted pick-up, he uneasily watched the massive space below the cab, expecting a dog to burst out of the shadows behind his oversized tires. As he climbed into the cab and slammed the door shut behind him, he breathed a sigh of relief, which turned to a gasp when something slammed against the rear window. In the mirror, he saw Heloise standing in the bed with her gun at the ready, tapping on the window to tell him to go.

Nervously fumbling with the keys, Brian started the truck and swung it towards the house, crossing the narrow road in a single truck length. His tires tore into the yard, leaving deep tracks in the grass behind him and spitting out chunks of earth in all directions. Brian slowed as he neared Garth, who awkwardly climbed into the bed, assisted by Heloise. When Heloise tapped on the window to signal that they were ready, Brian took off towards the house, making his way towards the balcony on the other side.

Melanie Richards pressed a torn scrap of pillow case against her face, soaking up blood and tears. Her face had been savagely bitten by one of the dogs, as had her hands when she tried to push the beast away, but thankfully several sets of hands had pushed the dogs away and pulled her to safety. She had never seen who had rescued her, but had regained consciousness in her bedroom, having passed out from shock and blood loss.

About a dozen of her party guests were crammed into the small room, and from what she had seen, they were the only ones still alive. Melanie wept as she thought of her friends who had come to help her bid the house farewell and had instead said goodbye to their own lives. The sobs contorted her face, widening the rips in her cheeks and bringing more tears, which mixed with the blood flowing down her face and dried on the pillow case she had taken off her bed.

Other guests were tying the bedsheets together, trying to form a rope long enough to reach from the balcony outside Melanie's door to the ground, just far enough below to induce a broken angle or leg from a jump. They had all seen Donald and several others attempt it, and now their half-eaten corpses littered the yard.

Sam and Eli were trying to hold the door shut against the merciless onslaught of the dogs. It sounded as if the dogs were throwing their bodies against the door, rattling the frame with each impact. Since she lived alone, Melanie had never bothered to put a lock on the century-old door, or even repair the hinges so it could sit comfortably in the frame, both of which she now regretted as her friends struggled to hold the door shut. Their strength waned after repulsing each hit, struggling each time to hold the door where it had been. The door itself seemed to be caving in from the impacts, the ancient wood visibly cracking and bending at places.

Melanie didn't know how much longer they could keep the dogs out. Jordan and Taylor were testing their rope of bedsheets with a tug, but found they ripped under even the slightest pressure. Melanie cursed herself for buying the thinnest sheets available.

A noise from outside pulled her out of her self-pity. Actually, a series of noises: a blasting, ascending series of tones that could have only been the modified horn of an obnoxiously big pick-up truck, and she knew only one person who had a vehicle like that.

She ran to the window to see Brian's monstrous pick-up parked just beneath the balcony. Brian was behind the wheel and two passengers were in the bed: one an overweight police officer in an ill-fitting uniform, the other a slim Hispanic woman in a black tactical suit. The cop was wiping sweat from his brow as he waved the people on the balcony towards the bed of the truck, brandishing a shotgun in his other hand. The woman kept watch on the area around the truck, aiming a silver-barreled rifle into the darkness.

Melanie screamed for the others, waving them towards the balcony with her blood-soaked pillow case like a matador waving his cloth. Jordan and Taylor led the charge to the balcony, lining up to climb over the railing so the police officer could help them down. As he lowered Taylor safely into the bed of Brian's truck, the Latino woman gave a small yell and raised her weapon at a dog charging out of the darkness. She fired her weapon, which turned out to be a dart gun. Whatever was in those darts must have been powerful, since the dog fell unconscious almost as soon as the tip struck its neck. More dogs rushed in, but the woman took care of each with a well-placed shot. The police officer continued to load people into the truck one at a time, but the balcony was filling with people waiting to get down.

More dogs were swarming the truck, but that didn't seem to have stopped them from attacking her bedroom door as well. Melanie turned back to see Sam and Eli still struggling to hold the door shut against the onslaught of dogs. Pushing her way inside past the crowd on the balcony, Melanie rushed to join them, hoping that together they could hold the door long enough to let everyone else escape.

For the first time behind the wheel of his truck, Brian felt completely useless. He watched helplessly through the rear window of the cab as Heloise picked off the approaching dogs one by one while Garth helped lower the party guests from the balcony. Following his instructions, the partiers would climb over the railing, then lower themselves until they were hanging from the edge of the balcony by their fingertips. This would bring them just low enough for the sheriff to bear hug them around the waist and lower them into the bed of the truck.

The work would have been much faster with two people, but someone had to keep the dogs from sneaking up on them, and Heloise's hands were already full with that. Brian wanted to get out and help them, maybe lower a second person while Garth was lowering the first, or maybe pick up the shotgun the sheriff had leaned against the wall of the bed and blast a few dogs alongside Heloise. But the sheriff had yelled at him when he had tried to get out of the truck before, wanting to be able to make an escape as quickly as possible in case they were overrun.

So, Brian was forced to sit helplessly behind the wheel of his truck, watching as other people helped with the heroics. It was too bad, since it looked as if the sheriff really needed the help: about half a dozen people still filled the balcony, and by the look of it they seemed to be growing desperate. Brian watched in his rearview as a pretty blonde in a Princess Jasmine costume that was more revealing than it was culturally appropriate climbed over the balcony railing next to a skinny redhead who the sheriff was already helping down.

"The dogs are breaking through!" the faux Princess Jasmine yelled. "I can hear them breaking down the door!"

"We'll get all of you out, don't worry!" the sheriff yelled back, sweat pouring down his face as he strained to lift the redhead into the truck.

The princess looked back as the sound of wood splintering came from inside the room.

"I'm gonna jump!" Princess Jasmine yelled, as desperately as if she meant to kill herself.

"Don't do that!" The sheriff yelled, setting the redhead down, "You'll break your goddamn legs and hold everybody up!"

Princess Jasmine seemed not to hear him, or tried not to. Brian looked out the window and saw her eyes calculating the distances to various landing spots, including the roof of his truck. He probably knew even before she did that she was going to try it. He was rolling down his window to tell her not to when she suddenly let go of the balcony, flying forward a lot faster than she had probably intended. She disappeared from sight over the roof of his truck and half a second later there came an enormous bang as the roof of his cab caved in. His windshield cracked under the impact, then again when her body rolled down the glass on its way to his hood. The metal crumpled beneath her body, which rolled into the grass with a heavy thud.

In the beams his headlights cast across the wide lawn, Brian saw several dogs running from the shadows, closing in on the point where Princess Jasmine had disappeared. Looking in the rearview, Brian saw Heloise, her hands already full with a wave of dogs approaching from the rear. Garth yelled, cursed, and sweated as he tried to push his way through the half dozen or so panicking young adults that filled the bed of the truck around him.

Neither of them would be able to make it in time. If Brian wanted to be a hero, now was the time. Suddenly, he wasn't so sure he wanted to, but before he could think twice, he was already swinging the passenger door open and climbing out. He heard the sheriff yelling somewhere behind him, but the pounding of his heart drowned out the words.

He found Princess Jasmine face down in the grass beside his right front tire. Her head seemed to be bleeding and, as the sheriff had predicted, one leg looked oddly twisted. Both ankles were swelling with blood.

But there was no time for a medical diagnosis now; the dogs were closing in. Brian shook the princess, trying to wake her up. When she didn't, he rolled her over, scooping his arms beneath her bare midriff to pick her up. She moaned a little, her arms instinctively closing around him as he lifted her up, but she didn't fully regain consciousness until he had turned back towards the truck.

Between them and the door was the biggest German shepherd Brian had ever seen. Its lips were pulled back in a snarl and its bare fangs were dripping with slime. Brian froze, knowing that he would have to move closer to the dog in order to get into the cab, and simultaneously knowing that to do so would awaken the anger of the dog and cause it to leap at them, probably ripping the princess from his arms before it decided to jump on him. So, he stood frozen, knowing only that by standing still he wouldn't risk the dog's anger.

Princess Jasmine chose just then to wake up. Shaking the blood-matted hair from her face, she looked around, first in confusion, then in fear when she saw the dog. As it opened its mouth in a growl, she opened her mouth in a scream. The sound almost made Brian drop her, it was so startling and loud, and its effect on the dog was even worse. After initially leaping back in terror, the animal recovered and prepared to jump forward. Brian squeezed Princess

Jasmine closer, partially to comfort her and partially to get her to stop screaming, but neither seemed to work. She clawed at his shoulders, screaming even louder than before.

Brian wanted to close his eyes, to pretend all of this wasn't happening, but he knew that a hero always faced his problems head-on, so he kept his eyes open as the dog prepared to leap at them, trying to turn Princess Jasmine away from the oncoming jaws in what he hoped wouldn't be a futile gesture.

As the dog leaped towards them, an enormous sound ripped through the night. A blast of red-hot shrapnel met the dog in mid-air, dissolving half its face and much of its torso. The body landed at Brian's feet, the flesh-stripped half of the skull grinning up at him. Princess Jasmine screamed even louder when she saw that, burying her head in his chest.

Turning back to the truck, Brian saw the sheriff pumping his shotgun, smoke still billowing from the barrel. "Don't just stand there all day, get back in the truck!" he yelled. Behind him, the people he had rescued were helping to lower the others still on the balcony while Heloise staved off an increasing wave of dogs.

As Brian lifted the princess into the cab, Garth joined Heloise in holding off the dogs. Soon the night was punctuated by one loud explosion of the shotgun after another, the silences in between filled by the gentle pffts of Heloise's dart gun.

Setting the princess in the center of his seat, Brian slammed the door shut behind them and began to climb over her. "You able to drive on that ankle?" he yelled when she slapped him away in protest.

"Oh, right, no," she said, looking embarrassed as she let him go.

He climbed into the driver's seat and dropped behind the wheel, impatiently drumming his hands on the dash as he watched the last of the partiers being lowered into the bed of his truck. Dogs were running towards the truck in all directions now, Garth and Heloise just barely holding them off.

"Thanks for coming after me," the blonde princess said in the silence between shotgun blasts. "I guess I owe you my life."

Brian waved the thought away. "Forget about it, it's what anyone would have done. You don't owe me anything." He looked out at the lawn through the spidery cracks in the glass. "But a new windshield might be nice."

Melanie breathed a sigh of relief as the last of her friends on the balcony was lowered into the truck. That left only herself, Sam, and Eli in the house. The two men were still holding the bedroom door shut against the onslaught of dogs, which had somehow grown worse even as the wave of dogs attacking the truck outside had grown larger. They had managed to keep the door closed against the attacking animals, but that would soon be impossible. The door itself was coming apart under the onslaught of the dogs, the bottom panels of the thin old wood breaking apart in large chunks. Soon the dogs would be able to stick their heads through the opening and nip at anyone close enough to keep the door shut.

Melanie ran towards the door, pulling the bloodied pillow case from her face. "You guys go for the truck," she said. "I'll hold the door shut until you're on."

"Are you crazy?" Eli exclaimed, the strands of his mullet wig flying as he turned to look at her. "You'll never be able to hold the door shut by yourself," Sam agreed, pressing his shoulder against the door.

"I don't need to hold the door shut all night, just for a few minutes while you guys run for the truck." She squeezed her way between them, pressing her hands against the door. "I'll be right behind you, now get going!"

"You know once you let go of this door, the dogs will be streaming in, right?" Sam asked, one eyebrow cocked beneath his jester's cap.

"Guess I'll just have to run faster than them then, now, won't I?" Melanie asked. "Now, get going! I'm not going to let any more of my friends get hurt because of me, and I am not taking no for an answer." She pushed her body against the door, leaving no room for the two men to hold on. Outside, the series of sharp, ascending tones came again.

"You sure you can hold them by yourself?" Sam asked as he began to let go.

She nodded, grimacing as she felt the full force of the attacking dogs outside for the first time. "Yeah. Now, get going."

Sam and Eli nodded and ran for the balcony.

Everyone he knew in Denver had made fun of Brian when he had customized his pick-up with lifted tires and extra suspension to hold up to two tons. But he was willing to bet money that none of them would be laughing if they could see his truck now, the extra-long bed filled to the brim with more than a dozen terrified party guests crawling over each other to find safety while a sheriff and an animal control officer stood on the edge of the bed trying to hold off waves of attacking dogs. The truck had sunk slightly under the added weight, but it would still drive. At least, Brian hoped it would.

The real problem was space, which seemed to be running out in the bed, just as two more men were climbing over the balcony railing. "Don't go yet!" one of them yelled, "Melanie's still inside!"

Brian grimaced, wondering how they could possibly fit everyone in his truck. Sliding open the window at the back of his cab, he yelled to the crowd of people pressed against the back wall of the cab, "Someone climb in here! We need to make some room!"

He instantly regretted his decision, and not just because it meant that Princess Jasmine had to slide to the far end of the bench seat to make room. A redheaded woman in a Princess Peach outfit tried to squeeze through the window, finding herself stuck halfway, her arms flailing around the bench seat while her legs tried to push off the crowd outside, which moved in the space she had vacated and pressed her legs to the wall, preventing her from moving.

As the crowd lowered the two men into the truck, Garth raised his shotgun towards another of the approaching dogs and pulled the trigger. He was greeted only with an unsatisfying click. "God damn it, Heloise, cover me while I reload!"

"I'll try!" Heloise yelled from the far corner of the cab, where she already had more targets than she could keep up with. She moved from one dog to the next, firing as quickly as possible and silently praying that her own ammunition wouldn't also run out.

"Melanie!" Eli yelled towards the balcony as the crowd helped lower him into the truck, "Time to go!"

Melanie heard his cries but was for a moment frozen at the door in panic, feeling the impact of one dog after another hitting the wood, imagining the impact they would hit her with.

In the truck, Brian drummed his hands impatiently on the wheel and blasted the horn again. In the rearview, he could see more dogs closing in, their ranks growing with only one shooter to hold them off. "Brian!" the sheriff yelled as he fumbled for shells from his belt. "We have to get going! If your friend's not here, that's her problem!"

Brian knew he was right. The dogs would soon be on them, and in greater numbers than Garth or Heloise could hold off. If he left now, he would be abandoning Melanie to die, but if he stayed, he would be dooming everyone in the truck. He threw the truck into gear but kept his foot on the brake, pounding the horn again in the last few seconds he had to make a decision.

This time, the sound got through to Melanie. Taking a deep breath, she abandoned the door and ran for the balcony. She was only halfway across the room when she heard the door burst open behind her. She tossed the bloodied pillow case over her shoulder, hoping it would be enough to distract the dogs. She heard them sniffing and tearing at the bloodied cloth, but she didn't dare slow down to look behind her.

On the ground below, the dogs were about to overrun the truck. "Brian!" Garth yelled again, his shaking hands struggling to force a shell into the shotgun, "If you don't get this truck moving right now, I will shoot you myself!"

This finally got Brian moving. He slammed on the gas and let off the brake in the same instant, bringing the truck to a lurching start that tossed the passengers in the bed against the rear wall of the cab. Princess Peach flew forward a few more inches, then wailed as she was wedged even further into the window. She screamed and scratched at Brian to help her, but he was beyond caring about that. He was holding the gas down and flying, leaving the dogs far behind.

"Wait!" screamed a familiar voice from behind them. Brian stepped on the brake as suddenly as he had stepped on the gas, bringing another wail from Princess Peach and more cries from the sea-sick passengers in the bed as they were slammed into the rear wall of his cab a second time. In his sideview he could see Melanie on the balcony, holding out her arms for help as she ran towards the railing.

More dogs were running towards them too, more than Heloise could keep off with her dart gun. There would be no time to lower Melanie down safely and she seemed to know it. As she climbed the railing just above the truck, the people in the bed raised their arms in unison, forming a protective net of hands. Brian was reminded of when Underoath had come to Denver when he was in high school, where a man in a cow costume had led a line of people crowd surfing across the massive stadium.

Melanie climbed the railing and jumped in a single motion, sailing through the air with her arms outstretched like some bizarre, bloodied angel. She fell into the protective net of hands, which bent down to take her weight, the crowd leaning down to lower her safely to the truck bed.

Brian slammed on the gas again, bracing himself for another lurching start which never came. He pressed the pedal to the floor and heard the engine roaring like a horrible monster, but the scene through the cracked windshield remained the same.

Finally, he realized what was happening: his sudden start and even more sudden stop, combined with the overloaded weight of his passengers, had sunk the tires into the soft earth, and now they were stuck. Keeping the gas pressed down, Brian quickly turned the wheel from side to side, hoping to find a patch of earth dry enough for the tires to get traction.

At the same time, Heloise was firing her darts into the approaching dogs. There were already more than she could handle when her worst fear came true. She pulled the trigger and the air canister hissed uselessly. She was out of darts. "Cover me, Sheriff!"

Garth grimaced. Having lost the shell he was loading in one of Brian's sudden stops, he was now fishing another one out of his belt. The truck was unprotected as more dogs swooped in from all directions.

"We've got company!" Eli yelled, pointing towards the balcony. Apparently, Melanie wasn't the only one who had realized she could jump from the balcony to the truck. An enormous Doberman that had followed her through the bedroom was now clambering over the railing, its mouth dripping slime as it prepared to leap onto the truck.

Garth pressed a single shell into the slide just as the dog made it over the railing. He raised his weapon as the dog began to fall towards the truck. Brian's tires finally turned enough to find hard earth and the truck took off, lurching forward at a crazy angle, throwing Garth's aim off the dog.

The dog, carried forward by its leap, was still lined up to land in the middle of the crowd, who screamed and cried as the dog fell towards them. Garth adjusted his posture to compensate for the changing angle and squeezed off his single shot.

The shell collided with the dog in midair, splitting open its belly and throwing it off its course. The people in the bed screamed as the dog's blood and guts rained down on them, but its body landed harmlessly behind the truck. Garth smirked as the truck left the dead dog behind, as well as the many living ones that still chased after them.

Brian kept his foot on the gas, ensuring the dogs had no hope of catching up. As he reached the narrow two-lane road, he turned left without slowing down and headed away from the mountains, speeding towards where he assumed the town would be. As he cruised down the street, his foot never for a second letting off the gas, all he could do was laugh. Even when the two princesses in his front seat shot dirty looks at him, he continued to laugh, an infectious grin growing from ear to ear.

He felt happy, he didn't want to explain it.

Derek had never before realized how long his upstairs hallway stretched. With each step, the shadowy corridor seemed to only extend further in front of him, its farthest end completely lost in darkness. Maybe it was only the disorienting effect of the swirling police lights, which entered the hallway through his open bedroom door, creating a narrow rectangle of red and blue which splashed across the wall for a moment before wiping itself away, replaced a moment later by a slightly different mix of colors, or perhaps it was the dread caused by the two barrels he could still feel pressed into his spine, but either way the effect was disorienting. His anxiety rose as he drew near the bedroom.

"Keep moving," Reeve growled, pushing him with both barrels. Derek hadn't noticed he had stopped, but the force of the barrels and the sudden stab of pain in his spine forced him to take a step forward. He landed in the opening of his bedroom door, holding on to the frame for support.

For a moment, the bedroom was only a sea of darkness, then a wave of multi-colored light washed through, illuminating two figures from behind. The first was recognizable from its silhouette alone: Hector's plump, rotund figure blocked out most of the middle window. The shape in front of him was an unrecognizable mass of shadow until the swirling police lights reached their zenith, bouncing off every surface, illuminating Alison.

Derek could see her hands and feet bound to the chair she sat in and the duct tape that ran across her mouth, but most of all he could see the pleading in her eyes, begging him for rescue in the seconds before the light faded. Above her, he saw Hector grinning wildly at him, the man's face becoming even more distorted as the shadows lengthened across it. Derek's fists clenched as he saw the last gleam of light reflect off the matte-black handgun Hector held to Alison's head.

"Derek, so nice of you to join us," Hector said from the new-fallen darkness.

"He had a gun on him, boss," Reeve said, pushing Derek into the bedroom.

"That was just in case things got crazy," Derek said, trying to be reassuring and instantly regretting it.

"Crazy?" Hector asked, astounded. As the lights came around again, Derek could see his eyebrow cocked in disbelief. He held Alison's head in one meaty hand, grinding the barrel of his gun into her temple with the other until her skin began to bleed. The first drops were made redder by the police lights that illuminated them. "What would I do that's crazy?" he asked, as if daring Derek to reply.

"That's enough, Hector," Derek intoned in a voice so confident it surprised even himself. "I'm willing to sign whatever you want, don't screw it up by hurting Alison."

The next strobe of the police lights revealed Hector's grin growing even wider. "I was hoping you would say that."

Reeve shoved Derek further into the room, where the spinning lights eventually revealed a stack of papers on his night stand. A heavy fountain pen lay next to the final page.

"No need to read it," Hector said as Derek turned over the pages, "it simply says you're turning over the land in Mexico to me. Free of charge, of course."

"Of course," Derek muttered as he pulled the thick cap off the heavy metal pen. Waiting for the lights to strobe again so he could see what he was doing, Derek turned to the last page.

As the light illuminated the heavy paper in swirling blues and reds, Derek began to sign his name, the blade-like tip of the pen gliding across the paper as nimbly as a skater on ice. Gripping the thick metal tube, Derek noticed that the pen even had Hector's name and address printed on the side. The bastard had thought of everything and feared nothing, Derek thought.

As he finished signing his name, a streak of motion near the door drew Derek's attention. Gracie's golden retriever stood in the doorway. As the lights washed across its face, Derek saw that the dog was no longer normal. Its face was pulled back in a vicious snarl which Derek had never seen on the animal before, and even after the light left its face, he could still see the eyes glowing in the darkness, the same eerie yellow as the Xolo's had been on the night Derek had run over the deer.

Since the animal's vicious snarl had been aimed at Reeve, who hadn't seemed to have noticed the beast, Derek said nothing. "Okay, all signed," he said, keeping his voice as calm and even as possible.

Hector replied with equal calmness. "Okay, Reeve, bring him over here. The bank won't accept the paperwork with his blood all over it."

Derek took the first few steps Reeve guided him on without question, until the full force of Hector's statement, and the pressure of the pistols still dug into his spine, made him realize what they had planned. With the signature they needed now obtained, they planned to kill him in his own bedroom. Once he was gone, they would undoubtedly do the same to Alison – or worse.

He froze, digging his heels into the carpet, keeping his body positioned between Reeve and the night stand. "Come on, fucker, we can do this the easy way-" Reeve growled, trying to push Derek aside with the pistols, "Or the hard-"

A low growl interrupted his sentence. Looking over his shoulder, Derek saw the valet's face in the next wave of light. The hard jawline was set in worry, the steely eyes pointed towards the ground. "God damn it, Reeve, I thought I told you to get rid of that mutt!" Hector yelled.

"I did! I don't know how he got back inside," Reeve yelled back, perhaps intentionally misunderstanding his master. As the dog moved in on him, Reeve pulled one of the pistols from Derek's back, keeping the other firmly pressed against his spine.

Derek turned his head over his shoulder to see the dog, its snarling face looking up at the valet, its eyes catching the strobing lights and seeming to turn an alarming red. Reeve raised his pistol above the golden head, as if to deliver a headshot between those horrible glowing eyes, but then seemed to think better of it. His hand wavered, then raised the pistol again, this time holding the butt of the handle towards the dog's head.

Reeve raised his arm, holding the gun like a hammer, then brought it down hard as if he intended to pistol whip the dog's face. Whatever his intentions were, he was far too slow. The dog's jaws snapped like one of the Hungry, Hungry Hippos that Derek had played with Gracie and Max not so long ago, catching the man's arm before he could complete the blow.

The jaws shut around his wrist and forearm. Derek saw blood flowing from the wrist as the dog's fangs tore through his skin, twisting the arm down like it was a chew toy. The trapped hand twisted uselessly, trying somehow to point the gun it held back at the dog, but the teeth were clamped just below the end of the palm, their grip preventing the hand from twisting back. The fangs dug deeper, the jaws grinding against tendon and bone.

Derek felt the pressure disappear from his spine and knew that Reeve, in desperation, had removed the gun from his back in order to aim it at the dog. This time, he would do more than pistol whip the beast. Derek knew this was his only chance to escape. Before he even knew what he was doing, he felt his hand wrapping around the heavy fountain pen, gripping the metal tube in his fist like a dagger. He whirled around, raising the pen over his head like one of the killers in the slasher movies he had watched in high school. The revolving lights gleamed off the steel tip.

Over the valet's shoulder, he saw Hector silhouetted by the lights. He had taken the pistol off Alison and was trying to aim it towards the dog, waving the gun wildly as the valet's struggling, thrashing body continually blocked his shot.

Reeve was focused entirely on the dog, his entire body twisted towards the animal. Cords stood out on his neck as he struggled to pull his hand free from the dog's mouth. The bulging veins on the twisted, exposed neck gave Derek his target. He brought the pen down hard, shuddering as he felt the metal tearing into flesh. Reeve screamed as the pen disappeared into his neck until half of Hector's name was obscured by his flesh. In the sudden shock, his body went limp.

Derek grabbed for the sheriff's gun and tried to pull it from Reeve's weakened hand, but found the man's fingers wrapped around the weapon much tighter than he expected. To his horror, he saw the hand twisting up towards him; Reeve was trying to point the gun at Derek. He tried to bend the arm back, but the valet was too strong for him to do more than hold him off for a few moments.

Reeve screamed again as a loud snap emerged from his other wrist, and Derek knew the dog had chewed through his tendon. The trapped hand went limp and the gun it held dropped to the floor. Derek considered stooping to pick it up, but that would have meant letting go of the hand that still held a gun.

As the lights strobed through the room again, Derek caught a glimpse of Hector over Reeve's shoulder. He was lining up another shot, but this one was aimed straight at Derek. As the light faded away, he heard a shot ring out and saw Hector briefly illuminated by the flare of his muzzle. Derek ducked and heard something pass directly over his head. An instant later there was an enormous crash as part of the wall behind him exploded. Derek felt plaster dust raining down on him.

He wanted to remain crouched, but the lights would be back in a few seconds and Hector would have his shot lined up. There was no way for Derek to rip the gun out of Reeve's hand, but perhaps there was a way to fire back at Hector. Using all of his strength, he put his weight on Reeve's arm in the same direction the man was trying to bend his arm. Reeve squeezed off a shot as Derek twisted his arm, but the bullet passed harmlessly in front of him, the heat tracing a line across his belly. Using Reeve's own strength and the element of surprise to his advantage, Derek was able to twist Reeve's arm up and backwards, so the gun was now facing into the darkness where Hector stood.

Clutching Reeve's fist in both of his, Derek aimed the gun towards the cluster of shadows. His only advantage over Hector was that while the other man had to wait until the lights came back to see his target, Derek had the advantage of the silvery moonlight through the windows silhouetting his target. Hector's silhouette, however, was one with that of Alison, and Derek couldn't be sure if he was lining up a torso shot on Hector or a headshot on his wife. Struggling to keep Reeve's hand still, he waited for the lights to come back.

When they did, Derek saw that Hector had also lined up his shot. The pistol was aimed just above Derek's head and there was no time for Derek to line up a better shot. Wrestling Reeve's sweaty finger out of the guard, Derek squeezed the trigger.

Hector's bicep and the window behind seemed to explode in tandem. Blood spewed out of both sides of the man's arm as his hand went limp, dropping the gun. Hector screamed in pain, making a futile effort to stop the bleeding by wrapping his hand around both wounds.

Derek had only a moment to savor his victory before he felt a sudden stab of pain in his bicep. At first, he thought the dog had given up on Reeve and was biting him instead, but in the last of the swirling light he saw that the valet was sinking his own teeth into Derek's shoulder. Derek screamed and pulled his arm away, leaving a chunk of flesh in the valet's mouth, but refused to give up his hold on the gun, which Reeve was beginning to bend towards Derek, the gun drawing ever closer to being within reach of him.

Derek was just barely able to match Reeve's strength and keep the gun at bay. The only advantage he had was in having both of his hands free. He used that to his advantage and pulled the pen from Reeve's neck with one hand, using all his strength to keep the gun away with the other.

There was another scream and a jet of blood that flowed over Derek's hand as he pulled the pen free. The strobing lights illuminated the blood and showed Derek his next target. Raging from the pain in his arm, Derek brought the pen down again as Reeve turned the gun towards him. The pen slid into Reeve's left eye, disappearing almost completely as blood and ocular fluid oozed around the metal.

Reeve's body went limp and the second gun dropped from his hand. Derek tossed him towards the large master closet that hung open nearby. The revolving lights showed him colliding with a rack of Derek's suits, which he brought to the floor as he struggled to regain his footing. The dog followed after him, its jaws closing around the fresh blood flowing from the man's useless hand. As the dog tackled him to the ground, Derek slammed the door shut and grabbed an old wooden chair, the twin to the one Alison was tied up in, pressing it under the knob, preventing either of them from getting out. The closet door rattled as Reeve desperately tried to escape, but the chair held the door in place. From inside came the sound of screams, then the rip of clothes and flesh as the dog tore into him.

Turning back before the light faded completely, Derek saw the two handguns on the floor, their finish gleaming. Derek remembered their location well enough to find them both in the darkness.

As the lights came on, he saw Hector performing his own search, his good hand patting the floor for the gun he had dropped. Derek aimed and fired as Hector's hand closed in on the weapon. A small section of the floor exploded between his fingers and the pistol, pushing the gun away. Only a warning, but it was enough for Hector. He looked up to see Derek, looking now like a gunslinger in some old western movie with a pistol in each hand, blood soaking his shirt from an open wound, his face deeply shadowed by the strobing lights. As the room fell into darkness, Hector dashed for the door, forgetting about the papers on the night stand, only praying he could escape before Derek killed him.

Derek let him go, knowing the wounded man could do no more harm. When he heard footsteps pounding down the stairs, Derek dropped the guns, ran to Alison, and pulled the tape off her mouth. "You know, you're actually quite the negotiator," she said as he began to loosen her ropes.

"Well, you know, when the stakes are high…" Derek trailed off, observing her face in the blue light that swept across the room. He dropped the ropes and kissed her, hoping nothing would interrupt this moment.

Hector's chest heaved and his arm poured blood as he ran out the front door. He no longer cared about the land in Mexico. The only thing that mattered now was survival. The limo was parked where they had left it on the street, but Reeve had the keys, and that psychopath Derek had locked him in the closet with a mad dog. The police cruiser that Derek must have stolen sat in the driveway, its engine still running and the driver's side door hanging open, as if beckoning him.

Hector clambered in, almost forgetting to close the door as he threw the car in reverse and flew out of the driveway. He felt the car momentarily rise on two wheels as he turned onto the street. There was a scrape of metal as he threw the car in drive before it had finished backing up, then he slammed on the gas and took off down the road. The police lights were still going, and that was good. He would keep them going until he reached the Mexican border, driving all night and day if he had to, never letting his foot off the gas.

He cursed himself for how sure of himself he had been. Now there was a printed contract with his name on it sitting in the middle of a crime scene, and a pen with his name on it jammed in the eye of his employee, who was surely dead by now. The two witnesses to his crimes would identify him immediately, and his life in America would be over.

But he still had friends in Mexico. They could help him get across the border, they would patch up his wound, which seemed to be bleeding more and more, and keep him hidden from the authorities if they came looking for him. He could still build his empire in Mexico. He held on to that hope as he flew down the road.

A single noise from the passenger seat dashed all of his hopes. It was a low growl, both instantly familiar and supremely menacing. In his haste to get in the car, he realized he hadn't even looked in the passenger seat. Now he was afraid to take his eyes off the road, both because of how fast he was going and because of what he might see in the seat next to him.

When the growling intensified and seemed to grow closer to his ear, he had to turn to look. In the faint glow from a passing streetlight, he saw the bare-skinned dog he had bought for Derek sitting in the passenger seat. It must have smelled its old master and climbed into the car looking for him. Now the only smell it seemed to be driven by was the scent of the blood pouring from Hector's arm. The beast's eyes glowed yellow as its mouth watered, anticipating the feast it would soon have.

Hector only had a moment to regret buying Derek the dog before the animal lunged at him.

Derek ran outside to find the patrol car gone. Alison, who he was leading by the hand, was the first to see it from where they stood in the driveway. "There!" she cried, pointing down the street. Derek followed her finger to the patrol car, its lights still flashing, swerving back and forth as it sped off down the road.

"Hector must have taken it, but why is he driving like that?" Alison asked.

Derek thought he knew, and the vague hints of struggling motion he could see inside the car seemed to confirm his suspicion. There was a final sharp turn and a spray of red liquid coated the inside of the windows. He saw the car heading straight for an electrical pole, making only the small, random turns of a vehicle out of control, not enough to throw it off its course.

Every window in the cruiser shattered as the vehicle collided with the pole, its hood crumpling as the pole severed at its base. In the moment before the pole fell forward onto the vehicle, Derek saw a thin, grey form wriggle out of one of the shattered windows and dash off into the darkness.

The cruiser's roof collapsed as the pole crushed it, sparks shooting from the live wires it brought down onto the metal. Hot sparks shot across the street as electricity flowed into the metal. A moment later, a terrific explosion ripped through the vehicle, blinding Derek for a moment with its sudden flash.

When his vision recovered, he saw the vehicle engulfed in flames, its gas tank having exploded after being caught by one of the sparks. The shattered driver's side door flew open and part of the fire seemed to break away from the rest. For a moment, Derek told himself he couldn't really be seeing Hector running across the street, that no one could possibly still be alive after all that. Then he heard the anguished screams echoing down the street and knew that it was real.

Perhaps because of the extra weight he carried or perhaps because of his fondness for cheap polyester suits, Hector seemed to be burning extremely hot. Reddish-orange flames covered his body, turning to blue as they arced around his head. He was running towards Derek, and at first Derek thought the man intended to have his final revenge, to bear hug Derek in a wall of flame, to pin him down until he suffocated in fire. But as his anguished cries continued, Derek thought that the man might be running to him for help, turning to his enemy for comfort in his final moments. Derek was tempted to run to him, though he was unsure what he could do to help.

Before he could step off the driveway, the screams suddenly cut off and Hector's flaming form fell to the ground, skidding for a few feet across the pavement before it came to a rest. Perhaps the smoke had filled his lungs, perhaps the pain and shock and exertion had given him a heart attack, or perhaps the suffering had grown too intense for him to bear, but in any case, Hector was dead. As Derek watched the corpse burn like some indecent bonfire in the street, and as the first scents of the charred carcass reached his nostrils, Derek found himself thinking that once the flames went out, the dogs would have a nice charred feast on their hands, and found that he didn't hate himself for thinking it.

Looking beyond the burning body, Derek saw that the flames from the car now illuminated the entire street. At the edge of the shadows, he saw the thin, grey form again, and this time he recognized it immediately. It was the Xolo, and it seemed to be staring back at him. Its eyes were glowing and Derek wasn't sure that was from the flames. He started forward, not sure what he would do even if he could catch the dog, but it had disappeared into the shadows before he even reached the edge of the driveway.

"It's heading towards the school," Alison said before Derek could think it.

He turned back to her, desperately trying to think of anything else the dog could be heading towards on the lonely county road it had followed. "I was never able to get a hold of the kids," Alison said, almost apologetically.

Without another word, Derek led her to the garage.

TWENTY-EIGHT

Because Derek had left his own car at the animal control center, they took Alison's minivan, Derek driving while Alison tried to patch the bite wound on his arm with the first-aid kit she always kept in the glove box. Steering the minivan around Hector's still-burning corpse, Derek was forced by the unfamiliar suspension to crank the wheel harder than he had intended, pulling his arm out of Alison's reach.

"Stay over here, will you? I don't want you bleeding all over my upholstery."

"Glad to know you're concerned about me."

She smiled through the bandages she held between her teeth to show she hadn't been serious. "There you go, all better," she said, clipping the gauze in place with a safety pin.

"Thanks, doc," he said, turning onto the county road that would eventually lead them to Sunnydale Elementary. "I didn't know you knew how to patch up a wound like that."

She shrugged, putting away what remained of the kit and snapping the lid shut. "Made me nervous not to know in case the kids got in trouble, so I took a few classes when you were on your business trips."

Derek didn't respond for a moment, unsure if this was intended as a rebuke. He was too busy searching the darkness anyways, keeping his eyes on the shadows at the edge of the road. "He's too fast," he heard himself muttering.

"Who's too fast?" Alison asked.

Derek realized his mind had wandered from their conversation. "The Xolo. If he is headed towards the school, he'll be there way before us."

Alison shrugged, looking as if she were trying to hide her concern. "We haven't seen anywhere else he could have gone. I'll try calling the school again."

While she did that, Derek scanned through the radio stations, trying to find any news reports about the dogs. Apparently, the news hadn't reached the radio stations, since all he heard were the same snippets of pop songs he had never heard before and rock songs he had heard too many times, all of them repeating in an endless loop.

Don't be stupid, he told himself, *radio stations don't even do news reports anymore*. They probably didn't even have real DJs anymore, just playlists curated by some algorithm with pre-recorded bits in between the songs, all of it beamed in by some huge conglomerate based in New York or LA. Still, the radio's lack of awareness of the situation felt disconcerting, as if the world were trying to pretend that their crisis wasn't happening. Warren Zevon singing "Werewolves of London" didn't help that feeling.

Derek snapped the radio off just as Alison hung up the phone. "No answer again, either from the school phone or from Ms. Lightheart's cell."

Although this news didn't surprise Derek, he still found himself stepping a little harder on the gas. "We'll be there in twenty minutes, maybe less," he said, looking at the clock.

"I just hope the kids can hold on that long," Allison said.

Max didn't know how much longer he could hold on.

The sloped roof of the play structure, which had never been easy to hold on to, was now slicked with sweat from the hours he had spent crouched on its edge, keeping his muscles tensed, since a single moment of relaxation could send him careening over the edge, to where the dogs still waited. His muscles were sore and stiff in a way he had never experienced before, but still he feared to move, watching the dogs pace the ground below.

Most of them seemed to be gathered around him. One or two dogs guarded each of the other groups of kids perched in trees or on the roofs of the other play structures, but seven or eight dogs stood patiently waiting below the high tower where they had Max trapped, while more milled around the blacktop nearby.

"They must be able to smell the Xolo on you," Gracie said from behind him, "from when it bit you. Its scent must have stuck in your hand."

Max looked down at the scars on his hand, disgusted with the thought of what they could contain. The idea of some part of that hideous animal staying inside him, maybe even permanently, made him want to puke. But it also gave him an idea.

He looked around at the other kids, most of whom were also struggling to stay where they were. Many of them were readjusting themselves every few minutes, trying and failing to find a comfortable spot on the branches or plastic roofs they had been perched on for most of the night. A few of them, wearing only light fall coats for the hour or so they had planned to be outside, were now shivering in the piercing late-night cold that was beginning to set in.

"We can't stay here all night," Max announced to anyone who would listen. "If we don't freeze to death, we'll eventually get tired, and then we'll fall to those fuckers." He waved a hand at the dogs, who stared up at him with hungry eyes.

"Someone will come rescue us," the rich-looking kid in the polo said, "they'll come for us soon."

"Bullshit they will!" Max yelled over a chorus of murmured agreement. "You all saw how many more of those things there were. They're probably overrunning the whole town right now! I'd bet no one will be able to get to us until tomorrow at least, even if the police haven't been wiped out."

No one said anything at first. There was nothing they could say: Max had spoken the truth they had all been too scared to admit.

Only Gracie had the courage to respond. "But we can't go down there, Maxie, they'll come after us."

Max was feeling so inspired he even overlooked the girlish nickname she had used for the first time in years. "No. They'll come after me."

Gracie's eyes widened in fear. She was smart for her age, Max had to admit that, and it seemed she understood immediately what he was planning. "Max, you can't! They'll catch up with you, they'll get you!"

"Only if I let them," he reassured her, "And I'm not about to do that."

He stood up uneasily on the plastic roof, bracing his feet as best he could. "Listen up, everyone," he announced, though most of them already were. "I'm gonna lead the dogs as far away as I can. When it's all clear, you guys make a break for the school. You'll be safe inside."

"No, Max, I can't-" Gracie tugged at the sleeve of his costume.

"You can!" he interrupted her. "You're the smartest one here, so I'm putting you in charge. You make sure everyone gets inside, then find a phone and call the police." He didn't ask if she could do all that, because he knew she could.

Gracie didn't seem as sure of herself, but she swallowed her fear and nodded in agreement.

Max turned back to the other kids, who were now carefully forcing themselves to standing positions, balancing on the thin roofs and thinner branches. "Okay, everyone, once the dogs are out of the way, move quickly but quietly. If they hear one noise, they'll come running back and this will all be for nothing." He saw the other kids nodding slowly, stretching their stiff limbs in anticipation of escape.

Stepping to the edge of the plastic roof, Max drew a deep breath. The dogs had gathered on the hard-packed floor of woodchips just beneath the tower on which he stood, but they had left the metal catwalks of the playground empty, probably because those would only lead their prey to the ground anyways. But the nearest catwalk led to another tower, this one free of kids and with the long branches of a tall oak tree overhanging its plastic roof. Max thought he could run to the tower and climb on the roof before the dogs had a chance to climb the catwalks and catch up with him.

Of course, that didn't take into account the possibility that at least one of the dogs was hiding underneath the plastic roof just beneath him, or inside the plastic tunnel he had to pass by on the way to the next tower, but that paranoid possibility did not occur to him until he had already jumped off the tower.

He landed on the metal with a thud that shook the entire catwalk. Looking back over his shoulder, he saw no hidden dogs emerging from inside the tower, but he did hear the dogs below running across the woodchips towards him. Max took off towards the next tower, giving the tunnel a wide berth. Paws clicked on the metal behind him, but he didn't dare to turn around. Their numbers and their speed seemed to increase as he drew nearer to the second tower, which seemed to draw farther away the harder he ran. Suddenly it loomed above him and the railing next to it was in his hands. Max climbed up, desperately rebalancing himself so he wouldn't fall to the floor of woodchips far below. He could hear more dogs behind him, but their sound was largely drowned out by the pounding of his heart.

Throwing himself upwards, Max just barely managed to catch the roof of the tower, hoping that the sweat on his palms wouldn't make him slide off. Whoever had designed this playground had obviously taken pains to prevent children from climbing onto the roof, and if Max hadn't been just a little old and a little tall for his grade, he probably wouldn't have been able to catch on to the lip of the roof, let alone simultaneously push himself off the railing. With the few inches of extra height the push gave him, he thrust his right arm forward, splaying his fingers and laying his arm flat across a section of the roof while his left hand clenched the overhanging lip.

The textured plastic sank into his skin, giving his right arm just enough grip to hold him in place while his feet shimmied up one of the metal poles that held up the roof. The black sneakers he had worn for his costume slid down the smooth metal, but he continuously kicked them back up. Eventually, one of his heels dug into a screw that stuck out between two sections of the pole. The metal tip tore through the soft rubber and dug painfully into his flesh, but it gave him just enough leverage to push himself up until he was waist level with the roof, grimacing the whole way as he put more of his weight onto the screw.

Still, it was less painful than what the dogs would do to him, especially now, with his body bent over the lip, his rear end thrust out appetizingly, and he let that motivate him. He reached for the pinnacle of the roof and managed to wrap one sweaty palm around the peak, bracing his other arm around a flat section of roof. He pulled his rear end over the lip just as the dogs reached him. He heard a set of jaws snap in mid-air just before his torso hit the roof. There was a moment of blind, instinctive panic as his feet kicked helplessly in mid-air. Max was sure they would soon feel the jaws of a leaping dog, but they only felt the reassuring slap of plastic.

Max turned around, laughing as he looked at the dogs below him. He had managed to attract the attention of almost all the dogs that had been gathered beneath him and Gracie, as well as many of the stragglers who had been wandering aimlessly over the blacktop. That still left too many gathered in clusters beneath the other groups of kids, who were still impatiently waiting for their chance to escape.

Wobbling as he balanced himself on the roof, Max stomped one foot on the thin plastic, shaking the roof so hard he was sure it would collapse. "Hey, you idiots! Come over here! You wanna fucking treat?!" he yelled, waving his arms over his head. That brought a few more of the dogs, who gathered with their friends beneath him, barking and jumping as casually as if they were waiting for a scrap to fall from their master's table.

Most of the dogs were now gathered beneath him, but there were still too many guarding the others. *They're following orders*, Max realized with horror. Even with the Xolo gone, they were carrying out the orders he had transmitted to them. The idea made Max sick, but also gave him an idea. Perhaps their orders were to prevent any of the children from escaping, but it was equally likely their main goal was to kill Max, in vengeance for first offending the Xolo by pulling his tail and then for later escaping his wrath, getting one of his dogs killed and revealing the location of the pack in the process. Max thought it was likely the dogs would abandon their posts if they thought there was a chance they would be able to kill him.

To actually jump to the ground would be suicide, especially with so many dogs directly beneath him, but he thought he had an idea. Stomping his feet on the plastic roof a few more times, he pulled the hood of his costume from his pocket, not entirely sure why he was doing it. He supposed having the hood out of his pocket give him slightly greater mobility, but he knew it was really to put himself in the mindset of a ninja, to make himself feel stealthy while he snuck along the branches overhead.

Holding back unpleasant memories of his escape from the abandoned house in the woods, Max leaped up and grabbed the thickest of the overhead branches. Reaching one hand over the other, he managed to pull himself along the branch until he was hanging in the air halfway between the play structure and the trunk of the tree, which stood next to an ancient wooden shed where the kids at recess liked to pretend naughty children were chained up. Max hoped to reach the base of the tree or the roof of the shed and lure the dogs to him from there.

Already, the plan seemed to be working: when he risked a look towards the playground, he saw dogs abandoning their posts beneath the other kids.

They ran beneath him and leaped at his legs as if they were dangling treats, which he supposed they were. Max would have thought the height of the branch would have made it impossible for the dogs to get anywhere near him, but the dogs leaped much higher than he would have thought possible, and his above-average height, combined with his above-average weight pulling down on the branch, brought his feet just low enough to be within range of the dogs.

He thrashed his feet when he felt teeth dig into the soles of his shoes, tearing away bits of rubber as he kicked them away. The frenetic motion caught the attention of more dogs, who saw him struggling and came running. Soon the entire pack was gathered beneath him, leaping and barking as they climbed over each other for the chance to eat him first. Max hurried faster on the branch, knowing it was only a matter of time before one of them leaped high enough to grab the hem of his pants or wrap its teeth around his calf.

He kept himself going with the realization that he had at least accomplished his mission. He risked a quick look towards the playground, not wanting to draw the dog's attention that way. With the dogs gone, the other kids were slowly climbing down from their hiding spots, lowering themselves gently off the plastic roofs or the higher branches of the trees. Across the playground, Max locked eyes with Gracie. He silently willed her to get moving, to lead the other kids to safety. She nodded as if he had sent her a conscious message and climbed down off the plastic roof, turning back once she had reached the catwalk to help the next kid down.

The desire for escape seemed to reach critical mass. As the children ahead of them climbed down, the kids still stuck on the plastic roofs or on the branches of trees grew impatient, shoving the kids ahead of them to speed their escape. One of them, the rich-looking kid in the dirtied polo, climbed to the far end of the roof he was trapped on, not following the slow-moving line of children to the catwalk just below, but awkwardly trying to lower himself onto the monkey bars on the other side of the tower. As he lowered himself down, his feet suddenly slipped beneath him, one foot sliding between two of the bars and tangling his ankle.

As he fell backwards, he let out a scream that echoed over the entire playground. The dogs turned at the scream, which was followed by the thud of his body hitting the ground. Most of the dogs took off towards the sound, sensing an easier meal. Max followed their path with his eyes, ending at the kid in the polo struggling to his feet. Just beyond him stood Gracie and the other kids in a wide-eyed cluster. They had reached the ground and seemed to be considering climbing back up the towers and trees they had just come from. But the dogs were closing in fast, too fast for them to climb up again.

"Run!" Max screamed. "Get inside!" At the same time, he began pulling on the branch above himself, hoping the dogs would be attracted enough by the sight of his dangling feet bouncing up and down to leave the other kids alone. The tactic worked with a few of the dogs, but most of them ran unheeding towards the other kids.

The kid in the polo saw them coming and ran towards the school. The sight of him coming around the play tower and booking it towards the school, pounding the pavement even on what must have been a sprained ankle, was enough to convince the other kids of the danger. They turned and ran towards the school like a flock of birds turning mid-flight. The dogs were already rounding the play structure, hot on their heels and gaining fast.

Max moved towards the shed, still hoping to distract at least a few of them. He pumped his shoulders, bouncing the branch up and down while he shouted at the dogs. More of them barked and leaped beneath him, but too many still pursued Gracie and the others, who were just barely keeping ahead as they crossed the pavement to the school. Max gave up his bouncing to focus on moving towards the trunk of the tree, where he thought he could attract more dogs in the hopes that they could climb to him.

He was most of the way there when the branch he was holding onto gave out. Maybe his bouncing had weakened the branch, or maybe his extra weight near the base of the branch had been too much, but either way he was falling through the air, the earth rapidly rising towards him. Thankfully, the roof of the shed was just below him. For a moment he thought it would save him, but before his mind could even coherently express that hope, he had crashed through the ancient wood, the roof of the shed giving way instantly beneath his weight, sending him tumbling into a pit of darkness.

———————————
———————————

Gracie risked a look over her shoulder. The dogs were just behind them, a single mass of bodies, a wave of teeth and claws. She looked back to the door ahead of them; it was close, but not close enough. Gracie veered off from the other kids, yelling at them to continue towards the door. She yelled to the dogs, trying to get them to follow her instead of the other kids. She slowed a little, hoping to give them an easier target.

When she risked another look over her shoulder, most of the dogs were following her, apparently preferring an easier meal to a more plentiful one. As she turned back to the school, she ran as fast as she could. Out of the corner of her eye, she saw the other kids disappearing through the door, the one they had come out from in what felt like another lifetime. Gracie kept her eyes on the second entrance just ahead, the one that led to the hall by the music classroom.

She nearly collided with the glass as she reached the door. Pulling on the nearest handle, she only succeeded in rattling the frame. In the jittering reflections, she saw the dogs approaching. Gracie felt panic about to overwhelm her, but pushed it down long enough to give the other handle a desperate pull. At first, she thought it was only her hopeful imagination creating the illusion of the door swinging open, but when she smelled the musty odor of the carpets, she knew she was safe. Gracie dashed inside and slammed the door shut, jumping back as a large black Labrador smashed into the door, rattling the frame.

Although the doors opened outwards towards the dogs, Gracie still searched the steel panels near the handles for a lock, but found nothing. Probably to keep a trouble-making kid from locking his friends out, she thought, thinking of her brother, who had saved them all.

The doors rattled harder as more dogs tried to break through the glass. Several stretched themselves against the panes, their claws brushing the handles, and Gracie's paranoid mind was sure they would find a way to open the doors. She looked around and saw a janitor's mop bucket in an alcove near the drinking fountains. Probably remembering some crappy action movie her dad and her brother had forced her to watch, Gracie pulled the mop from the bucket, leaving a trail of dripping water as she ran down the hall.

Pushing the mop through the handles, she observed with satisfaction as more dogs gathered around the door, shaking the glass as they threw themselves against it and bounced off. The door handles jostled and sometimes briefly separated, but were always stopped by the handle of the mop.

Gracie screamed as something settled on her shoulder. She turned to see the rich-looking kid in the polo wincing and pulling his hand back as her scream echoed down the tiled hall. More kids peered over his shoulder.

"Do you think the dogs will be able to break through the glass?" said a boy with brown hair and thick glasses.

"Naw, that's bullet-proof glass," the rich-looking kid reassured him. "My dad tells me nothing can break through it."

"Let's hope so," Gracie said. "Did everyone make it inside?"

A mousy girl with long red hair, who sat in the back of Gracie's class but who had never, so far as Gracie knew, spoken a word to anyone, now spoke up. "Yeah, everyone made it in," she said in a voice barely above a whisper, "everyone except your brother."

Gracie had suspected this, but hearing it aloud reignited her anxiety. Looking through the glass doors, she tried to see past the slobbering dogs that filled the panes, their drool quickly making the lower half of the view opaque. From this angle, Gracie was unable to see the playground, but she took the presence of this many dogs at the doors as a good sign.

If they had an easier meal elsewhere, they would have run to it by now.

Max came to on the hard-packed dirt floor of the shed. He didn't remember hitting the ground, but the pain in his bones told him it must have happened. As he forced himself to sit up, fragments of rotted wood rolled off his body. The moonlight pouring in through the opening his body had left in the roof glinted off of spades, blades, and shears, all of which he had missed by inches. He looked up at the moon framed by the remnants of the roof, an oddly beautiful scene until he thought that the dogs might be able to leap to the roof and climb into the shed through the opening. He leaped to his feet when he heard them outside, but quickly realized they weren't trying to leap. Instead, it sounded as if they were *digging*.

Looking at the shed's ramshackle door, he saw the thin streak of moonlight beneath it quickly widen as heaps of earth were tossed aside. Dirty paws moved in a blur through that gap, furiously tossing aside clods of earth. Occasionally a snout would press beneath the door, take a deep, purposeful sniff, and then pull out, instantly replaced by the furiously digging claws.

Max leaped on the nearest of the shelves lining the walls, hoping its wood wasn't as weak as that of the roof. It must not have been, since, although the wood creaked and groaned as he put his weight on it, it never collapsed. Max climbed to a smaller shelf higher on the wall, hearing the dogs tearing through the dirt behind him. He turned to see a large retriever, its golden fur matted with dirt, poking most of its body beneath the door. Max continued to climb the higher and increasingly narrower shelves, knocking tools and garden implements from them as he climbed. A few of these he picked up and threw down at the retriever, which was now pulling the rest of its body through the hole beneath the door.

As more dogs crawled in, Max threw garden shears, trowels, even a jar full of loose screws at them, anything that would slow their progress while he climbed through the hole in the roof. Reaching around the splintered fragments of wood, he grabbed what was left of the roof and pulled himself up. As he pushed his feet off the highest shelf, it finally gave way beneath his weight, the flimsy board pulling out of the wall and falling away beneath him.

As he dangled from the remaining chunk of the roof, his feet pumped in mid-air, searching for a foothold. He looked down over his shoulder to see the dogs, who had recovered from the small blows of the objects he had dropped on them and had begun to climb the shelves, were now splayed out on the floor, pinned beneath the shelf which had fallen from beneath him. Already they were recovering, pushing the shelf aside with their paws while they struggled to stand up.

Max needed a foothold in order to escape. He found one in a small shelf below the lone window in the shed, only a discarded end of lumber which had been nailed beneath the window to hold some lonely groundskeeper's meager collection of dying wildflowers in a childishly-made clay pot. Max kicked this pot aside as his right foot found the shelf. He smiled as the clay shattered over the head of a black lab, knocking the animal to the ground and leaving it with a crown of dirt and dying flowers.

Positioning his foot in the center of the flimsy shelf, Max pushed himself up, rising just high enough to grab one of the branches that crossed just above where the roof had been. Holding onto this branch with one hand and the remains of the roof with the other, he pulled himself into a sitting position on the roof, then climbed to the branch, leaving the dogs behind.

Again putting hand over hand on the branch, Max moved towards the trunk of the tree, hoping to find shelter among its branches. He stopped when he saw what he had most feared: a Doberman scrambling up the side of the trunk, its claws digging into the bark, giving it just enough leverage to reach the lowest branches. From there, Max knew it would only be a matter of a few jumps for the thing to reach any branch it wanted to.

Stretching an arm behind himself, Max turned around on the branch, wincing at the twisting pain in his shoulders. Moving away from the tree, he flung himself over the ruins of the shed, where yipping dogs leaped at him from the shelves, their heads too low to reach him on the branch. Following the branch across the open area before the playground, Max looked towards the school and saw that Gracie and the others were gone. At least they had made it inside, he thought with a smile.

Dogs leaped and barked while he rappelled towards the playground, but the branch held. He reached the highest play tower and let go of the branch as soon as it was safe. Landing hard on the plastic, he clutched the peak of the roof with the last of his strength. He realized this was the same tower he had been trapped on with Gracie only a few minutes before. He hadn't made it anywhere, but at least the others had made it inside. He smiled at that, his face sinking into the plastic with relief.

Now, he only hoped they could call for help while he still had the strength to hold on.

The road leading to Sunnydale Elementary was completely deserted. Derek wasn't sure whether to take that to mean that the trick or treaters and partiers had heard of the attack by the dogs and wisely decided to stay inside, or if the dogs had already torn through this area, killing everyone they had come across. Derek pushed this possibility from his mind and forced himself to focus on the road. If the dogs had attacked here, there was nothing he could do about it. He could only get to the school before another attack happened.

When he saw the truck coming over the hill, he at first thought it was a creation of his paranoid imagination. The mud coating the tires and splashed across half the white paint seemed incongruous with the immaculate finish on the rest of the vehicle, and the costumed revelers who poked their masked heads out of the cab in all directions formed an incredibly bizarre sight, like a truckload of demons escaping from hell. As he drew closer, he saw that one woman was stuck halfway through the window between the cab and the bed, her legs kicking, sending the skirt of her dress flying, adding a touch of mad hilarity to the scene. The only reassurance Derek had that the scene was real was the sight of the grim-faced sheriff standing watch in the back of the bed, his shotgun held above him like a conqueror's flag.

As the truck approached, Derek rolled down his window and flashed his headlights. The sheriff, seeing his face through the windshield, called to the driver to stop. As the absurdly lifted truck pulled up next to the SUV, Garth had to lean down to look into Derek's window. "Well, I see your negotiation went alright," he said with more than his usual understatement.

Derek nodded, not yet ready to discuss what had happened back at the house. "The Xolo crashed your cruiser, though. Long story."

"That's alright," Garth reassured him. "Did you happen to see where he went?"

"He's headed towards the school. We're going there now."

Garth nodded and straightened back up. "Then let me drop these kids off at the station and I'll be right behind you."

Derek was already pressing the gas, nodding to Garth as he headed off into the night. In the rearview, he saw Garth knocking on the roof of the cab, pointing ahead as if the young man in the skeleton costume could see him through the roof. As Garth led his team into the night, Derek looked forward into the darkness, wondering what he would find there.

Since the school had planned for the Halloween party to take place outside, most of the lights inside the building had been turned off, leaving only occasional pools of light to navigate by. Gracie led the others through the mostly darkened hallways, the corridors she walked every day made unfamiliar by the shadows. Thankfully, most of the lights between the entrance to the playground and Ms. Lightheart's classroom had been left on, leaving a trail of breadcrumbs for them to follow once they reached it from the back entrance they had been forced to use.

Finally, they found the classroom where most of the kids had left their jackets, backpacks, and buckets of candy. Gracie stepped across the rug of the show and tell area where this had all begun and crossed to Ms. Lightheart's desk, trying not to think about the fact that her favorite teacher would never again give them a lesson or lead them in show and tell.

On the desk, Gracie found two phones: one Ms. Lightheart's smartphone, the other the red plastic landline that the students called the "trouble phone," since it only seemed to go off when a student had to come to the principal's office or be taken away by their parents in the middle of the day. Since the smartphone was probably protected by a passcode, Gracie picked up the trouble phone, realizing for the first time how truly apt its name was, and began to punch the chunky plastic buttons embedded in the handset.

She had always complained when her mother had forced her to memorize their home phone number, as well as both her parent's cell phone numbers, groaning as her mother made her dial the numbers again and again on the ancient land line her parents kept in their bedroom until she knew them all by memory. Now she was thankful for the lessons, since her fingers flew naturally over the digits. But when she heard the hollow, endless ringing at the other end and imagined the land line echoing endlessly in her parent's empty house, she wondered if the lessons were worth it. Knowing who to call only helped if there was someone there to call, and for all she knew the dogs could have tracked down her parents the way they tracked down Max. The Xolo had left with many other dogs, after all.

Pushing the thought from her mind, she hung up and dialed the next number she had memorized.

Derek was almost to the school when his phone began ringing. Fumbling desperately in his jacket pocket to retrieve it, he almost swung Alison's minivan off the narrow country road. Alison screamed and grabbed the wheel, offering to grab the phone for him, but his fingers were already clutching the plastic case. He held the phone above the wheel, risking taking his eyes off the road in his mad need to know who was calling. When he saw the unsaved number he recognized as Sunnydale Elementary, he immediately slid the bar to answer.

"Dad? It's Gracie."

"Gracie? Are you alright?" Hearing her daughter's name, Alison leaned towards him to find out the same thing, but he was too distracted to think of putting the phone on speaker.

"I'm okay, but the dogs are here at school. They have Max trapped on the playground, but the rest of us are in Ms. Lightheart's classroom."

"Okay, just stay there. We're only a few blocks away. We'll come get you."

"Okay, Dad. I love you."

Derek had already hung up before he realized he had not said it back. He glanced at the phone, realizing he had to focus on his driving if he wanted to save his daughter. It was only when Alison spoke that he realized she hadn't heard the conversation. "Well, what's going on?" she demanded of him.

He quickly explained and together they discussed what to do. In the last few blocks before Sunnydale Elementary, they formed a plan that would save their children's lives, or doom their entire family.

When Gracie hung up with her dad, she told the other kids gathered around Ms. Lightheart's desk that her parents were almost there. "You should call the police too," the rich-looking kid half-suggested, half-demanded. "We need all the help we can get." He made it a demand instead of an offer because the phone which his parents had bought for him was now a useless chunk of plastic. He had forgotten to charge it before coming to the party, and the new Call of Duty update he had been downloading while they were outside had killed the battery.

Gracie didn't like his tone, but had to admit it was a good idea. She picked up the phone again and dialed the only three numbers that every kid in America has memorized. She again heard endless ringing, which was quickly replaced by a recorded message telling her that all circuits were busy. Gracie now had confirmation for the feeling that had crept over her when she had called her parent's landline, that what was happening here at Sunnydale Elementary was happening everywhere.

Just as the voice began to tell her again that all circuits were busy, the recording cut off with a sudden click, not even replaced by dial tone. As Gracie lowered the handset to try again, the bright red plastic suddenly disappeared in front of her, along with everything else. Only the screams from the kids around her assured her that it was the room, and not just her own eyes, which had suddenly gone dark.

This was further proof that the attack by the dogs was truly everywhere, even in the electrical system. As she dropped the useless plastic and listened to the screams, she wondered if her parents really would be able to rescue them.

Max tried to sit on the peaked roof of the play tower, but found his feet slipping on the plastic and the ridged roof impossible to find a seat on. He stood instead, even though his aching muscles screamed for rest after the exertion of distracting the dogs. At least that seemed to have been a success, judging by the large number of dogs that were now gathered around the doors to the school. That left very few dogs to guard Max, and he thought he might be able to escape, if he hadn't seen how quickly the dogs had gathered when they had heard the other kids hit the ground. For now, he could only stand watch, trying to see what the dogs were doing in the faint light of the halogens.

They seemed to be burrowing, as if they were trying to dig under the walls of the school. Max thought that might make sense in the mind of a dumb animal, but then he realized they weren't burrowing beneath the walls, but inside them, into some sort of vent covering on the side of the school. Their claws raked the rusted metal, which finally gave away at one corner as a screw snapped. A muscular German shepherd bit onto the hanging metal, bending the vent cover back until the other three screws snapped. Dropping the vent cover from its bloodied mouth, the shepherd led the other dogs into the small tunnel beyond.

Max leaned forward to watch, fascinated. He again had the impression of soldiers carrying out orders from their superior, only now the Xolo wasn't even present. The dedication and organization with which the dogs carried out their mission showed the power the Xolo had over their minds.

As the shepherd disappeared into the opening, Max suddenly realized that he had been so impressed with the way the dogs carried out their mission, he had forgotten entirely what that mission was. He desperately wished he had some way of warning Gracie that the dogs were coming, and he thought again of making a run for the school, but instantly heard a sound that made him stop.

From the vents came a sound like digging, accompanied by the scraping of metal and a pattering like falling plaster. Max had the idea that the dogs were digging through the wall of the vent in an attempt to get inside the school and, as if his thoughts had created it, there came a flash from inside the vent that silhouetted the madly dancing hind legs of the shepherd. The flash filled Max's vision, and for a moment he thought the darkness that followed was the result of total blindness.

But when he saw a few faint glimmers of moonlight outlining the school and playground, he realized that the dogs had somehow caused the power to go out by chewing through an electrical line. The smell of burnt flesh and fur told him that the shepherd had probably paid for this accomplishment with his life, but as his eyes slowly adjusted to the darkness, he saw the other dogs streaming into the vent, struggling to crawl over an obstruction that must have been the shepherd's corpse before wriggling and pushing their way inside. Again, he was struck by the selfless, military-like precision with which they carried out their orders, and again he feared for his sister's safety.

From inside the school, he heard the soft pattering of more chunks of plaster and then a louder crash as some part of the maintenance tunnel the dogs had entered fell aside. The sound made him want to run for the door, knowing that the dogs were now inside, but as his eyes adjusted to the darkness and he planned a route through the playground to the school, he heard a sound that again confirmed the precise, military-like organization of the dogs, a sound that sent a shiver through his spine when it emerged from the darkness that still filled most of the playground.

The sound that made his muscles clench and his teeth shake was the stealthy padding of a single set of paws, making slow, approaching circles around the tower where he now stood.

Order disappeared with the light. In the darkness, there was only fear and panic. Gracie had some small idea of what Ms. Lightheart had experienced every day of her short working life as she tried to calm the screaming, panicking students. In the thin light that managed to emerge through the small, filmy window in the far corner of the classroom like the glow from the lens of the classroom projector, she saw the silhouettes of the other kids descending into apes and circus animals, running around the room and climbing on the desks for God knew what reason. She yelled at them to stop, to calm down, but their shrieking voices drowned her out. Strangely, a smaller sound managed to capture their attention.

"Listen!" cried a panicked voice, its bearer invisible in the darkness. Surprisingly, the children did, a faint noise becoming louder as their voices dropped off one by one.

"It's the dogs!" another voice shrieked of the steadily growing clicking from the halls. At the sound of her voice, the clicking seemed to speed up and approach.

Gracie wanted to tell them that their shouting was attracting the dogs, but that would only draw attention to the problem, not the solution. "Shut the door!" Gracie shouted to anyone who would listen. She heard scrambling in the darkness as kids knocked over desks and chairs to get to the door. Feeling around on the desk, Gracie again found Ms. Lightheart's cellphone. It was useless for making calls, but perhaps it could still save them. Tapping the screen, she was greeted by the cryptic keypad. Beneath it were two buttons. Tapping one emitted a surprisingly bright beam of light from the back of the phone, which she shone towards the door to help the other kids.

The rich-looking kid in the polo slammed the door shut and searched the steel plate around the handle. "There's no lock!" he wailed in desperation, "it will open the minute they slam into it!"

"Move some of the desks in front of the door," Gracie said, pointing her light at a few nearby.

As the kids stacked desks and chairs in front of the door and the narrow, papered-over window that ran alongside it, Gracie heard the dogs just outside.

As the first desks were pushed against the inside of the frame, the kids felt the impact as the dogs threw themselves against the door, bulging the wood inwards, nearly knocking over the desks that had just been placed there.

Behind that noise was another, a steadily growing whine that grew into a piercing shriek. "That must be the police!" the rich-looking kid yelled hopefully, grabbing another chair to add to the pile. The noise grew stronger and more rhythmic, and in a moment its source became obvious when a faint red glow illuminated the room, suddenly revealing the faces of the kids.

"It's an emergency generator," the mousy redhaired girl said, "at least we'll have a little light."

The red light showed the other kids as little more than silhouettes, strange blurs almost indistinguishable from their background. Gracie kept the phone light up, adding to the thin light from the single, metal-caged red bulb at the back of the classroom. As she watched the red blurs scurrying across the room with more desks and chairs, nearly tripping on the folds of the heavy rug where they had sat for show and tell, Gracie realized with amazed wonder that it was in this room where the Xolo had had its first outburst of violence when Max had pulled its tail. She wondered how such a simple action could have led to all that had happened, and felt horror at being in the room where it had all started. She hoped this wasn't also where it would all end.

The school was dark when they arrived. The hollow lamp posts stood like useless sentries, and the long brick building, so charming in the sunlight, lurked in the shadows like an animal waiting to pounce, its dark bulk framed by the darker blackness of the mountains behind it. Derek swung the minivan into the long, curving drive usually reserved for school buses, his brights on just to see the curving sidewalk. The lights revealed only two cars in the enormous parking lot, one the principal's surprisingly flashy Buick in his trademark color, the other a beat-up minivan with its rear end covered in bumper stickers about liberal politics and religious tolerance which must have belonged to Ms. Lightheart.

As he slowed to a stop in front of the main entrance, Derek quickly reviewed the plan they had come up with, more to revive his own courage than to remind Alison. Since Gracie had told them that most of the kids were in

Ms. Lightheart's classroom, Derek would make his way there. Gracie had also said that Max was still trapped on the playground, so Alison would take the car around the back of the school to find him.

Between the two of them, they had three weapons: the revolver that Garth had given Derek, the Glock handgun that Hector had dropped when Derek shot him, and the smaller Walther that Reeve had been carrying. Derek still carried the sheriff's revolver, tucked into his belt so he could use the three shots remaining after he had used up Reeve's fully-loaded Walther. The Glock was, against Alison's wishes, tucked into the map compartment on the driver's side door, rattling uneasily as they drove despite Derek's attempts to secure it in place with Alison's seldom-used roadmaps of Colorado and the Denver area.

"That's just in case things get hairy," Derek concluded, motioning to the gun. Alison didn't seem to appreciate his joke at first, but slowly a grin spread across her face, and much-needed laughter burst forth, despite her efforts to restrain it, its power made more forceful by the long train of stresses and terrors that had suppressed all good feeling in her. Derek realized how much he had been thinking of the terrors inflicted by the dogs purely in terms of their effect on himself, of his guilt for letting the Xolo loose and his fear of losing his children, without thinking of Alison. He realized how rarely he expressed the feelings he had about her, and hoped that his coming back to rescue her had proved the depths of those feelings.

But there was no time to linger on those thoughts now. Alison was climbing out of the car to take her seat behind the wheel, and without a gun she could be at the mercy of any dogs that might be hiding in the darkness. He jumped out after her, leaving the door open and the engine running. They met in front of the car, nearly blinded by the glare of the brights, where Alison stopped him with a hand on his chest.

"Are you sure you don't want to wait for the sheriff?" she asked, pleading with him with her eyes.

He looked beyond her, into the empty darkness beyond the school, and swallowed his fear of what could be waiting there. "There might not be time. Who knows how long it will take the sheriff to get here, and the kids are in trouble now."

She nodded and pulled him close. "Just be careful," she said, wrapping her arms around him. He returned the gesture, ignoring every romantic impulse within him in order to keep his eyes open, still watchful for danger in the darkness.

"I didn't know you could be this brave," she said as if she could tell what he was doing, her words muffled by the folds of his shirt. As he looked over her shoulder, he saw their shadows elongated to impossible lengths in the headlights, their twin forms merged into one.

"I was going to tell you the same thing," he told her, pulling her away from him and moving his hands to her wrists, his fingers moving gently over the bruises left by the ropes. They locked eyes for a moment, but Derek only allowed himself a moment, knowing that to look any longer would convince him never to go inside.

As he stepped onto the sidewalk, he pulled out the Walther and turned off the safety. "Be careful!" Alison yelled after him.

"You too," he said, giving her a final look as she climbed behind the wheel.

As Derek traversed the impossibly long sidewalk from the street to the front door, which seemed to have tripled its length since he had dropped the kids off only a few hours before, he heard the minivan slide into gear and saw the headlights sweep across the front of the school, creating shadows that grew and bent and bowed behind every bush and tree.

Derek turned and watched as Alison piloted the minivan onto a sloping ramp in the sidewalk where, just last month, an ambulance had pulled up to the front door to take their son away. Instead of following the sidewalk, Alison swerved onto the lawn, leaving tracks in the brittle, late-fall grass. Derek watched until she disappeared around a corner of the building towards the fenced-off playground, then turned back towards the door.

Without the headlights, the darkness was almost overpowering, like a physical presence oppressively wrapped around him. Taking his phone from his pocket, Derek fumbled with the screen until a shockingly bright beam of light cut through the darkness. Sweeping the light and his gun around the lawn, Derek saw no dogs approaching. He breathed a sigh of relief until he realized that only meant there would be more dogs ahead, menacing the kids and lying in wait for him.

He exhaled slowly and pushed open one of the heavy glass doors.

Even the darkness outside the school couldn't prepare Derek for the tomb-like blackness inside. The faint red glow that buzzed from an exit sign above the door gave him hope for a few more emergency lights scattered throughout the building, the presence of which he inferred by the rumbling of a generator somewhere deep inside the building, but for now he had only his cell phone and the thin streaks of moonlight through the glass panes that surrounded the entryway.

Gently closing the door behind himself, Derek listened for a moment to the darkness. Hearing nothing but the hum of the generator and the buzzing of the exit sign, he cautiously raised his phone and cast the light around. The beam brought forward from the darkness glinting trophies, oddly distorted works of children's art, and photos of current and former classes. At the end of the trophy case that usually greeted visitors from the wall opposite the front door was a class photo that his daughter appeared in. All of these objects were made strangely frightening by the isolation and darkness that held them, and none of them would help on his quest, so Derek cast the beam to the left, away from the cluster of glass-walled offices where Principal Brown and his staff had watched the school's comings and goings from their lair.

Derek had only seen the inside of the school during a PTA meeting over the summer, and a second time under the guidance of the school's security officer who had quickly led him to the classroom where his son had been bitten. During both visits, he had been so rushed and his mind so filled with other concerns that he hadn't gotten much of a bearing on the school's layout, but he hoped he remembered enough to find his way to Ms. Lightheart's classroom.

As he came around the wall that held the trophy case, the view opened suddenly to the massive cafeteria, lit only by bands of moonlight from the few skylights that ran its length. On the far wall was an entrance to the gym on the other side and a raised stage that connected the two spaces, now cut off by a sliding wall. To his left was an entrance into the kitchen serving area, where his children and many others lined up to get their lunch each day. He hoped they would be able to again someday.

They will be able to, some part of his mind reminded him with surprising forcefulness, *you just have to keep moving*. Derek raised his gun and swept his phone around the cafeteria, revealing the round tables where the kids ate lunch. The sight of the plastic chairs overturned on the tables was strangely eerie in the harsh light of his phone, their crisscrossing metal legs giving the impression of bars in a prison.

At least it allowed him to shine his light under the tables and assure himself that nothing was hiding there. The gesture felt strangely childish, as if he deserved to be one of the students at this school, but it gave him the confidence to wind his way between the tables. Ahead of him, following an alcove formed by the backside of the trophy wall and a hallway filled with doors to the nurse's station and other school essentials, the room tapered to a point only as wide as the double sets of doors which hung open, the glow of a red emergency light revealing an intersection of the hallways that would lead him to the classrooms and eventually to Gracie.

The thought of her made him rush past the tables towards the doors, almost ignoring the chime from his phone until it crossed his mind that it could be a message from Gracie. Looking desperately at the screen, he saw only a reminder that he was at ten percent battery life and losing it quickly because of the flashlight. He grimaced and dismissed the message.

From behind him came an enormous crash. He spun on one heel, the beam from his phone glinting off the steel of a chair leg as it tumbled to the ground. On the table where it had rested stood an enormous mastiff, its bared teeth dripping with slime. Derek would have wondered where it came from, how it could have hidden underneath the tables or if it had snuck in from the gym or kitchen, but there was no time. The animal was preparing to lunge.

Raising the gun and the phone, Derek lined up a shot while blinding the dog. Instead of being dazed, the Mastiff grew enraged. As it leapt from the table, Derek squeezed off a shot, the bullet landing in the middle of the animal's exposed chest. More chairs tumbled to the ground as the dog flew back across the table. As the noise subsided, Derek could hear the animal's ragged breathing coming from both its mouth and the hole in its chest. The dog was still alive, but Derek doubted it would be getting up anytime soon. There was no sense in wasting a shot when he had so few remaining.

Instead, he turned back towards the double doors, being careful to sweep his light under the tables before he passed them. As it turned out, the danger he should have been looking out for was in a more obvious place. As he neared the open double doors, two dogs came running from the hallway beyond, appearing like visions of devils out of the red haze, probably attracted by the sound of his first shot. As they sighted him and quickly closed in, Derek dropped them with a bullet each, not bothering to check if they were still alive before moving through the double doors to the hallways.

He found himself at the corner of the main part of the building. He could see through the windows on the inner wall that he was in the hallway which wrapped around the library in a long rectangle, passing the music rooms and other large classrooms before connecting, at each of its other three corners, with a wing of classrooms. But which wing held Ms. Lightheart's room? Derek couldn't remember, and he didn't have time to explore and find out. Already he could hear more dogs approaching down the hallways. If he wasted time and had to fight more of them off, he would quickly run out of bullets before he had a chance to save Gracie.

Derek cursed himself, and not for the first time that night, for not giving Gracie a cellphone in case of emergencies. With the power out, he couldn't even call her back on the landline she had called him from just a short while ago. But the thought of a cellphone gave him a vague, hopeful idea and he pulled up the contacts on his cellphone, no longer concerned with the quickly fading battery life. Because of the glowing emergency lights in the hallway, he no longer needed the flashlight, but he left it on as he searched the contacts in case he suddenly needed to flee from the dogs he could still hear in the distant darkness. Finally, he found the number he was looking for and pressed the button to call.

Holding the cellphone to his ear, he was more delighted than he should have been to hear it begin to ring. As he waited for an answer, he stood in the middle of the intersection, turning in a slow circle to point his gun down each of the hallways in turn, feeling more exposed to danger than he ever had before.

———————————
———————————

Gracie was dragging a desk across the room when she heard the first shot. Letting the desk fall back to the floor, she stepped closer to the door to listen.

It sounded like someone was coming to rescue them at last, but if so, they might already be too late. Despite the kids stacking almost every desk and chair in the room in front of the door, the dogs were starting to get through. The door was buckled from the force of the dogs repeatedly throwing themselves against the wood, and the tall, narrow window that ran alongside it was cracked.

As Gracie listened to two more shots ring out, the lower pane of the window exploded inward, scattering shards of glass that sprayed between the legs of the stacked-up furniture and spread across the floor. Gracie felt a few shards hit her shins beneath the hem of her skirt. As she stepped back, she felt warm blood running down her legs and soaking her soaks.

Through the now-empty frame of the window, a yellow lab reared its head. The barricade prevented it from getting inside, but the dog quickly began to push the furniture aside with its teeth.

As the kids rushed to keep the barricade in place, Gracie barely noticed the phone she still carried vibrating in her hand. As she grabbed the leg of a chair with the hand that held the phone, the vibration rattled through the leg and into her other hand, giving her a feeling like she was being electrocuted. When she finally realized what was happening, she let go of the chair just long enough to look at the phone screen.

On the screen, she saw the words: MR. RAINS (GRACIE AND MAX). Smiling, she slid the bar to answer the call. "Dad?" she inquired hopefully.

"Gracie?!" He sounded panicked and out of breath. "Where's your teacher?"

"She's dead. The dogs got her. And they're about to get in the classroom. We put up a barricade but they're breaking through."

She heard him mumble a swear word under his breath. "Are you able to get out through the window?"

"I'll try," she told him, already running across the classroom. The latches on the old window were rusty and tried to resist being flipped up, and she had to pull on the crank until she thought it would break off, but finally the crank began to turn with a rusty grinding and the window lifted with an audible groan. There was a burst of suction as the rubber seal peeled back from the frame. The burst of fresh air that followed felt like freedom.

Still turning desperately on the crank, Gracie leaned over the window sill to look into the nook between the window and the next wing of the school. In the moonlight, all that was visible was a patch of sidewalk and a corner of brick wall. Gracie leaned down to the window, trying to see if the opening was big enough for her to fit through. "Okay, I think I can get out," she said into the phone, setting it down on the sill to free her hand.

As she pressed her hand against the screen, the shadows outside the window formed into the enormous head of a black dog. As it lunged towards her hand, she felt its hot breath and wet drool ooze through the screen. The dog's teeth scraped against the metal, giving her just enough time to pull her hand away before the teeth tore through the screen. The dog ripped an enormous section out of the screen and swallowed it before shoving its head through the hole. Gracie tried to push the window shut, but the dog's meaty neck was now over the sill. As she tried to push down on the window, the dog twisted its head and nipped at her wrist with its powerful jaws. With a small scream, Gracie leaped back.

The dog tried to push its way through the window, but was held back by the pane she had pressed down on its neck. The phone was still on the window sill, right beneath one of the large paws the dog rested on the frame. Gracie hesitated only a moment before leaping forward and snatching at the phone. The dog nipped at her hand as she sideswiped the phone, knocking it off the sill and against the leg of one of the few desks that still remained in place. Gracie dove for the floor and scooped it up.

"Gracie, are you still there?" Her father sounded breathless and terrified. She could hear his feet slapping against the tile as if he were running. The sound echoed harshly off the walls and into the phone.

"Yeah, I'm still here, Dad. There's a dog at the window, we can't get out that way!"

Again, she heard him mutter the swear word, louder this time. "Okay, just wait there for me, Gracie. You're going to have to tell me how to-" He suddenly cut himself off with another swear word, even louder this time and shouted directly into the phone. Gracie heard more gunshots, this time exploding directly in her ear over the phone, then echoing down the hall an instant later.

"Dad, are you okay?!" She heard him running even faster, his breath heavy and ragged. She was about to ask again when the line suddenly went dead. Down the hall, she heard more shots echoing. Gracie prayed that her father would be ok, but right now she also had to pray for herself, and for all of the other kids she had led into this classroom.

The black dog was forcing itself in through the window, gradually pushing the pane up while it dug its claws into the sill. She turned to the door to find the situation not much better. The yellow lab had managed to force itself most of the way through the window, pushing away the furniture that blocked its path. Kids rushed forward to hold the desks and chairs in place, a few of them grabbing the last remaining furniture and adding it to the pile.

Gracie shone a light to help their endeavors, not sure what else she could do. Feeling useless, she looked to the window, where the dog would soon be able to climb in, then to the door, where despite the other kid's best efforts, the yellow lab was pushing aside the desks. After that, who knew how many dogs would spill through the opening behind it?

There seemed to be no way out until Gracie thought back to the many times she had been bored in class, when it seemed like Ms. Lightheart's lectures would never end and she had fantasized about escaping from class, of making an exit that no one could miss and yet no one would be able to stop, a situation strangely parallel to her current one. When she was bored and wanted to escape from class, simply walking out the door wouldn't be dramatic enough, and to go out the window would be too difficult, so often, in her dreamy moods, Gracie had leaned back in her chair and imagined a far grander escape, of simply crawling into the ceiling and never coming back. It had always been an idle fantasy, a way to pass the time and nothing more, but as she looked towards the ceiling, she saw it could be their salvation.

"We need to stack more desks in front of the door!" the rich-looking kid in the polo said, leading the charge.

"No!" Gracie shouted, holding up her hand. "We need to stack them up over here!"

The other kids looked at her like she was crazy, but when they followed the beam of light from the phone towards the ceiling, they saw what she was looking at and began to nod their heads in agreement.

In a moment, all the kids were pulling desks and chairs from in front of the door and stacking them in a pyramid, hoping to reach the air vents in the ceiling which Gracie hoped could provide their escape.

Derek's footsteps slapped hard on the tile, nearly piercing his ear drums as they echoed off the locker-lined hallway like the sound of a bullet passing through its barrel. The sound seemed to fill his mind, but still couldn't drown out the sound of paws clicking behind him. He hung up the phone as they drew closer – Gracie didn't need to hear her father being killed on top of everything else.

As he ended the call, he risked slowing down to turn around and aim his gun at the two dogs just behind him. They were closer than he thought, close enough for him to see the whites of their fangs and the patch of pink flesh inside their gaping mouths. There was no time to think or even aim; he simply fired two shots, one for each of the dogs in the direction of the movement he saw, then took off running, not even bothering to check if he had killed the dogs, knowing it was enough to have simply scared them.

He thought of calling Gracie again, but he heard more dogs coming and knew she needed to focus on whatever was going on inside the classroom. Besides, he was nearing another corner and thought he knew the way now.

Heading around the corner, he cast his light down the hallway and found only a dead end. He turned back the way he had come, but heard more dogs approaching. Moving back into the hallway, he checked the few doors that lined each side. None of them were unlocked, and the dogs were getting closer.

Taking a stand at the end of the hallway, Derek crouched and raised his gun. In the red glow of the emergency lights, he saw the outlines of a pair of dogs appear at the end of the hallway. This time he carefully aimed at the center of their outlines, knowing he had the entire length of the hallway before they reached him. He took a deep breath as they rushed towards him, their growls echoing off the walls. When they had passed the first set of doors, Derek gripped the pistol with his other hand, carefully lined up his first shot and pulled the trigger.

The click that emanated from the pistol echoed even louder than the thundering of the dog's paws. Derek's mind filled with terror as he realized the pistol was empty. He felt stupid for not paying attention to how many bullets he had fired, but that thought wouldn't keep him alive to save Gracie. Throwing the empty pistol at the dogs in a desperate attempt to slow them down, he reached back into his belt for the sheriff's revolver.

In his cockiness, he had given away half the length of the hallway. Now, even the simple act of reaching for the revolver seemed to give them another quarter, as if the hall were growing shorter as they drew nearer. As he drew the revolver free, the first of the dogs was already leaping at him. As its shape grew to fill his vision, he pulled back the hammer.

The flash of the muzzle illuminated the dog's underbelly, briefly revealing an explosion of gore as the slug struck. The shape went flying back, revealing the red glow of the emergency lights again. The shape of the second dog was just beyond, preparing to lunge. Derek swung the revolver and cocked the hammer as the dog leaped at him. This time the dog's front claws were scratching him before he managed to pull the trigger.

The second dog flew back, hit the floor, and skidded for a moment before coming to a rest next to the first. Neither one moved or breathed. Derek let out a sigh of relief.

The relief didn't last long. He heard more dogs approaching down the hall, not one or two this time, but dozens, the thundering of their paws echoing off the walls and becoming an overwhelming cacophony.

Derek didn't need to open the revolver to know he had no chance against that many dogs. Garth hadn't given him any more than the six shots that were in the revolver to begin with, and he had fired three times back at the house. Killing the two dogs had left him with only one shot. As he listened to the dogs approaching, he thought about using it on himself, but then he thought of Gracie. He had to try to rescue her as long as it was within his power to do so.

Even if he had no chance of fighting the dogs, maybe he could evade them long enough to get to Gracie. Knowing that he still had some time before the dogs reached him, he cast his light again on the doors in the hallway, studying them more carefully this time. Two of them led to bathrooms while a third led to a janitor's closet between. All three seemed like certain dead ends, but a door on the other side of the hall seemed more promising. The simple metal sign read simply: BASEMENT ENTRANCE, NO STUDENT ADMITTANCE.

"Good thing I'm not a student," Derek said, smiling to himself. He figured the basement must run beneath the entire school; perhaps there would be another entrance to the main level somewhere near Ms. Lightheart's classroom. At the very least, it seemed like a better option than waiting for the dogs.

As he suspected, the door was locked. He jammed his shoulder against the door a few times with no effect. He had just begun to kick at the handle when he heard the dogs again, much closer now. Looking back at the corner behind him, he saw the silhouettes of several dogs boiling over each other.

With a shrug, Derek raised the gun and fired at the lock. The sound echoed back by the metal was so loud it drowned out the sound of the lock exploding, its fragments bouncing silently off the wall. The door swung open, revealing a pit of darkness that even his phone light did nothing to penetrate.

Hearing the dogs approaching, Derek plunged himself into the darkness, nearly slipping on the metal that immediately greeted him. Spinning on his toes at the edge of the platform, Derek pushed the door shut behind him just as the first of the dogs appeared through the thin crack between the door and the frame. Holding the door shut, he felt the metal rattle as the dogs threw themselves against it. He knew that if he let go of the door, it would swing open and they would come flooding in, eager to destroy him.

Shining the light with his free hand, he saw that, although the lock had been blown to pieces, the handle had remained intact. It was a half-rectangle of metal protruding only a few inches from the door, with a corresponding half-rectangle on the wall where a lock could be slid in. When Derek slid the revolver through the handle, the long barrel easily reached through both handles, preventing the door from opening. As he let go of the gun, the weapon sat easily in the handle. The dogs continued to rattle the door, but to no avail.

Breathing a sigh of relief, Derek turned back to the darkness. Trying a light switch on the wall next to him, he immediately felt foolish, remembering that the power was out. "Right," he muttered to himself, using his phone light to make his way down the metal flight of stairs, which projected over a rough cement floor in a curving tunnel of red brick.

He had just reached the floor when his light began to flash. For one desperate, hopeful moment he thought the flash meant that Gracie was calling him back, but then the flashlight blinked out again and did not come back. Derek desperately smashed the buttons on the side of the phone to no effect. He realized he had drained the battery and again cursed himself for not charging it before he left to drop off the kids, regretting every search he had made for fresh stories about the dogs and every video he had watched of their news coverage. In his frustration, he threw the now-useless chunk of plastic aside, not even thinking about how much was left on his payment plan or how much it would cost to replace it, a consideration that would have shocked him even a few weeks ago.

In the darkness, he heard the phone hit the wall only a few feet from him and shatter. He only now realized he could not see the phone; the darkness was absolute and overpowering. "At least there are no dogs down here," he almost said into the darkness, but held himself back. There was no need to tempt fate.

All that mattered was finding light, then finding Gracie. Holding his now-empty hands in front of him like the groping monster in some B-movie he remembered seeing on late-night TV, Derek stumbled forward into the darkness, searching blindly for a way out.

By the time the dogs broke in, most of the kids were already in the vents. The pyramid of desks and chairs they had hastily built wobbled and leaned under every new arrival, and at first the kids had rushed to climb the stack so quickly that Gracie had been forced to take on the role of a traffic controller, waving kids onto the pyramid one at a time, holding the others back at its base, waiting with desperate impatience even while she heard the dogs crashing through what remained of their barrier.

The rich-looking kid in the polo had made sure he was the first to climb the stack, clambering up the uneven layers of desk tops and chair bottoms before anyone else could. When he had reached the top of the wobbling pile, he had stood uneasily on the topmost desk, swaying and almost falling as he pushed on the vent in the middle of the ceiling. The wobbling had increased with his strain, until Gracie had thought he was going to tip the pile over and ruin their entire plan, but suddenly he had given a final, larger wobble, coming closer than ever to tipping over as his weight redistributed while the vent cover lifted out of the ceiling.

Gracie and the others had ducked as he dropped the cover carelessly to the floor. When she had looked back, his legs were already disappearing into the vent. As she had heard the scuffling of his body against the metal, the sounds gradually heading towards the wall and into the next classroom, she had let go of her secret fear that the vents would be unable to hold their weight.

Now her only concern was getting everyone out before the dogs got in. As the last of the kids climbed the stack of desks, which had become disordered and unstable from the weight of those who had come before, a clattering from the door told her that what remained of their barrier had fallen aside. Gracie looked back to see the yellow lab, its length now fully inside the classroom, buried under the stack of desks it had just managed to knock over. Already the dog was struggling out from underneath the desks, and more dogs were streaming in through the narrow window behind it.

Gracie leaped onto the first layer of desks, no longer worried about overburdening them with her weight. The desks swayed and wobbled as she clambered to the top, but she didn't dare slow down. As Gracie reached the top, the mousy girl with long red hair was climbing into the vent, her stockinged legs disappearing into the opening as Gracie climbed onto the last desk.

She was the only person left in the classroom now, and the dogs seemed to know it. She heard them climbing the desks behind her, their spindly legs struggling over the uneven surface, but still growing closer. Gracie scrambled onto the last desk and desperately grasped for the opening, not sure she could pull herself up in time. As she reached up, a thin set of arms reached down, grasping her own and pulling her to safety.

Gracie looked up to see the mousy redhaired girl smiling down at her. Gracie smiled back as the girl pulled her to safety. Once she was inside the vent, Gracie grasped the edges of the opening and pulled herself up. Hearing the dogs still behind her, she looked down to see the yellow lab scrambling for the summit of the pile of desks. The entrance to the vent was only a few feet above its snout, close enough for the dog to jump inside.

Hating herself for doing it, Gracie stretched her leg and kicked the topmost desk, tilting it far enough askew to make the entire pile unsteady. Confused, the lab still tried to mount the topmost desk, which slid out from underneath him. The desk rolled down the pile with a mighty crash, the lab tumbling after. Their combined weight quickly destabilized the entire pile, which came crashing down on the other dogs that had flooded the classroom.

Gracie felt a twinge of guilt as she heard the dogs yelping and saw them buried beneath the falling furniture. She forced herself to remember the horrible things they had done and would do again if she let them and swallowed her guilt. At least she and her classmates were all safe now, and only had to find a way out through the vents.

As she pulled her legs back inside the vent and turned around, Gracie realized that might be harder than she had thought. The vents were almost entirely dark, with only a small red glow coming from the opening behind her. She still had Ms. Lightheart's cell phone, and she pulled it out now, shining the light ahead of her. The kids ahead nearly filled the vent, preventing her from seeing much.

"Pass the light up here." Gracie recognized the demanding, entitled voice of the boy in the polo echoing down the vent. She supposed it was a good idea no matter how much she resented his tone, and she handed the phone to the mousy girl in front of her, the light still on. The beam bounced off the rivets and ridges of the vent as the phone was passed from hand to hand until it finally stopped, presumably in the rich-looking boy's hands.

Around the silhouettes of the other kids, Gracie could see the beam waving around an intersection of the vents. "So which way do we go?" the boy in the polo called back, his confidence faltering now that he had been given responsibility.

"Whichever way will lead us out of here!" the redhaired girl cried unhelpfully.

"Just keep going straight," Gracie said more evenly. "It's bound to lead us out eventually. If we can get to the roof, we can wait there until help arrives."

The light bobbed up and down and the sound of fabric brushing metal came as the boy in the polo began to move. The other kids followed and soon Gracie was following them, fearful of being left alone in the dark. The sound of them all moving in sync created a cacophony inside the narrow metal tube, a sound which Gracie was sure was echoing out through the vent covers that lined the passage ahead.

As they crossed a vent that overlooked the hallway outside Ms. Lightheart's classroom, Gracie saw the dogs on the floor below, following the sounds of the children inside.

As Alison piloted her minivan around the outermost corner of the school, she was immediately greeted by a chain-link fence that stretched from the edge of the building to the end of the woods that reached to the mountains. She slowed, not sure if her car could even make it through the fence, then noticed a gate, presumably used for riding lawnmowers and other equipment, swinging open in the breeze. Pushing the gas pedal to the floor, she centered on the half-open gate, not caring if the metal damaged her finish or cracked her headlights, a thought that would have been unimaginable to her only a few hours before.

Her minivan hit the gate with a mighty crash. Alison barely felt the impact, but heard the scream of metal on metal. The gate swung open as far as it could go, then snapped back, scraping the side of the van as she passed. Alison winced at the long, grating noise, but drove on uncaring.

As she rounded the next corner and came within sight of the playground, she instantly realized she shouldn't have been so cavalier about smashing her headlights. The back of the school was shrouded in almost total darkness, as if her headlights were creating the small circles of reality she could see out of the endless void around them. She flipped on the brights, bringing the entire fairy castle of the playground into existence.

At first, she saw nothing, but a flash of movement made her realize she had been looking too low. Max was lying on top of the highest tower, waving his arms desperately. She wondered why he didn't climb down to reach her, but knew he wouldn't from the childish way he clung to the tower with his free hand. The last time she had seen him like that was when he was two years old and had accidentally knocked over the glass of wine Derek was sipping while he finished work, spilling the liquid across the plans for his latest development, ruining weeks' worth of work in a single accidental step. Derek had lost his temper, a rarity even then, and had yelled at the hapless boy for hours. Alison, just recovering from giving birth to Gracie, hadn't had the energy to stop him, so she had stood by, only acting as her son's support by letting him hold her hand and press his head against her hip for safety. The way he had looked when she glanced down to comfort him was almost exactly the way he looked now, clinging to the plastic roof of the tower.

Since she knew Max wouldn't come to her, Alison drove to him. Gritting her teeth and gripping the steering wheel, she pressed on the gas, the car juddering as it bounced over the wood frame that held the playground's sand. The car fishtailed as the tires sank, spewing sand that she could hear bouncing off the glass and metal. The engine roared as she retook control of the car, turning into the swerve to pilot the car beneath the tower where Max stood.

As the car came to a rest beneath the lowest platform, Alison fingered the Glock in the map compartment, considering getting out to meet Max until she considered why he was hiding on top of the tower in the first place. Taking her hand off the door handle, she looked up through the windshield to see Max carefully climbing down the poles that held up the plastic roof. Sudden inspiration came to her and she pressed a button on the control panel above the rearview mirror, listening to the moon roof above the back seat slide open.

A moment later, there was a heavy thump as a section of the roof just above her caved in slightly. More thumps led towards the moonroof as Alison looked towards the backseat. Max dropped through the opening, not bothering to lower himself in, landing perfectly in the center of the bench seats. His face was pale and haggard, his hair sticking to the sides of his head in wet clumps.

Alison reached around her seat to take his hand. "Are you alright?"

Instead of answering, Max pointed straight ahead and screamed. Alison turned to see a golden retriever jumping onto the hood and dashing up the windshield. Too late, she realized she hadn't closed the moon roof. There was no time to do it now, the dog would be at the opening before the automatic servo could close the panel.

As the roof above her caved in again, Alison stomped on the gas pedal harder than she ever had in her life, but the car didn't move at all. The engine whined as the tires spun in the sand, kicking up plumes that coated the side windows. In the rearview, she saw Max look up towards the opening above him and shriek in terror at what he saw there. She was about to reach back for him, to let off the gas and leap into the backseat to cover him with her body as best she could, when the rear tires, having finally spit up enough sand, dug into whatever material lay beneath all that sand and began to move. The car was thrown forward so suddenly that Alison nearly lost her grip on the wheel. Alison swerved through the playground, narrowly missing the next tower.

As she swerved, she heard a yelp from above and saw in the rearview a streak of gold falling past the rear window. A moment later, there was a heavy thump, then another yelp. Alison risked another glance in the rearview and saw the golden retriever in the sand, struggling to regain its feet. She thought for a moment about putting the car in reverse and running the dog over, but thought better of it. The dog couldn't harm them now, and she would only risk crashing her car.

Gripping the wheel as the car bounced over the wood frame surrounding the playground, Alison pressed the button to close the moon roof and slowed the car to a halt. "Are you okay?" she asked Max again, turning back to him.

He stared at her for a long moment, then began to laugh. "Yeah, I'm okay now. Thanks to you." He sat up from where he had begun to recline on the seat, a troubled look crossing his face. "But Gracie and the others are still inside! We need to help them!"

Alison held up a hand to calm him down. "It's okay. Your father went inside to find them."

Max only looked more concerned. "By himself? The dogs are in there, they're gonna get him! We have to go after him!"

Alison had to physically stop him from climbing out of the car. "No, Max. Your father's expecting us to be out here. Once he finds Gracie, we're his way out. If we go in there too, the entire plan could be screwed up."

"But all the dogs went in there! He doesn't know what he's heading into!"

Alison almost reached for the Glock, wondering to herself what she could do with it. But she didn't know how to use the thing; she would only make things worse. Instead, she reached for her cell phone and called Derek, telling herself she was only checking in on him. Instead of a comforting ring tone, the phone went instantly to voicemail. "Hi, you've reached Derek Rains," he said in a voice cheerier than any she had heard from him in months.

"He wouldn't have turned the phone off," she said to herself.

"Maybe the battery died," Max said from the backseat.

"Let's hope that's all it is," Alison muttered, putting the car in gear. "I'm going to do a loop around the building. Hopefully your father finds his way out soon."

Derek was lost in the endless darkness.

He had walked for what felt like hours, feeling his way along by trailing one hand against the smooth, cold brick, keeping the other out ahead of him in case of a sudden obstacle in the impenetrable darkness. For how long he had been walking, he would have thought that his eyes would have eventually adjusted to the darkness, but even now, the world ahead of him remained the same endless blackness. He figured his eyes couldn't adjust when there was absolutely no light for them to adjust to. He was in the basement of the earth, somewhere no light could penetrate.

Unlike upstairs, there didn't seem to be any emergency lights anywhere in the basement. He figured the emergency lights had been intended for the kids, that the designers had figured that anyone down here in a power outage would have their own light. That probably meant there was a flashlight somewhere down here in the darkness. The thought gave him hope, and the hope kept him crawling forward through the darkness.

A sudden sound in the darkness froze him, and made him lose all hope. It started as a simple tapping, like metal hitting metal, which was quickly repeated in the echoing darkness. The sound could have been anything, but his paranoid mind quickly invented a story, which was supported a moment later by the sound of a heavy door creaking open. He knew then that his story had been right, that the gun he had placed to block the door had been knocked off the handle by the repeated attacks of the dogs and bounced down the steps, allowing the door to open. This story was further confirmed by an even more horrible sound an instant later: the heavy padding of dozens of paws, clicking on their way down the stairs.

Derek held still in the darkness, hoping the dogs wouldn't be able to hear him. His hopes were immediately disappointed when he heard the dogs turn in unison, the clicking of their pads quickly growing louder. Derek realized they had an advantage in being able to smell him, and maybe even see in the dark, while he was helpless to use any of his senses except hearing, which wouldn't tell him anything except that he was about to die. He turned and ran, no longer bothering to keep one hand along the wall. He kept both arms straight out, heedless of danger as he barreled into darkness.

When it first came into view, he thought the red light ahead of him was only in his mind, a symptom of his intense fear overtaking his visual cortex. But soon he began to distinguish the outlines of bricks and the shape of the hall curving ahead of him. As he rounded that curve, he realized that there was a faint light ahead, perhaps the only emergency light in the entire basement.

He ran faster, motivated as much by having a goal ahead as by the sound of the dogs behind him.

As he reached the lighted area, Derek realized it was a workshop of sorts for the school's custodians. He also realized this was the end of the hall. A workbench was built along one wall, scattered with small tools and half-finished projects. The red light was glowing from an enclosed bulb above this bench. At the end of the hall was an enormous storeroom, its heavy steel door hanging open. Derek quickly scanned the work table, noting ironically that there were several flashlights on the bench. *Of course,* he thought, *you find 'em now that you don't need 'em.* There were also several tools, all of them too small to be effective as weapons.

The best thing he found was a large, red fire extinguisher, which he gripped with both hands as he pulled it from its hooks above the workbench. He raised the weapon, feeling its weight, wondering if it would be enough to fight off the dogs. As he heard them trampling down the hallway, their footsteps thunderous in the cavernous space, he knew it would not. He considered locking himself inside the heavy-doored storeroom, but knew that would only delay the inevitable, that without a cellphone he would run out of air in the unventilated space long before someone found him.

He was looking around for another weapon when a better idea suddenly struck him. Grinning to himself, he opened the steel door of the storeroom until it touched the edge of the workbench, then used the cracked leather seat of a stool as a step to climb on top of the bench, kicking the stool over after he had climbed up. Unhooking the hose from the body of the extinguisher, he sprayed a flood of white foam across the floor in front of the entrance to the storeroom, covering every inch of the surface.

Once all that was coming out of the extinguisher was hissing air, Derek began to strike the empty cylinder against the steel door, relishing the high, ringing sound that echoed down the hall. "Come get me, you fuckers!" he yelled to the dogs, which he could still hear charging down the hallway. As they drew closer, he struck the door harder with the empty extinguisher, yelling louder and more profanely at the dogs. Eventually they came in sight, charging around the corner. The yellow lab that led the pack looked up and saw Derek on the table, but it was already too late.

Derek beamed as the dog's paws slipped in the foam, its legs splaying underneath it. The dog slid across the foam-coated floor, more dogs following after, their tiny legs flying out from underneath them as their bodies slid across the floor. The traction from their initial speed was enough to carry them across the floor, and soon their bodies were gliding into the waiting mouth of the storeroom.

His grin widening, Derek pushed the door shut from where he stood, then leaped to the floor, moving slowly so he wouldn't slip on the foam himself. As he pushed the door shut the rest of the way, he heard the dogs scrambling to their feet, struggling to regain their footing in the foam. As he tried to turn the lock, a golden snout pressed itself between the door and the frame, preventing him from closing the door all the way. As he pressed against the snout, he felt more dogs throw their weight against the door, their claws scratching the metal.

Pressing one knee against the door, Derek raised his other foot, balancing carefully on the foot that slid against the foam. Bringing his raised foot down hard, Derek stomped on the snout hard enough to make blood spray from the nostrils. As he brought his foot down again, the snout pulled back, snuffling blood.

With the doorway clear, Derek pushed the door shut, straining against the weight the dogs threw against the door. As the door settled against the frame, he turned the lock and stepped back, catching his breath as he struggled to keep his footing.

Relief was just starting to flood over his body when he heard the growling behind him. He turned slowly, unsure whether one of the dogs had managed to avoid slipping in the foam, or if there had simply been a lone straggler who had only just now caught up with the rest. Either way, when he turned, he saw a German shepherd with blood clotted around its mouth.

The animal growled again and began to charge forward. Derek raised his hand to block the thing, but stopped when he saw that it wasn't moving forward. Instead, the animal was pinwheeling wildly on the slippery foam, remaining in place even as it tried to force itself to run harder. Derek found the sight so comical that for a moment he forgot to react, or even try to escape, only stood there watching the dog in open-mouthed amazement. Eventually, the furiously spinning paws splashed away enough of the rancid foam to clear four patches of floor, enough to give the dog traction.

As the shepherd lunged towards him, Derek instinctively raised the empty extinguisher and swung it at the blonde and black head. The cylinder connected with a hard thump and a metallic ring. The dog fell to the ground, finally sliding across the foam. As Derek's own breathing calmed, he heard the shepherd's ragged breaths continuing. Derek raised the extinguisher, debating whether he could really hurt an animal when it didn't present an immediate threat, but when he considered what might happen if the animal woke up and caught him unaware while he was making his way out of the darkened tunnels, he overcame his resistance and brought the cylinder down hard, extinguishing the animal's life.

His bloody deed done, Derek crossed carefully to the workbench, stepping slowly so he wouldn't slip on the foam. As he walked, the extinguisher he still carried dripped a trail of blood, which dried quickly as it mixed with the foam. Setting the extinguisher by its bloody base on the bench, Derek picked up the largest of the flashlights he had seen, a long, heavy one of silver metal, like the ones police used.

After testing the light to make sure it worked, Derek stuffed a few blue work rags into his pockets, to wipe off his shoes once he left this area, so he wouldn't be slipping and squeaking during his entire walk back through the school. He took a few steps away from the bench, then came back and stuffed another flashlight in his back pocket, too scared by his previous experiences not to err on the side of caution.

Picking up his extinguisher with the hand not holding the silver flashlight, he grimaced at the sensation of having to physically peel the cylinder from the table, and almost gagged at the circle of drying blood it left behind. Doing his best to ignore these sensations, he stepped carefully out of the field of foam, then wiped off his shoes and the base of the extinguisher, leaving the soaked rags behind, next to the body of the dead dog. He could still hear the living ones scratching and howling at the door of the store room, muffled by the heavy steel. Derek turned away, knowing that in the airless room, they wouldn't be alive much longer.

Tuning out their howls and screams, Derek walked into the darkness with a newfound sense of confidence, shining his flashlight ahead of him to seek out the path back to the upper floor of the school, where he would find Gracie and the others.

As Garth waved the terrified partiers across the empty dirt parking lot, he kept an eye out for approaching dogs. The only vehicle in the lot was Brian's mud-spattered, once-white pick-up truck, and the only person inside the station was Garth's elderly dispatcher, Maria, who stood in the doorway, waving the partiers inside. The other officers and their accompanying vehicles were scattered across town, assisting with any one of the dozens of emergencies the dogs had brought on.

But there was one emergency that none of them were responding to, that Garth knew he would have to see to personally, and for that he would need a vehicle. He approached the young man in the skeleton costume, who was currently busy pulling a plump woman in a princess costume from the rear window of his cab while a blonde in an even skimpier outfit looked on.

"Sorry, Brian, gonna have to commandeer your truck. Eminent domain, ya know."

Brian pulled the young woman free and looked up at the sheriff. "Well shit, ya're gonna need a driver."

Garth looked at Heloise, who was coming out of the station with the fully-loaded shotgun and sidearm that Garth had approved for Maria to give her, Heloise's ammo for her dart gun being in short supply. She also carried more ammo and a fresh sidearm for Garth. Heloise looked back at him and shrugged.

Garth looked back at the young man and nodded, motioning him inside the cab. The blonde in the skimpy Arabic costume clasped her hands together, her eyes growing watery as she watched the young man, who was still wearing his skull mask over the top of his head, climb into the truck. Garth waved for the young woman to get inside as he climbed into the bed of the truck alongside Heloise.

"You know, Heloise, I never thought I would be caught dead inside one of these lifted trucks," the sheriff growled, huffing as he dropped his bulk inside the truck bed.

She shrugged, checking the chamber of her shotgun. "Who knows, sheriff, the night is young; you might get your chance."

Garth gave her a dry laugh as the truck roared to life and the two princesses jiggled their way inside the station, Maria locking the front door behind them.

"Very reassuring," Garth growled.

The truck spewed fumes and kicked fresh mud from its tires as they took off across the parking lot.

Gracie scrambled to keep up with the light as the other kids moved around an angle in the vent. Navigating by the faint glints on the burnished metal, Gracie pulled herself around the corner. The others were already at the far end of the length of vent ahead of her, following the boy in the polo, who was shining the flashlight around another bend.

As Gracie pushed herself down the vent, a scent came to her that was strangely familiar, both revolting and comforting at the same time. Ahead, the boy in the polo disappeared around another corner, taking the light with him. The other kids followed, completely ignoring another path to the right which seemed to be completely lost in darkness. As Gracie, bringing up the rear of the pack, passed this opening, she caught sight of faint red bars of light coming through a grate at the end of a long stretch of vent.

More intriguing than that, though, was the smell, which suddenly grew much more powerful as she passed the opening. The associations with the smell were strong enough to make her stop at the intersection, breathing in a lungful of the air, trying to place the smell. In a moment, she had it. "Hey guys, come back here!" she yelled to the others, who were already disappearing around the corner ahead.

Gracie sat still, afraid of being left in the dark, even more afraid of missing their best chance at escape. The mousy redhaired girl stuck her head around the corner, looking back at Gracie. "Hurry up, Gracie, everyone's way up ahead!"

"Yeah, well they're going the wrong way!" Gracie cried, "The exit is this way."

"How do you know?" the girl spat through her braces.

"Because I'm following my nose," Gracie said with a grin, making her way down the other passage.

Behind her, she heard the redhaired girl crying to the others to come back. "Gracie! Where are you going?"

"The cafeteria!" Gracie called back. "The main entrance is just beyond that." As she crawled further down the vent, the scent became even stronger: the sickly-sweet smell of frozen hamburgers and years of baked-on grease. The smell simultaneously made her nauseous at the thought of eating that stuff and nostalgic at the memories of sitting around one of the circular tables in the cafeteria with her friends, enjoying one of their few breaks from the school day.

As she drew nearer to the vent cover, Gracie could see the cafeteria far below, much further away than she had expected. Behind her, she heard the others crawling back, the vent tunnel turning into a cacophonous stream of noise as the children all tried to bunch together at the end of the passage.

"Gracie, what are you doing?" the boy in the polo yelled, too loud.

"We can get out this way!" Gracie whispered back, letting the echoes off the narrow metal tunnel carry her voice.

"I thought we wanted to get to the roof!" the boy roared. "What if they hear us when we climb down?"

"Well, they definitely will if you keep shouting!" she hissed. "Besides, we don't actually know if the vents will lead us to the roof. For all we know, we could be crawling around all night while my dad waits for us outside."

"Well, then you go on ahead and look if you're so damn sure!" he yelled back, but continued crawling towards her.

As the other kids crawled down the vent towards her, Gracie felt the tunnel shaking, their collective weight straining the metal frame. She tried to picture the outside of the vent in her mind, the metal tunnel she had seen running along the ceiling of the cafeteria a hundred times by now, but had never consciously noticed. Now that she thought about it, she found that she could visualize the vent hanging from the ceiling, suspended only by a few metal braces. The whole thing had looked pretty flimsy, designed to hold up the weight of a cloud of hot air, not a herd of stampeding children.

Gracie held up one hand, trying to stop the children from coming any closer. "Wait, wait, the vent can't hold us all!" she cried. But it was already too late.

The vent tilted to one side, slamming Gracie against the metal grill. The other kids screamed as they were dropped against the wall, which dented outwards beneath their weight. Over their screams, Gracie heard the pling of the bolts that had formerly held up the brace hitting the floor far below. In the next moment, she heard another of the braces snap and felt the vent continue to tilt.

Screaming at the other kids to turn around, Gracie tried to move towards them. The other kids hurried ahead of her, clogging the vent as they crawled over each other. The vent continued to shake beneath them, more agitated by their sudden movement than relieved by the loss of their weight. As Gracie crawled forward, she suddenly felt herself sliding, her fingers scratching against the smooth metal, failing to find purchase. The mousy girl looked back and saw that Gracie was in trouble. She reached out to help, but was too far away to do much of anything. Still, Gracie couldn't help but instinctively reach out, their hands trying to grasp across a dozen feet of empty air.

At first Gracie couldn't figure out what was wrong with the sight of the girl ahead of her, but when she realized that the girl was sliding away, appearing to change shape like a character in one of the old video games her dad sometimes played late at night, who seemed to switch dimensions as they turned, Gracie thought she was passing out, overwhelmed by the terror and exhaustion of the night, her vision disappearing into a tunnel. Then a dropping, sinking feeling in her stomach made her realize that she was in fact more awake than she had been all night. She soon realized that she was literally dropping, the world around her reframing itself as the narrow tunnel of the vent plummeted towards the ground.

Gracie pressed her hands and feet against the walls, bracing herself for the inevitable impact. The vent filled with noise as the metal bent ahead of her, quickly bringing the others out of view. Finally, she was left alone, tumbling endlessly through the dark.

After what felt like an eternity of searching the tunnels by the bright but narrow beam of the flashlight, Derek was unsure whether he had unknowingly passed the entrance to the main floor or had not yet reached it. All of the doorways looked the same and when he had been heading here in the dark he hadn't noticed any of them. He had thought for sure that he would see his discarded gun on the floor and the damaged door hanging open, but he couldn't be sure that the door hadn't swung shut on its own just as easily as it had swung open, and that the gun hadn't fallen into one of the drains along the floor or beneath one of the shelves that lined the walls. Meanwhile, while he was busy dallying around in the basement, he also couldn't be sure that hordes of dogs weren't tearing his daughter and her friends apart.

He forced himself to push that thought out of his mind. He was only letting panic get the best of him, the same way that he didn't realize that he had only been in the basement for a short while, the apparent time extended by his lack of a clock or any external signs of the time.

Still, he had to get out of here sooner rather than later. When he passed the next flight of steps, he climbed to the top to read the small metal sign on the inside of the door. GYM ENTRANCE, the sign read in neat white lettering on a red background. The gym connected to the cafeteria; he could find his way back into the school, and from there to Gracie's classroom. Derek had no idea how the twisting basement corridor had somehow brought him to the other side of the school, but he didn't care to question it. Maybe the darkness had disoriented him more than he had realized; either way, he pushed the door open and cautiously poked his head inside, momentarily setting down the extinguisher he still carried in order to hold the door.

Shining his flashlight around the cavernous space revealed nothing. A red exit sign glowed from the darkness to his right, and Derek carefully closed the basement door behind himself, wincing at the loud squeaks his shoes made as he crossed the gym floor, the sounds made louder by the darkness. When he reached a pair of double doors that he thought should lead to the cafeteria, Derek pressed his ear against the metal for a moment to make sure he couldn't hear anything on the other side. When he heard only the gentle buzzing of the exit sign, Derek gently pushed the door open.

Crossing through the cafeteria again, Derek saw no movement, but made sure to give the tables a wide berth. As he neared the hallway that led to the classrooms, Derek suddenly heard a noise that made him spin on his heels. At first, he thought the dogs had snuck up on him again, but the sound was muffled, as if they were in another room, and strangely echoed. As he cast his light around and saw nothing, he eventually realized that the sound was coming from above him, near the ceiling. He cast his light up and saw a vent duct suspended from the ceiling by the thinnest of metal straps. At the same moment, he heard the sound of children's voices yelling back and forth.

One of them was Gracie's. Derek ran towards the vent, crawling on top of one of the tables in a desperate attempt to be closer to her. Before he could say a word, the voices above turned to screams as the vent began to tilt crazily. Derek saw the bolt from one of the metal straps fly out as if launched by an air cannon hidden in the ceiling. The bolt slammed into the ground next to the table, raising a puff of dust from the floor tile it shattered. The entire supporting band bent back, allowing the vent to tilt even further. A moment later, another bolt shot out of the next band, slamming into Derek's shoulder with the force of a bullet. He nearly dropped the flashlight as his hand flew to his shoulder, then jumped off the table as the vent came crashing down.

He heard the children inside screaming as the vent hit the floor, ending up propped on one of the tables like some insane slide. That metaphor turned out to be apt, as he heard the rushing of clothes against metal and the tinny scream of a child quickly plummeting down the fallen vent. From the torn opening at the end, a small form burst out and skidded a few feet across the floor before coming to a rest.

Shining his flashlight on the form, Derek instantly recognized Gracie's tiara and what remained of her dress. She turned as he called her name, and held out her arms like a toddler as he reached to pick her up. "Are you okay?!" he called as he scooped her up, instinctively searching her for injuries.

"I'm okay, Dad," she told him, pushing his hands away, "but we need to get out of here before the dogs come back."

Derek smiled. Gracie had always been more levelheaded, more focused on the immediate situation, than even her parents. "You're right, honey. How many more kids are in the vent?"

Gracie screwed up her face, trying to think. "Two dozen maybe?"

"More than can fit in Mom's van. But the police are on the way."

Turning back to the vent, Gracie called into it like it was a soup-can phone in a treehouse. "You hear that, guys? Help is on the way; you can climb down!"

From inside the vent, there was a chorus of cheered voices and sudden rustling as the kids lined up to get down. Made nervous by the loud, echoing noises, Derek cast his light around, searching for danger. He saw nothing in the cavernous cafeteria, but he did hear something: a low, rumbling growl far behind him, quickly joined by another.

Derek turned to see several dogs gathering in the space between where he and Gracie stood and the hallway to the classrooms. Instinctively, he clapped a hand over Gracie's mouth, silencing her summons to her classmates. "Stay up there!" he risked yelling to the kids above, hearing them getting ready to come down the vent. "The dogs are down here. Find a way to the roof and wait for help!"

He heard a thousand confused questions shouted from above, but ignored them all, dragging Gracie towards the front door, his hand still over her mouth. When she began to move with him, he dropped his hand and took hers, running by her side towards the front door.

As they rounded the wall that blocked off the entrance to the school, they saw more dogs waiting in the atrium, turning towards them with mouthfuls of bare fangs as Derek's light shined on them, their teeth and eyes responding with an equal glow.

Derek skidded to a halt on the tile floor, holding up a hand to stop Gracie. For a moment, they stood frozen, their eyes locked with the dogs'. A sound behind them snapped Derek into action. He turned to see more dogs slowly closing in, cutting off their escape through the cafeteria. Derek remembered there were other doors in the gym which he assumed led outside and turned that way, only to find more dogs closing in on that side, stalking slowly forward, as if enjoying the hunt. They were surrounded on three sides, the cafeteria wall pressing close on the fourth. Derek squeezed Gracie's hand, unsure what else he could do.

As usual, she had other ideas. "Come on!" Gracie yelled, pulling him by the hand. She led him to the small door that led to the kitchen, where the kids usually lined up to receive their lunches. As he squeezed through the doorway behind her, he pulled the door shut behind them, blocking the entryway before the dogs arrived. Derek felt self-congratulatory until he saw the red glow of the exit sign across the room and saw that there was a second door into the kitchen. It was probably where the kids exited once they had picked up their food.

He was rushing towards this other door when an enormous rottweiler burst in through the frame, sniffing the air for a moment before turning towards Derek. He froze as its lips peeled back, revealing dripping fangs. In the glow of the red light, he saw more dogs approaching.

Gracie grabbed his arm and pulled him back. "This way!" She instinctively guided him in the darkness. Even before he shone his light on the steel counter where the kids would line up to receive their meals, Gracie was ducking under a metal flap that would allow cafeteria workers through. Derek thought of jumping over the counter, then quit kidding himself and paused to lift the flap, even though the time it took might literally kill him.

Needing to free up a hand to lift the flap, Derek turned and threw the bloody fire extinguisher he still carried across the floor, rolling it towards the approaching dogs. They stumbled and tripped as they tried to get out of the way of the rolling cylinder, but Derek didn't stay to watch. Raising the flap with his now-free hand, he followed Gracie into the kitchen, shining his flashlight on the narrow aisles between the enormous island grills and the shelves of pots and pans.

Gracie was already halfway across the kitchen, racing towards a loading dock at the back of the kitchen, where she had probably observed countless boxes of frozen pizzas and pre-made tortilla bowls being delivered while she was waiting in line. Derek followed her through the aisles, hearing the dogs just behind them. As they passed a wire rack full of heavy pots and pans, Derek stopped and pulled on the rack, watching the dogs gain on him as he struggled to reach the tipping point. Just as the rottweiler passed beneath the lowest shelf, Derek gave a final heave and felt the rack began to tip. Pots and pans fell from the shelves, knocking the dog to the floor. The rack tumbled after it, burying the dog and blocking the path of the next few, but only for a moment. Derek saw the dogs scrambling to climb over the fallen shelf, their legs getting stuck between the thin wire of the shelves. As Derek turned to follow Gracie again, he saw a dog leap onto the stove that ran down the center of the room. As he dashed for the loading dock, Derek heard its paws clicking on the metal grills.

Ahead, stacks of boxes separated the loading dock from the kitchen. Beyond were two rolling cargo doors, both locked and shuttered, with a single steel door to the left. Gracie was just reaching the boxes when she turned back. She looked from Derek to something just over his shoulder with a look of pure fright. He didn't need her to tell him that the dog on the stove was gaining on him. He could hear the clicking footsteps catching up with him.

"Get outside, Gracie!" Derek yelled, "Don't look back!"

Once again, she had her own ideas. Stepping to the edge of the long island that ran the length of the kitchen, she fiddled with the knobs on the gas stove. Derek saw the blue flame spark to life in the darkness. He only hoped the dog didn't see it as well, or at least didn't understand its meaning.

Scooping up Gracie as he passed, Derek sprinted past the end of the kitchen into the loading dock. Behind him, he heard the clicking stop and the dog howling in pain. As he passed a stack of frozen pizzas that almost reached the ceiling, Derek paused long enough to look back, unable to stop himself from smirking at the sight of the dog trying to simultaneously pull back all four of its paws. Feeling Gracie tug at his arm, Derek knocked the stack of boxes over, creating another obstacle for the dog as it finally leapt to the ground.

Slamming into the crash bar, Derek threw open the single steel door without thinking of what might be on the other side. As he found himself and Gracie on a metal platform in the cold night air, Derek slammed the door shut behind them, shuddering at the sound of dogs colliding with the metal on the other side.

Taking Gracie by the hand, Derek led her down the short flight of steps and around the concrete lip of the loading dock. They were in a parking lot on the back side of the school, chain-link separating the gravel from the woods beyond. Derek had no idea which way led to the front of the school, and Alison's minivan was nowhere in sight. He led Gracie in the direction he hoped was right, then suddenly stopped.

A jet-black mastiff stood in the parking lot ahead of them, almost invisible against the pavement. Only the pink circle of its slowly opening mouth was growing more visible. That, and the subtle yellow glow of its eyes.

"Get behind me, Gracie," Derek whispered, not sure what his next move would be. For once, Gracie listened, moving behind him and pushing her face into the small of his back. Derek held her tight as he heard the dog's low growling quickly building in intensity. He scanned the empty parking lot, but saw nowhere they could go. Empty asphalt stretched in all directions, and the dog would run them down before they could get far. All he could do was hold Gracie and squeeze his eyes shut.

In the darkness, he heard the growling growing closer. A second growling joined it, growing louder and closer. Soon the second growling had completely overtaken the first, its sound completely changing as it grew closer, becoming a rhythmic, mechanical whine.

Derek opened his eyes and was immediately blinded by the headlights of Alison's minivan. He threw up his arms in futile defense, thinking for a moment that they were going to die at the moment of their rescue. Then the van swerved, heading directly towards the dog. The dog made an almost comical squeal as the bumper collided with it, sending the suddenly helpless form flying through the air. The minivan screeched to a halt where the dog had stood, the side door sliding open. Derek was relieved to see Max inside, Alison poking her head behind the driver's seat. "Come on, come on!" Max yelled like one of the soldiers in the war movies he liked, waving them across the thirty or so feet of pavement that separated them from the van.

Derek pushed Gracie forward, then froze at a sound behind them. This time he knew it was really growling, and it was horribly familiar. He turned to confirm what he had already seen in his mind's eye: the Xolo, it eyes glowing in the darkness, its mouth pulled up in what looked like a crooked, knowing smile.

Behind him, he felt Gracie tugging at his sleeve. He pushed her away, shoving her towards the car. "Go, Gracie. Run!"

"Are you crazy? That thing will run us down!" Alison was already swinging the van towards them, but would never make it before the Xolo sprinted on them.

Derek turned back to Gracie. "Run one of us down." He saw fear building in her eyes, but pushed her towards the van. "Go!"

She hesitated only a moment before taking off for the van. Derek sprinted in the other direction, making for the chain-link fence and the stretch of woods beyond. Turning back halfway, he saw that his plan had already failed. The Xolo was sprinting after Gracie, who was still ten feet or more from Max's outstretched arms.

"Hey! I'm the one you want!" Derek yelled, shining the flashlight in the Xolo's eyes. For an instant, the dog's eyes glowed even brighter. The Xolo stopped in its tracks, confused by the flash of light. Derek flashed the light as he watched Gracie dash towards the van. The dog paused for a moment, then cast its gaze on Derek. Even without the flashlight, its eyes seemed to glow brighter as it focused on him, and Derek had the sickening, horrible realization that the dog recognized him.

"Come on! Come on, come get me!" Derek yelled, waving the flashlight. He started to run backwards, still making for the fence. As the Xolo began to run, Derek threw the flashlight, which shattered on the pavement just ahead of the dog, then turned and sprinted for the fence.

In the van, Max pulled Gracie inside and slid the door shut. "What about Dad?" Gracie cried.

Alison watched him through the windshield as he reached the fence and began to climb, a scrambling, athletic motion she never knew he was capable of. She pumped the gas, hoping she could run the Xolo over too, possessed by a mad certainty that would undo all of this, would take all the pain of the last months away, but the dog was already following Derek up the fence, using its claws to scale the chain-link in a way that Alison never knew any dog was capable of.

Alison stopped the van as Derek dropped himself off the other side of the fence, landing hard on the ground and half-rolling, half-tumbling down a steep hill to the woods beyond. The dog somehow swung itself over the top of the fence, landing much more gracefully on all four legs and giving chase.

Alison turned back to the kids, unsure what she should do next. Over Gracie's head, she saw the mud-spattered pick-up truck that she and Derek had passed on the road in another lifetime. In the bed, she saw the sheriff and the animal catcher, weapons at the ready. Alison sped the van towards them, meeting the truck in the middle of the parking lot.

"The kids alright?" Garth asked as she rolled down the window.

"Gracie and Max are alright, but the rest of the kids are-"

"-The rest of the kids are still inside!" Gracie interrupted, leaning over Alison. "They're in the air vents, looking for a way to get to the roof."

Garth gave a puzzled look towards the collection of air conditioning units that huddled menacingly on the roof, then looked back at the van, even more confused. "Is Derek with them?"

"He ran into the woods," Alison said desperately, pointing beyond the fence. "The Xolo is after him!"

Garth looked at the woods and nodded, then looked back at the animal catcher. "Think you can stay here and take care of those kids?"

The young woman in the black tactical uniform looked determined but confused. "Where are you going?"

The sheriff looked off into the woods. "I'm going after Derek. And that damn dog."

Without waiting for a response, the sheriff slung his shotgun over his back and took off for the woods.

TWENTY-NINE

As he ran into the darkened woods, Derek was glad he had thought to grab a second flashlight while he was in the school. Without breaking his stride as he ducked amongst the furthest branches, he fumbled with the flashlight tucked into his back pocket, pulling it free and shining the light ahead of him just before he collided with an enormous oak tree. Ducking around the tree, he cast a look back for the Xolo, but saw nothing. Even the edge of the forest was already obscured by the ancient, vine-tangled branches, but he certainly heard something: a stealthy, decisive padding, sneaking around the edge of the woods just beyond the reach of his flashlight.

And it was growing closer.

Derek crashed through brush and shrubs, unsure of where he was going, only knowing he had to lead the Xolo away from the kids. It was like some primitive instinct, as ancient as the ones that gave the dog its bloodlust and hunting skills. He knew that wherever he was leading the dog, it was certain to end in death. He could only hope it would be death for the dog.

Garth Chambers dropped heavily to the ground. He hadn't climbed a fence since he was in high school, and right now every muscle in his body was reminding him why. He wanted to pause to catch his breath already, but the whole point of throwing himself over the fence was to catch up with Derek. If he waited, the dog would catch up with Derek first.

Raising his shotgun, Garth slid down the muddy embankment to the edge of the woods. As he reached the trees, he heard gunshots ringing out behind him. He paused, one hand resting on the trunk of a tree, and considered going back. But the shots continued in an unabated stream, and so did the cries of triumph that accompanied them.

Garth was needed more in the woods: Derek was alone and unarmed, and he had the main creature after him. If nothing else, Garth had a chance to end this whole thing by finishing the dog off.

If it doesn't finish you first, the voice inside his head said. Garth pushed that voice away, telling himself it was just the pain in his body talking. As he set off into the woods, it talked pretty fucking loudly, sending creaks from every single one of his joints, but Garth pushed that away too, just hoping the noise wasn't loud enough to attract the cholo, or whatever the fuck the thing was called.

Whatever it was, Garth was gonna kill it. Of that, he was pretty damn sure.

As he plunged into the brush, the gunshots continued behind him.

It was Gracie who first saw the kids on the roof. At the suggestion of the woman in the tactical suit, who had hastily introduced herself as Heloise, Alison had pulled her minivan alongside the school's side entrance, while the man in the skeleton costume who was driving the pick-up truck brought his own vehicle just behind hers.

Heloise stood in the bed of the truck, keeping watch over the front lawn of the school, a flashlight in one hand and a shotgun in the other, the dart gun Alison had seen her with earlier apparently abandoned. Alison also kept her gaze outside, her fingers nervously playing over the Glock she still didn't know if she would be able to shoot.

That left only Max and Gracie and the man in the skeleton costume to look out for the kids, but the man seemed more interested in nervously checking his phone and his radio for updates than paying attention to his current situation. So, it was Gracie who spotted them first, looking up through the moon roof towards the top of the school, pointing and screaming for her mother just as she had when she was a baby.

Pulling herself into the middle row of seats, Alison looked up to see a huddled, desperate pack of shadows leaning over the edge of the roof. The white pick-up truck was parked beneath a ladder built into the wall, which ran from the rim of the roof to halfway down the building. When he saw the kids, the man in the skeleton costume jumped out of his truck and climbed into the bed, quickly freeing a ladder hooked to the side of the bed. This he balanced on the floor of the bed and leaned against the brick wall. It didn't reach as far as the enormous ladder that the designers had intended for the custodial staff to bring from some distant shed so that kids wouldn't be able to access the roof. Those designers probably never could have imagined that their design was now having the opposite effect.

Climbing as high as the ladder would carry him, Brian waved for the kids to come down, encouraging them to climb to the bottom of the cage-encased ladder where he could reach them. Alison thought of climbing out of the car to help the kids down when a sudden flash of light and a sound like thunder made her dive for the floor. When she regained her courage enough to look out the back window, she saw Heloise pumping her shotgun, smoke still pouring from the barrel.

Getting back into the driver's seat, Alison looked out the window and saw a horde of dogs approaching. One was lying dead in the grass, blood pouring out between clumps of matted fur, but more were coming, much more than Heloise would be able to handle, especially with such a slow-firing weapon.

From the backseat, Gracie was calling out. "We have to get the other kids down, come on, Max!" She was already pulling her brother towards the door.

Alison slammed the button on the door handle, locking them in. "You are staying right here!" she yelled into the rearview.

"But mom, we have to help them!"

Alison was already rolling her window down. "We will." Reluctantly, Alison pulled the Glock from the map compartment. Gracie cowered back, as if she thought Alison might use the weapon on her.

Balancing her arm on the window frame, Alison lined up a shot. The dogs were storming towards them, a seemingly unstoppable horde, but she had to at least try to hold them off until the man in the skeleton costume could get the last of the kids down. In her sideview, she could already see him beginning to lower children into the bed of his truck.

As the dogs rushed towards her, Alison took a deep breath and opened fire.

Somewhere in the distance, there was gunfire. The sound was tinny, muffled even more by the distance than by the all-encompassing shroud of leaves surrounding Derek, which also made it impossible to tell which direction the shots were coming from. That didn't matter now; all that mattered was killing the Xolo.

But first he had to find it, and he had the feeling that it was going to find him first. The noises of its approach had stopped some time ago, whether minutes or hours Derek no longer knew or cared. He was uncomfortably reminded of his experience in the school's basement, and of how many advantages the dog had over him in the dark.

Can't think of that now, he reminded himself, *can only think of how you're going to kill this thing*. That part of the plan he hadn't thought of when he had run off into the woods. His only thought then had been leading the dog away from his family. He desperately wished he still had one of his guns, or at least something besides a flashlight.

Taking a step into the underbrush, the earth suddenly gave way beneath him. He tumbled forward, crashing through the branches and leaves, which parted like a curtain to reveal a new world of darkness beyond.

Derek tumbled down a steep slope of dirt, his body bouncing off rocks and thick roots. Several times his head nearly collided with a tree, but he was unable to control his fall, only picking up speed as he tumbled down the hill towards an unknown destination.

As suddenly as he had started, his plummet stopped, coming to rest on a flat plain of dirt. Derek picked himself up, wincing at the pain with every movement, and took in his surroundings. As he saw what was in front of him, a grin spread across his face. Suddenly, he was glad for his fall, because it had led him to what he knew would be the solution to all his problems.

Ahead of him lay the instrument of the Xolo's destruction.

Another dog hit the ground, but more were streaming in. Alison tried to line up another shot, but her hands were shaking and her eyes were filled with tears. As much as she had never liked dogs, had even hated the hairless one when Derek had first brought it home, she still couldn't stand to see them die, especially when it was by her own hand.

Still, there was no other way to hold the dogs off until the kids were rescued. Risking a quick glance in the sideview mirror, she saw Brian lifting another child off the ladder, but there were still so many more lined up on the roof, and the cage-lined ladder leading up the wall was crammed with students kicking and shoving each other to get down.

Alison couldn't think about that now. If she let the dogs get any closer, they would quickly overwhelm the vehicles, attacking the children before they had a chance to escape. "Cover me!" she heard Heloise yell from the bed of the pick-up truck, dropping her shotgun to load in more shells. Alison didn't know what else she could do; there were already far more dogs than she could handle. She lined up a shot and fired at the first dog in her sightline, dropping it. More rushed in to take its place.

If they didn't get the kids out soon, they would quickly be overwhelmed.

The ravine stretched before Derek as far as he could see in both directions. The unbroken forest on the other side was almost lost in the distance. When he dared to step close enough to the edge to see down, the bottom of the ravine was only a hazy collection of half-visible rocks scattered along a barely flowing stream. Until now, Derek had no idea that a ravine like this existed anywhere in Sunnydale, but he was glad to have discovered it now. One way or another, he had decided, the Xolo was going in that ravine, and it would never be able to get out.

Until then, he would need something to defend himself. Casting the flashlight beam around, he found only a long branch fallen from a nearby tree. Picking it up, he found it still solid and strong, not yet beset by the rot and corruption that seemed to be creeping over the entire forest. Breaking the stick to a manageable size over his knee, Derek scooped up a large flat rock from the edge of the chasm and began striking one end of the branch, hoping that his futile strikes would eventually whittle it to a point. He had only seen this done in movies, but if cavemen could figure out how to do it, he should be able to, for Christ's sake, he could run a company, he could plan a community, but he couldn't figure out how to-

A sound from the woods interrupted his thoughts. It was just a small sound, the tiniest rustling, but Derek knew what it meant. The Xolo was somewhere in the trees that lined the edge of the ravine. Derek thought of shining his light between the trunks, but it would make no difference. Sooner or later, the Xolo would make itself known. He was only wasting time that could be better spent preparing for its eventual attack.

Tucking the flashlight under his arm, Derek continued to whittle down the stick, forming a rough approximation of a point. Between every strike, he cast a glance at the woods, watching for sudden streaks of movement. They never came, but as he whittled the stick to the finest point he thought would be possible, he saw a slight glow emerge from the darkness. Two ovals of yellow light glowed dully, their black centers focused on him. Derek felt himself getting sucked into those eyes, until he remembered what had happened in the school parking lot and realized how he could snap himself out of it.

Taking the flashlight from under his arm, he shone the beam in the direction of the eyes, drowning out the yellow glow in the brighter gleam of the reflected flashlight. The pale, thin body revealed by the flashlight drew back, its spindly legs trying to backpedal into the forest.

For some reason, the sight of the creature trying to escape after it had spent so long tracking him down made Derek irrationally angry. Letting the spear rest against his shoulder, Derek hurled the rock as hard as he could, and surprised himself by actually making contact with the pale dome of the Xolo's skull.

The dog winced and drew back even further, then seemed to shake off the impact. Moving forward out of the underbrush, the dog growled and bent towards the ground, preparing to lunge. Derek kept his flashlight on those glowing yellow eyes, readying the spear with his free hand.

The creature rushed forward, moving almost instantly past the beam of the flashlight. As Derek rushed to keep the beam even with the dog's eyes, he felt himself losing control of his body, felt his will and consciousness being absorbed into the dog's eyes. He wanted to give up, to let the dog attack him, then all of his troubles would be over.

Then he remembered Gracie and Max and Alison. What right did he have to abandon them? Their troubles would be going on long after he was gone, assuming that the dogs didn't kill them right after they had finished him. Keeping his family in the front of his mind, Derek raised the flashlight in one hand, drowning out the glow of the Xolo's eyes, while holding the tip of the spear up with the other hand, bracing the back end of the spear against the ground.

The dog leapt at him, apparently blinded by the flashlight. Derek managed to keep the light focused directly on its eyes as it sailed through the air towards him. He lowered the spear, lining it up directly with the pale underbelly of the dog.

There was a sickening ripping sound as the dog's belly settled over the spear, the point sinking into its flesh and raising a ring of blood that was shockingly red against the dog's pale skin. The bulk of the dog's body, its forward momentum undeterred by the spear, slammed into Derek, knocking him off his feet. He was sure that he and the dog would go tumbling off the edge of the cliff, so it was almost a relief when his back slammed painfully into a ledge of rock. His flashlight tumbled from his hand, rolling across the angled rock and tumbling into the ravine, which he saw was only a few inches to his left. He heard the flashlight bouncing against outcroppings of rock on its way down before hitting the bottom far below.

With the light gone, he could see the Xolo's eyes more clearly than ever, their piercing glow overwhelming his vision. He was only brought back to reality by the painful swiping of the thing's claws against his chest and legs. The dog was still struggling to get closer to him, impaling itself further on the spear to do so. Pinned down by the weight of the dog above him, Derek could only close his eyes, turning his head away from those hypnotic eyes. He felt warm gusts of breath as the thing's jaws reached towards him, warm drool and hot blood dripping onto his cheek. The claws dug deeper into his flesh, the jaws snapped only inches from his face, but still the dog continued to struggle towards him, blood running down the spear as the thing further impaled itself.

Mustering strength he didn't know he had, Derek pushed up on the spear, driving the point even further into the dog, raising its body away from his own. He felt the claws still reach towards him, desperately tearing at his clothes and skin.

Rolling onto his side, Derek braced his elbows against the ground, raising his forearms to lift the spear. His hands almost slipped on the welter of fresh blood that ran down the wooden shaft, but he managed to hold on long enough to lift the dog away from him. The dog reached out its front paws, leaving one last swipe across the middle of his chest.

With a final heave, Derek threw the dog over the edge of the cliff. Its claws scratched at the rocky ledge, but found no purchase. Derek heard an almost desperate whimper dying away on the wind, then the surprisingly light thump of the dog hitting the rocks below. Then all was quiet.

Derek realized with sudden shock that this was the end of the whole thing. It felt surreal, strangely anti-climactic, despite all that had led up to this moment. Nervous energy that he hadn't even realized had been building up inside him suddenly began to pour out of him, pulsating from his body into the rocks below, becoming visible as steam that poured from every inch of him into the quickly chilling night air.

Derek wanted to take in that air forever. He let his limbs uncoil, his muscles relax, feeling the night for what it was. The clouds above parted, revealing the full moon, which seemed shockingly close. Derek stared into its eyes, feeling like he was as far away from his situation as the craters that made up that face. Suddenly, the grim unreality of the last few months came crashing down around him, the pain and horror that would stay with him for the rest of his life, clawing at his mind the same way the Xolo had clawed at his flesh. Even now, he could still hear those claws scratching in his mind...

The soft whimpering that accompanied the scratches made him realize the sound wasn't merely in his mind. The whimpers echoed up through the ravine, and he could hear the small sounds of rocks being dislodged by the dog's paws. Somehow, the thing was still alive!

Carefully, Derek crawled to the edge of the ravine and looked over. The flashlight he had dropped was shattered, but still working, its beam splayed across the broken form of the dog. The Xolo's limbs were bent at odd angles and huge rips ran across its flesh, stress marks from the impact of its fall. The flashlight beam just barely caught one of its eyes, which still glowed yellow.

Derek found himself locked in its gaze, his eyes again unable to look away from the Xolo's. As Derek looked into that eye, he was reminded of the first time he had seen them glowing, when the dog had stooped over the dying deer in the roadway and absorbed its lifeforce. Now, the Xolo itself was the dying animal, its life force leaking out of it in the form of steam from its mouth and from the tears that lined its body.

As the steam drifted up to Derek, he smelled its sickly-sweet odor. It reminded him of the scent of an antique censer in an ancient temple he seemed to remember from ten thousand years ago, a temple bathed in light as yellow as the Xolo's eyes. Ancient priests hustled around the temple, preparing a young woman for sacrifice. The Xolo was nowhere in sight. As Derek looked around for it, he realized that he was looking from the vantage point of the throne where the Xolo had presided the last time he was here. He felt the jewel-bedecked robe draped around his shoulders and knew that this was a dangerous dream he was being trapped in.

Throwing the robe aside as a physical symbol of his disgust, Derek stood up from the throne and immediately found himself back in the cold night air, about to step over the edge of the cliff. Pulling himself back, he collapsed to his knees, waving away the steam that still billowed up from the ravine. Still tasting the sickly-sweet scent in his mouth, Derek leaned over the cliff and spit into the ravine until the taste was gone.

Below, he saw the Xolo's small movements come to a stop. He locked eyes with the dog again, but this time he was not pulled into them. He saw only a weakly reflected vision of ancient temples and high priests in the dog's eye, a vision that slowly faded along with the light inside those eyes. As the light went out completely, the eye closed. Steam poured out of the body for another moment, then dissipated. The body was still and peaceful, almost beautiful in the moonlight. As Derek looked down on it, the flashlight blinked, buzzed, and went out, obscuring the body in shadow.

Dragging himself away from the edge of the ravine, Derek turned himself over painfully and collapsed again on the flat shelf of rock, looking up at the moon. The full moon reminded him of the strange visions the Xolo had given him, and soon those visions were running through his head again, mingling with the world around him. He didn't even realize he was dreaming until a voice called him out of sleep. It was a stern, desperate, familiar voice, but still, he didn't want to call back to it. He didn't have the energy to get up or walk out of this forest; all he wanted to do was lie on this cliff and sleep.

The voice called his name again, making sleep impossible. He realized that he was cold and alone, that if he let the owner of that voice pass him by, he might never be found, only sleep here until the rocks beneath him sucked all the heat from his body and he died. When the voice called again, he feebly called back, using the last of his strength to project an answer. After a few calls back and forth, the sheriff emerged from the woods, his uniform covered in briars and dead leaves. He shined his flashlight on Derek, a hot sun that obliterated his vision after the darkness he had been in all night.

"You alright, Derek?" the sheriff asked.

He nodded weakly.

"Where's the Xolo?"

Derek didn't think he had the energy, but he raised his hand and pointed over the edge of the cliff. A look of concern on his face, Garth stepped over Derek and looked down into the ravine. Sweeping his light along the bottom, he nodded and looked pleased. "So, it's over then."

"Let's hope so." Derek's voice sounded like it could fade away at any moment.

"Come on, let's get you back. You feel well enough to stand?"

"Maybe if you give me a hand."

The sheriff laughed and extended one. "Alright, I guess you earned it, hero."

Derek groaned as Garth helped him to his feet. He leaned on the sheriff as they began to walk out of the forest, Garth finding the way with his flashlight. "You sure you know your way out of here?" Derek asked.

"I found my way in, didn't I?"

"So did I, doesn't mean I know my way out."

"Well, I didn't have a dog chasing me."

Derek laughed, the sound uncomfortably loud in the darkness.

Ahead, he noticed that the gunshots were silent now, and had been for some time, having faded out while he was distracted with the Xolo, no doubt. That was either very good, or very bad. They would only know for sure once they had escaped from this forest.

THIRTY

Because neither Derek nor Garth had the energy to climb the fence again, they walked the length of it until they found a gate that allowed the school's custodians to step outside the schoolyard and trim the vines and weeds that threatened to wrap around the chain-link. The extra distance added considerably to their time getting back, but not hearing any signs of struggle ahead, they took the walk as a much-needed break. As they approached the gate, Garth took out his revolver to shoot off the lock, but found it sealed only with a simple latch. Throwing the gate open, they crossed the wide, empty asphalt lot, Garth supporting Derek and both of them scanning the darkness for dogs.

They saw the dogs when they reached the front of the school. But instead of the snarling, attacking horde they had come to expect, they found the dogs wandering aimlessly, almost confused, around the parking lot. The white pickup truck and Alison's minivan were parked against one wall of the school, beneath a utility ladder built into the wall, where Brian had leaned his own ladder against the wall and was now taking down the last of the kids. The bed and cab of his truck, as well as the back seats of Alison's minivan, were now filled with kids.

Heloise still stood watch over the vehicles. When she saw Derek and Garth approaching, she lowered her shotgun and waved, calling out to both of them. Derek was worried she would also attract the attention of the dogs, but they continued to wander the parking lot, seeming to pay no mind to the humans.

Alison climbed out of the driver's seat of the minivan, carelessly stuffing the spent Glock into the map compartment as she rushed out of the vehicle. Dashing across the parking lot, she swept Derek up in a hug, taking him out of Garth's arms and into her own. "I'm so glad you're okay," she whispered into his ear.

"I'm glad you're okay, too," he whispered back, "all of you." Over her shoulder, he saw Max and Gracie had followed her across the parking lot.

"You should have seen it, Dad," Max said, more excited than Derek had heard him in months, "Mom dropped all the dogs that were coming at us like she was the Terminator!" He made gun firing motions with both his hands, squeezing one eye shut.

Derek followed the aim of the guns he was making with his fingers and saw several dogs laid out on the asphalt, some obviously blown apart with a shotgun, but others with expertly aimed holes in their necks and heads. Alison looked ashamed, dropping her gaze from Derek's. "I had to do it, honey, it was the only way to protect the kids."

Derek squeezed the back of her neck. "You're right, honey, it was the only way." Looking over at the kids, he waved them back towards the van. "You guys shouldn't be out here, it's not safe."

"It's okay, Dad," Gracie told him confidently, "I think it's all over now." She waved a hand at the dogs. "They just stopped attacking a while ago, just a little bit after the Xolo chased you into the woods."

"Yeah, I think I know why," Derek said uneasily. He still wanted to get Gracie safely away from here, but as he pushed her towards the van, he saw something that he knew would make that impossible. The last time he had seen her new golden retriever, Derek had locked him in the closet with Reeve, where the dog was ripping the bodyguard to shreds. Apparently, the dog had finished his work there, and had even managed to knock aside the chair Derek had hastily placed in front of the door, because now he was calmly crossing the parking lot towards Gracie.

Although the dog looked calm and friendly, the dried blood matted around his mouth was a stark reminder of what he was capable of. Derek tried to pull Gracie back, but she was already running towards the dog, her arms spread wide. Derek winced as she threw her arms around its neck, but the dog only nuzzled her, spreading a little bit of dried blood on her neck. Despite that disgusting detail, the scene was undeniably sweet as the girl and her dog reunited. The other dogs drew nearer, cautiously curious about what the humans were up to, seeming to forget the violence done against them just as easily as they had forgotten the violence they had been trying to inflict on the humans just moments before.

Derek let out a deep breath. Whatever psychic influence had taken control of the dogs had died with the Xolo. Things could get back to normal now, or at least as normal as they ever could be.

Evidently, other people had figured that out, too. Echoing off the hard brick of the school building, he heard further evidence of the return to normalcy, a sign that the emergency was disappearing everywhere. Echoing off the school was the sound of sirens, quickly approaching in the night.

EPILOGUE

Derek strode through the temple, a dagger clutched in his hands. A gentle breeze tugged at the jewel-bedecked robe slung over his shoulders, making the linens separating the chambers into flowing ghosts that revealed just enough of the neighboring rooms to excite his paranoia. Pressing the handle of the dagger to his chest, Derek cast aside the next linen, revealing only darkness. He let out a breath he hadn't been aware of withholding.

Although Derek told himself it was only the darkness that made him nervous, he knew there was only thing he feared to see in the shadows.

As he pushed another linen aside, he found it. Instead of regally standing guard over the main chamber, the Xolo was now in the position of the victim, strapped to the stone altar with straps of cracked leather restraining its body and binding its spindly limbs.

Derek knew what he had to do. As he marched towards the altar, he had never been more aware of being in his body, of the fact that he was seeing through his own eyes. He raised the dagger, holding it above the Xolo's heart. As the blade came into view, he could see his hand aging before his eyes, the flesh growing wrinkled and mottled. As he brought the blade down, the entire temple grew older, the cyclopean stones chipping and weathering before his eyes, the vines that wound between them snaking to the floor in seconds, widening the gaps between the stones as they expanded, the plants themselves growing gray and crumbling to dust in an instant, leaving gaps where the stones collapsed on themselves.

Realizing he had never heard the Xolo cry out, Derek looked down to see only the dog's skeleton on the altar, the rusted dagger resting between two ribs. An enormous stone tumbled from the ceiling and destroyed the altar, crushing the bones into dust. Derek looked up to see stones tumbling on him from all directions. He held up his hands as if that would provide some sort of protection.

As the final stones filled the space around him, entombing Derek forever, he woke up in an unfamiliar darkness. After a long moment of straining his eyes, Derek finally recognized the darkened living room of his new home. Moving boxes cluttered the corners, forming dens of deeper shadow from which the denizen of his nightmares still peered.

His body ached as he forced himself off the couch where he had fallen asleep. Even though it had been more than a year, the scars lining his chest and arms still burned, as if the Xolo had made them only yesterday. Pushing aside the coffee table that still held the stacks of land deeds and floor plans he had been reviewing before he fell asleep, Derek fumbled for a while to find the unfamiliar lamp. When he finally switched it on, the blinding light made him realize just how dark the room had been, and wonder how late it was.

When he finally found it among the papers on the table, Derek's phone told him it was just before midnight, but he was almost distracted from the time by the slew of messages and notifications that crowded his screen. Clearing them all, Derek stuffed the phone in his pocket and made his way unsteadily towards the front door.

Ever since they had moved back to Illinois, Derek had been drowning in questions that needed to be answered and issues that needed to be resolved. As if moving into the new house didn't keep him busy enough, he was working full time designing sustainable housing to help ease Chicago's homelessness crisis, and the constant demands of the job would have overwhelmed him if he hadn't been so passionate about it.

Still, the job was a massive drain on his energy. But things could have been worse, he had to remind himself constantly. Once he had sold the old house, as well as all of the undeveloped land in the old neighborhood to a group of his former investors who wanted his name off the property, he had donated most of the proceeds to the survivors of the dog attacks. He had done this mostly out of guilt, but it seemed to have headed off the inevitable lawsuits that would have otherwise kept him in court (and in Colorado) for the next several years. He had also given away his land in Mexico, donating it back to the local Yoreme people, who were using it to build both housing and a community center for their tribe.

Both moves had lightened his conscience over unleashing the Xolo on the world, but had also lightened his wallet enough to make him worry about how he was going to support his family long-term. Thankfully, he didn't have to worry about that for now. As he crossed into the living room, he nearly tripped over a box of books newly arrived from Alison's publisher. Even though Derek had seen the cover a million times during the approval process, he still couldn't help picking up the topmost shrink-wrapped copy and giving it an admiring glance. Alison's name was printed in bold red type above the title: A VENETIAN ROMANCE. Below that, an oil painting of a lusty maiden escaping from a castle, chased by a figure in tattered men's clothing of the eighteenth century. Derek still couldn't stand to look at that figure's face, which to him looked more like a dog than a wolf, and had glowing red eyes that seemed to peer into him.

With cover art like that, it was sure to be a bestseller, and apparently her publishers thought the same. The advance they had paid her was enough to take care of their down payment, and they had already contracted her to write another. As he passed the study at the front of the house, Derek saw the faint glow beneath the door and heard the clacking of her fingers on the keyboard. He had no idea how she had found the time to write the first one, but now that she didn't have a day job to worry about, she was certainly finding time for the second one.

Trying not to disturb her, Derek snuck past the office to the front door. Light also emerged from the small window on that door, and Derek's first thought was that Max had taken up smoking again, but as he swung the door open to catch him in the act, he only found the boy sitting peacefully on the swinging bench outside, staring out at the darkness beyond the porch. Even as he closed the door behind himself, Derek didn't smell the lingering mechanical scent of his vape pen.

"Everything alright, Max?"

The boy only shrugged. "Couldn't sleep. Thought some fresh air might help."

"You must've been reading my mind." Max made room as Derek took a seat on the bench. Beyond the yellow circle of the porchlight, the cornfields across the street were only shifting shades of darkness accompanied by a soft hiss of wind through the fallen stalks. Buying this mid-century farm house had seemed like a great idea when they were looking for a place to escape Colorado and start fresh, and the fields of corn that surrounded the house in all directions (once worked by the former owner of this house, but now long since bought out by a conglomerate from Chicago) had seemed like a peaceful and beautiful view. But at night, the unbroken darkness that settled in around the house, combined with the sound of the wind hissing through the crops, made Derek uneasy, knowing what could be hiding in those fields and shadows.

"Have you been having any more bad dreams?" he asked Max, partly out of concern for the boy and partly for himself.

Max shifted a little. "Not really," he said, but the way he scratched at the scars on his hand told Derek otherwise.

He decided to change the subject, knowing it wouldn't help to push Max on anything. The boy had been opening up more and more since their move, and Derek didn't want to ruin that.

"It's okay," was all Max said when Derek asked him how he liked his new school.

Derek sighed. "What about your sister?"

At that, Max seemed to light up. "She seems to really like it. She's making a lot of new friends."

"Glad to hear it."

Max slid off the bench, still uncomfortable about spending time around his father. Derek thought he might just have to get used to that for the next decade or so. "Have a good night, Dad." Derek smiled at that. That little bit of courtesy, and the earnest way it had been said, was progress at least.

Derek had been staring out into the darkness alone for only a few minutes when his phone rang. He pulled it from his pocket, wincing at the pain as his scars scraped against the denim, then sighed when he looked at the phone. The name on the screen was one he had tried not to think about for months, not because he didn't like it, but because of the associations it brought up.

At last, he worked up the courage to answer. "How's it going, Garth?"

The sheriff's voice sounded halting and uncertain, but just as clear and powerful as ever. "See you're having trouble sleeping, too."

"Eh, I've got bad dreams."

"Tell me about it. How are things with the family?"

"Things are good. The kids are adjusting to their new school, Alison's hard at work on the new book."

"Good. Speaking of which, I got the signed copy she sent me. Be sure to thank her for that. I never met a famous author before; just don't tell her I haven't had time to read it yet."

"Why not?" Derek laughed, "Haven't you retired yet like you said you were gonna?"

"Eh, I haven't had time for that either. Gotta find a replacement first."

That took the smile off Derek's face. Knowing what had happened to the deputy who was supposed to replace Garth, the topic was uncomfortably close to the one thing Derek wanted to avoid discussing.

Garth apparently had other plans. "I'm assuming you know why I'm calling?"

Derek tried not to let his slow exhale be heard over the phone. "I'm guessing it wasn't just to thank Alison for the book?"

Garth laughed, but there was no amusement in it. "I'm sure you saw the stories on the news?" Derek had tried not to, but after what had happened, the constant news coverage was inescapable. As winter had begun to set in, animals had been found in the woods outside Sunnydale, mutilated beyond recognition. At first the police had tried to downplay the cases as natural, the work of aggressive bears getting out of their natural habitat, but last week a man in his sixties snowshoeing alone had been found torn to shreds. The early reports from the medical director had said the bites were consistent with that of a dog.

"Could have been a wolf, too," Derek heard himself saying flatly. Even he didn't believe it.

"Yeah, maybe and maybe not. Obviously, there's a big push to deal with this now, and I can't say I don't see the urgency. But everyone's putting pressure on animal control and I want it to remain a police matter."

"Isn't Heloise still in charge over there?"

"Naw, she decided to come over to my team. Guess she decided she wanted to make a real difference instead," he said with a laugh.

"Well, that's great. She'll be a wonderful asset."

"We needed to do a little repairing of the ranks anyways. You remember that kid Brian? The one who drove the truck that rescued all those kids? I offered him a job, too, and he jumped at the chance. He was doing some shit job at a gym or something before that."

"Sounds like you've got a great team, then." There was a long pause. "But if you need my help, you know I'm happy to offer it," he said reluctantly.

"I'm glad you offered." Even through the phone, Derek could hear the sheriff's smarmy grin. "I have a theory I've been dying to try out."

"This is all starting to sound a little familiar. I thought we all agreed the Xolo was definitely dead? Those government guys even came and took the body. Unless you think they cooked something up…"

Garth cut him off. "I've actually got something a little simpler in mind. The Xolo had that whole pack of dogs out in the woods with him for weeks, right?"

"Yeah, but they all came back, right?"

"All the ones that were pets did, yeah. Except for the ones we had to kill. But there were tons of dogs out there. The ones from the shelter, the ones from that dogfighting ring, who knows what else. None of those were documented before. We rounded up a bunch of 'em, but who knows? It's possible one got by us. Especially if it had a reason to hide."

"A reason like what?"

"Like she was having puppies."

Derek's mouth went dry. "You think… the Xolo…"

"Like I said, it's a theory."

"Well, I'll help you test it. I'll make arrangements with work tomorrow and head out in the morning."

Garth thanked him and hung up. Derek sat in the darkness, scratching the scars on his hands. He had thought that the burning was only brought on by his dream, but perhaps it was something else. Perhaps it was a sense of purpose, of knowing that there was still something out there that their maker was connected with. Derek shuddered at the thought. If that sense of connection could be passed down genetically, he wondered what else could.

Stepping off the porch and into the front yard, he looked up at the window, beyond which Gracie was sleeping peacefully with the golden retriever in her arms. The dog had been normal ever since the incident, but who knew if the power the Xolo had once had over it could be regained. Derek told himself that was unlikely, that if there were new dogs that were half-Xolo, their control over other dogs would have to be reasserted again.

Unless he could stop it. If that sense of connection still existed between the offspring of the Xolo and the bites their descendant had inflicted, then perhaps they would still be drawn to him as the Xolo had been. Perhaps he could use that to destroy the dogs before they caused any more harm.

Another thought was still nagging at him. If there really were more dogs that were half-Xolo, and his mind had already seemed to accept that as a certainty, then what was the other half? Suddenly, he no longer wanted to be outside alone in the darkness. Turning off the porch light, Derek locked the door behind himself.

The door to the study hung open, and the room was dark. Alison must have gone to bed while he was outside. Instead of keeping her up all night with his inevitable tossing and turning, Derek headed back to the couch, which he approached with trepidation.

Sleep meant dreams, and now that he knew his dreams were more than just the echoes of bad memories, he wasn't so sure he could face them. He had to drown them out with determination, he told himself. He had defeated this evil before; he could defeat it again. At least, that's what he tried to tell himself.

Besides, he told himself as he flopped down on the couch, dreams didn't mean a thing.

The End
October 2019-May 2022
Forest Lake, Hugo, and Saint Paul, MN